D0261099

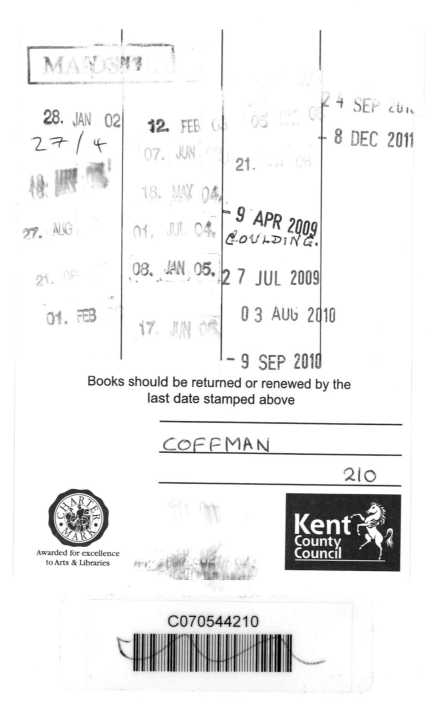

MAIDSTONE

28. JAN 02
27/4
18. MAY
27. AUG
21.
01. FEB

12. FEB
07. JUN
18. MAY 04,
01. JUL 04,
08. JAN 05,
17. JUN

05
21.

24 SEP
- 8 DEC 2011

- 9 APR 2009
GOULDING.
2 7 JUL 2009
0 3 AUG 2010
- 9 SEP 2010

Books should be returned or renewed by the
last date stamped above

COFFMAN

210

Charter Mark
Awarded for excellence
to Arts & Libraries

Kent
County
Council

C070544210

# THE
# LOMBARD
# CAVALCADE

# THE LOMBARD CAVALCADE

## Virginia Coffman

G. K. Hall & Co. • Chivers Press
Thorndike, Maine USA  Bath, England

CO70544210

This Large Print edition is published by G.K. Hall & Co., USA
and by Chivers Press, England.

Published in 2001 in the U.S. by arrangement with
Pinder Lane & Garon-Brooke Associates, Ltd.

Published in 2001 in the U.K. by arrangement with
the Author.

U.S. Hardcover  0-7838-9400-7 (Core Series Edition)
U.K. Hardcover 0-7540-1618-8 (Windsor Large Print)

Copyright © 1982 by Virginia Coffman

All rights reserved.

The text of this Large Print edition is unabridged.
Other aspects of the book may vary from the original edition.

Set in 16 pt. Plantin by Myrna S. Raven.

Printed in the United States on permanent paper.

**British Library Cataloguing-in-Publication Data available**

**Library of Congress Cataloging-in-Publication Data**

Coffman, Virginia.
   The Lombard cavalcade : a novel / by Virginia Coffman.
     p.  cm.
   ISBN 0-7838-9400-7 (lg. print : hc : alk. paper)
   I. Title.
PS3553.O415 L6  2001
  813′.54—dc21                   00-069119

For Donnie and Johnny Always

# BOOK ONE

# Chapter One

The prickle on the back of her neck warned her that the two guards at the Cambon entrance to the Hôtel Ritz had noticed her. She could imagine their hard, steely eyes following her, though their helmets would remain immobile.

She lowered her head and shook it until the bright golden strands of her hair fell carelessly about her piquant face. Bracing herself, she slung her string bag with its meager contents over her shoulder and fell into her exaggerated, pigeon-toed walk. It had worked before, making her look clumsy and half-witted. Even her bare legs lost their trim, shapely look and her hair fell loosely to conceal her blue, almond-shaped eyes. A lower jaw gone deliberately slack completed the picture of ungainliness.

She had devised the trick for herself after an encounter with a German soldier three years ago. She knew too well what an enemy in uniform could do, especially if he was drunk and the girl was alone.

It had taken place one warm, autumn night shortly after her mother's funeral. Her brother Carl had said he would be working late at the Ministry of Education, although she knew now that he had probably been at a meeting of his cell in the French Resistance. Jany had gone out by herself against her brother's orders to light a candle and pray for the peace of Maman's soul. Germans wearing the black and silver lightning slash on their shoulders blocked the way west toward the old St. Roch Church. The mere sight of the SS men terrified the fourteen-year-old. Wishing she'd heeded her brother's warning, she hurried off in a different direction, remembering that the concierge had told her "the Boche are polite and respectful around Notre Dame." She'd hoped they would be so that night.

It was a long walk to the church and she had to be back in their tiny apartment before curfew — sometimes *they* shot people caught out after nine o'clock. But she made it safely to the end of the rue St. Honore and over the pont au Change to the Cité, reaching the dark facade of Notre Dame a little before dark.

On entering the cold, damp interior of the church, she was surprised to find several others sitting in the shadows, mostly women, but also a surprising number of German soldiers. It was not a warm or comforting place, but as she looked up into the massive darkness she felt that Maman was not really gone forever. She felt that something of her mother had become a part of all the thousands who, through the centuries, had worshipped here as she had. Jany wondered if she might be looking down from that enormous dark, trying in vain to comfort her desolate daughter.

The young girl felt better after she left the great cathedral and began her long walk home. Her candle had been as fine and straight, its flame as bright as any of the others burning on that October night.

Ahead of her at a corner café she saw the *patron*

stacking wicker chairs on the tables, getting ready to close in time for curfew. Realizing how much farther she had to go, she began to run just as a German soldier came out of the café, obviously drunk. He was having trouble belting his coat, fumbling with the buckle more than seemed necessary. At this stage of the Occupation Jany had seen few drunken Germans — they were under strict orders not to imbibe. But this one was definitely drunk. Not very young, either. He had mislaid his peaked cap somewhere and Jany was meanly amused to note that he was going bald.

Served him right. *Sale Boche!*

He looked her over as she approached and she heard him mutter something. By this time she knew it was too late, but she started to cross the street toward the forbidding walls of the great city hospital, the Hôtel Dieu. The soldier, not willing to let her get away, put one arm out. Scared but angry too, she kicked his leg as high up as she could reach. It wasn't high enough. He chuckled and put out his other arm, imprisoning her against the rough cloth of his sleeves. She tried to escape under his arms but he backed her against the wall of the café. Exhaling the strong stench of beer, he began to nuzzle her neck.

She screamed in shock and disgust, but his thin mouth persistently pressed her lips shut. His hands moved over her body, unbuttoning her close-fitting princess coat. She tried to wriggle away but his hands were everywhere, over her stomach and lean, childish hips until they reached her groin, his coarse fingers poking between her stiff, thin legs. Horrified, she attempted to scream again, but only heard gurgling noises caught in her throat.

Like a messenger from heaven — maybe Maman — the *patron of* the café called out.

"You like another beer, monsieur? The girl, she will wait. What do you say?"

The soldier drew back briefly, looked around, debated, and Jany, seizing her chance, made a dash for the pont d'Arcole, running as she had never run before until she reached the Right Bank and was heading for home.

She never again made the mistake of being caught near curfew on a dark street.

Today, in front of the two Hôtel Ritz guards, she wanted as always to taunt them with the color of their uniforms:

*. . . String beans . . . Dirty string-bean Boches! . . .*

But she didn't say it out loud. Not any more. When the armies of the Third Reich first came swinging along the Champs-Elysées four years ago, showing off their military power in the wake of dusty, unshaven, exhausted Frenchmen with dead eyes, Jany had been thirteen, flaunting a child's ignorant courage.

Her voice shrill and high-pitched, she'd yelled, *"Haricot Vert! Sale Boche!"* at every German she saw until her brother had cupped his hand over her mouth to silence her.

"Quiet! You don't fight the Boche with words," he'd said.

It was a hard lesson for an impulsive, self-assured girl like Jany to learn. If the Wehrmacht had begun its occupation with excellent manners, the arrival of the SS with "question rooms" that were not quite soundproof ended any expectation that the entire French population would remain docile.

Coming home from the market this warm, hazy July day in 1944, the fourth year of what her intellectual brother Carl called "our Babylonian captivity," Jany had been dreaming about food. The collection of onions, dirt-covered beets, and several flower bulbs of unknown variety in her string bag didn't offer much inspiration, but Jany had a vivid memory and she spent much time daydreaming about the past — a glorious, food-filled past without rationing.

When she thought back to the years before the war, the shops with their colorful piles of vegetables and silvery fish and bright, fresh meat seemed more beautiful to her than all the art looted by the enemy. Her memories of meals at home with her mother and brother were among her favorites. No Olympian ambrosia could match the succulence of the *boeuf bourguignon* prepared by Jany's ex-movie star mother, Olga Rey. And the sole she prepared with the world's most delicious herbed sauce . . . nobody knew what Maman Olga had put in it. It looked creamy but it was no garden variety of *béchamel* sauce.

Olga Rey had died during the first year of the Occupation. Carl blamed the Germans. It was his theory that her heart attack might have been prevented with the right diet, but then, Carl blamed everything on the enemy. He had served in the army for ten months before the fall of France, and couldn't forget the shame of that armistice. Jany was terrified now by his secret, late-night rendezvous that she knew had nothing to do with the kinds of affairs that ought to occupy a sensuous young man of twenty-six. Now and then he dated some of the girls who belonged to his particular Resistance group, but all too often he was off on risky political errands in and around Paris long after curfew.

Jany always tried to make their mealtimes and home life pleasant. She adored her brother, but still she feared what he might do during his bitter moments when he sat brooding about the fate of their country.

Turning the corner past a café where several Frenchmen chatted or calmly read Nazi-censored newspapers, Jany looked back and saw that the German soldiers had lost interest in the little French girl with the awkward walk and silly expression. They were motionless again, staring straight ahead. She thought that they must be uncomfortable, standing there in those metal helmets and heavy uniforms.

It was the first time she'd ever thought of them as human, and even at that it was difficult to think of Kurt Friedrich, Jany's anti-Nazi German father, as related to those robots stationed before every important building in Paris — it was these same robots that had murdered him in 1938.

Jany resumed her normal, lilting stride when she reached the ancient rue St. Honore and headed for home, no longer upset by the German signs in the shops she passed. Most of the merchandise, from vases to gloves, was looted by Occupation forces or paid for by scrip that was practically worthless. Jany wondered if anything beautiful would be left in Paris by the time the enemy retreated.

Of one thing she was sure: they *would* retreat. They were on the run in North Africa, in Italy, in Russia. Any day Paris would wake up to find the enemy rolling eastward, their hideous, hobnailed boots marching across the cobbles for the last time.

Meanwhile, there was noon dinner to be prepared for Carl and the most important item, the bread, was missing. If she had only been higher in the line of women at the bakery, she might have gotten a chunk of the hard, black bread before the shop ran out. Though rationed severely, Parisians had to have their *baguette*. Like ancient Roman soldiers, they demanded bread before meat, even before wine. Sometimes Jany dreamed of the lean, crusty white loaves Maman had sent her to buy before the war. But these were no longer available.

She turned in at the narrow, dark passage between the Café St. Just and a shop selling tiny, painted lead figures. Somebody had bought the charming little set of musketeers since Jany passed the shop this morning on her way to the fishmonger's. She hoped the buyer would give them a good home. She would always remember those three gloriously caparisoned little lead figures sprawled around a table, raising tankards to the damnation of the cardinal's guards. Gone now, Jany thought, probably off to delight some German child.

Like so many others in Paris, the passage opened into a tiny, square courtyard. The bricked court was bordered by potted plants belonging to the ground-floor tenants. In the center was a Second Empire fountain no longer used, except by the local cats. Two staircases, at the north and south ends of the courtyard, wound upward to the first floor and then beyond to the garret apartments under the mansard roof.

For ten years Jany and Carl had shared with their mother the south apartment on the first floor. They were the illegitimate product of a liaison between their mother when she was a star of silent films, and Kurt Friedrich, a young leading man who had gone on to greener pastures in his native Austria, marrying a rich American woman named Brooke Lombard. Illegitimacy had never troubled Jany very much. She and Carl were accepted by Olga's acting friends in their childhood, and Friedrich made no objection to their using his name.

Since the Occupation, all social standards had changed anyway. One either collaborated, or endured, or resisted. There were friends in each group who had no interest in whether the Church recognized their birth or not — they had more important things to think about.

Jany never knew her father although before her birth he had often visited Olga Rey and Carl in their Paris apartment, even sending small gifts and money at times. But that show of generosity stopped abruptly when Jany was born, perhaps because it was about that time that he married the rich divorcée, Brooke Lombard, and disappeared from their lives.

During the first years of her life Jany had heard from Carl what a scoundrel their father was. The loss of his father — the exciting visitor who talked to him and playacted for him — was a great blow to the boy.

Then, magically, in 1938, at the time the Nazis marched into Vienna, Carl heard a broadcast on the radio and suddenly thought their father to be a respected war hero. Jany, who was eleven then, couldn't quite understand how Kurt Friedrich — a man she'd never met — could suddenly become the wonderful father he was in Carl's eyes.

Still, the radio broadcast had been exciting. Carl and Maman huddled around the big loudspeaker, absorbing every word of the program that originated from Zurich. Maman, who had still followed all the movie gossip, pricked up her ears at the name of Leo Prysing, Hollywood's genius successor to Thalberg and Selznick. The producer was being interviewed by an English correspondent after the death of Prysing's brother in Vienna.

"Prysing is thanking the people who tried to rescue his brother after the Nazi takeover of Austria," Olga explained to Carl. "I could swear he mentioned your father's name — there it is again!"

Leo Prysing's deep-pitched, powerful voice was saying, ". . . I'm referring of course, to one of Austria's unsung, unsuspected anti-Nazi heroes, Kurt Friedrich."

The interviewer hesitantly mentioned that "my broadcasting associates in Vienna list Kurt Friedrich as a well-known Nazi sympathizer."

Prysing had explained that Kurt Friedrich, now safe in London, was the son of a Jewish father and had secretly worked for "his people."

Jany would always remember how Carl asked their mother, without inflection, "Is it true? Was our grandfather Jewish?"

Jany wondered if her brother was shocked by

17

this disclosure. It would be uncharacteristic of Carl, especially since most of their friends with theatrical parents were Jews.

Olga Rey shrugged. "If so, your father never knew, and I'm sure he never had any suspicion of his Jewish blood."

Leo Prysing ended the interview with the hope of meeting Kurt Friedrich in London where, presumably, he was safe.

Carl's gray eyes lit up. The fact that their father had failed to save the movie magnate's fugitive brother was less important to him than his heroic attempt to do so. In Carl's mind, he no longer needed to despise his father. It became clear to him alone that the reason his father hadn't visited him and Jany during their childhood was because of his anti-Nazi activities. He hadn't wanted to involve them.

Months later, when word came to Paris of Kurt Friedrich's death in a Berlin riot, Carl wore a black mourning band around his arm and told Jany that their father had died an anti-Nazi hero.

"Why did he go back to the Reich where they hated him?" Jany asked, sensibly.

It was Olga who made an odd suggestion. "Maybe he never left. Is it not possible that Leo Prysing's interview was released too soon?"

"You mean before papa could get out?" Jany had asked. "How could that have happened?"

Maman hadn't answered.

But Carl, blinded by his need to respect the father who once abandoned him, could see no possibility of wrongdoing. "My father was a hero. All the world knows that — everyone has heard about Prysing's broadcast."

Jany was proud of Carl's loyalty and asked no more questions about it, but privately she wondered why their mother never mentioned their father's name again.

Had she resented her ex-lover's martyred status? Or did she secretly doubt that he was actually a hero?

Not that it mattered to Jany. Losing Maman Olga was a great blow for her, and it made Carl's life even more precious to Jany. He was all she had.

Jany unlocked the door into the shadowy, boxlike hall and dropped her groceries off in the tiny kitchen which had been a powdering closet a hundred years ago. A window that offered a view of the court below had been cut into the wall above the two-burner gas stove. On a July day a surprising amount of light shone through the room where Jany couldn't even find space for a table and two chairs. Jany and Carl ate their meals in the living room.

It was hot today, window or not. She pursed her lips and blew loose strands of blonde hair off her forehead. Her face was damp. All that nervousness about the soldiers, the running up the stairs, the eternal worry about how to make a decent noon dinner for poor Carl — no wonder she was sweating.

While she washed and changed into a three-year-old voile dress that wasn't quite styled for a seventeen-year-old figure, she decided on onion soup for dinner. She could make do with the heels of bread left over from yesterday's loaf and add some of the seasonings that Olga Rey had taught her to use so cleverly.

Maybe the flower bulbs would give the soup more body, she thought. It was worth a try. Rumor had it that the Dutch were living on tulip bulbs and little else. She wished she could identify what variety of flower she was about to stew. No matter — they would be sacrificed to a good purpose — her hardworking brother's noon meal.

Only minutes after twelve, Carl, a clerk at the Ministry of Education, bounded up the stairs. Although he was light-footed as always, Jany sensed that something must have happened — she knew how quiet he could be and how he had a disconcerting habit of appearing where one didn't expect him. She thought that this quality must serve him well in what she was certain must be his Resistance work.

On this July day he couldn't conceal his excitement. His gray eyes, almost the color of slate, were usually hard to read. Girls found him mysterious and sexy, but complained to Jany that they could never guess his thoughts — it seemed as though he was always thinking about something distant and secretive — something far removed from whomever he was with. Since he often looked this way to Jany, she saw nothing unusual about it.

He burst into the kitchen, lifted Jany off the floor and swung her around with an uncharacteristic exuberance. Her worn shoes hit the cupboard under the burners before her shrieks made him set her down. She fended him off with her wooden spoon.

"You're crazy. You nearly made me spill the soup." A short time later, when he offered no explanation for his exuberance she asked, "What's

20

happened? Has the invasion started?"

He quickly calmed down to his usual cool self, but his hard, slender body was still tense. He took a deep breath and reached behind her for the half-empty beaujolais bottle on the shelf. It was hard to get even *vin ordinaire* these days, though Jany carefully saved their ration tickets for Carl's sake.

"Thirsty. I ran all the way."

She watched him pour wine into a sturdy little bistro glass and drink it down while he held the bottle's neck between two fingers.

"You always tell *me* not to run," she reminded him angrily. "You know how violent *they* get when they see one of us running."

"Sorry." He was seldom sloppy but he swiped the back of his hand over his mouth now after returning the bottle to its place. "The Boches are sending new reinforcements to the Normandy front. They must be desperate. The Allies are on the march. Mark me, Jany. They will be in Paris before autumn. You will see. And there is a rumor . . . it's fantastic." After the strain of having to live a double life for so long, his passionate belief in the liberation of France as opposed to his pretense of collaboration in his office, he was now happy for the first time in many months. "They were quarreling in my office today in German. An SS and an army captain. I heard that there was an attempt to blow up Hitler. He was hurt. The SS insisted it was true. But you know how the SS and the Wehrmacht, the regular army, are always feuding. The captain refused to believe it. But it's true. I feel it."

After all the hopes, the disappointments, the

constant presence of the hated enemy, something had finally happened. The liberation *must* be in sight, Jany thought, and cried out for joy. Carl waved her to silence.

"That new concierge. I'd swear she is Gestapo. Listen!" He drew her across to the living room where he slept at night. Its narrow windows with their miniature, wrought-iron balconies opened on the busy rue St. Honore. The windows were closed today to keep the heat out, but a heavy camion rolled by, its earthshaking rumble punctuated by the raucous blare of car horns.

Jany noted the way her brother glanced quickly at the window. His tension scared her — what could it mean?

"It's just traffic . . . isn't it?"

He nodded but he pushed one window open a few inches and looked out, taking care not to be seen by anyone on the street below. He finally relaxed, then turned to her.

"These days, wheels mean Germans, but not today. Now, Jany, there are going to be some very bad times before it's over. The Boches may be more deadly, and they will be everywhere. Himmler's SS already has more power. He is even dictating to the Wehrmacht."

She gulped the air nervously.

"Don't tell me anything, please, Carl. I'd betray it. I'm sure to."

He shook her gently. "No, *chèrie*. I don't want you involved. Ever. So you must never see or hear anything that I may do. And don't let them use you if anything happens . . ."

"Don't say it."

"I must. I have . . . dealings with other groups. The Front Nationale are Communist. At this moment we need them. They need us. But the day will come when we must beat them to the post, unless we want Monsieur Stalin sitting in the Elysée Palace."

Jany had always known Carl's present mistress, Danielle deBrett, was a Red. But it never occurred to Jany that the passionate Resistance worker who was a French native would actually sell out her country to the Russians.

Danielle had been much different when she first met Carl at school in the Paris Lycée. Much more interested in enticing men for her own self-interests than her politics, she and Carl were well-matched, especially for the steamy tussles they engaged in so frequently.

Jany understood his attraction to the voluptuous girl, but she longed for him to meet someone more respectable, someone with less dangerous attachments. Danielle would never be the elegant, respectful wife he would eventually marry. Long ago in 1939, when he proudly started off to guard the impregnable Maginot line, Danielle's silly flirtation with her Communist friends at the Sorbonne had seemed so harmless that Carl had joked with Jany and their mother about it — the university had always been the setting for radical confrontations that were never cause for alarm. But the bitter Armistice of 1940 had hardened him, so much so that he'd sworn to help restore his country's honor, no matter what methods he had to use.

When he learned that sex meant no more to Danielle than a brief physical thrill that she

23

frequently indulged in with others, his romantic interest quickly waned and she became another weapon for his use. Most of her friends were working to replace the Nazi dictatorship of France with a Communist leader. In those four years of the Occupation Carl learned well how to use Danielle for his own purposes as she used men to hers.

Trembling a little, Jany sat down on Carl's sleeping-couch. Two springs were broken and she rose abruptly, wondering how her brother was able to sleep on it at all. Jany had a whole list of resolves for the time when the war ended. Some day she and Carl would be rich and he could have a real bed in his very own bedroom. Then they would eat soup without flower bulbs.

But now two worry lines persisted above his tawny eyebrows as he looked into her eyes. She had never seen him more serious, not even that afternoon in the spring of 1940 when his unit was demobilized.

"It's not finished yet. Only *they* think so," he'd said to Maman and Jany in a strange, hoarse voice.

Watching him now, she promised again to be cautious. Her mouth felt dry as she reached for his hand. The terror was coming back, creeping through her body, making her hands icy in spite of the sultry air. "Carl, I get so scared at times. I mean, if anything happened to you, what would I do?"

He pretended amusement at the tragic look on her face, but he squeezed her fingers in understanding.

"I'll be around. But some day — maybe soon — you are going to be surrounded by dozens of hopeful lovers. Then I'll remind you of how important I am, and you'll laugh."

"Never!"

"Wait and see." Obviously, he wanted to find a subject far removed from dangerous missions and secret identities. "Well then, are we to have dinner? Or have the Boches closed the last *boulangerie?*"

He brought her chair to the little round table and seated himself, as usual, on the couch.

She decided not to tell him about the flower bulbs just yet, and brought the soufflé dishes out of the oven with the cheese melting over the ugly, dark crusts and into the soup below. Hoping he wouldn't notice anything unusual, she watched him take up his spoon and dip it into the toasted cheese and bread on top. She laughed at the stringy cheese and applauded his neat disposal of it before he dipped into the soup underneath.

"Good?"

"Mm-hm."

She began to eat. It *was* pretty good, and for a moment she felt proud of herself. Then she saw him wince as he changed his position. It angered her to see how he was forced to make do with that awful couch. In Maman's day Jany and Carl had both shared the couch at mealtimes.

Having given it a great deal of thought, she announced, "When I get married, it's going to be to someone terribly rich and powerful. And on the day he takes me to the Mairie for the civil service, I shall demand a decent bed for you."

That made him laugh. He wasn't able to stop until he bit into something hard and made a face. Rubbing his cheek, he took out a bit of solid substance on his spoon and examined it.

"Peculiar tasting onion. Doesn't cook up, does it?"

She passed the matter off without emphasis. "Very likely you bit into a tulip. Or maybe a hyacinth. I must not have cooked them enough."

He took it well. "So, now I may expect to sprout tulips." He pinched his tooth, announced no harm had been done, and went on eating.

They did not mention the war or the Resistance again. Jany had a theory that if she asked nothing, she wouldn't know any secrets to betray.

After dinner Carl went back to work and didn't return home until long after the supper hour. He hadn't even stopped for an aperitif at the café just below their front windows, owned by their long-time friend, Pierre St. Just. He looked worried, or maybe only distracted, but such signs always gave her bad dreams.

During this time of the Occupation, her evenings were filled with anxiety and moments of nerve-wracking terror. Peering out the window, waiting for Carl's return, she babbled to herself in vain. "Holy-Mary-full-of-grace, don't let him be caught, please . . . please . . ."

And yet, she didn't have any definite idea of what he actually *was* doing when he wasn't filing or recording or taking letters in the Right Bank annex to the Ministry of Education, where he worked. Before the Occupation it used to thrill Jany to walk under the bright, snapping tricolor over the entrance foyer. Now she never went there. To do so meant she would have to walk under the blood-red banner and swastika of the Third Reich, and she could almost feel its tentacles reaching down to engulf her. It was bad enough seeing the swastika outside the massive Hôtel de Crillon, the Meurice, and even the sacred Ritz.

She was most scared in the blue hours of early morning. That was when an ominous voice inside insisted that the big red-and-black swastika flag was never going to leave. The war which France had already lost would go on forever.

But when daylight came she looked up through the narrow window at the chimney pots, counted the dirty, gray sparrows alighting and taking off from the rain gutters and she'd think to herself, "Something nice could happen today. It's been so long, it must change soon."

Mostly out of habit, but what her brother considered superstition, she remembered to say a prayer each night and to reach for her mother's rosary, which she kept under her pillow.

By the time she got up in the morning she felt optimistic. Things were going to change for the better. They had to.

# Chapter Two

The Nazi flag still hung limp but omnipresent in the July air throughout Paris; yet Jany felt surprisingly cheered by the thought that somewhere along the coast of Normandy brave men and women were working this very minute to conquer that blood-red flag. In doing so, they would free Paris. She didn't think so much about the rest of France. Like most Parisians, she felt that the city *was* France. She hugged her thin arms at the prospect of what must come, and she banished to the back of her mind the gnawing thought that the closer the Allies came to Paris, the more danger there would be of destroying the city, with everything in it that she loved.

Meanwhile, just to stay on her good side and try to keep the concierge from suspecting Carl of aiding the Resistance, Jany went very early to the *boulangerie,* waiting for the shutters to be opened, and was able to buy two chunks of the ersatz bread. She intended one for Madame Charpentier, the concierge, who occupied the rooms opening off the dark passage at the foot of the stairs.

The woman had taken over the post recently, following a traffic accident to her ancient, crabby predecessor who had a habit of drinking too much. It was his misfortune to fall, while in one of his drunken stupors, under the wheels of the Mercedes in which the current German commander of Paris rode. In some ways Madame

Charpentier was an improvement. Jany found her to be super-patriotic to her beloved France and less formidable in demeanor, compared to the old concierge. Because she yearned for someone she could trust besides Carl, it was always upsetting to Jany when he made caustic, accusatory remarks about the woman. "Probably sells information . . . She's very likely Gestapo . . . Never trust her, Jany. Never!"

Jany returned from her special fish market near the end of the rue St. Honore feeling a new surge of confidence in the future. Along the narrow, winding street the excitement seemed to be transmitted from Frenchman to Frenchman. She was sure they knew about the landing of the Allies along the Normandy coast, although it was not something to be discussed aloud — anyone might be a paid agent for the Gestapo.

The German soldiers she passed appeared oblivious to any hint of their fallibility. They were well-behaved and seldom rude, but their arrogant stance hadn't diminished. She tried not to look at them, but couldn't resist sneaking a glance now and then, the way she would have given a tiger in the zoological gardens a fascinated, though cautious, stare.

She was just passing an ancient building, once the townhouse of a noble family, when a slim, dark young civilian limped out under the porte cochère and onto the sidewalk. Perhaps an ex-soldier, she thought. Walking backward as he studied the eighteenth-century facade, he bumped into Jany. Swinging around, he apologized in excellent French that was almost, but not quite, without accent.

He was dark enough to be Neapolitan, but she had seen brunet Germans before, even Germans with this man's good looks, and she didn't think he was Italian.

He went right on, apparently confident of his accent. "I have hurt you, mademoiselle? I do beg your pardon. I was admiring the mansion. Handsome, is it not?"

Handsome. In spite of a small web of white scars across his left jaw and throat, he was everything she considered handsome. Not many men in Paris today looked like this stranger. His smoky blue eyes enticed her in spite of her suspicions about his nationality. It would be sickening to become acquainted and later find out he was one of the enemy.

"It was nothing, monsieur . . . *pardon*. Let me pass, if you please?" She knew better than to remain on the sidewalk chattering with a stranger, even a Frenchman who made her insides churn and tighten. She had been brought up very properly by a mother who insisted that the sins of the mothers should not be repeated by the daughters.

The young man made an extravagant gesture, a sweeping bow that both amused and thrilled her. She remembered the little lead musketeers and felt like their patroness, Queen Anne of Austria. Although she had been told by Danielle deBrett that "men find feminine giggles unattractive," she giggled anyway at his gesture, then nodded regally before she started past him. Coming toward her, walking two abreast, she spotted four German soldiers, and the lightness of the moment was immediately lost. To her relief they ignored her, but from force of habit she dropped her eyes and decided it best to quickly move on.

A few steps behind her the young man was now in their path. She heard the sarcastic exchange between the two leading Germans and knew they were referring to the stranger. "Here's one more cowardly French rabbit." She looked back. Perhaps they hoped to shame the man.

The young man grinned but the Germans had lost their sense of humor. Their ringleader, seeing his harmless smile, demanded to see his papers. Jany watched the handsome stranger carefully as they looked over his papers and questioned him. In spite of his superficial ease, she wasn't surprised to see that he had clenched his free hand into a white-knuckled fist.

The soldiers passed his papers around among them. Could there be something wrong with them, Jany wondered. A horrible thought. He might end up in one of those Gestapo "question rooms." People said that if you walked by at certain hours you could hear the screams of terror. She remembered the crisscross of white scars along the stranger's left jaw and throat. Had he been questioned before?

On a sudden, reckless impulse, Jany shocked herself by pushing between two of the Germans and asking the stranger, "Is there any trouble, *chèri?*" She gave the Germans a huge, wobbly smile, showing all her teeth. "He is harmless, messieurs."

Her loyalty, or her concern, seemed to move the soldiers. No longer able to make more of the papers that were obviously in order, a couple of them shrugged and looked away. Their leader slapped them back into the stranger's hand, saluted Jany with a meticulous click of heels, and passed around them on the sidewalk, followed by the others, all exchanging amused, slightly sardonic glances, if only to save face.

The young man took her in his arms and kissed her exuberantly for their benefit, paying no attention to her embarrassed struggles which mostly came from habit and the stern teachings of her mother and Carl. The pressure of his mouth on hers was unnerving, it was so hard and persistent.

When he finally let her go she was sure that his eyes were laughing. He'd found her prim resistance funny. Or maybe he'd guessed the shocking way in which he'd stirred her. She drew herself up and looked into the young man's eyes.

"No need to playact," she said in her most sophisticated voice. "They aren't looking any more."

"That's a pity." He took her pointed chin in his palm and assured her, "I could go on playacting like that for the rest of the day. Can't we find some other Jerries?"

So! He was no Frenchman at all and he had made his first mistake. Her amusement at discovering the truth faded, though the sensuous aura about him remained to excite her. She knew that he was still in great danger, and looked around nervously.

Aware that he had betrayed himself, he muttered, "Christ!" and added, "It was the Jerry business, wasn't it?"

She nodded. "You must be most careful about such things. You are English?"

32

His grin was as engaging as she had suspected it would be. "Something tells me I've been hanging around Piccadilly too long. I'm a Californian. San Francisco, to be exact." He waited until a woman with a string bag had passed. "I'm no hero parachuting in to save the nation, if that's what you're thinking. I'm a director. We make propaganda movies. To build up morale, you know. We were strafed somewhere this side of Orléans and bailed out. I was picked up by . . ." For the first time he hesitated.

"I know. Maybe the FFI. Resistance. *Forces Français de l'Interieur.* My brother knows . . . I'm sorry. I shouldn't have said that."

He took her string bag and limped along beside her. "Only in my case they called themselves Partisans something or other. Communists. Not that I asked questions. They were expecting some agent who didn't show up. I pulled some ligaments in my foot. That cow pasture was harder than I expected. Tell me. Is my French really that bad?"

"No, no. You could fool a German easily. But a Frenchman might know. Did your Maquis friends send you to a safe house here in Paris?"

"Nothing to it," he said, nodding. "A highly respectable lawyer and his wife. They live on the ground floor of that handsome townhouse over there. That's where I got my papers and this French suit."

Along with everything else, he'd escaped the Germans which, to Jany, made him a hero. Maman had always warned her that there was no such thing as a Prince Charming. But Jany had found one.

"It's so exciting. I never dreamed I would meet a cinema director. What is your name? Have I seen any of your movies?"

"Tony Lombard. You would have to look fast to see my name on the screen before the war. But these papers say I'm 'Antoine Lenoir.' Veteran of the 137th Infantry. French, of course. Wounded at LaPanne during the Dunkirk rout — to explain this." He gestured carelessly toward his neck and the tiny pattern of white scars just visible above his collar.

She was curious about where the scars came from but obviously he was sensitive about them, so she refrained from asking. She tried to think of some reason why she should not walk away and leave him. She couldn't bear the thought that they might never see each other again. There would never be two Tony Lombards in her small, circum-scribed world.

"Can you get back safely? I mean, wherever you came from?" Jany asked.

"More recently, London. The maître — that's what they call lawyers here —"

"Yes, I know."

"Sorry. At any rate, the maître says they will get me out disguised as a carrot. Or maybe it was a turnip. Something like that."

She laughed, but the very idea of the danger she knew was involved scared her.

"Every day terrifies me," she said, "I'm so afraid something will happen to Carl."

His eyebrows shot up. "Your husband?"

She hoped this meant that he was disappointed. "My brother," she replied.

34

"I don't much like the name Karl." He studied her string bag and then her face. "You wouldn't be German, would you?"

She hastened to reassure him. "It's Carl with a *C*. Half German. Our father was an anti-Nazi. Some Gestapo bullies beat him to death in the street on the night they called *Kristallnacht*."

"I'm sorry," he said as they moved along the sidewalk. "Are we walking in the right direction?"

"For what?" she asked, confused.

"You live on this street?"

There was no way to prolong the time with him. "We live beyond the next crossing," she said, regretting it. "On that side of the street. You see the Café St. Just? We live in the court behind the café. One flight up. On the first floor." She realized she might be offering more information than he wanted or needed. "That is to say, if you have trouble and need help," she added stiffly.

"Bless you." His carefree, breezy manner softened. He gave her her bag of groceries and made the same sweeping gesture for her to pass in front of him as she started across the street. "You have already saved me once. You are very *sucre*."

She laughed. "I doubt it. If you like, monsieur, you may say I am *gentile*. But 'sugar' — never. Ask my brother."

"Have I made another mistake? My French teacher will never forgive me. *Adieu*, mademoiselle."

"*Au 'voir*, monsieur."

She had already stepped into the gutter and was crossing the street when he called after her, "I don't know your name."

"Jany!" she cried as two bicycles zoomed past. He waved to her.

"*Au revoir*, Janine."

He had misunderstood her name. Too late now, she thought. He'd already turned and was on his way.

She stopped in front of the café and watched as he limped away. Where was he going? Did he have other friends besides the lawyer and his wife who would help him?

On her way up to the Friedrich apartment, she remembered the concierge and knocked at Madame Charpentier's door after a quick glance over her shoulder. She had never liked the dark passage at the foot of the stairs. When she was a child Carl and his friends had played Seek and Find with her, never guessing the terror she felt when they left her blindfolded in this passage that smelled of urine and trash and sour wine.

Madame Charpentier opened the door so rapidly it was almost as if she had been waiting for Jany. Madame was tall and buxom for a French woman, with breasts tightly encased in a black material that looked like shiny, fraying rayon. Her height gave her the advantage. She appeared to look down on Jany, who put on an eager, humble smile that was far from sincere.

"I'm so glad I caught you before you went to the market, madame."

The woman put her hands on her hips. Her body seemed to swell up in a way meant to be friendly but which was actually alarming in its effect.

"Ah well, then. It is Mademoiselle Friedrich.

How may I help you?"

She did not spit out the German name as most French people did these days. Maybe Carl was right. Maybe she did spy for the Gestapo.

"I had good luck at the *boulangerie*, madame. Can you use an extra loaf of bread?"

It was hardly a loaf and far from the trim, white, prewar *baguettes*, but Madame accepted it with a friendly display of false teeth and unnaturally pale gums.

"You are kind, mademoiselle. I accept. Your handsome brother is doing well these days? He works such long hours. One wonders."

She took the chunk of black bread in hands that smelled of the stock she was boiling down for a poached fish. Madame's table, carefully placed by her window on the little court, would be graced by fresh-caught river trout or salmon. Or sole. Jany's mouth watered at the thought. But she managed to put on a show of pleasure at surrendering the hard-won bread.

"One wonders," Madame repeated, her darting olive eyes busy over every betraying muscle in Jany's face. "Why must the young man work so hard? Is the Ministry of Education so busy now?"

Fear for Carl's safety made Jany adept at lying. She poured out the explanation with nervous haste.

"They wish to teach the children about German history, I believe. There are discussions every night about what is to be included. Of . . . of the war with Prussia in my grandmother's time. And the Great War of 1914."

Madame's hands went up in the air.

37

"A matter most disgusting. That we should teach our children the bloody history of the Boche! What next, I ask you? The Bible according to Adolf Schicklgruber?"

Jany did not fall into that trap, if it was a trap. She put on her innocent, helpless look, neither agreeing or disagreeing.

"Carl only does what he is told, madame. He does not wish to make trouble." She started up the stairs.

"There is about him a quality, mademoiselle," the concierge called out. "I do not think it is cowardice I see in his eyes."

As Jany kept going, Madame bellowed up the stairwell, "You must not be afraid to confide in me, *ma petite*. I am a good Frenchwoman, I hope. Tell your brother he should not work so late. It looks bad, coming in at all hours. One of these nights they will pick him up for breaking the curfew, and then he will be shot if there have been any acts of sabotage that evening. Remember to tell him."

Jany leaned over the splintering bannister.

"Tell his girl, madame. He and Mademoiselle deBrett prefer her apartment. I think it is me they wish to avoid."

"Ah! So that's the way it is. He has surrendered to that woman. I have seen her visit here. Well, so it is. All the good-looking males are taken," she muttered and went inside, slamming the door.

Jany almost fell into the little hall of their apartment, weak with relief. Madame Charpentier might not be a spy after all; maybe she was just an oversexed Frenchwoman who saw an attractive young male like Carl slipping out of her reach.

She dropped her bag in the kitchen and rushed to the street windows, but of course, there was no sign of the American. Tony Lombard had limped far out of sight by now. Remembering the excitement he had aroused in her, she felt a bit of sympathy for Madame in her craving for a man.

# Chapter Three

The damned ankle was giving him fits.

Tony Lombard came to a stop in the shadow of the Madeleine Church. He balanced himself with one arm against a kiosk and raised his right foot from the paving stones. He found himself sweating from the pain. Or maybe it was just the sultry July day.

"Lost," he decided. "I'm one block from the most famous place in town and I've gotten off the track."

He knew why. That girl with the golden hair and the blue eyes. Funny kid. At twenty-five he could afford to regard "Janine" as a child. A sweet child who make him think of grassy dells and soft, downy violets hidden from the sun. In spite of his theatrical performance — the passionate kiss bestowed for the benefit of the German soldiers — the girl with her innocent demeanor reminded him a little of his daughter. Eve Andrea was not quite three years old, born in Hawaii only weeks before Pearl Harbor, but something he saw in Andrea's big, trusting eyes with their silken lashes was also there in the way this "Janine" had looked at him.

Andrea was very precious, the only person in the world who he knew loved him first and best. His wife, a highly successful actress, had a set of priorities that put her career first, Andrea second and her husband last. Eden Ware, without being beautiful, had managed her exciting personality and talent for touching the heart into a career in which she had been nominated twice for an Oscar, both times for Best Supporting Actress. There were few things in life she wanted more than to be nominated for Best Actress. Tony often thought this elusive, career-driven woman with her flaming red hair fascinated him because he could never fully understand her. She was eight years his senior, but instead of hiding the fact, as one might expect, she used it as a kind of shield to keep him from ever possessing her completely.

He remembered the first time he had gotten to Eden. It was precisely the way he had dreamed of having her, in the crazy "Valentino-Modern" apartment she rented on Franklin Avenue above Hollywood Boulevard.

Eden had been wildly excited, a hangover from her successful escape the night of the *Anschluss* when Hitler's hordes marched into Vienna in March of 1938. She and Tony's aunt Brooke and his father, Steve, had been involved in what she called "an international caper" which included Eden's boss, Leo Prysing, in some mysterious way.

Tony remembered that he hadn't cared much to hear about it, but he had noticed how exciting Eden Ware could be. He had first known her as a girl, but the early years of her career spent in Europe, starving, playing bit parts in sex-exploitation "art" films, and living freely had given her a strange new luster.

So he had walked her across the avenue from a party in Leo Prysing's suite, hoping to make love to her because . . . hadn't a few Frenchmen been there before him?

41

In Eden's spacious, one-room bachelor apartment things moved rapidly. He and Eden got to laughing over her wall-bed which fell down when the hall door opened. Eden bounced on the mattress, deciding no harm had been done to the springs, and Tony joined her. There was a childish tussle which ended when he rolled on top of her, held her down on the bed and began to explore her wide, enticing mouth with his tongue. She fought him, sometimes playfully, sometimes with a surprising violence.

When he managed to get his fly open while keeping her in a tight embrace — no easy feat — he entered her with a sense of triumph. Her body accepted him after a struggle of resistance that Tony found even more exciting.

Still writhing in what seemed more like a wrestling match than lovemaking, they had reached their passionate climax in unison. That night marked the beginning of what was to become the pattern of their lives together: all problems were solved, at least temporarily, by their perfect sex life. Maybe that's why their baby, Eve Andrea, was so perfect.

But the basic problem of the relationship was only blurred by their physical success. The many glorious hours spent in bed together didn't make it disappear. Tony knew they were both self-centered, and understood that, for his part, he wanted nothing more than to overcome and pass beyond his father's fame. It seemed to be passed down through the generations, this competition among the Lombards. There was his father's success and renown in the world of real estate and high finance, his mother's work in movies as a writer for her old friend, Leo Prysing, and his cousin Alec's success in the radio broadcasting business. With these as role models it was naturally expected that Tony, too, would excel at something.

In his youth he had achieved a fame of sorts, especially because of his popularity among women, but this began to pall for him even before his marriage to Eden. Then Andrea's birth, one of the few high points of his life, was followed within weeks by his injuries from a low-strafing Zero on its way to Pearl Harbor.

Eden had been great during those weeks of his convalescence. But as soon as he was on his feet again, she resumed her career. She was hailed for her War Bond tours, her USO tours to North Africa and her visits to army hospitals. More and more, Tony felt like the first failure in three generations of Lombards. He wangled a job as assistant director with movie producer Leo Prysing's London unit during the Blitz, but it was a job that separated him from his equally busy wife and, of course, his daughter.

When Tony and Eden did get together, about the only thing they shared, aside from Andrea, was their enjoyment of each other in bed.

It seemed unnatural that only sex and a longtime mutual understanding held him and Eden together. There must be more to a marriage than sex, he reasoned, in spite of Heather Burkett's comment to him long ago, before she married Alec.

"You haven't the biggest prick in the world," she'd said, "but it's the best."

He had accepted the compliment, half-believing she meant it. It was a long time ago, before Heather married Alec, and especially, before Eden.

Lately, when he tried to reason with Eden at various times, or to point out that they should think of settling down to live life like a normal family she reminded him of her seniority in age.

"Don't be silly, darling. You knew what I was and who I was when you married me. I'm too old to look starry-eyed at you. I know more of the world than you do. God knows, I've lived in it a lot longer."

How could he answer that? Yes, he thought, the little French girl, Janine, was at the opposite pole from Eden Ware Lombard. She seemed so sweet and giving, perhaps easily possessed. Not much of a challenge to a hardened man-about-women, but enchanting nonetheless. He realized then that the womanizer in him had been left somewhere along the hard road to this moment.

Just for a minute there he had been thinking like the old Tony Lombard, without regard to anything but a momentary delight. It surprised him that he had begun to doubt himself, even to ask himself what that lovely, innocent girl was thinking and feeling.

And what was Eden doing today, halfway across the world in the safe haven of Hollywood? He had been hopeful about seeing her soon when she talked about doing the location shooting for her new film in bomb-scarred London. Leo Prysing had cast her as a lead in his new war film, all about gallant entertainers in London during the Blitz.

But the idea of sending her to London had gone sour when production costs mounted, due to the efforts to get government cooperation for the aerial sequences. Tony knew it would never occur to his wife to back out of the film so she might join him. She was too professional for that.

He considered the time difference between Paris and California. She must have heard by now that a plane photographing the progress of the invasion had gone down somewhere in Northern France, and her husband, a second unit director for Prysing Productions, was presumed captured or dead. She would care, he knew that. Eden loved him. But she probably wouldn't be shattered — she would still carry on.

He looked around.

"Where the hell do I go from here?"

He had passed muster with the cold, business-like Partisan who first rescued him, and then had been easily transformed into Antoine Lenoir by Maître Mercier, but there was still one more hurdle, Danielle deBrett. "That's the Paris contact. I am to give her the code name Icarus." Not very subtle. Icarus was the ambitious young man who flew with wax wings that melted near the sun . . . he hoped that the Germans didn't study much Greek mythology.

"Between St. Honore and Rivoli," the lean, tough little Maquis leader had told him, "Just off Concorde." Well, that was only a block away. He took a deep breath and started down the spacious rue Royale after glancing across the street at the subtle facade of Maxim's. He wondered how many years and how much blood would be spilled before

45

the war ended and he could bring Eden for a glamorous evening at the famous restaurant.

It would be just like Eden to say, "No thanks. There's a little café I'll take you to, near the boule Mich, upstairs, with newspapers for tablecloths. The food is marvelous."

Yes. That would be Eden. She had always been there — no matter where it was — before him. There was nothing he could introduce her to for the first time.

Suddenly a lovely face flashed across his memory. The little golden French girl, Janine. What a kick she would get out of Maxim's! Like most Parisians, she probably had taken the belle epoque restaurant for granted without ever having been as far as the sacred foyer. She was about as unlike Eden as he could imagine. Curious that she should linger in his memory. An ordinary little girl, though beautiful for her age, with some sweet, naive quality. Good Lord, he thought. A virginal quality. A quaint idea, but very appealing.

The place de la Concorde spread out before him in the sunlight, that rare combination of the monumental and the elegant.

Continuing on, he turned to the left and limped along under the Rivoli arcades, counting the small side streets that would have intrigued him by their charm in the old days. He found his way at last, came into a street behind the rue de Rivoli and walked boldly into the tiny Café au Coin, nestled in an ell between two buildings where the street made a sharp right turn. There were two tables out on the sidewalk but he ignored the customers seated there. A German soldier and a French-looking girl had their heads together, oblivious to the busy traffic only a hundred yards away, while at the other table an old man wearing a beret was picking his teeth and studying the dregs of his vermouth glass.

Inside, two workmen with hands stained by either whitewash or plaster sat at the table for six. Tony slipped into the chair farthest from them. They were talking in a dialect so rapidly he couldn't understand most of it. It sounded as though they had some complaint about their foreman.

The café owner, dressed in a black waistcoat and sleeveholders, ambled up to Tony's end of the long table.

"M'sieur desires the specialty of the day?"

Tony nodded. The French girl had given him a complex about what he had always considered to be his excellent French. He put one hand over his mouth, appearing to bite his thumbnail in order to muffle his pronunciation. Leaning down to rub his throbbing ankle, he felt tired and yet high-keyed. He knew his wits were dulled by the long hours since he had parachuted out over the cow pasture near Orléans. The strange, yet welcome group that had surrounded him with their triangle of shaded lights were positive the crew of his reconnaissance plane would be rescued by members of another cell. But he had neither seen nor heard of the whereabouts of any of them since the order to bail out, and could only hope that they hadn't broken their necks or been betrayed into SS hands.

"Where is Mademoiselle Danielle?" Tony asked.

The patron polished his end of the table with a

dirty cloth, shrugging in reply. "A wine for m'sieur?"

"*Ordinaire.*"

"*Naturellement. Rouge?*"

Tony nodded again, concentrating on his nails, even though he wasn't the nail-biting type. That was more like his cousin Alec, who was currently the top American correspondent in London for Universal Broadcasting Company. Alec was a good egg in his own sour way. He would probably believe Tony had been lost with the plane and deliver one of his dry, yet oddly stirring eulogies that night. Wish I could hear it, Tony thought wryly, remembering how Tom Sawyer, sneaked home to hear all the nice things said about him that never would have been said of the living boy.

Tony had a somewhat similar reputation. He hoped Eden wouldn't suffer too much, thinking he was gone. But she had her career and the baby to keep her busy. His little love, his Eve Andrea, would be sorry if she thought she would never see her "dada" again. And he knew his own mother would care deeply, though she seldom showed it. It was hard to know about his father. Tony wasn't sure if the fierce competitiveness between the Lombard males was strong enough to overshadow their caring for one another.

Tony winced as a shot of pain jammed its way up and down his leg. He welcomed the wine which appeared promptly in its little carafe. Good, drinkable table wine. He poured and drank fast. He may have been imagining it, but thought he felt better at once. Getting on to business, he started to bring up the name of Danielle deBrett again when the patron arrived to serve him a steaming dish of the day's special — the portions were modest, but the food was nonetheless delicious. He hadn't tasted the long, dark strings of green beans since his last visit to France before the war, but he could never forget their succulent taste.

Tony's hands shook slightly. He hadn't realized how hungry he was. Before asking again about the deBrett woman, he took a forkful of the dark green beans, winding them up and enjoying the taste as well as memories of past feasts. Between the wine and the pure pleasure of the food, he felt much more like his normal, lively self, able to cope with anything, even the sexy brunette beauty whose hips were swiveling between the tables and bringing her either toward the open door or to him.

Looking around, he saw that the patron had moved away, and was now in the area of the two plasterers. They included him in their intense argument on working conditions. The German Occupation seemed to have no part in their complaint. Luckily, they had no interest in Tony, because the brunette beauty proved to be Danielle deBrett. She slipped into a chair and leaned toward Tony, providing a full view of her pendulous breasts. With some interest he observed that if she breathed deeply enough her large, dark nipples would be exposed at this inopportune moment, at least for him. He grinned but took care to go on eating. Might as well get off on the right foot. Business first, pleasure — some other time.

"Good," he said in French, indicating the dish rather than the bosom.

"Of course. Why not?"

Her voice did not match her looks. It was harsh and abrasive. To his surprise her wide, sexy mouth repulsed him a little. "You want me?"

He felt like saying "Not offhand," but managed his best quizzical look. "We have mutual friends, no? The Icarus family. You are Mademoiselle deBrett?"

"Danielle. Yes, I know the family. Especially the old man. Fat Paul, we call him. Was he helpful to you?"

He immediately saw that she was testing him.

"Must be one of those private family jokes. The Paul I know is very small, lean as a whippet. And hardly older than I am."

She reached for his tin spoon, dipped it into the rice, chewed and swallowed while gazing into his eyes.

"Well, then. The report. Are we to receive the support of the Churchill government? With the landings in Normandy we comrades must know we are to take Paris from the Gaullists when Liberation comes."

Good God! She really believed he was the Communist courier they had been expecting. He started to deny it, then wondered if she and her Red friends would betray him if they were to discover that they hadn't saved one of their own kind, after all.

"I'm not privy to the Privy Council," he joked, and seeing the cold veil that seemed to descend over her eyes, he added quickly, "You may know, the old man chose to support the Partisans in the Balkans. That seems to show which way Churchill's choices run."

"That is something," she agreed. "And the money?"

"The money." He repeated the words to gain time. These Resistance bands, Communist-Partisan or Gaullist or somewhere in between, were always short of cash. It was a built-in condition of the species.

"Well?"

Still thinking about the eulogy his cousin Alec Huntington would be punching out just about now, he started to use Alec's name as that of a fellow "comrade," but it occurred to him that these Partisans had radios too and were sure to have heard his broadcasts. Occasionally, Alex had been the means of sending coded messages to the French Underground. Another name popped into his head, that of Roger Games, the best cinematographer Prysing Productions had. At the last minute he had been scrubbed from the mission so he could concentrate on some RAF training scenes.

"Roger Games has the package, unless it's spilled all over the Norman countryside. Bailed out just before me. I don't know what happened to the poor fellow."

"The devil you say! If he was taken, and with all those francs!"

He could afford to be nonchalant. They weren't his francs. He had a sneaking suspicion that the Communist courier they were waiting for had turned capitalist and remained in England with the money.

"Maybe he landed nearer the coast. He's liable

51

to show up any hour."

But he thought to himself, Nobody will be more surprised than yours truly if he does!

A shadow crossed the doorway. The two plasterers started to get up for their return to work, then sat down again, very slowly. Tony and Danielle looked around at the doorway. An agent of the French Police strolled in, followed by two Germans in uniform. Not the gray-green of the Wehrmacht. From the way Danielle sucked in her breath, Tony recognized trouble. He made out the double lightning strokes on the shoulders of their uniforms. These were the first SS he had seen since the beginning of the war. Like the evil, black-clad gang of a B-western, they looked every bit as formidable as they were reputed to be.

The patron hurried to serve them but the younger, taller of the two waved him aside imperiously. In a loud voice and speaking German, he demanded of the two laborers their papers.

The French agent translated. What surprised Tony was that the stocky little man's manner was just as arrogant as the Germans'. Tony was forced to correct his idea that all citizens of occupied democratic countries were defiant anti-Nazis. The two men brought out their identity papers with unsteady hands, though their papers seemed to be in order. Tony could understand that very well. He shared their nervousness, but with greater reason.

The shorter German looked civilized. Tony might have met him at Berlin's elegant Adlon Hotel before the war, but the large, younger one was the arrogant, bullying type — a carbon copy of all the Martin Koslecks and Kurt Katches who currently populated the anti-Nazi movies on American screens.

They moved on to Danielle who leered at them insolently as she pulled her papers out of her low-cut, gathered blouse which seemed to amuse the older SS officer. The younger one's heavy, brutal face did not crack a smile, though it was clear that he was interested in what he saw.

"*À bas le Générale de Gaulle!*" she called out with what Tony thought might be perfect honesty. The worst obstacle to a Communist takeover of Paris was not the Germans, but a lanky French exile with a parrot's beak and a voice that had stirred millions of his countrymen with his "flame of resistance" and his passionate vow, "France has lost the battle, but not the war." No Communist leader had risen to the eloquence of the arrogant, imperious de Gaulle.

Tony disliked Brigadier General Charles de Gaulle as he disliked all men of spirit who made him feel inferior, but if the FFI was to serve in the liberation of France, there was only one logical leader of a free France — "Le Grand Charles," as many English and Americans in London called him.

The heavy-faced Gestapo agent stared, sputtered a laugh and then agreed with Danielle in German. Tony noticed that this time it was the older German who did not laugh. His eyes narrowed slightly as he regarded Danielle with suspicion. To take the man's attention from her, Tony handed up his papers.

"Is it permitted to ask why you are inspecting papers now, monsieur?" he asked.

The young one, still interested in Danielle's cleavage and her bold shout, made a gesture, dismissing his question. Tony now noticed the French police agent for the first time. To his surprise, the man's squirrel-cheeks had reddened at Danielle's anti-Gaullist cry and Tony began to respect him more.

The second SS officer, too, was seeing more than had been intended. As the first German handed him the girl's papers, the older one made a remark in French, watching her carefully.

"Gaullist saboteurs are being dropped to destroy the city. Perhaps you would harbor them?"

"Who? Me?"

Danielle spat only inches from his polished boots. In spite of himself, he shifted his boot toes slightly. It was a small movement, but it symbolized retreat and Tony was relieved out of all proportion for the gesture.

"Where do you live, you?" the first SS officer asked Tony in German.

Danielle looked at Tony, while the older German and the French agent seemed to concentrate on him. He had waited a fraction of time for Danielle to speak up. She didn't, the bitch. If he wasn't mistaken, she seemed amused by the spot he was in. Remembering suddenly a very different kind of girl he had met earlier, he rose to the occasion brilliantly, he thought.

"I live on the rue St. Honore. Above the Café St. Just."

For some reason, this satisfied the Germans. Only now Danielle deBrett seemed upset. After the boots of the SS had clicked off down the street, it was Danielle who spoke first.

"Don't tell me you've met Carl and Jany so soon. A small world, indeed, monsieur. I thought your contacts in Paris were Maître Mercier and his woman."

Now it was Tony's turn to shrug and play it cool, while she stared with her mouth open. She didn't like it, and he couldn't help but wonder why.

"Well, I'm off to the Café St. Just. My lodgings, as it were," he said, getting up to leave, having convinced her he was the Communist courier he was expected to be.

But secretly he found it unpleasant, if not dangerous, that this coldblooded beauty should know of the little virgin of the Café St. Just.

# Chapter Four

Strand Beach, California.

Eden Ware Lombard was on location. They had made seven takes and she still hadn't reacted properly, which was most unlike Eden, who usually hit the mark on the first few tries.

The boy with the clapper snapped it in front of the camera, reminding everybody on the set and all the avid fans beyond the camera's range that Eden Ware had gone up on her lines again.

Chastising herself for these memory lapses, the first in her career, Eden grinned and ran her hands through her fine, red hair, making it stand on end, to the delight of her fans. They saw beyond her appearance to the uniquely fascinating woman who needed no Hollywood makeup to charm — it was her sparkling personality, her ability to move an audience to laughter or tears, and her refreshing manner of never taking herself too seriously that endeared her to so many.

Framing Eden's well-known face with its fantastic bone structure, her uncontrollable hair was oddly attractive. She apologized, aware as always of the inconvenience to the crew.

"Sorry, boys. Don't know where my brains are today. If anybody can rustle up some scotch the armed forces haven't siphoned off, it'll be my treat after shooting. You've put up with a lot of crap this afternoon."

Everyone was embarrassingly solicitous.

"Mr. Lombard's going to be all right, Eden. Anybody'd feel the same in your shoes."

"Don't worry, kid," someone else called out, "Old Tony's too ornery to die."

Several British advisers on the set had been through it themselves. They were more aware of Tony's chances and were less boisterous, but Eden appreciated their cool honesty.

"We've had a bit of luck now and then, Miss Ware. The whole French countryside is honey-combed with Underground agents. Look at how they got me out."

"Quite true, Miss Ware," an RAF man agreed. "Remember Ronnie Lenox from up border way? Rescued by something called the Maquis. All French. All anti-Nazis. Live like animals in the forest, they say. But by George, they got Ronnie out."

She finally made the shot on the ninth take and was through for the day. Her numerous retakes were costly for the film that was already running over-budget, but this was overlooked as the crew tried to cheer her. Everyone had a different story of a friend who had returned after a miraculous rescue, though it was never a tale of someone captured by the Nazis, or someone who had broken his neck on landing.

Throughout the encouraging chatter around her, questions continued to needle their way through her brain. *Tony, did you make it? Forty-eight hours since Alec called me. We ought to know. We ought to feel it, somehow.*

But she felt nothing but a gripping fear that she might never see Tony again.

"I won't think about that," she told herself firmly. "I'll think of Tony and me, the perfection of what we had. *No. What we have* . . . how we enjoy each other, sympathize with and understand each other's ambitions, our drives and passions. And our little Andrea . . . such a perfect marriage as ours can't end this soon."

While she ran through her lines in a love scene with her leading man, a 4F, she pretended he was Tony, with his knowing, skilled hands, and his marvelous timing. Tony always knew just how much foreplay she needed. The memory of his lips and his graceful fingers exploring the deepest erogenous areas of her body was enough to give her large, expressive eyes a look now that startled her less-than-sensual partner.

During a break she tried calling Alec again, but getting through to London in wartime and to a man as busy as Alec seemed to be increasingly harder as the war blazed onward — to what? Pray God, its conclusion, Eden thought silently.

Steve Lombard arrived before the crew struck the beach set and headed back home to Prysing's Hollywood unit studios. Eden had always liked her father-in-law, and he was never more welcome than at this moment. A man of strength and ruddy good looks, even at fifty, he was still her idol as he had been when she was a young actress living in Paris, before the war. Luckily for her eventual marriage to Tony, she and Steve had never consummated the feelings they had briefly felt for each other. It was the one thing Tony never would have forgiven.

He greeted her with his usual frankness.

"You sure are a mess. You mean to tell me your fans pay to see you looking like that?"

Eden carelessly smoothed down her hair and licked sand off her lips. "Okay. Now I'm decent. Have you heard about what happened? When will he be rescued?"

Before he could say anything she saw the answer in Steve's eyes. She also saw that he was trying to put on a good front but there were new lines in his face and an unfamiliar tension in his tall, athletic body. He took her arms and pinned them to her sides, quieting her. "I know you're worried, honey. It's Pearl Harbor all over again. Only this time I'm so damned helpless. There's no way I can get to him . . . even if he is hurt."

Tony had been driving his father to a breakfast meeting with Admiral Kimmel that Sunday morning in December of '41 when the car was strafed by a Zero headed for Battleship Row at Pearl. Badly cut about the neck and jaw by glass, Tony had been raced to a plantation hospital by his father and his life was miraculously saved.

In the present emergency Steve Lombard felt that he was a failure. He didn't even know whether his son was alive. Trying to encourage himself as well as Eden, he said, "It's too early. It takes time to plan those things from the French side. They can't trust everyone, you know — the whole Resistance is infiltrated with pro-Nazis."

"But the Channel is only twenty-six miles across. When I used to make the Calais crossing I could see the French coastline from Dover. I mean . . . couldn't a lobsterman, or a cod fisherman or someone row him across?"

59

"Honey, you know as well as I do that the French coast is full of bloody fighting. And if it isn't, it's swarming with Nazis . . . By the way, your fans will be watching the way you take this."

"Who cares?" she muttered. "Just tell me if you know what happened . . ."

He'd always admired her incredible spirit. As she stood there in a one-piece, harlequin-patterned swimsuit, with an egg-beater hairdo, her trim legs sprinkled with sand, her high cheekbones shiny, she was apparently oblivious to what must have been a hundred excited fans gaping at her. Eden did what she wanted, lived as she wanted, and cared for no one's opinion about how she did it. She was Eden Ware, the exciting movie personality — but did she really care for her husband as much as she cared for her daughter and her career?

Steve was beginning to believe that perhaps she did, and respected her a great deal more for that assurance.

"The plane crashed," he explained, "and we know it was hit by some flak. It was tracked somewhere over Normandy. They don't know what caused the crash yet." His mouth betrayed him by twitching a little. "They were still shooting film after they got the action stuff. If they bailed out, some were bound to make it. Law of averages."

"If the Gestapo doesn't get them."

"Yes."

"Do you think the Gestapo would kill Tony?"

"I don't think so, honey. There's nothing he can tell them, and they'll see that he's not carrying anything like money or ammunition. If they did get him they'd take him as a prisoner of war, most likely."

"Oh, God!"

But of course, it was better than some of the unspoken alternatives.

Steve caught out of the corner of his eye two spinsterish women as they walked through the unofficial barricade of crewmen and made a beeline for Eden.

"I loved all your pictures, Miss Ware," gushed one woman wearing green eye shadow and bobby sox. "Would you autograph this picture for me? I got it at the United Artists film exchange."

Not at all to Steve's surprise, Eden Ware, the movie star, quickly recovered from her upset. "Of course I will," she said with her full-lipped grin, "It'll be my pleasure. How do you want it to read?"

Nobody had a pen. Eden turned to Steve who fumbled in his pocket and finally produced the gold pen that Randi had given him last Christmas. While Eden was signing her second picture, she called Steve's attention to the eight-by-ten glossy.

"Good Lord! This is a still from *Journey*. That sure brings back memories, doesn't it, Steve?"

Although some of the fans who had gathered overheard her remark, only Steven understood her allusion to the true story behind Leo Prysing's 1939 anti-Nazi film, *Journey*, an adventure actually involving Steve, Eden and Leo Prysing himself, with only a few fictional changes made. Steve didn't like to think about the original event. Leo never mentioned it, and it was surprising for Steve to hear Eden bring it up of her own accord. Apparently, it didn't bother her.

Eden make no excuse to her fans once she decided she'd wasted enough time. She mistakenly handed the gold pen back to a young boy in swim trunks, waved good-bye to the crowd, and sprinted off toward the cement boardwalk. The studio had rented the front apartment of a twenties court facing the boardwalk for Eden's dressing room and Stephen was still studying the front of the old court a short time later when she came out in a ghastly pair of wide-legged, flowered beach pajamas and a halter top. Her hair was twisted into a meager French knot, but it was neat and on her looked chic. Steven knew that in spite of the "star" side of her he liked her and understood perfectly why his popular son had pursued Eden Ware all the way to the altar.

"You look wonderful," he said, his tone suggesting surprise.

"Compared to what?" she answered, teasingly.

"How are you getting home?"

"With the crew. What made you give that little court such an x-ray eye?"

He gave the white stucco place one last glance.

"I owned those very apartments back in the twenties. Randi and I spent our honeymoon in this town. Or the town that was, before the '33 quake. Let me drive you into Hollywood. Then I'm heading out to the airport."

"Back to San Francisco?"

They walked along, arm in arm, up the steep little side street to Ocean Avenue and the garage. "No, Randi thought I'd better go on from here if I could make the connections."

She knew instantly what he meant. "You're flying to London?"

"From Washington. I pulled a few strings, called in some markers. They're getting me on General Berryman's plane tomorrow. I'll try to get through to Randi from London the minute I hear anything. Too bad you can't join her and Brooke in San Francisco. Alec called his mother, of course, so between Alec and me, you girls will be kept well-informed."

It seemed the best idea, under the circumstances. Today's scenes were her last for the weekend. She wouldn't be called until Tuesday. Her only hesitation was Randi Lombard. Eden felt that Randi had never been too fond of her. Maybe she suspected that there was something between her husband and herself in Paris in '38. Or maybe it was just the usual jealousy between mother and daughter-in-law over a son and husband. Or maybe, Eden thought to herself, it's my own jealousy. Randi is everything I ever wanted to be. *She should have been the movie star, with her elegant looks and glamorous personality.* An awareness of her own physical flaws had long ago convinced Eden Ware that since she couldn't change them, she would play them up, make the most of them. She figured that in that way she would disarm criticism — and it had worked. But it didn't stop her from wishing she were as attractive a woman as Randi Lombard.

*Good God! I'm jealous, that's all. I'm the problem, not Randi.*

"Maybe I'll fly up to San Francisco tomorrow morning with the baby. Then we can all get your calls together. That is, if Randi won't mind."

He was enthusiastic. "She'd love it. The whole

family will be dying to see my little granddaughter."

"Thanks loads."

He ignored her friendly sarcasm and started to help her into his Cadillac but she already had the door open.

"You should lock your car doors, father-in-law. Even in this haven for the elderly, there still may be someone out there hungry for a used Cadillac."

He snorted, boosted her onto the seat and went around to the driver's side. He said nothing until they were headed out of town, past hills planted with oil derricks and toward the Los Angeles Highway.

"Thinking about Tony?" she asked at last.

He glanced at her. "About Tony. And about that time in Paris when I visited the attic dump you lived in on the Ile St. Louis."

"Where we found Leo Prysing waiting for us, big as life. That was some experience, wasn't it? Vienna and the *Anschluss*. And that horrible train ride with the Nazis breathing down our necks."

"Do you ever — ?" He started over. "Does your conscience ever bother you? Did you ever have bad dreams about that?"

She raised herself from a slouch. "About Kurt Friedrich?"

"I know it doesn't bother Leo. I've mentioned it once or twice and he has absolutely no reaction, except maybe pleasure."

She snapped, "I don't blame him. Leo is a realist."

"An Old Testament realist. Sometimes he scares me."

"Steve! You're kidding. I've never lost one

night's sleep over the Friedrich thing." She looked at him in the dim light of passing cars. He had always been completely in command. She knew that even Tony was awed by his father's accomplishments in real estate, financial affairs, and then in the Allied cause. These days Steve Lombard was on the receiving end of secret information concerning international affairs. Probably because he knew where the Washington bodies were buried. If they didn't scare him, nothing would.

"It's pretty obvious that Kurt didn't know he was Jewish," Steve said. "I suppose that Nazi mother of his went out of her way to keep it a secret. Funny that Leo Prysing never brought it up. They worked together in Hollywood for years."

"With Kurt spouting off his anti-Semitic slime? Leo's too smart for that — he knows it would have cost him a leading man. But he used that knowledge when it counted. I'll say that for Leo."

"You're hard, Eden. Maybe that's what Tony sees in you. Tony was spoiled young. He could get anything or anyone he wanted until you came along. You'll never be conquered."

She was unexpectedly furious. "That's a rotten thing to say. I'm just as vulnerable as the next woman."

This curious defense sounded ridiculous, even to her. She knew it was untrue.

They had little more to say until they reached Eden's Spanish-style apartment house on Franklin Avenue, a block above Hollywood Boulevard. As Tony Lombard's wife, her official home was either the old Lombard mansion on San Francisco's Nob Hill or her birthplace, the Ware estate on Oahu's

65

windward coast, outside Honolulu. But those who knew Eden well contacted her at the Hollywood apartment she'd had since she was single, with its "bachelor" look in both size and decor — a large living room complete with Moorish archways and a sexy "Valentino" couch, a dressing room, bath and what purported to be a kitchen, about three-by-six feet. This had always been her idea of heaven. She entertained on the floor and had dozens of cushions and hassocks stored away for just that purpose. People who couldn't cross their legs Yoga-style seldom paid her return visits.

It was in this apartment that Tony camped out with Eden, telling her it made him feel "like a stud with a call girl." She hoped that was meant as a compliment. Entering the shabby romantic little foyer and ducking under the first dark, oaken arch, Eden felt Tony's presence vividly. She remembered how he joked about their romantic gestures toward each other because she did, but he remained the more romantic of the two.

Eden reasoned that a man with Tony's looks and popularity could afford to show his vulnerable, romantic side. And when she and Tony came in under this Moorish arch during their infrequent nights together, he would grab her, sweep her into his arms, and give her a sexy, Valentino-type kiss. She would never forget their first night together . . . Tony was incredibly sexy and suave in his technique, but for some reason his furtive attention made her giddy and she found herself giggling at his initial overtures. Tony found this delightful and they were soon wrapped around each other in a night of passionate, uninhibited lovemaking.

And now that he was gone, she missed him with a poignant ache every time she came home from the studio and entered her lair.

Someone else evidently missed him as much. After five months of separation from her father, little Eve Andrea still raised her small, dark head every time the corridor door opened and wobbled across the wide living room with her arms outstretched.

"Dada? Dada?"

Eden hurried toward her. "Not yet, sweetheart. But someone else almost as nice. I've brought granddada to see you."

Andrea was easily satisfied. "Granddada!" she screamed, and held her arms out to her grandfather who lifted her up and swung her over his head so high she could almost touch the dark beams. She squealed with delight, screaming, "Mo', mo'," and Steve obligingly swung her up again.

"She is so easily distracted, even from her father," Eden said with a sigh to her baby-sitter, a pretty young movie hopeful.

"Oh, no, Miss Ware! Nobody could ever forget Tony. I mean — Mr. Ware."

"Lombard," Steve put in, holding Andrea straight up in the air by her ankles.

The baby-sitter gracefully touched her fingers to her moist lips and hunched her shoulders in mock apology.

"What a goof! I'm sorry, Miss Ware. But I guess we're just used to your name. I mean, well, you know Hollywood . . . Have they heard anything about Tony yet?"

Eden was used to everyone's familiarity in Hollywood but it still annoyed Steve. He scowled and set his granddaughter on her feet on the floor. She clung to his leg.

"More, granpa."

"No, sweetheart." He bent and kissed her small, round cheek. "Got to go out and find dada and bring him home to his best girl."

Eden raised her head and gave him a look.

"His best girls," he amended. "Well, Eden, I'll try to get through to everybody at the Nob Hill house. You be there. Even if I don't get you, Alec will — Brooke says he's been very good about phoning. Technically, it's not easy at this time, and God knows that sister of mine never gave Alec reason for any filial devotion when he was growing up."

Eden thought Alec Huntington had become quite self-sufficient in handling his feckless, pleasure-loving mother. He understood her so well that he had deliberately married a pretty, self-centered, flirtatious girl exactly like her. Alec was Eden's friend. But she knew he didn't deserve sympathy and would despise it anyway — he knew what he was doing.

Steve took her hand. "I'm not coming back here without Tony, you know. I'm going to make those Krauts cough him up, if they've got him."

"Thank you, Steve."

She started to press her cheek to his in the Hollywood way. He had moved his head at the same time and they came together in an unexpectedly warm kiss that brought back memories both would like to have forgotten — it was difficult for them to think of their Paris days, no matter how unfulfilled,

68

without also thinking of the Friedrich affair. That was enough to quell any romantic notions.

Under the interested gaze of the baby-sitter, Eden quickly broke away, telling him a lame good-bye.

"And Steve," she added, "if there's one person who can bring him home, I know it's you."

He grinned fleetingly. "That's what Randi said. I think she's got the idea I'll buy up France to get him."

"Wouldn't put it past you."

With Andrea's hand in hers Eden walked the baby after him to the hallway. They watched him duck under the archway at the point where three tile steps led down to the sunken lobby with its decor copied from Spain's Alhambra, complete with a dry fountain. He looked back, waved to Andrea, then raised two fingers in Churchill's famous victory sign.

Eden tried to borrow from his optimism but could only wonder if Steve Lombard was really as confident as he appeared. A deep, ominous depression began to form in the back of her mind — if Steve couldn't bring Tony back, who could?

# Chapter Five

Three days a week Jany Friedrich took typing lessons in an office on the rue des Saussies, just off the Faubourg St. Honore in the Eighth Arrondissement. Carl didn't like her to go there because it was too close to the areas taken over by the SS. Whenever Jany had to pass under the sign of the swastika on its bloody background, she would stare at the sidewalk, concentrating on the layers of the pro-Nazi newspaper, *Paris-Soir*, which covered the hole in her shoe sole.

Sometimes she encountered SS men, both in and out of uniform. The terror they aroused in her had nothing to do with the sexual fears she associated with the average German soldier. Furthermore, it was the Gestapo who ordered her off the sidewalk, unlike the regular German army, some of whose members seemed to find her attractive before she went into her pigeon-toed routine. Unlike some of her fellow class members, she had never heard any of the horrible sounds from the SS building that she'd been told about — inhuman noises, the sounds of people in agony. But she knew they existed.

Remembering the description by a girl in her class, she shuddered that July afternoon, carefully crossing the street after class in order to avoid even the shadow of the building, its flag and its SS guards. A good-natured boy from her class, Georges Binet, too stout for his height and his sixteen years, called to her from a table at the little terrasse where he sat.

"Where are you off to, Jany? Come and talk." He raised the strainer from his glass. "See? A *citron pressé*. I'll squeeze the lemon for you myself."

She smiled but refused, tilting her head toward the building across the street.

"Too close to them."

"Ah! They won't be here long. I know a secret. Sit and talk. I'll tell you."

"Well . . ."

Georges' invitation *was* tempting — sometimes she got lonely for company her own age. Everything about her life since Maman's death had become so restricted, so serious. It was good to be with the jolly fat boy who had nothing to do with the Resistance, the FFI, the Partisans-Tireurs, or an other dangerous group. She sat down on the wire-backed chair but turned it a little, so she wouldn't have to look across the street. She could still hear the flag though, snapping briskly in the afternoon breeze, a reminder of *their* presence.

Georges licked his spoon and waved it at her.

"You won't believe this. Real sugar. Know why? Because *they* come to this café. Food is always better where the Germans do business. Ever notice that?"

She started to get up. It felt obscene and horrible to be sitting where the Gestapo came to get their beer and coffee. But Georges' pudgy, sweating hand stopped her.

"Don't. They might notice you and think you're a Red."

Quoting her brother she whispered fiercely. "Do

you mean only the Communists have the right to hate the Nazis?"

Nevertheless, she looked around nervously and sat down again; allowing him to order a lemonade for her. While they waited for the tiny water pitcher, the sugar, strainer and lemon, he looked at his wristwatch ostentatiously.

"Got to be at the dentist's in five minutes. How do you like my birthday present?" He held up his wrist for her admiration which she gave him wholeheartedly, though the little leather strap was stretched to its final notch. "It was my father's idea. My mother wanted to get me a new coat."

Fingering it, she said wistfully, "I wish we had the money for one. Carl's watch stopped running almost two months ago. He had it repaired but it still doesn't keep good time." Her eyes sparkled at a thought. "If I were rich, I'd get Carl a new watch and I'd wear lovely clothes by Chanel and Schiaparelli."

A man of the world, Georges reminded her, "Schiap is out of business now. You'd never look right in high fashion anyhow. Besides, you'll never be rich. What can you do? Type on a machine? Machine typists don't get rich."

"Then I'll marry a rich man. The richest I can find. And have a lovely kitchen and all the fresh food and fish and meat and poultry we can eat."

Georges was offended by such crass materialism.

"I certainly wouldn't marry you. The girl my parents choose will love me, not my money . . . not that I have any money," he added on reflection.

Georges' friendly honesty brightened her spirits.

She laughed and began to squeeze the lemon the waiter set down with all its trappings. Once she had the *citron pressé* ready to drink and had taken a moment to luxuriate in the shiny little crystals of real sugar, she was ready to carry on their conversation.

"Are you going to let your parents choose your wife, the way your grandfathers did?" she asked.

"Why not? They've had practice. They know life. Grandfather was born while Paris was under siege from the Boche in 1870. Father was in the Great War against the Boche and now this war. They've seen life."

"And the Boche," she added gloomily.

"Oh, they're not so bad. I just grin at them. They've never been nasty to me. Some day they'll go home. They always do."

Getting back to essentials, she asked him what kind of girl he hoped they would choose for him. He guzzled the last of his lemonade and studied all the shabbily dressed girls who passed the café tables swinging their hips.

"Well then, first, she must be a good cook. That is understood."

"Georges, you are so romantic."

"At the Lycée they said one must put things in their proper perspective. That's all I do." He startled her by groaning suddenly. He set his heavy jaw, winced and rubbed his cheek in a gingerly way. "Hope he doesn't draw it out. I need all my teeth. I chew a lot."

She glanced around. "You're going to be late for your appointment, aren't you?"

He checked the time again and jumped up in a

panic. "I'm late already. *Pardon,* Jany." He pushed his chair out of the way, scudding it along the floor, and started out to the street.

Ever aware of Carl's warning, Jany called out, "Don't run, Georges. They mustn't see you running."

But it was too late. The fat boy had already passed between the outer tables on the sidewalk, clumsily knocking against a Frenchman drinking a vermouth and reading the paper. Georges headed across the street, loping along at an angle toward the dentist's office.

Jany returned to the *citron pressé.* When no one was looking she wet her forefinger and stuck it in the grains of sugar that had scattered onto the table. She still had her finger in her mouth, savoring the all too infrequent taste of something sweet when she heard an auto backfire in the street. Then she heard the second backfire within a second or two of the first sharp, crackling sound. Now there were screams. It seemed to Jany that the world had stopped. Pedestrians hurried past the café. Traffic piled up in the street. With her heart thumping in her breast Jany rushed to where a crowd was forming.

Georges shouldn't have run. It always looked suspicious to the Germans. They shot first, asked questions later. Georges Binet lay on his back in the middle of the street, a huge bundle with pudgy hands spread-eagled and his eyes wide open, as if questioning this death that had come upon him so suddenly. It took a long time for anyone to see the blood. It was a small trail seeping out from under Georges' head. No one went near him. They all stood back, expressionless, terrified of drawing attention to themselves until one of the uniformed guards in front of the SS headquarters strode over to the boy, kicking him over face down with a polished boot. While he examined Georges he carried his rifle barrel pointed down at the dead boy.

His contemptuous gesture in kicking him produced what the death itself had not brought from the crowd, a low growl, a curious canine sound that seemed to come from many throats. A second Nazi guard moved out, rifle in hand. It was impossible to pin down the source of the sound. In their anger a contagion had swept the crowd.

"Clear the street," the second guard ordered, first in German and then in French. A few people turned and left the scene, but many only backed away, still staring. It seemed to Jany, watching in a daze, that there was menace in every French face, that a small spark dropped at any moment could ignite the entire city. Such a revolt now, without the strength and ammunition of the Allied armies, would mean a holocaust. Jany had heard Carl say it too often, that they would need the Allies on their side before they brought on another Warsaw.

Black-uniformed SS and plainclothesmen were drawn out of the headquarters to the street.

"He was running. Damned saboteur!" one of the guards said in German.

Those around Jany who understood German repeated this aloud with obscene gestures that clearly said they didn't believe it. It seemed to her that the most important thing in the world was to make everyone understand what had really happened, and she found herself babbling to anyone who would listen.

"He had a toothache. He was late for the dentist. He had a tooth . . . a tooth . . ." She couldn't go on.

Somebody patted her shoulder. "Go home, girl. This is no place for you."

But Jany continued to tell the story. It was important to her that everyone should know it was all a mistake. Georges hadn't meant to run. At his weight he couldn't run fast anyway. People kept shoving her along between them, unwilling to listen.

"He was going to the dentist, that's all."

A brisk but kindly woman led her out of the morass as far as the Faubourg.

"Go along home, child. Tell your mother all you feel. She will tell you this is nothing. This is the Boche. Go along."

But there was nothing to go home to. She would simply return to the apartment and walk up and down and remember things. She should have been kinder to poor Georges. There ought to have been some way that she could have sensed what would happen and stopped him.

Yet she felt guilty in another way . . . If he hadn't seen me on the sidewalk and bought me a *citron pressé* he'd have gotten to the dentist on time. . . . And it was that disturbing thought that she couldn't put out of her mind.

Tony Lombard returned to the house of Maître Mercier to ask his advice about getting back across the Channel but the lawyer and his wife were gone, and the old, nervous-looking concierge said the maître had gone to the law courts. Tony debated

76

going over on the Ile de la Cité to the courts, but with his throbbing ankle he didn't think he could make it.

He had just turned away and was limping out through the porte cochère onto the busy rue St. Honore when the old man bustled out after him, obviously tense about something.

"Monsieur. These things I forget sometimes. I was to ask the name of Monsieur. And where to find Monsieur when the maître returns."

Tony heard little warning bells in his head. The old man couldn't be terrified of Maître Mercier, a kind person who seemed incapable of terrifying anyone, including any opponent he might face in court. Something else must have frightened the old man. The lawyer was gone, and so was his wife. Maybe a coincidence — or maybe the Gestapo had them. In which case the Germans would have given the concierge instructions to report the name of every visitor.

He looked around. The whole thing must have been quickly done. Neither German nor French agents had yet been assigned to question the Merciers' visitors. Tony knew he had to act fast — it could happen any minute, as soon as they pried whatever information they wished from the Merciers.

He said casually, "I am Etienne Lomard. The maître's nephew from Brittany." Etienne was French for Stephen. Curious that he should choose his father's name. Wish fulfillment? Absurd. He had never wanted to be Steve Lombard. Luckily, he named a place far enough from Paris that might explain his slight accent. With his best smile he said, "I'd hoped to borrow a few francs, just until I get on my feet. Do you think I'd have a chance, monsieur? Or should I forget it?"

The question gave the old man an air of superiority.

"Well then, it may be." But his attitude changed suddenly when he seemed to recall his instructions. "I may help, perhaps. If Monsieur will return a little later."

"Wonderful. When?"

"Soon. Very soon. If Monsieur can wait inside, I will make a call on the telephone at once."

*I'll bet!*

"Excellent. You are a gem. Let me get rid of the woman I left in the café next door. I'll be back in five minutes. Again, many thanks."

He shook the old man's gnarled hand and walked away, gritting his teeth and forcing himself not to limp. He looked back. The old man seemed uncertain whether to trot after him or go inside and call his contacts. As soon as Tony was past the first sidewalk table, the old concierge trotted into the big Mercier house. Once inside the café Tony moved past the zinc bar to the sign marked WC over a curtained area.

Beyond the curtain was a steep, dark staircase, lighted somewhere in the basement by a fifteen-watt globe. Hoping for the best, he went down and peered into the toilet area. A turkish toilet, it wasn't too clean, and consisted of a hole in the middle of the tiled floor. No exit doors here.

The WC itself had no door. He looked around and found an unlighted door opening onto an outside flight of stairs. These hugged the wall of the narrow Mercier garden. Fortunately, only one window of the Mercier house looked out on the garden and the area behind the café. He watched the window for a few minutes. Satisfied that no one was looking out, he made a beeline across the area littered with an inordinate amount of cabbage leaves and other decaying produce.

Weaving his way through the maze of narrow openings behind other buildings on the block, he reached a cross street and was out on the rue St. Honore again. He looked back. No one seemed to be watching him.

The girl Janine lived above the Café St. Just. He thought he could make it that far. The trouble was, he had heard about the strict upbringing of French girls who belonged to good families. If he came marching up to the door — well, crawling — she might jump to all the wrong conclusions. Maybe if he assumed a nice, proper, almost fatherly attitude . . . Politically, her reaction gave him the hope that he would be accepted, although they would certainly be aware of the deadly consequences if the Occupation authorities were to guess his presence there.

Still, a few hours would help, just to rest his ankle. After all, something else would turn up. It always did.

"Well, here goes. Janine, I hope your family has your charitable instincts."

He strolled along, figuring his limp was going to be less obvious if he walked slowly. He wanted to melt into the crowd, become a blurred part of the populace around him, not call attention to himself. He glanced over his shoulder again. No men in uniform. Of course, there might be plain-clothesmen; you could never be sure.

A block later Tony began to relax, feeling he was for the moment out of danger. By nature an optimist, he took a few long, deep breaths and reminded himself that so far his luck had remained true. Never in his almost twenty-five years had it failed him. According to his mother, he was born under a lucky configuration of signs. When two of the crew bailed out from the plane ahead of him and he had come up the "unlucky third," as the pilot had called him, he still knew he would survive. He hadn't been quite so sure for a few minutes in that field when the strange, shadowy figures holding flashlights formed a triangle around him. But even the lines in his palms told him he would always win out in times of stress.

Finally he stood across the street from the Café St. Just, only a few yards from temporary safety. No one had followed him. He crossed the street and started through the narrow passage that emptied into a square, brick-lined courtyard about as large as a tablecloth. It was all characteristically French and he loved it. Things about Paris intrigued him because they brought back memories of the marvelous imitations he had known from his childhood in San Francisco.

I'm homesick, he thought ironically, and I've only been gone five months. It's ridiculous. I'll be home in a few weeks. There has to be a way of getting across the Channel. All I have to do is blend into the crowd . . . and hope Janine's family will help.

He stood in the small court for a minute or two,

considering. There was a moldy-looking staircase on the far side of the court, but the girl had said "over the café." It must be the closed staircase, a few feet to his right. He stuck his head in and almost collided nose to nose with a buxom Frenchwoman. She must have seen him coming. Not bad looking, either. She reminded him of Stella Burkett, the ambitious housekeeper who worked for his family during his boyhood. Stella had done well, maneuvering her daughter, Heather, into position as the wife of his cousin, Alec. He thought that the woman seemed always to know exactly what she was doing, too.

The Frenchwoman's forbidding facade melted perceptibly. "Are you lost, monsieur? May I assist you? A pleasure."

"I certainly hope so, Madame —"

"Charpentier. You wish to see me?"

He was perceptive enough to realize that the idea pleased her. Maybe it would be helpful to him later.

"You are most kind, Madame Charpentier. I am just here from Gascony to see my cousin Janine."

Madame sniffed but kept smiling.

"Janine? Little Jany, yes. She is never called Janine."

Mistake number one. This woman was sharp.

"So my little cousin's nickname has changed again," he said. "As a child she insisted she be called Janine. Ah, but madame, we are of the world, you and I. We understand how fickle children can be."

Madame Charpentier preened herself at being linked with him in age. "But you have missed your cousin. She is at her typing class. I suggest, monsieur, you wait here just a very short time until she returns. You would not wish to miss her again."

Thank God she hadn't slammed the door in his face when she told him Janine — no, Jany — was gone.

"Madame, you are all kindness. I hope my cousin's family will be as understanding."

Madame's dark eyebrows gathered slightly, and her opaque olive eyes sharpened just a fraction.

"Her family, monsieur?"

Since he knew nothing whatever about her family, he knew he'd better tread carefully.

"Our mutual family back in . . ." Making it far from Brittany, in case the police tracked "Etienne Lomard" from the Mercier house, he thought of Cyrano de Bergerac and d'Artagnan and said Gascony instead. But what the hell cities were there in Gascony? "Back in Peyrac." Where did that come from? "I mean to say, I was told by my family to visit my cousin the day I arrived and I am two days late."

"But you have not mentioned your cousin, Carl," she said knowledgeably. "It is one of those family feuds, no?"

Of course. The brother named Carl. Or Karl. He had forgotten all about her brother. Maybe the fellow was a collaborationist. If so, would his sister protect a strange and potential enemy as she had on the street for him? He sensed that he was getting into a quagmire here.

"Not a feud, so to speak — political arguments, mostly."

She stood aside and gestured for him to enter

her small, overheated room with its window over-looking the courtyard on which someone from the northern garret rooms was at present dumping the contents of a dustpan and a mop. The flat smelled strongly of urine. Tony suspected there was a used chamber pot somewhere in the room, probably under the faded couch.

I'm getting awfully fussy, he thought, considering that I could be picked up any minute and land in a German concentration camp if it weren't for people like this.

"Sit. Sit. If you please." Madame bustled around her tiny kitchen and brought out a green bottle that looked like a vinegar cruet. "Do you drink ouzo, monsieur? I had a friend from Athens. He used to bring me ouzo. The war frightened him away. He went back to Athens and found the Boche there, too. I found it amusing, that."

He accepted the ouzo in something rather like a Swedish schnapps glass but sipped it carefully, aware that the woman had more on her mind than sex. He must be guarded; she was not a fool.

"You like?"

"Very much," he lied. "I hope I do not take your time from something more important."

She sat on a stiff, cane-bottomed chair opposite him, studying him over the rim of her glass.

"Not at all, monsieur. You say that you and Monsieur Carl, your cousin, quarrel over politics. It is so often the case. He has a young mistress who, I believe, is a Communist. Perhaps Monsieur Carl is also a Communist, and you do not approve. One can only admire your resistance to this hideous cancer."

"Very true," he agreed, but added hastily, "not that Carl is a Communist. Far from it." He hoped he was telling the truth.

"Really . . ." she hesitated, "as you say." Madame Charpentier continued to sip her ouzo, all the while studying him between sips. He would have been more comfortable with her if he thought she were only interested in sex. That would be simple enough to handle, with no threatening political consequences.

"You have not told me your name, monsieur. Certainly you are not one of the Boche. You have not the face for it."

He didn't know what to say to that. "Etienne Lomard" would be disastrous. But "Antoine Lenoir," the name he had papers for, seemed to fit him well and had a certain legitimate air to it. Of course a lot depended on whether Maître Mercier was being forced to betray him — if so, the papers would be worthless.

"Certainly not, madame. Lenoir. Antoine Lenoir. I was invalided out at LaPanne, during the 1940 retreat."

She accepted this, but thoughtfully. It struck him that she was very professional about it. He took a cigarette from the Florentine leather box she offered. Curiously enough, with the war going on and the cost, they were American Lucky Strikes. Although meant to impress him, they only added to his suspicions about her.

"I hope my presence here won't anger Monsieur Charpentier."

Madame blinked.

Returning the leather cigarette box to her, he let

his hand briefly rest on hers.

"Jealousy would be quite understandable in any man who was your husband. Forgive me, madame, but I could hardly blame him."

Her fingers followed his when they retreated. Her smile reminded him of a content, purring feline.

"I am not offended, monsieur. But I am a widow. Tell me, please, just between us. I do believe Monsieur Carl is working for the Resistance. If not, then the Communists, or the Gaullists, or some other group. Which is it?"

Damn her! In spite of all his efforts, she went marching on, nipping at him and his "cousins."

"I doubt it. Carl is pretty wrapped up in himself. He's not the heroic type."

"Not that I think it's wrong," she hastened to assure him. "I think we should all be proud of him. Don't you agree?"

"He'd be a fool to do it. And in my family there are no fools."

She started to say something, to persist in the matter, but she stopped abruptly with her hand raised.

"Shh! Your little cousin is in the passage." She opened the door a few inches, motioned him to join her.

He did so, and smelled a strong perfume mingled with the woman's body odor. It should have been unpleasant, but he was suddenly aware that Madame Charpentier did have a sensual aura. He backed away, then saw the girl Jany running up the stairs to the flat above. She looked as if she were crying and her hair looked disheveled, bouncing around her pretty, flushed face. The sight of her weeping moved him to a surprising degree.

"*Pardon,* madame." He wedged himself between Madame Charpentier and the doorway, dashed out and up the stairs after the girl.

He caught her as she was fumbling to unlock the door that opened off the second landing, called the "first floor" on the Continent. She gave a soft, scared little scream and he quickly reassured her with some of the same tenderness he felt toward his daughter.

"Don't be frightened, Jany. It's me. Your old — new friend, Tony Lenoir. Everything's okay. Please don't cry."

The door was open now. He found himself inside the minuscule foyer-hallway with her, caressing her straggled hair, looking down into her tear-stained face and trying to cheer her up.

"He d-died . . . just like that. Right in the m-middle of the street . . ." Her big eyes, ringed with long wet lashes, stared up at him. "He had a toothache. That's all."

"I know," he said, trying to calm her, though he didn't have the vaguest idea what she was talking about.

"Poor G-Georges!" she cried into his shoulder, hardly aware of his arm around her. "It was all my fault." He went on consoling her, but in his present plight he was selfish enough to hope she would recover soon. They might be tracking him down at this minute, and he would need a little cooperation.

"Who did all this?" he asked finally.

"They did. The Boche."

It was shocking, but it encouraged him to tell her more of the truth about himself.

"Jany, do you want them to shoot me in the street, too?"

She raised her tousled head sharply. "No! Oh, no!"

At this unlucky moment they were shaken by the crash of the door as it was pushed open.

"Let her go or I'll kill you!" a male voice demanded in a low-pitched French fury.

Tony released the girl with as much dignity as he could muster, and knew without a doubt that the furious fellow standing before him was her brother, Carl, whose good will was as important to him as his politics.

# Chapter Six

Every time Eden approached the old Lombard house on San Francisco's Nob Hill, she remembered the fairy tales of her childhood. This was the castle on the slippery Glass Mountain. For Glass Mountain she substituted the California Street hill. Her own coach, chugging up the hill, carrying her and Andrea, was a Yellow Cab, as usual.

Inside the big, solid stone mansion that had survived both the earthquake and the fire, the Lombard women reigned. There were usually at least two in residence.

Technically, the house belonged to Steve, his sister Brooke, and their one-time housekeeper, Stella Burkett, whose daughter had married Brooke's son, Alec. But family tradition kept it in the center of the Lombard empire. Stella Burkett was in England looking after her daughter, so that left Brooke, to whom the great house had become a haven where she returned to lick her wounds after each of her marriages. The last, to Kurt Friedrich, had left her a widow in 1938, and as far as Eden could see, Brooke now belatedly turned to Alec, her son by her first marriage. She looked forward to each of his calls from London, and would get on all the local radio stations to read his letters containing eyewitness reports of Britain in wartime.

Still, it seemed odd to think of Brooke Lombard

Huntington Ware Friedrich without a man under her spell. Eden understood the woman and had liked her since girlhood, when Brooke was briefly married to Dr. Nigel Ware, Eden's father.

Eden's feelings for Randi Lombard, the other reigning queen of the mansion, were quite different. Respect and admiration about summed it up. What disturbed her most was that she never did know exactly what her mother-in-law was thinking.

The cab climbed up to the Taylor Street level where it passed the Mark Hopkins and Fairmont Hotels, skidded on the cable car tracks, to Andrea's delight, and moved slightly to the right. One block beyond the driver pulled up in front of the big gates and wrought-iron fence that set the two-story Lombard mansion apart from its skyscraper neighbors. Back in the early Gold Rush days "Mad Tony" Lombard had fortuitously staked his claim on what was to become half a block of prime real estate on the classiest peak in town. Before Steve Lombard, the heir to the age-darkened stone house, claimed his inheritance, two splendid wings were built, housing the ballroom that was essential in the nineties, an equally grand dining room, and other heavily ornamented Victorian rooms. It had taken the war bride, Randi Gallegher, with her marriage in 1918 to AEF hero, Stephen Lombard, to give the house a lighter, more modern aspect. During Randi's reign Brooke had often boasted that she had maneuvered the marriage because she felt that Randi, her college friend at the time, would make an excellent "unpaid housekeeper." Eden sensed that it was one of those family jokes with just enough truth in it to annoy the leading players.

Before Eden got out of the cab with the excited Andrea, Brooke Lombard came out, waving and hallooing as if she were a girl of sixteen. The tiny network of lines around her eyes was more prominent because she persisted in using too much powder, but at a slight distance she looked very little older than the popular, auburn-haired beauty who came to Hawaii in 1922 and added Eden's father to her string of conquests. Her marcelled hair remained a deep, glorious auburn with a little help from her hairdressers, but she swung her head around so much, tilting and laughing and tossing, the curls almost sprang out by themselves in charming ringlets. Eden did not envy her the beauty but certainly envied her the hair.

The two women happily embraced before Brooke turned to Andrea.

"And here's my big girl. Say hello to your great-aunt Brooke." She lifted Andrea who clutched her around the neck delightedly.

"Honey, say 'Hello, Great-aunt Brooke.' "

" 'Lo, G'ant Booke."

The two women laughed and went up the walk together. "By the way," Brooke said, "Alec tells me there's every hope."

Eden's eyes widened and her pulse quickened with the news. Oh, God, Eden thought to herself, Tony was too vital, too young to be snuffed out so easily. *Let Alec be right.*

Tony almost always felt that he would win, no matter what happened. But he hadn't seen Europe in the thirties as Eden had. He hadn't seen the insidious rise of totalitarian powers month by month until it was stretched to year by year. He hadn't seen the tired, disillusioned people of Europe. Tony would just know he was going to survive. After all, wasn't he a Lombard of Nob Hill?

Brooke was holding Andrea in the crook of one arm while Eden clutched Brooke's other plump hand.

"They know what happened, he parachuted. And I just know he landed safely," Eden said.

Brooke winced at her unflagging optimism.

"Don't worry, Alec will get him out. And now that Steve is in England — well! Between my brother and my son, they wouldn't dare hold Tony prisoner."

Eden felt the maddening impatience Brooke Lombard inspired in some people when she fluctuated from one extreme to the other. She had become hopeful only to lose all hope in the space of the few seconds it took to walk into the dark, slightly gloomy Victorian house.

"You mean, they don't know anything else yet?"

"No, dear, but it'll come any day now." She flashed her girlish grin, wide-lipped and punctuated by a giggle. "You and Alec aren't the only ones in the family with a public following. You should see the fan mail I get every time I read one of his letters on the radio. It's mostly from all those poor mothers with sons stationed overseas."

"I'm sure you could be the biggest star of us all, Brooke. Just wait until television comes in . . . What does Randi think? Is she hopeful?"

They climbed the heavy, oaken front staircase which was more impressive than it was graceful.

Brooke was briefly confused but eager to express her sister-in-law's opinion.

"Oh, Randi thinks I've done wonders. She went down to the station with us last Sunday night. Sam Liversedge, my banker-beau, and me. I was on the air locally right after Jack Benny. Isn't that something?"

"No. I meant what does Randi think about Tony? The chances of his rescue."

Randi called to them from the head of the stairs.

"Is that you, Eden? Is the baby with you? I was worried about your flight in all this fog."

"But honey," Brooke put in. "It's always like this in the summer. I've flown in fog before and I'm not the least bit afraid of it."

After twenty-six years Randi had learned to ignore her sister-in-law's extraneous comments. She took Eden's hand, kissed her cheek lightly, kissed Andrea who was still in Brooke's arms, and walked along the upper hall with Eden. Brooke trotted behind the two women, her cheek against Andrea's but pursuing her own thoughts.

"As soon as Tony gets home, station KHO wants him to appear," Brooke said. "I'm to interview him. My nephew is our newest hero, you know."

"Have you heard anything new? Has Steve been able to call you yet?" Eden asked Randi.

"Nothing so far, he says. He had to leave for Folkstone. While we were talking, a rumor came in. One of the men on the plane may have been brought in. The cinematographer, I think. But like I said, it's only a rumor."

Eden looked at her. Randi's ageless face, coolly

classical, was framed by the sand-gold hair that had once blown long and free but was now coiled loosely in a French twist. It was hard to detect her anguish from her outward manner. Only her long, slender fingers, flexing nervously, betrayed any anxiety.

Eden tried to find hope in her mother-in-law's report.

"Randi, couldn't that be what happened to Tony? Or maybe he was picked up by the Resistance? They would try to get him across the Channel, wouldn't they?"

"It seems very likely." Randi smiled and tickled young Andrea under the chin. At this the child held out her arms to her "Gam-maw Wandi."

While Randi was kissing her enthusiastic granddaughter, Eden brought her overnight case into the bedroom she and Tony shared whenever they stayed "at the museum." Everything in it reminded her of Tony — the dressing area and new bathroom "just for us," as Tony had boasted, the enormous bed with no head or footboard, as Tony wanted it. The worn carpet was the only period piece he would accept. It had been in his grandmother Bridget Gallegher's bedroom where she had lived out her last days until she was carried off, most unwillingly, of a liver ailment.

Randi took Andrea in and looked around the room. "Is everything all right?"

"Sure. No! Do you realize we went through this on December 7 when Tony was hit?" Eden hurled her handbag across the bed. "Why? What's the point of Tony being saved then only to have this happen to him? Hasn't he endured enough?

Randi, you don't think he's dead . . ."

"Never!" Randi said sharply. "God wouldn't be so cruel."

"God? God must be pretty busy these days. He's spreading Himself thin. Bataan and Corregidor. Guadalcanal and Burma and all those monstrous Jap prison camps. Europe is behind Nazi bars. And their prison camps are just as bad as the Pacific ones, they say. And what about North Africa? Hell, God can't be bothered with one poor, unlucky soul like my Tony."

In the doorway Brooke was shocked at this blasphemous outpouring, but Randi understood. She set Andrea down on the big bed and touched Eden's shoulder in a gingerly way.

"He is alive, and free. Because . . ." She broke off unable to give a plausible answer beyond her firm belief that her son could not die so young. She just didn't believe it possible.

"Because Steve says so?"

Randi colored faintly. She hadn't forgotten her old suspicions of an affair between her husband and Eden Ware.

"I can't explain it. I simply believe."

"Alec said he would call this evening," Brooke put in eagerly. "That's tomorrow morning in London. He can tell us what Steve found at Folkstone. Alec's been so concerned . . . he was always fond of his cousin Tony, you know."

"What does Leo think of all this?" Randi asked Eden.

Eden shrugged. "Haven't heard from him. He took off for London last week before any of this happened. He was anxious to see the shots Tony was supervising beyond the battle area." As Eden had suspected, Randi found as much relief in this as she had expressed over her husband's presence in London. The business relationship between Randi and Leo Prysing dated back many years, and she was confident he wouldn't let her down. But Eden wasn't so sure about Leo.

The way he handled the business with Kurt Friedrich proved him to be ruthless, devious and vengeful. Still, Eden approved of Leo's actions in that unpleasant business since she understood what had compelled him to do what he did. Of course, not even Randi nor the rest of the family knew much about the Friedrich affair — just as well.

In spite of Randi's conviction, Eden's clash of hopes and fears, and Brooke's bubbling optimism, all three women were unnerved by the jangle of the phone ringing through the various connections in the house. Eden had hoped the call would come through Tony's phone number, which would mean Tony himself was calling. No such luck.

Miss Thorgerson, the lean, lank, soft-hearted housekeeper, came to report that "a gentleman" was calling "Mrs. Stephen" from long distance. She stayed to entertain young Andrea while each of the women rushed to various telephone extensions.

"Randi speaking. Is it you, Steve?"

All kinds of squawking interfered but no one could mistake Leo Prysing's low, booming voice, so different from Steve Lombard's pleasant baritone lilt that had converted a good many fence-sitters to the Allied cause before Pearl Harbor.

"Leo here. Look, sweetheart —" Randi could fancy seeing Brooke's eyebrows shoot up at his familiarity that was based only on a long personal and professional relationship. "The news isn't too good."

At this Randi heard Brooke gasp while Eden let out a little animal cry like a moan. She herself felt the old-fashioned black receiver shaking in her hand. Her grasp tightened. It couldn't be . . . to have him spared at Pearl Harbor only to lose him in a plane crash . . .

"Do you have any real news? Where is Steve?"

"At the Channel. They brought in the pilot. He was badly burned. Died before the Maquis reached him. They're pretty tough Resistance fighters. They managed to ship him across in a dory or something. The fisherman said two other bodies were found by the Germans. From the description they gave me one of them seems to have been my cinematographer, Bill Atherton."

She was hoarse and had to clear her throat.

"But you don't know if Tony is the other one."

"That's right. The only other one besides Tony not accounted for is my second camera boy. But the Maquis doesn't know everything. It was a dark night and the Germans didn't stay around long. Just lugged the bodies off. But money talks, Randi. Steve and I will get together on this and find out something one way or the other."

Eden cut in abruptly with an hysterical edge to her voice. "I'm going over. I want to be there. I can't stand this waiting."

"No!" Leo Prysing's voice was like a whiplash. "There's no way for you to help, Eden. Believe me,

I understand how you feel, but you'll only be in the way. Leave it to Steve and me. We'll get him back. Money talks."

"You repeat yourself." Randi's voice, in contrast to his and Eden's, was very low and cold, with an edge to it that she herself scarcely recognized. "What it boils down to is you have no certain knowledge, either way, and you're not sure you can get it."

"True. Randi, I'd give my right arm not to have sent Tony on that assignment. But since those Pearl Harbor injuries kept him out of the service, he's been devil-bent to do something heroic. Supervising these action sequences seemed to fit him. He got sore as hell when I wanted to send Sergei Eisenman."

Randi said nothing, but Eden broke down suddenly. "God, I know. He talked about it all the time. I should have gone to New York with him to see him off. I should have . . ."

Randi couldn't take much more of Eden's hysteria — it was beginning to affect her.

"Leo, tell Steve or Alec to let us know the minute you find out anything," she said, and hung up.

Randi held her left hand in her right and slowly massaged her fingers that had cramped from gripping the phone so tightly. As she stood alone considering her son's fate, she was scarcely aware of the sound of Eden's and Brooke's footsteps as they rushed to join her.

# Chapter Seven

Tony slowly lightened his grip on the girl, though she seemed weak and ready to fall — she had felt especially fragile in his arms. It was one of the few times in Tony's carefree life when he felt really needed, and in spite of Carl's angry threat, he felt wonderfully alive.

However, the brother did pose a problem. Tony said the only thing he could think of without sounding too ridiculous.

"Look, this isn't what it appears to be. Your sister has had a bad shock."

Carl grabbed his shoulder. He wasn't kidding. His thin hands were steely, like his slender body. He was about Tony's size but righteous anger gave him added strength. In another second or two Tony would be spun onto the floor. It was Jany who saved the day. Reaching for Carl, she went into his arms and hindered his action.

"They shot Georges. Right in the street. It was all my fault. He was going to the dentist and they shot him."

Carl was so bewildered he forgot his anger, staring over his sister's head at the intruder.

"Georges was shot because he went to the dentist? And who is this? Are you Georges?"

Tony breathed more easily. Since the jump two nights ago he hadn't been quite in shape for a wrestling match with a self-righteous young

Frenchman. Or was the fellow German? He couldn't be too sure yet.

Jany shook her head, blinking away the tears irritably.

"No, Carl. You aren't listening. This is Monsieur Antoine Lenoir. He helped me. On the street. After Georges was shot."

Still confused, Carl turned to Tony for help. "Just who is Georges?"

Before Jany could add to her explanation, Tony tried to straighten things out.

"Georges was a friend of Jany's. The Gestapo must have shot the boy while he was on his way to the dentist."

Carl patted his sister's shoulder absently. "Belongs to the Binet family, I think. A fat boy, not too bright. I know his father . . . a good patriot." He frowned at the betrayal of his own feelings. "Like all of us. A good Frenchman, that is to say. Are you all right now, Jany?"

"Yes, don't worry about me. I just don't want you to fight with Monsieur Lenoir. He was shot down —" Tony tensed up. Which story would she tell? "— at LaPanne." Relief. "So you see, he's a patriot, too. In reality, I mean."

Again Tony became aware of the brother's slightly lowered eyelids, as if he were studying and analyzing this new patriot. Carl was not unattractive, with his thin, high-boned face, the planes like his sister's, though his mouth was straight and uncompromising and his narrow chin looked stubborn. Tony suspected those heavy-lidded gray eyes could be dangerous and, like his mouth, uncompromising.

The idea was to get him on Tony's side. Did the fellow know anything about the Underground in Paris? If he was Danielle deBrett's boyfriend, he was probably a Communist. That would pose a big problem. Danielle had made it clear that if you didn't play the game their way, not only would there be no help, but they just might turn you over to the Gestapo.

Carl offered his hand. "Many thanks, monsieur. We must meet again and compare notes on our service days."

It was definitely a cue for Tony to leave. He took the hand Carl offered, trying to find an excuse, any excuse to remain. But his tired mind had blanked out.

"A pleasure, Monsieur Carl." There seemed to be no last name.

He limped to the little hall, remembered Madame Charpentier and without any ulterior motive, stopped long enough to warn them.

"Your landlady is very curious about you two."

"Landlady?" Carl repeated with a quick glance at his sister.

That was a slip. He corrected himself. "My mistake. She is probably only the concierge. Madame Charpentier thinks you, Monsieur Carl, are either a Communist member of the Franc-Tireur-Partisans, or a Gaullist, or even a collaborationist. She has a persistent curiosity."

"What a pity to disappoint her! And here I am, none of those exalted beings. Only a peaceful member of an occupied country."

"Exactly. I told her so. *Au 'voir*, mademoiselle. Monsieur."

He had gotten to the door and turned to close it but Carl was there behind him, ready to shut him out of the apartment. It was then that Tony saw the name on a little card inserted in a slot in the door: Carl Rey Friedrich.

"Friedrich?" Tony stopped, astonished by the coincidence. "Your name is Friedrich?"

Carl had grown suspicious again. "Certainly. Were you not aware?"

"I had no idea. It is my aunt Brooke's married name. They lived in Vienna until the *Anschluss* when Hitler marched into Austria."

"But Carl," Jany burst out, "Father was in —" She noticed her brother shake his head as if to warn her. "Well, he was," she ended, less enthusiastically.

Hoping this might help his own case, Tony made the most of the information.

"Kurt Friedrich was my uncle by marriage. He died in 1938. Do you think we might be related?"

Reaching over Tony's shoulder, Carl closed the front door tightly. His stern expression hadn't changed.

"Your aunt is named 'Brooke'? An English word, that."

Tony could only be grateful that Carl Friedrich wasn't an SS questioner. He knew he had blundered into that one. Maybe because he was so damned tired. He leaned back against the door, grinning weakly.

"Right. Flowing little rivers. Come to think of it, Aunt Brooke does flow on and on."

"You have a French I find most strange. You were not born to it, I think. You are not Antoine Lenoir. Who are you?"

101

Passing Carl, who made no effort to bar his way, Tony limped back into the living room and fell onto the old couch with a sigh. He explained in English.

"God! I am tired. Excuse me, but I've got to take it easy for a few minutes. I'm about dead." He raised his hand, though neither of the Friedrichs were trying to stop him. They simply stared. "Don't worry. I'll be on my way. Just give me a little time."

Jany, filled with compassion, said, "Carl, he looks bad. He is so tired and something happened to his foot."

"Ankle, honey," he corrected her, between set teeth. He could hardly get the words out but unfortunately they were loud enough for Carl Friedrich to hear and resent them.

"Call her that again and I will turn you in to the police myself." He stood over Tony on the couch like an avenging angel, speaking softly but menacingly.

The whole situation was beginning to give Tony a guilt complex, not just for calling the girl the innocuous "honey," but because he hadn't yet tried to get word to his own family about his rescue. If, of course, it should prove to be a rescue. He had to find a way, somehow, to let Eden and Andrea and his mother know he was all right. On the other hand, he would make a sizable bet that his father was flexing his power-muscles somewhere right now, trying to learn of his whereabouts.

It was Jany again who intervened. "No, Carl. He's a hero. He parachuted to save France. Ask him. He is from the Free French in London, from

102

your beloved General de Gaulle."

This was embarrassingly untrue. She had gotten excited again, and mixed things up, almost as if Tony meant as much as her beloved "Georges," that poor sucker who was probably the love of her teenage life. She was too sweet to go on like this over somebody who hoped he would soon be on his way back to London and the United States. Back to Eden and his baby Andrea.

Maybe her brother sensed it. Regardless, he certainly didn't trust anybody who gave any attention to his little sister.

"Is it true what Jany says of you? That you parachuted to join the FFI inside France?"

"I'm the hero, all right. That is, I parachuted."

Tony tried to look alert, eyes wide with interest, mouth fixed in an absurd smile, but he was almost too tired to care. Even four years ago, after the strafing by the Zero pilot at Pearl Harbor, he hadn't felt like this. Naturally "dear old dad," noble hero that he was, had come to the rescue. But today it was Tony alone who had to fend for himself, and he wasn't sure his casual, flip personality was working its usual charm.

Carl Friedrich had begun to look more puzzled than suspicious, which was encouraging. He reached out, pressing the back of his hand against Tony's forehead.

"He has a temperature, I think."

"Should we get a doctor, Carl? How about the one you used when I had a bad cough last winter? Dr. Steinburg is a safe man."

"Too safe," her brother snapped. "He was in the shipment to Germany this spring. The accursed

Boche. We almost had the right palms greased to free him but he was unexpectedly moved out in a cattle car with a hundred others."

Tony kept his eyes closed. At least Carl Friedrich realized that he was on their side and would not turn him over to the Germans. It was the first important step.

"I can't seem to keep . . . eyes open," Tony murmured. He hoped that would prevent them from calling a doctor who could be a potential spy — especially since he had no doubt that the old man at the Mercier house had already set the Gestapo on him with a full description. They were probably scouring the street for him at this minute.

"He's dead!" Jany whispered, her voice rising in a wail. He had a strong urge to rise up and kiss away the concern on that sweet face. Luckily, he refrained. Her brother would kill him, at the very least.

Carl scoffed at her fears. "Certainly not. His pulse is regular. He may have a slight fever, but that's understandable, after the jump."

So he had begun to believe. There was a brief silence. Lying there "unconscious," Tony could hear the traffic and assertive Wehrmacht auto horns out on the street, but he was more impressed by Jany's reaction, the way she had sucked in her breath. By this time Tony didn't care whether her brother knew his real history or not. He wasn't going to get anywhere without Carl Friedrich's help. That talk about the doctor being carted off by the Nazis, and Friedrich's attempt to save him satisfied Tony that the young man was in the Resistance.

"What are you going to do about him?" Jany asked.

"First get me a wet cloth for his head. The question is, what was his mission? If he was carrying ammunition or messages, they were obviously for the Communists. He has nothing on him now except these papers and about fifty francs — old francs. *Liberté, Egalité, Fraternité.* Look, Jany." He raised his voice. "Always remember," he said when she returned with the wet cloth, "this is our money. Not that Vichy trash. *Famille, Travail, Patrie.* An obscenity, that."

The unexpected cold of the rough towel that Carl laid on Tony's forehead almost made him jump, but he restrained his body with an effort. He appreciated their help, but wished they would wrap the soggy cloth around his ankle, which felt as if it were on fire.

Jany then asked her brother what Tony himself was aching to know. "Do you think he was found by Communists? If he was does that mean he is a Communist, too? But the Communists are also fighting the Boche."

"My innocent, if he were a Communist he would not have been abandoned in Paris. Evidently, they are not sure of him. Or — they are sure. They either discovered he is one of us, a Gaullist, or dropped by the Boche to infiltrate our groups."

"Then he is one of you." She leaned over Tony, her hair like bright golden threads tickling his nose. It was all he could do to keep from sneezing, while another part of him was definitely aroused by her nearness.

Carl took the soggy towel off, to Tony's relief. The moisture had begun to trickle down his neck.

"I must think," Carl said, "I'd best talk to someone."

"Not Danielle, please. You know what she would do if he turned out to be anti-Communist."

"Trust me to know Danielle's thinking processes. I can't act on my own completely in this," he reminded her stiffly. "It looks very much as though we must let him rest here for the night, in any case."

Thank God for that, Tony thought to himself. Now, if only I could get word to Eden or Alec one other problem would be solved.

Meanwhile, he had never been more exhausted, and with no effort at all fell asleep for the first time in three nights. Dozing off, he remembered his easy, cocky boast to Alec Huntington about sixty hours ago when they were drinking together in Alec's little hotel in Richmond outside London.

"I'll be back before this time tomorrow. And with film you wouldn't believe. Leo will have to make me a full-fledged director."

Just before Tony had left for the airfield, Alec's gorgeous but dimwitted wife Heather had been hanging around. Either she or her mother had determined long ago that she should marry into the family of her mother's employers — an admirable ambition and in the best Cinderella tradition. The unseemly and rather obvious thing was, she didn't care which of the cousins she married, so long as the money and the fame were there. When Tony coolly told her to forget marriage, she had fallen into Alec's waiting arms.

But she still hung around Tony, making Tony uncomfortable over how Alec might react to her attentiveness to him. Alec seemed not to notice it, but he had always played his emotions close to his vest. He was odd in a way, not easily understood. Maybe he really loved the beauty who, in Tony's eyes, resembled a flower of sorts — an overblown rose. All in all, Heather was nothing like the exciting, unpredictable, unattainable Eden. And certainly not like the sincere young girl watching over him now, who genuinely cared about what happened to him.

He slept. Sometime in the early evening he thought that Jany Friedrich was leaning over him, her charming, disheveled hair in his face, and she was kissing him. It must have been a dream. A delightful one, but it was a highly unlikely thing to have happened, with that dragon brother of hers guarding her.

A little later, after his dream about Jany kissing him, Tony was awakened by the sound of voices arguing in French — a man and a woman. Not Jany Friedrich, but he knew that voice . . . of course, the delectable Danielle, who almost betrayed him to the Gestapo. He strained to hear what she was saying.

"Why is it you don't want to see me? You expect me to turn around and go, just like that?" He heard fingers snapping, then Carl said something.

She persisted. "Well then, why can I not enter? Am I not good enough for your precious little sister? I could say something to the SS and by the time the Gestapo got finished with her, your precious little sister would be as common as I am, I assure you."

This aroused even Tony to an unusual degree of protectiveness, as if the woman had threatened

Andrea. He swung his legs down to get off the couch but got no further before he heard the resounding sting of palm against flesh. Carl Friedrich must have slapped Danielle. Understandable, but not advisable, under the circumstances. Tony decided he had better get into the fracas before they all wound up in a cattle car bound for the Fatherland.

# Chapter Eight

Alec Huntington had made the quick drive out to Richmond, hoping to spend an hour or two with Heather before he checked back to London for his evening broadcast. Uncle Steve and everyone knew where to find him, if they got word about Tony, so he decided to make the trip.

He only hoped for the best for his cousin, even though Tony had been his bête noire from childhood. Tony Lombard, always the popular charmer. Things came easily to him, always had. Even Tony's last name was lucky. The man who was to become Tony's father had returned from the Great War a hero. Alec's father, a Canadian, had died hideously of the effects of mustard gas after Ypres in 1915.

Tony hadn't married Heather Burkett, perhaps because she'd never fully recovered from the trauma she suffered in the Strand earthquake in 1933. After that, she could never be left alone, or she'd go into queer white silence that was close to catalepsy. At times like this she seemed to relive the moments when she had been imprisoned alone in a room with the door jammed and the whole side wall of the building gone. The wall had swelled outward at the first tremor, then shattered and rained down upon the street eight stories below. After such an experience, ten-year-old Heather would never again feel safe alone.

Regardless of her fears, Alec had wanted her

from the time he first saw her, partly, as he well knew, because she was as beautiful as his own mother had been. But for Heather, when she couldn't get Tony it was just as well for her to take the Huntington name, which was just as good and established for far longer, too.

Alec had no trouble overlooking Heather's earlier preference for Tony. In her, he saw the mold of a woman much like his mother — silly, sometimes cunning as a spider, yet curiously enchanting. Although Alec was always the devoted son, Brooke had never quite loved Alec in his youth, especially after her handsome little nephew, Tony Lombard, was born. But now, since her son had become "someone," she received Alec's overseas calls with enthusiasm and excitement. In her late-blooming pride she forgot the early years when she couldn't be bothered with her son.

Alec knew instinctively it would be the same with Heather, too. Eventually, she too would see that Alec was indispensible. But not if Tony died a heroic death on a flight over the war area, even though it was only made to get footage for a Prysing film.

With Tony's death almost certain, Alec couldn't help but feel a certain ambivalence toward his cousin. Although he genuinely liked him, as most people did, he was tired of being overshadowed by the appeal of Tony's good looks and personal charm.

Alec parked his aging Ford on the grassy bluff above the Thames and made his precarious way across the road to the little Tudor-style, half-timbered hotel that had gradually come to be the home of several Americans currently stationed in Britain.

Leo Prysing had taken over three bedrooms on the second floor, refurbished two of them for his offices and kept the suite on a permanent basis, though his main headquarters was still in Culver City, California.

To Alec's surprise, Stella Burkett met him in the lobby of the hotel. When he married Heather he had known that he would be saddled with her fiercely aggressive mother. In a large household she could be useful, as she had proven to be in the Nob Hill mansion. In the present situation, to quote his British friends, she was "a bit much." All the same, he shared with Stella Burkett an unbreakable bond — their love for Heather.

He found her pacing up and down the narrow, paneled lobby. Evidently, she had been waiting for him. A handsome woman in her late forties, she might have been ten years older. On seeing him she lurched forward to grab Alec's arm. He immediately knew there was trouble.

"You didn't leave Heather alone, did you?" he asked anxiously.

"You know me better than that, Alec. She's up there preening for the great Prysing."

That relieved him. Every time he left her he wondered if he would return to find her in that state of white terror he'd come to know so well. He especially worried when the Luftwaffe bombers droned across the sky headed for their London targets. But the sound didn't seem to bother her. Even when she was caught at a Hotel Savoy party during one of the fire raids she had behaved well. It was only when she was left alone, after her experience during the Southern California earthquake, that the paralyzing fear seemed to take control.

Alec hurried his steps. "I'll go and rescue Leo before he finds he's been wangled into signing a new star."

"She *could* be a star, too. She's that pretty. A lot prettier than Tony's wife, wouldn't you say?"

They were going up the little staircase beside the reception desk. Although Alec didn't disagree with his mother-in-law's reasoning, he said, "I'd be the last man to notice Eden's looks. We've been friends since we were both kids."

"I forgot. Her being so much older than my Heather and all."

He saw through that remark and decided to ignore it. Stella Burkett was always in there pitching.

"Why were you waiting for me downstairs?"

He had hoped to spend some time alone with his wife before returning for his evening broadcast. Any delay meant driving through blacked-out London — no easy job for anyone not born a Cockney.

"A dumb idea, I guess. Me figuring I'd spare you, and all that."

*"What is it?"*

"They'll all be there. Mr. Steve and Mr. Prysing . . . with the news."

Alec was surprised by his own relief.

"They've found my cousin. Alive?" He watched her face in the light from the window at the end of the hall. The truth came then like a body blow. "Not alive?"

"The French fisherman got the description of

one of the bodies the Germans picked up. There's a rumor the Germans shot a couple of the crew as they parachuted down. Anyway, they say it sounds like it's Mr. Tony."

"God!"

He hadn't really believed it could happen to Tony Lombard. Not lucky Tony. How often in his boyhood he had envied that handsome, laughing, spoiled little cousin of his. Not, of course, to the point of wishing him any harm. The Pearl Harbor injuries had turned out just the way Alex thought they would, with twenty-two-year-old Tony rising like a phoenix from the ashes, more handsome and luckier than ever. For the kid to go like this, only three years later, a broken, shot-up body to be picked up by the enemy — it made Alec sick. It was unnatural. He knew Eden would suffer, but his mother would suffer more. In their quiet way, holding in all emotions, Alec and his Aunt Randi understood each other very well.

At the door of the Huntingtons' little two-room "suite" Stella put her arm out, barring him for a moment.

"There'll be a problem for you, Mr. Alec." He was still "Mr." to her. "My girl ain't — hasn't been told about Mr. Tony yet. It's me own thought they're waiting for you to do the dirty work. Thought you'd ought to know."

He grimaced at the idea. He had never been quite sure about the extent of his wife's feelings for his cousin. Squaring his shoulders, he walked into the lounge, as it was called in the fashion of country British. Uncle Steve stood by the windows that looked out across the road to the grassy bluff where Alec had parked his car. Beyond was a steep, green drop to the valley of the winding Thames. For all his strength and athletic build, Uncle Steve looked older, haggard to Alec's anxious eye. Steve had tried to take the place of Alec's dead father and now Alec found himself more deeply moved by his pain and that of Aunt Randi than by any other aspect of the tragedy.

Leo Prysing, a chunky, muscular man with an electrifying presence, commanded attention whenever he chose to do so. Far from handsome, with a large face, grizzled curly hair, and a voice often harsh with authority, the aura of power about him made him seem to have sex appeal, whether he did or not. Alec, who analyzed people in his own quiet way, often felt that power and authority had more sensuous appeal for women than all the good looks and charm that men like Leo Prysing lacked. Prysing made up for these shortcomings in other ways. On rare occasions he revealed a gentleness tinged with irony, and at such times it was impossible to resist his spell, as numerous women who had fallen under it knew. Not quite so rare was his streak of ruthlessness that showed itself when he was crossed.

He seemed to be in one of his gentle moods with Heather, who fussed over his coat, produced a thread from his shoulder and held it up proudly, pinched between thumb and forefinger. Alec quickly noticed that she was trying to ignore the serious thrust of Prysing's conversation.

"Oh, let's not talk about planes and crashes and those awful things," she said. "Do tell me how you choose the actresses in your movies."

114

"Now, Mrs. Huntington . . ."

"Heather. For goodness sake, my name is Heather. What do your girls — I mean your stars — have to do to get a part? Are the screen tests hard?"

"The camera would have no trouble with you, Mrs. Huntington. But I'm afraid the hours would. Do you like getting up at four or five?"

"A.M. or P.M.?"

Alec smiled at that. Neither he nor Stella Burkett moved from the doorway, she because her daughter's wiles fascinated her, and Alec because they filled him with amusement, tenderness and a certain sense of superiority.

Slapping her hand playfully, Leo went on. "You have to get out to Culver City, be in makeup, hairdo and wardrobe by nine o'clock, six days a week, shooting — on the average — until six at night. Then it's home for dinner, learn tomorrow's lines and off to bed, for that five A.M. alarm clock."

She wrinkled her small, delicate nose. "Well, I just wouldn't work Saturdays. That's all."

"Then you wouldn't be a Prysing star."

She looked around and, spotting Alec, held out her arms to him. "Alec, sweetie! This man is a slave driver. You never told me that."

He leaned over and kissed her in a perfunctory way because the others were watching. Still, she clung to him. Alec was well aware that most people wondered what the gorgeous young girl had seen in the quiet broadcaster of middle height, no outstanding features, and only an unsuspected strength. He wore glasses now for his work, and they didn't help promote the image of a glamorous war correspondent. Though aware that his mild-mannered personality caused some people to consider him weak, Alec had developed a strength of character that didn't permit him to doubt himself or his convictions.

Leo saw from Alec's expression that he had heard the news. Steve turned away to stare out the window again, his fingers drumming nervously on the windowpane.

"Is it certain?" Alec asked no one in particular.

"It's not certain, so forget it," Steve said without moving.

Alec and Leo exchanged glances.

Leo shrugged. "The description fits."

Heather asked innocently, before Alec could pursue it any further, "What fits?" She slowly removed her hands from around Alec's neck. "Not Tony. He promised to come back. Right in this room. On this couch, he promised me. You remember, Alec." Her voice took on the childish petulance that obviously disturbed the two older men. Leo stirred, showing signs of getting ready for a hasty departure. Steve's mouth twisted. He blinked and looked out the window again.

As always, Heather turned to her husband for reassurance.

"He shouldn't do that to me when he promised."

In his calm, quiet way, Alec said, "Heather, you remember all the people who were killed when the Blitz was on? They didn't want to leave you and me either. Sometimes we have to hurt people by leaving them."

Leo got up. "I'll do what I can. Steve, you're going to keep checking?"

Steve looked at him blankly. "What else? I've still got some contacts. I know an ex-Communist who has been briefing the government on their workings in the Maquis. The liberation of France, particularly Paris, will require them as well as the legitimate government of Free France. He thinks he can find out if Tony is alive."

Leo laughed harshly. "Does anyone know what *is* going to be the legitimate government of France after the Liberation?"

"It depends on which group gets control of Paris when the uprising comes." It always surprised the others present that Alec could talk politics and still act like a disciplinarian to his wife. "Stop sniveling, Heather. You know better than that. You're a big girl now."

"She can't help it," Stella Burkett objected. "Don't be cruel."

Heather swung around on her mother. "Don't you dare call Alec cruel." She was back in his arms, kneading his shoulders with her fists. "You won't let them leave me alone, will you, darling?"

Although Alec remained coolly reserved while slipping her arms off his neck, he couldn't help feeling a secret satisfaction that Leo and Steve and Stella should see just how much this beautiful creature loved plain, unexciting, dull Alec.

He kept an arm around her and looked across the room at his uncle. This was the hard part, the part he dreaded.

"I believe I must say something on my broadcast soon. Shall I make it tonight?"

"Christ, no!"

Everyone looked at Steve. A quick smile flickered on and off. He immediately recovered from his outburst and apologized. "Guess I overreacted. But if it's all the same to you, Alec, I'd appreciate your giving me a few more days."

"Sure, Uncle Steve. I'd just as soon not rush into it, anyway. Let's take the gamble. After all, he may be a prisoner somewhere. And we can't be a hundred percent sure the witnesses are reliable." He paused, aware that Leo had been eyeing him with a kind of cynical disapproval. "Of course, the competition may mention Tony," he added, now ashamed of his sudden pollyanna attitude, "BBC asked me this morning why I had been keeping the story under wraps."

"Then you'll give us time?"

Alec nodded. A denial would have stuck in his throat.

Leo joined Steve. "I'll go along with you. You headed for the Channel again? I've got to get my second camera crew out of there. The Nasties have been blasting the daylights out of the ports."

The two men left together.

Ignoring her mother, Heather drew Alec toward her.

"Alec, honey, I'm cold. Make me warm."

After half a dozen years of marriage Alec still couldn't get used to his wife's sexual overtures in front of her mother. But Stella Burkett knew when to retire gracefully. She slipped out the door and down the hall to her room where, as Alec was aware, she would order up whatever ale was available and drink until he called her to take his place with her daughter.

Like a great many people whose every thought revolved around themselves, Heather was better at foreplay than she was during an orgasm. He sometimes wondered if she ever had one. But she was remarkably skilled in satisfying Alec and all too willing to encourage his enjoyment. Probably she found it an excellent way to control Alec and maintain his interest. Despite her beauty, she was perfectly aware of his importance to her well-being.

She drew him down on her on the old double bed and began to caress him, at the same time unbuckling his belt, sensuously raising his shirttails before whispering, "Come . . . come . . ."

Within moments the allure of his wife's body and their caresses allowed him to blot out, at least temporarily, all the painful thoughts that plagued him throughout his long, nerve-wracking day.

It was dusk before he left for London, after having brought in Stella to stay with Heather while he was gone. He always dreaded that look on her face when he was leaving, the way the blood drained from her cheeks and she sat up, usually on her knees, her body stiff, her golden cat's-eyes glazed.

"Don't leave me alone — please."

"Here's your mother, dear. You'll be fine. I'll be back after the all clear, whenever that is."

At the sight of Stella Burkett Heather relaxed at once, the color returning to her porcelain face.

"Ma, wait 'til I tell you," she said, gleefully. "Before you and Alec came, Mr. Prysing was promising to make me a star. He said I was a natural."

"That's nice," Stella said drily.

Driving back into the appalling wreckage of London's East End dock area, Alec reminded himself that the worst part of his own job was coming up. Somehow, he had to eulogize a fallen hero, the son of an internationally-known American, while still giving the impression that, against all evidence, Tony was still alive. He knew that BBC and CBS would mention Tony as a casualty.

Curiously, Heather hadn't once mentioned Tony Lombard after her initial reaction. Still, he couldn't help but wonder if she had been thinking about Tony all along.

# Chapter Nine

Having Tony Lombard in the apartment with her provided Jany Friedrich with the most exciting hours of her life. But she knew she had to be careful while Carl was around. He still didn't entirely trust the man whose presence was a deadly danger to Carl and his sister. There were several possibilities, all of which Jany denied indignantly.

The dashing, injured parachutist could be a German plant, Carl argued. He could be a Communist plant, since the Communists in France hated the Gaullist Free French only a little less then they hated the Germans. The Communists knew that when the Occupation ended their ultimate competition for control would be the Free French government in exile, born that dark day in 1940 when a little-known French general had escaped to London and broadcast the defiance of free Frenchmen.

Neither Carl nor Jany had heard the actual broadcast, but the words became his Bible and during the following four years he had firmly entrenched himself in those Resistance cells taking their orders from the emissaries of Charles de Gaulle. For this reason there was no chance of thinking Tony Lombard was a Gaullist. Carl would know better.

In spite of his stern politics, though, Carl could be a dear. Jany was touched by the way he had helped Tony and let him rest on his own bed. Late in the afternoon Carl had gone out to visit the Binet family and see how he might help after the murder of young Georges.

Jany tried to stay away from the couch where Tony Lombard slept but his nearness fascinated her. As the afternoon wore on and the room grew more stuffy, she decided Monsieur Tony was suffering. She stood beside the couch watching him, aching to touch him. Why not? His fever might have risen. She had to find out. It was the only decent thing to do.

His forehead was damp, but that could be from the stifling room. Though he didn't seem to have any fever, he groaned. She figured that his ankle must have been giving him pain. She took her brother's wet cloth, knelt beside the couch and raised Tony's trouser leg to wrap the cloth around his swollen, badly bruised ankle. The pain lines smoothed out of his forehead. This accomplished, she got to her feet again and moved to the head of the couch. He had nice hair. Dark and shining — well, it would shine if he didn't have to keep jumping into Normandy pastures. She leaned over him, and astonished herself by brushing his forehead with her lips. The touch thrilled her. She had never felt like this in her entire life.

The closest sensation was the pulse-pounding excitement she felt when she sat huddled in the darkness of a cinema, imagining she was up there on the screen in the arms of Monsieur Boyer, Monsieur Power, or best of all, the Irish Monsieur Flynn. Although Tony Lombard had a little of Power's lean, dark, gentlemanly appearance, he seemed more in character like the devilish Errol. The combination was irresistible to a girl reared by an ex-movie star mother, who spent all her pocket money in the movie houses of Paris.

He stirred under her touch but did not wake up.

She propped her elbows on the head of the couch, rested her chin in one palm and put together some more movie dreams in which Tony Lombard climbed castle walls merely to kiss her. She knew all about sex but wasn't quite sure she liked the idea. Except — maybe — with Boyer or Flynn or Tony Lombard.

She heard Carl come back just before suppertime and ducked into her bedroom. She knew his strict rules for her behavior. She knew he wouldn't chastise her, though he might be very angry with Monsieur Tony.

Not unexpectedly, he was feeling depressed, but tried to be cheerful for Jany's sake.

"They're taking it very well. Monsieur Binet wanted to do something stupid. I think I persuaded him to turn that passion to a good use. We are going to need him against the Boches when Liberation comes."

"And the Reds?" She didn't like Danielle deBrett and took every opportunity to hint that Danielle should not be let in on the secret plans of the Gaullist and the Centrist Undergrounds.

Emotionally, he might not share her feelings about Danielie but he agreed that the sexy Communist runner should not know they were harboring a mysterious American. Or was Monsieur Tony British, after all?

"The Reds aren't to know about this fellow.

That specifically includes Danielle. By the way, how is Lombard?" He went over and looked at Tony. "He must go in the morning. It won't be safe for us. Possibly not for him either." He considered Tony's shirt and trousers and examined his shoes. "Jany?"

His tone made her anxious. "Yes? What is it?"

"Who did he say gave him these clothes? They are all French."

She hurried on with what she knew. "Monsieur Tony was coming out of a big town house on St. Honore. The one that was the Hôtel Udine-Mercier before the war."

"I know the place. A lawyer, one of the Merciers, lives there. We suspect he has been counterfeiting passports and papers for Communist refugees. We can use him eventually, in spite of his politics. He means well."

His eyes narrowed. He went around the end of the couch and opened the curtains a little way, studying the narrow, airless street below.

"There are two Gestapo pulling out from the curb. They've been somewhere up the street . . . I wonder."

"Oh, Carl, no!"

"Be glad, *chèrie*. They are passing us."

He sat down to supper and they talked in low voices with an occasional glance at Tony on the couch.

"He'll be hungry when he awakens," Carl said unexpectedly. "Is there enough? Perhaps eggs, you think? And a salad of tomatoes. I saw some today."

She felt warmly excited inside. To have Carl talking about Monsieur Tony with such generosity, it answered all her dreams.

"Not the egg, Carl. I'm saving that for your breakfast."

He smiled. "Well, in that case . . ."

She cleared the dishes, very quietly, and was in the bedroom mending stockings when she heard a brisk knocking on the door of the flat. The sharp sound cut through the long streaks of late sunlight in the rooms. She got up from the bed, went to the bedroom door and opened it. She felt tight, cold hands closing around her heart. She knew that Carl was eternally in danger. And now there was Monsieur Tony as well.

*Please . . . please don't let it be the police.*

Carl's voice was low. He seldom raised it, yet there were times when Jany thought her beloved brother could sound positively sinister. This was the tone of his voice now, telling his visitor, Danielle deBrett, that he couldn't spend time with her. He had other things to do.

Suddenly, Jany saw Monsieur Tony limp past her partly opened door, headed for the argument between Carl and Mademoiselle deBrett. Horrified, Jany threw their bedroom door open and started out into the living room, then restrained herself, remembering Carl's warning never to interfere with his visitors.

It thrilled her to see how brave Tony Lombard was, limping up to Danielle deBrett, bold as could be. It would be hard to say who was more surprised, Carl or Danielle. Carl, at least, covered his uneasiness with an expression of extreme boredom.

"You are awake, Antoine? I thought you wanted

silence for your nap. Mademoiselle deBrett, may I present my cousin, Antoine Lenoir?"

Danielle showed all her dark allure as she took the hand Tony offered with a flourish.

"Ah, Monsieur Lenoir, it was my thought I would find you here. You must explain to Carl that I am a safe one, that you were sent to me. The Gestapo came around with the hungry nose and you ran away. But you belong to the Party. You are safe. And I too, though I belong to the people, I am to be trusted. You see, Carl? Look at his face and see the truth."

Hating herself for obeying the black-haired bitch, Jany looked at Tony Lombard. From his look there was no doubt that he was confirming what she said, although Tony didn't appreciate Danielle's disclosure that he knew her. Carl was less quick to behave as Danielle had expected.

"Is it true?" he asked in that tone full of quiet menace, "you are a courier for the Franc-Tireur, the Partisans?"

Tony's smile and shrug were too innocent. They revealed too much of the mischief that was part of his nature.

"Mademoiselle is right. Her friends rescued me. I am not a parachutist by profession. Matter of fact, I only made five jumps before this. Sort of a rehearsal, you might say. But I am not the man her friends were waiting for."

"He says he did not bring the money," Danielle explained to Carl. "The Party needs it, desperately. That is the difficulty. No one would understand better than you, *mon chèr.* Your own cell is desperate for money, no?"

126

In spite of the sultry evening Jany was chilled to see the way Carl's flat cheek muscles set stiffly; yet he managed to respond without special emphasis.

"I am sure it would be, if I were involved in the Resistance. I am not such a fool. You must know that, if you know me at all."

Danielle's throaty laugh grated against Jany's nerves. Danielle worked her seductive wiles further, running her fingers along Carl's sleeve. He was unresponsive, so she moved her fingers slowly to Tony who gave her the grin she had expected.

"Yes, yes," she murmured. "It is understood. Carl is, in fact, a collaborator. But not in the way I have said. He is a lover of the Boches. Being of German blood himself, it is natural." She laughed again.

Tony looked from one to the other. Jany thought he seemed puzzled and was beginning to question his own position. Maybe he believed Danielle's heavy-handed joking.

She joined the group, anxious to reassure Monsieur Tony.

"It isn't true, that. My brother would never, never collaborate. Why, he hates the Germans more than Mademoiselle deBrett ever could."

Tony was plainly relieved, and Danielle burst out laughing at Jany's betrayal of her brother, but Carl replied calmly.

"It is normal to hate the Boches. It does not make one a spy for the Resistance. I am a simple clerk who lets others perform the heroics. I will stand by and applaud them."

Jany had already realized her betrayal and was growing more nervous by the minute. She trusted

Danielle even less than Carl did.

"Mademoiselle, you know my brother is a man of peace. If he were in the Resistance, we would have more to eat than we do now. Monsieur Tony is injured. He needs rest." To her great relief, Tony nodded obediently when she turned to him. "You should not be up. You need your rest."

He understood at once and became the sickly patient.

"Thank you, Cousin Jany." He excused himself with all the charm he could muster and limped back to the couch.

Danielle deBrett looked annoyed, uncertain about how to deal with the young man who purported to be a Communist courier. What baffled her more was that his cousins seemed unaware of his political persuasions. No matter, she thought, possibly this Lenoir could be used to sway Carl to the side of the Reds. "Carl, are you with us, or are you one of these slugs who call themselves Frenchmen but do nothing to free France of the Boches?"

Infuriated by this insult to her brother, Jany pushed her thin young body between him and Danielle.

"How dare you, you . . . you Red! Don't you dare call my brother names just because he wants peace. He's kind and good and gentle and does no one harm. I don't want him to be shot like Georges. Georges was shot because he was late for the dentist."

Unable to control her excitement, she pushed Danielle who responded with a most disagreeable smirk. Sensing trouble, Carl quickly took Jany by the shoulders.

"All right, *chèrie*, be calm. Danielle means us no harm. Danielle — say something."

"Of course, Carl. *Ma petite* Jany, we are fooling, your brother and I. Sometimes we talk like this, but we would never betray each other. We know we will need each other when the Allies come to free Paris. Carl knows we must work together until the day Paris is free. Then —" Again the fleshy shrug, the oily smile. "Do I read correctly, Carl? You and your poor beaten, rejected democracy."

"Aren't we getting political again?" Tony Lombard put in, trying to neutralize the conversation. "I thought the French spent all their time talking sex."

Beset on all sides by these spiteful remarks and Tony's attempts at jokes, Carl managed to keep his temper. He opened the door.

"Danielle, good night. Another day we will discuss politics."

"As you say, Carl. We will discuss it again. Not politics, no. But the money which Monsieur Lenoir was to have brought us. *Bon soir, mon amour.*"

Jany would have slammed the door after her but Carl closed it gently. She knew he was thinking of Madame Charpentier. He was careful. That was one of the reasons he had managed to survive so long in the Resistance.

Carl leaned back against the door with his eyes closed. Jany felt all the relief and also the apprehension of the moment. But Tony limped over to a chair, fell into it and began to rub his ankle.

"That's one obstacle removed," he said cheerfully, "I've been worried about our Commie friends."

"Not quite removed." Carl opened his eyes and followed Jany and Tony into the living room. "*Chèrie,* would you make some coffee? I need to think. Plans must be made."

In the kitchen Jany spooned in ground coffee while she listened to the conversation drifting in from the living room. Tony wasn't letting Carl's threatening manner upset him, though she kept peeking in to watch them when things got a little tense.

"I'm not actually a Communist, you know," Tony tried to assure him. "I'm an American — a movie director by trade." Carl's tawny eyebrows raised. "Well," Tony amended, "make that an assistant director. A small group of us working for an American producer wanted to get some of the actual fighting on film. We caught some flak and got off course. You know the rest. I parachuted out and landed in a pasture somewhere. Danielle's friends got to me before the Germans did, thank God. They were expecting a delivery of ammunition and money. When they mistook me for their courier, I decided to go along with it." He winced. "I wonder if I could trouble you for a cool, wet cloth. This damned ankle is making a little trouble. Anyway, that's how I met Mercier and Danielle and got the phony papers."

In the kitchen Carl passed Jany as he went for the washcloth. "Be kind to him, Carl, please." She whispered. "He's telling the truth. I'm sure of it."

Carl looked at her quickly. She flashed her most naive smile. He pinched her nose.

"Even handsome people can lie, you know."

But she was sure she could count on him to help

Monsieur Tony. Carl was back in the kitchen a moment later.

"Is there any of the eel pie left? He says he had to leave his lunch today. Gestapo took his appetite and he hasn't eaten since sometime yesterday."

Happily, Jany rescued the remains of supper and started to reheat the pie. Then she brought in the coffee, which made the American yelp. Carl drank the thick black stuff, watching Tony with some amusement.

"You find our coffee a trifle strong?"

"Not at all. Marvelous stuff. Puts hair on the chest." He went on drinking valiantly. He must have been aware of Carl's close observation. Once he had emptied the little cup, he said, "I'm not going to be able to dig up the money deBrett and her gang are looking for. Not unless I charge it to ransom and have my family cough it up."

"Your French is adequate, but your expressions are curious. If you're to pose as our cousin, you will have to stop using those strange words. *Cough up,* and the like."

"Sorry about that. Guess I forgot myself. Ah, food," he exclaimed, as Jany brought in a serving of the pie. "I'm famished. It smells delicious. What is it?"

Before Jany could explain Carl said, "Just a meat pie."

"Eel," Jany added.

Tony dropped his fork, but picked it up again and started to investigate the succulent, juicy contents under the crust. As he began to eat, they could see that he was pleasantly surprised.

Carl waited until he was halfway through his

meal before bringing up business again.

"You mention that your family has money. Is it possible that they might get guns for us?"

"Who are *us?*"

"We must defend Paris. And ourselves, when the Allies come. The Germans will be merciless if there is a siege."

Tony looked at his fork and touched the sharp ends of the tines, considering the proposition.

"If you rise, they will destroy the city. Look at Warsaw and Rotterdam and a dozen others. They won't spare Paris just because it's Paris. It's the Commies who want the rising. They aren't interested in preserving your city. The Party wants control. The Maquis leaders boasted about it to me."

"They won't get it," Carl said. "Not if we have the weapons. And all Maquis are not Reds."

Clearly, this gave Tony Lombard the opening he was looking for.

"If I could get word back to London about my safety, I might be able to arrange something. My producer has influence. He would notify my parents and family. My father might even fly to London to make arrangements. He pulls some weight. But I will have to get word to them — they probably think I'm dead. It depends on whether the camera crew or the pilot made it back safely."

Carl sat thoughtfully considering the options. Jany was sure he knew ways of getting word to the London Gaullist committee. But if Tony Lombard was a plant, he could destroy not only Carl, but the entire Resistance cell in which Carl was involved. Jany knew the American was just what he claimed to be, but she didn't blame her brother for his suspicions.

"Carl, couldn't we send some kind of message to London and let them know?"

"By the mails? And past the censors? We do not live in a free French republic."

"No. I meant — I don't know what. It was just an idea."

Tony also had an idea which he canceled out as he talked. "My producer is well known. He may even be respected by the Germans — oh, damn! Leo Prysing is a Jew. You may have heard what happened to his brother and sister-in-law."

Jany started. "Carl, he said Leo Prysing."

"I heard." Even Carl had been aroused to display his feelings. "Monsieur Lombard, you know Leo Prysing? The producer of the cinema who was in Zurich in 1938?"

"Of course I do; I work for him. What have I been telling you? Anyway, what difference does it make?"

Carl got up excitedly. "It makes all the difference. If mother and I had not heard the broadcast Leo Prysing made from Zurich we would never have known that my father was a hero. He was an anti-Nazi working inside the Reich. That's the most dangerous work possible." He swung around to Tony. "I hated him for many years. He deserted us when little Jany was born. Shortly after he married a rich American woman."

"My aunt Brooke."

"Yes, but don't you see? It was all a part of the image he projected in Vienna and Berlin, to cover his anti-Nazi efforts. And if Leo Prysing had not made that speech praising father, I would never have known."

Jany, who had never known her father, was pleased over Carl's revelation because it made him happy. But her emotions were far enough removed from her father to give her a more objective view, and it seemed to Jany that Tony Lombard was not quite as impressed by Leo's praise of the dear "hero," Kurt Friedrich.

"That's great," Tony said, after a slight hesitation. "Then you see I'm telling you the truth. If you know someone with connections, someone with a radio, you can get a message through to Leo Prysing. He was due back in London this week."

Carl walked up and down, making plans.

"One day, after the Liberation, I would like to meet Monsieur Prysing. I want to learn as much as I can about my father. Meanwhile —" He slapped Tony on the back. "It is almost time for the London broadcast. We only have a few minutes. The Boches will be getting what you call a fix on us."

Tony wrapped the soggy cloth around his ankle and followed Carl into the tiny kitchen. Jany watched, breathless. She was aware of a creeping doubt. What if the dashing Yankee really could betray Carl? It wasn't like Carl to be so trusting, all on account of their father, a cipher in Jany's young life.

From the back of the vegetable shelves Carl produced a radio, a small, complex box quite unlike the radio and loudspeaker they owned before the Occupation. Carl and others working in his department had been asked to turn in their radios, which Carl did at once. Jany understood gradually that his compliance with all German orders was deliberate. He wanted no suspicion drawn to him and his cell of Resistance workers.

Carl glanced at his wristwatch. He scowled, twisted the little dial, and from within an aura of static a voice came through, speaking in an English that was difficult for Jany to make out.

"American," Carl explained, while she strained to understand.

Tony, however, was delighted. "That newscaster is my cousin, Alec Huntington. He's based in London as a war correspondent. Never thought I'd be so glad to hear his voice."

"We're late," Carl said, interrupting him, "I'm afraid my watch is slow. It's nearly over."

Tony listened with his head close to the radio.

"Same old Alec. Seems like years since I've seen him. What I wouldn't give to be back there having an ale with the gang!"

Jany felt a sharp letdown, but the two men had their heads together, busily translating Alec's news. His last items were clearly coded. Tony and Carl discussed various translations, some of them ludicrous, while Alec's calm, not quite monotonous voice continued the report.

"The cat keeps all her feathers . . . I repeat, the cat keeps all her feathers. Nine times nine will be ninety-nine. The squirrels and the goat meet at the squire's barn. The squirrels and the . . ."

To Jany it sounded very silly, even though she knew the nonsensical remarks meant something serious. But nobody was fooled — the Germans would know it was a code. Since the two men had crowded her out of the kitchen, she sauntered back into the living room. The room was still hot and she opened the windows to breathe in a little of the night air. Several seconds had passed before she noticed the big cruising van, ominous with its flaring swastika flags. It was followed by a small, open truck that looked like the American jeep she had seen exhibited after its capture near Dunkirk. Swastika flags flapped from the truck as well. The van was tracking down the illicit radio broadcasts, and would certainly make it rough on anyone they caught with a radio, whether they were broadcasting or not. From her angle she could see that the truck following the van carried reinforcement troops. Her heart in her throat, Jany didn't bother to close the windows but rushed back to the kitchen to warn the two men as they huddled, unaware, around the receiver.

# Chapter Ten

"Gestapo looking for transmissions," she whispered urgently at the entrance to the kitchen.

Though Carl was only receiving, the mere presence of Gestapo, this time surprisingly supplemented by German soldiers, was enough to spell out the imminent danger. Carl stuck the little radio back into the vegetable bin and piled up dirty rags, turnips and celery root, then added the discarded ends of vegetables so it appeared to be nothing more than garbage. He pushed Tony out of the kitchen with a warning.

"If they stop here, say nothing. Only answer. I work for the Ministry of Education. They trust me."

Tony recited quickly, "I'm the cousin from Gascony. My papers say I was wounded at LaPanne during the retreat from Dunkirk."

Jany slipped away to the foyer door and opened it a few inches. Peering out, she saw Madame Charpentier talking to several Germans at the foot of the stairs. So they had stopped at their building. They must be suspicious of someone. Madame Charpentier sounded very friendly to them. Jany was still huddled there listening when Tony came up behind her. "Easy, honey," he whispered, feeling the tension in her young shoulders. "Let me handle this."

Carl was at her other side. "What are you going to do?" he said, addressing Tony over her head.

"Nothing stupid, I hope."

"Me? Stupid? You've got to be kidding. Seems to me the best defense is a good offense. If I'm curious in a friendly way, they aren't going to think I'm hiding something. I'll make a fuss over Madame, your concierge."

Carl ignored this. "They've separated for the search. Too late for any of your wiles now, my dear cousin," Carl said as the soldiers branched out. "Besides, such unnatural confidence would strike them as suspicious."

"But to hide behind the door, scared to death! What if we were to leave the door open and wait for them on the top stair? You know, act simply curious."

Carl considered this and nodded. Obviously Tony's trouble was going to be too much bravura, too little caution. Jany, on the other hand, was so terrified she could offer no suggestions, but only obeyed Carl's instructions to keep calm with abrupt nods. The sound of boot heels ringing on the bricks of the courtyard carried up to where they waited. The tension mounting, Jany prayed under her breath. In an abstract way she was aware of the precision in those sounds.

It seemed an eternity before she heard the ring of the jackboots on the stairs. Tony Lombard was at the open door, gazing down at the black uniforms with interest and curiosity, or at least a good pretense of it. To Jany, the faces looked like the faces of all men in uniform. Even when Carl mildly protested, she refused to find any difference between the SS, Gestapo or otherwise, and the gray-green of the Wehrmacht, the German army.

She was shaking badly, unlike her brother, who had cultivated a slight, but acceptable uneasiness that suited these situations.

Tony beamed at the spectral faces floating like pale Halloween masks in the dark of the stairwell.

"Good evening, messieurs. How does the search go?"

They were a quartet with no interest in small talk. The soldier nearest him thrust him aside with an elbow and what looked to Jany like the corner of a well-loaded pistol holster. She tried never to look at their sidearms, but the second officer unsnapped his holster flap and the gun was there, a dark, heavy thing pointed right at Tony Lombard's kidneys.

The four Germans plunged through the foyer into the living room. Two soldiers went into Jany's bedroom. Passing Carl, they showed him even more contempt than they'd shown Tony. Tony tried to follow them but the lean one in the lead with the gun swung around and jabbed the blunt business end into his side, at the same time giving him a sharp order in German. Tony had sense enough to stay back.

The tall Wehrmacht officer, somewhere between fifty and sixty, with thinning, straight gray hair and an unexpectedly voluptuous mouth, made his way to the head of the little troop. He appeared contemptuous of the black-clad Gestapo with whom he was so uncharacteristically working. Jany had never seen an army officer taking over a search of residence. Usually, the French police cooperated with the Gestapo in such matters.

The officer's manners were good and Jany wondered if this was a deliberate plot of some kind or a sincere effort to be friendly. Because he held himself ramrod straight, his politeness was even more unnerving to Jany. He spoke French very well with only a Germanic twist to his phrases.

"So this is your room, little one. My daughter's apartment, it resembles very much. You attend school, yes?"

"I attend typing class, monsieur."

"*Oberstlieutenant.* That is to say, Lieutenant Colonel Walthur von Leidersdorf." He clicked his heels and she had a dangerous impulse to laugh. "In this modest little room I am sure we will find nothing . . . Hansberger, is she not the image of my little Erika?" To demonstrate, he put one arm around her, hugging her shoulders in a fatherly way. His hand was cold and his fingers were unusually long, the forefinger nearly the length of the middle one. Abnormal, she thought, but took care not to shudder.

The two Gestapo agents exchanged cynical glances but the short, fat soldier called Hansberger agreed. He watched her, his eyes like raisins pressed into his doughy face.

"Ja, Herr Oberstlieutenant. Like Fraulein von Leidersdorf."

The Gestapo pair next concentrated on the living room, the kitchen and foyer. They began to throw around cushions while Tony kibitzed, getting in the way at every turn. It seemed strange to Jany that they looked so harmless, like simple German burghers. Carl had moved to the bedroom doorway and watched his sister as she stood with the officer. In spite of all his pleasantries,

Lieutenant Colonel von Leidersdorf tore off the embroidered bed coverlet and then felt under the mattress, all the while assuring Jany, "You should be living in the Reich, mademoiselle. We would do much better for you. My daughter soon joins the hospital staff in Darmstadt. We have many opportunities for ambitious and dedicated young females."

"Is it not *Kinder, Kirche und Küchen,* Herr Oberstleutnant?" Carl remarked innocently.

Stay out of it, Carl, Jany thought silently. Don't try to be clever. But she was too frightened to open her mouth.

Von Leidersdorf looked at him, really seeing him for the first time.

"You speak very well German. Where did you learn it?"

"In the Lycée, of course, monsieur."

Jany ventured, "Carl?"

The officer was pleased. "A good German name. What is the rest?"

"Carl Friedrich, monsieur. I am with the Ministry of Education."

Slowly, the German smoothed the bed, gave it a pat, set Maman's old satin slipper chair back in place and gave the lowboy and mirror no more than a cursory glance. He turned back to the doorway and tapped Carl on the shoulder.

"So you are the Friedrich. We hear good things about you. You cooperate. It is intelligent, that. When we have completed the pacification and this tiresome war is over, you must visit the Reich. I personally guarantee you will receive a warm welcome."

"You are most kind, Herr Oberstlieutenant."

The officer started past him in an excellent mood. He stopped briefly in the doorway to look Jany over from head to foot.

"And you will bring your little sister, naturally. She will be an excellent companion for my Erika. Such a golden maiden! Like our Aryan goddesses, yes. You must certainly not come without — what is the name, mademoiselle?"

She managed to get it out in a breathy whisper.

"Jany Rey Friedrich, monsieur."

Tony watched Carl's fingers tighten into his palm. He moved toward the two men just as the German laughed, "But why should we wait until you visit the Reich? We have this warm, French summer ahead of us." He bowed stiffly to Jany, saluted Carl, set his peaked cap back on, and made a sweeping gesture to his men. "We are finished."

The Gestapo pair responded slowly but they obeyed, leaving the living room a shambles. Tony followed them to the door, bolting it after them. When he turned to Jany he saw that she was staring at her brother. Carl's skin looked ash gray. But the natural gray of his eyes seemed to burn like coals. "What in God's name was an army lieutenant colonel doing in a job like this? Are we being specially watched?"

"He said he insulted Himmler, which is nice. But I don't like him anyway," Jany said.

Tony tried to relieve the tension of the moment.

"Don't worry. With the invasion on, our fatherly oberstlieutenant will be too busy to worry about Jany."

Jany took Carl's hand. He looked down at it,

smiled faintly and relaxed.

"Very true," Carl said, "but for us it has been four years of this. And even now, so close to freedom, the greatest danger is coming. The Boches have been under orders. Except for the Gestapo and some of the elite SS, they are on good behavior. When the Allies close in the Wehrmacht will become the tigers they've been throughout the rest of Europe."

Jany tried to break the ominous mood.

"Help me, both of you. They are always so destructive. They opened the tear in the couch cover again. I mended it only a week or so ago. Now, it's to be done all over again."

Tony was his cheerful self. "Glad to help," Tony said cheerfully. "I think I'd do anything for you two after that narrow escape. Where do you want the china closet moved? I was in an earthquake once where every wine glass in the damned closet toppled over on me."

"An earthquake!" Jany shivered. "I couldn't bear a place where the earth moves. That could be dangerous."

Her remark struck the two men as riotously funny under the circumstances, and they both pitched in to help her, still chuckling.

With three pairs of hands and an abundance of good spirits, they soon had the flat in order again. Carl dug the last of his vermouth out of the cupboard and they all drank to the arrival of the Allies and a return of the tricolor. Tony couldn't understand the absurd restriction on the display of their flag.

"The *tricoleur* arouses too much passion in a

Frenchman. It always has," Carl said.

"And woman," Jany added, filling her cordial glass a second time.

"And women. However, I would wager that every household in France has one hidden away, ready to bring it out on the day of Liberation."

"And the Friedrichs?"

"But of course." Carl peeled back the thread-bare crimson carpet which looked hot and dusty on this summer night. Jany had basted the blue, white and red flag flat out onto the carpet backing in one corner of the room. "We never walk here. This little area is sacred soil, like our mother's grave."

It was nearly midnight when Carl asked Tony Lombard what he knew about Kurt Friedrich.

"Did you meet him often? Did you know of his work in the German Underground?"

Jany had been listening eagerly to Carl's questions about Tony's parachute jumps, especially the one over Normandy, but it was late and whenever Carl got off on his favorite pastime — vindicating their father — she lost interest. She was about to close her eyes now but something hesitant in Tony's voice and manner aroused her curiosity. She saw at once that Carl was so wrapped up in the glory of the martyred Kurt Friedrich that his usually astute senses were blunted. Jany, however, could see that Tony was suddenly giving a lot of attention to his drink.

"I met him once at the house. I mean home. At the Nob Hill house, while they were visiting San Francisco. I was pretty young and he was heavily involved in politics. And Aunt Brooke, of course.

They were visiting San Francisco . . . seemed to be showing each other off. I was pretty young, as I say. He didn't strike me one way or another." He finished off his drink, and as if he suddenly remembered something, he said brightly, "He was very good-looking. He was in a lot of Leo Prysing's silent movies when I was in my tricycle years."

"Father knew our mother back in his very young period," Carl said dreamily, to Jany's surprise. Maybe it was the effect of the vermouth . . . "I was born in 1918. But Maman didn't believe in marriage. It would have been disastrous to her career. She was a famous silent film star, too — Olga Rey."

"I knew Olga Rey," Tony said. "Not personally, but I saw all her films. I was crazy about her. Eden even met her in the Royal Hawaiian Hotel once."

"Who's Eden?" Carl asked with nostalgic interest.

He had caught the American off-guard. Tony laughed uncomfortably. "Didn't I tell you? I thought I had. The Lombards are a big family. Randi and Steve and Brooke in the older generation; Eden and Heather and Andrea, and Alec and me in the present generation."

"And Kurt Friedrich," Carl added, "until your aunt left Vienna in 1938." It was almost an accusation.

"Oh, she left, all right. The night Hitler's gang marched in."

"*Anschluss.*"

"Right. Anyway, my father and Eden went to get her out, along with Leo Prysing's family." He studied the dregs in his glass. "Leo's family didn't make it. But you know about that."

145

"Did your aunt Brooke love my father, do you think?" Carl asked.

"Wow! You should have seen her fuss over him when they visited the Nob Hill house. But you couldn't expect her to stick around and entertain the führer's gang in Vienna."

Hoping to keep the peace, Jany cut in. "She didn't know father was really against the Nazis, don't you see?"

This explanation satisfied Carl if only because he ached to be satisfied.

"If you could describe Monsieur Prysing's broadcast, how he knew my father was a hero . . ." He slapped his knee, "But my father helped his wife and your family to escape. I'd forgotten. That may be how Leo Prysing knew about his courage and his anti-Nazi work."

Tony seemed anxious to foster this idea. "Yes, which made your father's death at the hands of the Nazis all the more tragic, if you'll pardon my bringing it up."

"It's all right, I've come to accept it now. He was murdered by a street gang on *Kristallnacht,* the night when the Nazis raged through the streets destroying property — everything they could get their hands on — and murdering Jews. My father had Jewish blood. God only knows why he returned to the Reich after Leo mentioned that in his broadcast praising him for his efforts."

Tony started to pour from the empty vermouth bottle, put an eye up to the bottle, laughed and set it back on the round, oak dining table.

"We sure killed that. And poor Jany has been sitting here listening to us jaw away while yawning

146

her head off. Maybe I'd better figure some place to sleep tonight. I can see there's precious little room in here."

Carl looked around, considering. "Have you ever slept on a floor?"

"Practically grew up on floors. Nothing to it. I haven't been draftable, thanks to this." His fingers briefly lingered over the network of white scars on his neck and across his jawbone. "All the same, I've been sleeping out quite a lot lately." He grinned. "I can always sleep in the bathtub."

"We don't have a bathtub," Carl said evenly. "You've seen the WC next door. We share it with the flat on the east side of the courtyard. There is no — what you call — bathroom."

"In that case, step aside, folks. I've seen harder floors than this one. And it may be cooler than a bed would be. You may have done more than save my life today. You've kept me out of the hands of the Gestapo."

"Do you mean to say you think Danielle would have betrayed you? I doubt it. There would be too much involved for her and her Partisans."

"The place where they furnished my papers. Maître Mercier. If they have him, and he talks, I'd have been done for before this. I can only hope he destroyed any evidence before he was taken."

"He destroyed it," Carl remarked drily. "If he hadn't, you wouldn't be here now."

"In any case, if I had returned to the Mercier house, I've got a pretty good idea I'd be lying on a different floor tonight. And no carpet. But there is one more favor you can do for me, if you will."

"I refuse to walk into that Gestapo nest for you."

147

It was the kind of black humor that Jany didn't appreciate, but it didn't seem to bother Tony.

"Quite. But seriously, I've got to get back across the Channel. I know your people have done it for others."

"I haven't, personally. A Gaullist agent was dropped in April and the plane picked up two RAF. I imagine they reached London safely."

"Great. If you have any connections, I'd certainly appreciate it. The Gestapo is going to catch on to me sooner or later."

Carl nodded. "Did Danielle's Communist friends promise to get you back?"

"They did before the young lady decided I might not be one of them. If you could get through by radio to London, I know Leo Prysing would send word to my family. Then I could be picked up by plane when they're making a flight, maybe an arms drop. After all, I don't want my heirs spending my insurance quite yet."

"Carl, couldn't you?" Jany said, "I mean, I know you can't give Tony all the details, but you did get a message through to General de Gaulle's headquarters once through that old lady who transmitted . . ."

"Jany!"

"I'm sorry." It was a stupid thing to do. Jany had forgotten that the woman was killed, and there was no point in getting Tony's hopes up needlessly.

"I have no connections," Carl explained to Tony, "unless one of my superiors agrees that the message should he sent. It would compromise the cell. Surely you can see that. First they must check you out in London and be certain of your affiliation.

Understand, you would not be the first great industrialist's son who turned to the Reds or the Fascists."

Tony seemed more upset by the reference to being a "great industrialist's son" than the difficulty of getting across the Channel. "I do have an identity of my own, quite separate from my father's. He's in Washington, or San Francisco, or Guadalcanal with his own problems to worry about."

Carl shrugged. Neither Jany nor Tony could be sure how much Carl felt he could afford to betray in protecting Tony.

In spite of all the tensions of the day, Jany went to bed in an ecstasy of hope. She was in love for the first time in her life. She was certain there would never be anyone like Tony Lombard. And here he was, sleeping under her own roof. All her ideas of marrying a rich, powerful man in order to help Carl went sailing into oblivion. She would marry Tony even if he was poor.

And he was so close, out in the next room, stretched out on the living-room floor, using a mended sheet and Carl's own pillow. She went to the WC twice that night just so she could pass Tony. She was very quiet, and wore her best blue voile wrapper over her nightgown. She told herself she only wanted to look at him, not touch him.

The second time she passed he reached out and caught her bare ankle. She felt the prickle of excitement clear through her body. She looked down at him and saw in his eyes a warm, even tender look in the faint light that seeped in between the drapes. But she saw something else that he couldn't hide. She knew enough about men since the Occupation to recognize sexual desire when she saw it. This was the first time she welcomed it.

His thumb massaged her ankle, very gently at first, but with a persistence that inflamed her. She was aware of sensations in her loins that she had never known before. She trembled. Her knees felt watery, as if all her strength were gone. In another minute she would drop down beside him, let his body cover hers, his hands draw away her wrapper and gown. And then?

Maybe I'm growing up, finally, she thought, and all because of Monsieur Tony. He had aroused her body so that she would welcome his caresses instead of dreading them as she did when she passed the enemy soldiers and the dreaded SS on the streets.

Her brother turned on the couch, coughed and went back to sleep.

Jany pulled away from Tony's hand because it was expected of her, though she wished Carl weren't there. Tony let her go. He was only kidding, after all. She looked down and saw his perky grin. She loved his easy way, even in his present danger from Danielle's group as well as from the Germans. Hearing Carl turn again, she hurried off and closed her door.

In the privacy of her room she hugged herself ecstatically, pretending Monsieur Tony's arms were prowling over her body, admiring, caressing, enjoying her budding flesh. She sighed, debated whether to mention this delightful moment to her confessor, and went back to bed, undecided.

She gave some earnest prayers of thanks that

both Carl and Tony had passed the first acid test. The Gestapo, as well as the German army, had examined their papers without finding anything suspicious about them. Ordinarily, the German army would have nothing to do with such matters, so it was even more encouraging that no one had found anything wrong with the false papers. She wondered if the tall, gray-haired officer with the daughter in Darmstadt had influenced them to go easy on Jany's relations. For some reason the idea that the lieutenant colonel may have favored them because of Jany made him all the more terrifying. She'd heard Carl tell her often enough not to let them notice her, to become part of the crowd, not to call attention to herself.

But the danger was over, for the moment.

The next morning Carl, who shared politics with the owner of the Café St. Just, took Tony off to introduce his "cousin from Gascony." Pierre St. Just, the café owner, said it was a good idea for everyone to learn to accept "Monsieur Lenoir" now that the American was on Gestapo records as a member of the Friedrich family.

Jany spent a dream-filled afternoon at typing class, making more mistakes than ever, and counting the minutes until she could get back home to the flat. And Tony.

She hurried home so fast that she beat Tony, who had been captured by Madame Charpentier and invited to share a glass of ouzo. When Jany reached her own door she found stuck in the door latch a small, stiff bouquet of enchanting Parma violets, the faded flowers with the exquisite scent. Happily wondering if Tony had left them for her,

she took out the card. Her forgotten terror immediately returned. Across the top was scrawled in
French:

My little one, these suit you. With them I
send my deepest admiration for your beauty
and sweetness. Until we meet again,
WALTHUR VON LEIDERSDORF.

# Chapter Eleven

The first flat statement of Anthony Lombard's death came from BBC, followed within twelve hours by the London broadcast of CBS.

There was the eyewitness report and evidence by two members of a Communist cell of the Maquis. They had made their way to London to demand arms for the Resistance fighters under their control. They wanted nothing to go to any other group of the Resistance, and were especially vocal about not giving aid to the Gaullist committee stationed in London. While they were in a demanding mood, they insisted that Leo Prysing start production on a propaganda film which would be released through Prysing's usual distribution organization, United Artists, in America. Since Leo and Steve Lombard had already been warned by the British government that no such propaganda movie would be acceptable and anything remotely like one would be censored before it started, there wasn't too much of a deal they could make with the two Partisans.

Leandre Thibaud, a clever, ferretlike man with strong Marxist leanings, dropped strong hints to Prysing. "If we were to receive the arms from the British or the Yankees — it makes no matter — and we have proof that our specified film is in production, we may be able to find a few missing men who parachuted into Normandy. We may even find several of the bodies, if you wish proof.

What do you say, messieurs?"

Leo was dry and noncommittal. "I take it you've been turned down by the British government." He knew perfectly well they had been, but he and Steve were anxious to pursue the hint that they might know something about Tony.

Steve was less calm. "Look, do you know anything, or don't you? What exactly are we buying?"

Thibaud shrugged. "We are determined that the Allies shall recognize the Front Nationale — CNR — the Partisans, Franc-Tireurs . . ."

"All Communist, of course."

Thibaud's chin raised. "All Frenchmen," he said proudly.

"But you don't represent *all* Frenchmen."

Thibaud waved a hand as if to sweep away the producer and his cynicism. He turned to Steve who was walking up and down, obviously trying to decide whether to trust the two Resistance couriers or not.

"You, monsieur, they say are very rich. You also make speeches that are much broadcast and you write articles of Allied propaganda that are much read."

"Do you know my son is missing over France?"

"Many are missing. Shall I tell you of my own family? Two sons and a daughter. All in the Resistance. My wife and others were shipped off like cattle to Germany. No one knows if we will see her again. It may be we can find your son for the price we named. And only for that price."

Though dejected, Steve had his first inkling of hope. "Can you at least say whether or not you've heard the name? Anthony Lombard. No one calls him anything but Tony."

Thibaud's companion, a tough, bearded fisherman, shoved a fist in Prysing's face. He poured out his anger in French heavily accented with his native Breton dialect.

"You make the cinema. You tell the world of us, what we do to save France. The French are nothing. The Gaullists, they are Fascists in all but name. We are the saviors of France. You must say so in the cinema."

"Isn't there some way we can compromise with them?" Steve asked Leo quietly.

"Steve, I'd make the damned film tomorrow. Hell, I'd make it tonight, but we've got two governments that won't let us release it. We'd be recognizing the Communists as the legitimate government of France. Now, see here, fellows, if it's money you want, we'll talk turkey."

"Silver. Always the silver," the Breton howled. "You insult us. It's arms we need, but we also have pride. Thibaud, you speak. I cannot. The CNR is recognized, or nothing. This Anthony Lombard is dead. Tell that, Thibaud."

While Leo argued with Thibaud, trying to convince him that money would be of far greater use, Steve grabbed the big Breton's blue blouse.

"What do you mean, he's dead? This isn't something you've seen yourself."

The Breton objected to this manhandling. His hammer fist shot out, but Steve caught it over the wrist and cracked the Breton across the jaw, sending him stumbling backward into Leo's desk. By the time Leo and Thibaud got between them the Breton was out of control.

"No more. I kill him next. You tell the truth, Thibaud. No waiting. Tell about the things we have. Evidence, you call it. It says this Ant'ony is dead."

Thibaud backed away, looked at Leo's harsh features and then at Steve, whose anger had faded into a hushed suspense. Feeling desperate, Steve had fleeting thoughts of grabbing the Breton's calloused hands and pleading if necessary. He didn't want to see his last hopes of finding Tony go because he had lost his temper.

He tried once more. "Look here, you mentioned proofs. Proofs of what?"

The Breton pushed his small comrade. "They can do nothing for us. We show the proofs, no?"

Reluctantly Thibaud picked up the old wicker suitcase he had left by the door. He reached into his cuff. A second later a knife blade snapped out of its pocket sheath and he sliced off the frayed hemp that held the case together. A bundle of clothing fell out. Steve immediately spotted it — the khaki without insignia was not a uniform, but a specially tailored jumpsuit which seemed to be Tony's. The leather jacket was definitely his, though the initials had been ripped off.

Leo guessed from Steve's expression and his stiff, nervous fingers that he had recognized the clothing. There were few stains. A bad one across the right ankle, small spots along the collar.

"Bleeding of the nose and the ankle," Thibaud explained, less belligerently. "Quite natural from the fall, and from the Boches. The cap too is here."

Steve carefully threw the jumpsuit over one arm and picked up the cap. He touched it gingerly, re-

156

membering the first time he and Randi had given Tony a cap to wear, complete with a stiff bill. Randi had placed it properly on his dark, tousled hair, but he had removed it with a mischievous smile and tilted it back jauntily.

Steve could imagine him wearing it that way the day he left on his last journey.

"How do I know for sure he's . . . gone?" He still couldn't bring himself to use that word. It went against his optimistic hopes, his lifetime of confidence.

Thibaud gave the Breton a quick look. Then he nodded and laughed shortly. "The body was stripped by the Boches, monsieur. We have other clothing, too. We save it for the survivors one day. The Boches shot the two men as they descended."

Steve made a twisted, choking sound and turned away, still carrying the billed black cap and the rest of the clothing. Leo, too, was badly shaken, but forced himself to say something.

"There are explanations. Maybe he changed his clothes. He might have been found by Maquis, Free French fighters, anyone. He sure as hell wouldn't keep this outfit on. I don't see any holes in it. If he was shot, there'd be signs."

"I have said two parachutists were shot as they descended. The clothing is from one of those two. It was a head shot, about here." Thibaud tapped his temple boastfully, as if he wanted to insure their suffering, to make them believe the worst. He beckoned to the Breton and they started for the door with the empty suitcase. In the doorway Thibaud flipped a salute.

"Keep the rags. When you look at them, think of

what you lose. We will get arms from others. When this war is done, those who have refused us will find themselves the enemies of the French People's Republic."

Leo went out in the hall after them, and watched as they approached Alec Huntington, who was leaving for his London office, a temporary building in the West End that hadn't received a hit in over a month. A fire-bombing had destroyed the original quarters of UBC.

Heather had made him late, as usual, but Alec recognized the connection between the two strangely dressed men, obviously not among Leo's crew.

When they were through talking, the Breton gave Steve the clenched fist salute and turned to follow his comrade, who'd left abruptly.

"Have they seen Tony?" Alec asked as he approached Leo.

Leo shook his head, made a gesture toward Steve and was silent as Alec went over to his uncle.

"I don't know. They gave me this." Steve showed him Tony's clothes but didn't let it out of his hands. "They said he was shot before he hit the ground." His strong voice that he moved thousands in the last six years sounded vague, uncertain. "I don't believe it. There are dozens of explanations."

Alec and Leo looked at the jumpsuit in Steve's arms, along with the cap and a green-and-black cotton kerchief jammed into the patch pocket on the thigh of the jumpsuit. There were faint sweat stains where it had been creased and worn around Tony's neck.

"He could have changed his clothes," Alec muttered. "If he was rescued, they would have gotten rid of the clothes first. Unless they intended to bargain with them, which they obviously did."

Heather's presence close behind Alec made him start.

"Oh, you've found Tony's clothes. What a coincidence!"

"Coincidence?" Leo repeated impatiently.

"Well, of course. Didn't I tell you? I dreamed about Tony last night." She tucked her hand in Alec's arm. "He was dressed like he used to be in San Francisco, too. You know, in that green turtleneck sweater I always adored on him." She gazed around, her lovely eyes wide and misty. "You all think he's dead, but he can't be. How could he come to me in my dream if he was dead?"

Alec glanced at his uncle, but Heather's assurance had come too late. Steve fingered all that remained to him of his son, his young rival who had been his great link to the past and the future. He kept running the flat of his hand over the creased scarf. "I'll have to tell Randi and Eden."

Alec felt timid with his uncle for the first time in years. "Shall I put the call through?"

Steve shook his head. "It's got to come from me."

An hour later, making his way through the crowd around the sandbagged entrance to UBC's temporary headquarters, Alec was told by his backup man that two members of the French Communist Party had been refused arms by the British and United States governments.

"They're being told that we don't distribute

weapons to civilians in the occupied countries. Especially Commie civilians. They're liable to turn them on the populace."

"No wonder those two Reds were so sore."

There was overwhelming evidence of Tony's death between the eyewitness accounts and recovery of his clothes. Not Steve, Alec nor Leo felt they could take the two French agents at their word — they may have told their gruesome story out of sheer revenge.

"By the by, Alec, BBC has just given out that your cousin is a goner. They're basing it on some sort of conclusive evidence. Damned sorry, old boy. Are you going to announce it yourself?"

Until the word got out on the air, it seemed that Tony Lombard was still alive. But Alec felt that once he broadcast the news, any last hope would be gone.

Reluctantly, he faced the fact that he had put it off as long as possible.

"Okay, throw out the business about the U.S. girding its loins and the cut in rations. Then I'll go on with the coverage about Steve Lombard's son. That's how he'll be known, anyway. Poor devil."

Tony Lombard's priorities were changing rapidly. When he landed in that French meadow his primary goal had been to avoid the German army. Then, once he felt the Occupation accepted his credentials, his priorities shifted again: first, how to get word to his family of his safety, and second, how to get out of France in one piece.

His latest priority was in many ways the most complicated. He had made love to many women, but had purposely avoided becoming involved with virgins. Their naiveté didn't attract him, and from what he'd been told by male acquaintances, they tended to be overly possessive and quick to turn into shrews. In contrast, Eden Ware was the perfect woman for him — always unattainable, slightly superior and condescending, yet yielding to him in bed in the most bawdy way.

And now there was Jany Friedrich who destroyed all his preconceived notions of the attractions that a lovely, sweet, unspoiled virgin might have for a man. Jany was unattainable in a different way. Even if she had been taken in passion there would still be a quality about her that made her different from any woman he had ever met. Purity?

Because she was the antithesis of Jany Friedrich, Madame Charpentier always brought to mind Jany's qualities. She managed to be in her doorway whenever Tony came home from the market, or after escorting Jany to her typing class.

"*Bon jour*, Monsieur Lenoir. Any luck today in finding a job? A pity for so well qualified a young man. How is the turned ankle?"

He shook the hand she offered.

"Perfectly fit. You are kindness itself, madame, but no. In the end, I may have to go back to Brittany empty-handed."

"Brittany, Monsieur? And here am I, thinking you were a Gascon."

Damn!

"But what else, madame? Even a Gascon may work in Brittany."

She tapped her finger on his knuckles.

"Not on the coast. Unless, my friend, you are

employed by the Boches. One hears that the field SS, the Waffen SS, as they call it, is inducting certain specially chosen Frenchmen into their ranks. Would you be one of those chosen, monsieur?"

He put one hand against the wall beside her, smiling into her big, handsome face.

"My friend — and I do hope we are friends — I'm not clever enough for the Boches. I am only a poor Gascon with an eye for beauty. It is my vice."

He leaned forward until barely an inch separated his face from hers. She responded with bated breath and would have proceeded from there, but he pretended to make a confused recovery and stepped back.

"Your pardon, madame. I have no right, after your kindness to me. I presume, and it was wrong of me."

She was obviously disappointed but managed to retreat with dignity. Shrugging her meaty shoulders, she said on a sour note, "Many thanks. I am treated as if I were a simpering child like the Friedrich girl."

"And so you are, madame. Although not simpering. Never that. But all the respect that little Jany inspires is certainly yours."

"*Eh, bien,* to be sure. *Bon jour,* monsieur."

He breathed a little easier as he went up the stairs. The woman worried him. She was sharp, and he couldn't help but wonder if she knew more than she pretended. How far would he have to go to keep her silent about her suspicions?

One thing was certain. He must stop making stupid mistakes. It wasn't just a case of getting himself jailed, maybe tortured and killed. He would be bringing down the same fate on Jany and her brother.

With mixed feelings, Tony resolved to get back to London and his work, no matter what. He couldn't take any more chances of exposing the Friedrichs. Besides, there was his own family, too, on the other side.

He felt the necessity of leaving more acutely when Jany met him at the door with her radiant smile and transparent delight. Her greeting gave him a warm sensation of being welcomed home that he had never felt with Eden, nor had he ever known he missed it. His emotions were beginning to interfere with his common sense. He knew he must tell Carl, and especially Jany, that he had a family, a wife and daughter whom he also loved. That word "also" scared him. Had it actually gone that far without a single consummation of his feelings for Jany?

He decided that evening he would mention once again the importance of getting the news to London that he was alive and well. He felt guilty, knowing the suffering he must be causing his parents and family. Now as he thought of Andrea he immediately remembered Jany's sweet concern, her wonderful eyes that looked proud one minute, adoring the next. Andrea would probably be like that one day.

He hoped to God that by 1960 Andrea would come of age in a peaceful world. For himself he had never expected calm and peace. In fact, a certain excitement always seemed necessary in his life. But for Andrea it had to be different.

And for Jany Friedrich?

When he grew impatient and hounded Carl to let him help in the activities of the Resistance, even to run errands or deliver messages, it was Jany's patience, her friendly consolation that made it all bearable.

After greeting him so affectionately she returned to the kitchen and, seeming to be nervous, started to kid with him playfully.

"So, it's only you. Now I must return to my work."

"My ego is in shreds. Only me, indeed. Or do I misinterpret your elegant French?"

She dropped the old copper kettle. It rattled on the sinkboard but she ignored it as she reached for Tony's hands.

"I did not mean it, truly. Not to you. I was so happy all through class today, thinking that when I came home you would be here."

He was deeply moved and at the same time, alarmed. He knew he could not bear to hurt her. He shook her hands cheerfully.

"And here I am and Carl will be home soon. Then the Three Musketeers will be together again. That is, if Carl doesn't have to run all over town on another mysterious errand." He saw then that she was especially nervous today.

"Jany, what is it? Tell me all about it. Did they shoot somebody again?"

He pulled her to him. She wasn't crying, thank God, but she was in a might shaky condition. She accepted his strength, allowing him to draw her lissome body close. Emotionally, she was only a child, he kept reminding himself, but his own emotions were hardly under control.

She seemed to accept him as she would have accepted Carl's support. When he repeated her name she tried to reassure him.

"Nothing happened, really. But that Boche was standing outside the SS headquarters today. The one who called himself a lieutenant colonel."

"Maybe he had business there. Since the assassination attempt, Himmler has gotten his hands on more power. He'll even be ordering the army around in no time."

She shook her head. Her golden curls tickled his nose, making him sneeze. They both laughed, forgetting her concern, if only for a moment.

"No, Tony," she went on, "he was watching me. I know it. Then he followed me until I reached the place Beauvais. The traffic stopped him, and I ran the rest of the way home. Tony, he knows where I live. I just know he'll come again."

Tony was startled by the sudden, hot fury that welled up inside.

"I'd kill him before I'd let him hurt you. You know that."

"Do I?" The innocent question reflected in her big eyes troubled him.

"Jany, you are one of the dearest . . ." He moistened his lips and began again. "One of the dearest people in my life. I don't care what it takes — neither Carl nor I will ever let him hurt you. You should know that. I couldn't bear the thought of anyone touching you."

She lifted her head from his shoulder. Her lips were warm and eager, so close that they brushed his mouth. He touched her lips lightly with his finger. They were hot with desire, and he felt ashamed for having aroused such a feeling in this young, innocent girl. Ashamed, yet overwhelmed by the realization that in spite of her age and lack of experience, she was capable of sharing his own passion that threatened to take control.

She clung to his body while they kissed. A part of him was still standing off, aware that this was a despicable act on his part, considering that she knew nothing about Eden and Andrea.

But she was here, in his arms, her lips parted for his, and he was weak enough to take what he hungered for. How soft and dear she was! He felt like a boy with his first love. Almost of their own volition, his fingers moved across her throat and then down to her bosom.

Her breasts were beautifully shaped, rounded, not too large, but with the nipples prominent beneath her thin cotton dress. She must have been wearing a camisole of some kind, but no bra. The feel of her excited him wildly.

He wanted to put his lips to her firm, young breasts that shivered in her ecstasy. He wanted to drink some of that wonderful, vibrant innocence from her nipples, to give himself to her, bury his manhood in the soft places of her body. She would yield, he knew. Her bed was so close, just beyond an open door, and she trusted him.

It was this thought alone that jarred him back into reality. He raised his hands gently from her breasts to her shoulders, kissed her small nose and let her go. She stumbled a little and fell against the wall, but as he reached out to catch her, she warded him off.

"Carl is coming at any time. He wouldn't understand. He still thinks I'm a child. He doesn't know I'm old enough to be married."

*Married.* Tony winced at the simplicity of her dream. While she returned to the kitchen and Tony lingered casually in the hall, he reminded himself that there must be no more of this. Not so long as his own life was hopelessly entangled with someone else, miles away.

He knew he had to tell Jany and Carl the truth about his life, and soon, when the right moment came.

But even with the easy, brotherly manner he practiced toward Jany there were times when things almost got out of hand. Any remark he made, no matter how innocuous, now acquired a serious meaning.

One evening while he enjoyed Jany's onion and flower bulb soup, he said, "Now, there's something I love."

Jany flushed and looked away but Carl frowned. "You love easily, my friend."

"No, I mean it. Very few chefs earn my patronage, much less my love. But this soup is glorious. There was a sous-chef on the *Normandie* who prepared a potage a little like this. You know the *Normandie*?"

Jany clapped her hands. "I wish I could have sailed on her. The greatest, loveliest ship ever built."

"Of course," Carl put in. "She was French. That's why the Americans sank her."

Tony saw that he was getting into hot water. He tried to get out of it, delicately.

"I wouldn't go that far. The *Normandie* caught

fire at her New York dock. She capsized after she was waterlogged."

"The same thing."

"Carl, do be kind. Tony didn't personally sink the *Normandie*."

Her soft voice soothed the two men. Carl went into the kitchen and uncovered the radio for the evening broadcast.

"Time for BBC or your London friend. Which will you have?"

Tony followed him after helping Jany remove the dishes from the table. While the men listened to the squawk of the wireless, Jany went to the living-room window, knelt on the couch and looked out at the street traffic which was still busy, thanks to the German military, who seemed especially active tonight.

She wondered if all those trucks, interspersed occasionally with a gleaming Mercedes and even heavier wagons, were bound for the Normandy fighting. The idea of German panic was thrilling.

Behind her Tony and Carl silenced each other, pointing out that the plain, undramatic voice of Alexander Huntington was coming through between the spitting static: ". . . on every front, from the U.S. fleet's hard-won victory in the battle of the Philippine Sea to the mopping-up process in the Rome area . . . With the fall of Minsk hundreds of thousands of German troops have surrendered to our great Russian ally . . ."

Carl and Tony gave a cheer that would have done credit to a touchdown victory in Tony's college days at Berkeley. Jany waved them to silence.

"Do be still. Madame will hear you."

She took the dish towel and began to wipe cups while she listened in the doorway and continued to keep an eye on the street.

The two men huddled close to the little box with mental images of the Allies marching under the Arc de Triomphe and down the Champs-Elysées in a week or so.

Alec's broadcast continued. "But with the inevitable victory . . ."

He cleared his throat but did not strain for a dramatic note in his voice. "There is the price to pay. This correspondent has lost a close friend and relative, a companion from boyhood, who was shot down in late June over the Normandy countryside while carrying out his duties as second unit director for a Prysing Productions tribute to the Allied invasion of Fortress Europe."

Carl grinned. "Is that you? You're a hero, my friend."

Alec's voice went on inexorably: "Anthony Lombard, known to all as Tony, was the only son of Stephen Lombard, the international financier who is best known in Europe as the prime mover for aid to Britain and France during the dark days of America's isolationist policy. Tony Lombard is also survived by his mother, and by his wife, popular film star Eden Ware, and their two and a half-year-old daughter. See you at sundown, Tony . . ."

Carl said nothing, but kept gazing at the radio. He didn't even look around when his sister dropped a cup, breaking it.

"Maman's best set," she moaned. "The handle

just broke off. I'll never be able to put it together again." Her mother brought to mind, she cried softly to herself as she stooped to pick up the pieces of delicate Limoges.

# Chapter Twelve

The afternoon after she saw the last dailies run in Leo Prysing's private projection room at the studio, Eden Ware left for her family's estate in Hawaii with Andrea. She just didn't feel she could cope any longer with the mourning household in San Francisco. Randi was her usual noble, unflinching self, carefully hiding her real feelings. Brooke, on the contrary, wept rivers, as she had when Kurt Friedrich was killed, and then would salve her pain by acting capriciously or taking up a new male hobby. She might even dash off to London as Eden had tried to do, and that would make Eden hate her — something that so far the two women had managed to avoid in their long relationship, beginning with Brooke's quick wooing, winning and divorcing of Eden's father when she was a young girl. Now the one thing forbidden to Eden by her boss and her father-in-law was permission to fly to London on top priority, and she would be damned if Brooke would go in her place.

It would serve no purpose, they'd said. Once Steve had sent Tony's clothes home, the evidence seemed clear. Their presence was the final blow. They were so like Tony, the jaunty cap, and the carefully tailored jumpsuit that must have fitted him superbly. She looked often at the pale bloodstains on the collar and leg of the jumpsuit; the sight of them made her suffer and she felt she deserved to suffer. Guiltily she reminded herself of how she had treated him with such indifference, except for the times they were locked in passion. She knew now that she'd taken his love for granted, and wished she could undo the many times she'd treated him so casually.

Coupled with this guilt Eden felt a ferocious hatred for the Nazis and a desire to do something more than just accept what had happened. But even Steve seemed to know when he was licked.

All the same, Eden was sure that if she could work with Steve and maybe Alec in London she might at least get Tony's body back. The worst of her fears was that his body might be desecrated by the enemy.

"No, that's one worry you won't have," Leo reminded her brusquely on his return to Hollywood the day before she decided to leave. "They wouldn't bother with that. They'd just throw the bodies in a pile somewhere and burn them. Believe me, there are a hell of a lot of them over in Normandy right now. It isn't as if he's the first victim."

She knew that his callous tone and brutal candor were the products of his past. He would never forget the fate of his brother and sister-in-law on the night of the *Anschluss*.

Days and weeks passed, and when Eden was unable to gain passage to London, she tried pulling some strings again until she finally got on a cargo plane for Honolulu. She still nurtured an outside hope that somehow Tony would turn up alive. Maybe if she went home, those old Hawaiian gods of her childhood would save Tony. She knew she was being superstitious, but she had nothing else to cling to.

On December 7, 1941, with the exception of Tony, Andrea and her stepsister, Chiye Akina, she lost everyone she cared for who lived in Hawaii. Whenever the Lombards talked of home, what immediately came to Eden's mind was the golden shore of Oahu's windward coast and the long, low wooden house with its comfortable lanai and its many windows, the jalousies open to the trade winds and the warm climate.

Eden's arrival was quite different during wartime with the sky, the sea and the Kamehameha Highway crowded with vehicles all claiming high priority privilege. Normally she made a grand, dramatic entrance on the magnificent white passenger liner, the *Lorelei*. Oddly enough, though, Eden's renown in Hawaii was not as a movie star, but as the daughter of Dr. Nigel Ware, her highly respected father.

Dr. Ware and his wife, Tamiko, had been two of Oahu's best-loved citizens. Eden had been especially fond of Tamiko since she was the only mother she ever knew — for her own mother had died when she was very young. During the bombing raid on Pearl Harbor, Eden's father, stepmother and Chiye's fiancé had been caught in the attack on a plantation hospital. The traumatic effect of their deaths was only blunted for Eden by her concern for Tony, who was seriously wounded in the raid.

At that time Andrea was only three weeks old. By the time Tony returned to the Ware house on the windward coast, the loss of her beloved father and stepmother had become more bearable for Eden. Tony was alive. That was the most important thing. She knew she could cope as long as her immediate family was safe and sound. And so Eden, always the pragmatist, counted her blessings, accepted her losses, and resumed her career with reasonable ease.

Arriving now at an obscure air field outside Honolulu, unnoticed and hastily moved out of the way for important cargo arrivals, Eden sighed nostalgically for the old, remembered morning arrivals on the *Lorelei*, serenaded under the Aloha Tower by the Royal Hawaiian Band. For a moment she felt very much alone. Carefully taking Andrea's hand, she started across the field to the group of wooden shacks hastily put up since 1941.

Nothing looked familiar. She hadn't been home for two years, since 1942. Movie after movie and three USO tours from Alaska to North Africa had kept her and Tony from the Islands where they spent their honeymoon, where Andrea was conceived, and which Tony persisted in referring to as "the summer place." Tony never could adjust to being away from the mainland for too long, especially San Francisco — his foggy, hilly, chauvinistic San Francisco. God knew what would happen if he couldn't return every few months to the Golden Gate, "to clean out my lungs with that good old white morning fog," he'd often said.

Now he was gone. Happy, cocky Tony, without ever having returned to breathe that foggy air he loved so much.

Andrea shook her hand. "Where's dada?"

Eden said huskily, "He went away for a while,

honey. I told you that. Remember?"

"G'an says I'll see dada some day. When's that?"

Eden had no religious faith and yet it choked her to deny Andrea's pathetic hope. A part of her still wanted to believe that some day Tony *would* nonchalantly stroll in, give her a casual kiss, and lift Andrea, swing her up around her warm little waist-line, and demand, "Who's my favorite girl? Who loves dada?"

There were times when Eden was sure Tony loved the baby more than he loved her, but she wouldn't be surprised if he did. Eden knew with a growing sense of guilt that she had often put her life at Prysing Productions before her home life. Perhaps she hadn't been intended to marry. But that had nothing to do with the passion and love she knew without a doubt she felt for Tony. Especially the passion — when it came to that there was no one Eden had ever met like Tony Lombard. And Andrea was the beautiful result. But they had always been good companions, too. They genuinely liked each other.

*Tony darling, no one so full of life could be snuffed out like that. It's not fair. Not fair . . .*

"I don't know when you will see dada. You must hope very hard. And never forget dada in your prayers. Maybe he will hear."

"God'll hear, mommy?"

"No! I meant . . . yes. God might hear."

Her depression lifted suddenly as she heard a familiar voice call to her from the parking lot across the busy highway.

"Eden! Andrea! This way."

Her Japanese-American stepsister, Chiye Akina,

slender, simply but impeccably dressed, waved to them from the running board of the old Chevrolet. Chiye stepped down and started toward the highway with half a dozen flower leis on her arm. Eden and Chiye embraced with Andrea between them, hugging her godmother's slim left leg.

"Mommy, look. Aunt Chee's bare."

The beautiful Chiye, who seldom displayed her innermost emotions, lifted the child and kissed her pink cheek. "No one wears stockings in the Territory, sweetheart. Nor will you." As she set the child down, Chiye's eyes searched Eden's. She dropped the fragrant carnation, pink *Plumeria* and rare *Pikake* leis over Eden's head. "Are you all right? You look tired."

Eden shrugged and got into the front seat of the car with Andrea, also bedecked in leis which she fingered with more curiosity than pleasure.

"You got through it when your Jim, dad and Tamiko went," she reminded Chiye. "They say the pain goes too, after a while."

Chiye nodded. Her richly curved lips were set tight, making her look older than her thirty-three years. She backed out of the parking space, carefully avoiding the high line of scarlet hibiscus bushes, and they were soon on their way home across the island.

The frantic activity along the Fort de Russy area and Kalakaua Avenue in the Waikiki district took Eden's mind off her loss for a few minutes. She had never seen so many summer whites going in and out of the hotels. Uniforms were everywhere, the men swarming under the coco palms along with bright-clad, leggy girls, across the fabled Royal Hawaiian grounds, posing for snapshots in front of the big hibiscus bushes or under the old-fashioned marquee of the Moana Hotel. Eden was pointing out the landmarks to Andrea when Chiye startled her with a sudden outburst, especially apropos of Eden's earlier thoughts.

"How ungrateful I was with Jim Nagumo! I took him for granted. I received, but never gave anything in return. I was even wrong about Japan. Remember how sure I was that Jim and Steve Lombard and the others were just warmongers? And it was my beloved Japan that killed him. But it's too late for regrets now."

"You weren't the only one who wanted peace, Chiye. But when it comes to regrets, I lead the pack. If I had it to do over again, I'd be so different."

Chiye didn't say anything, which made Eden wonder if she thought Tony also had been taken for granted. But Chiye often kept her opinions to herself, except when the subject was politics. Before Pearl Harbor, she had been vociferously pro-Japanese. But a friendship begun in infancy between the two girls had never been shadowed through the years, not even when their countries went to war. Though often apart, they had never permitted themselves to doubt each other's devotion. In the old days they quarreled like most sisters, but there was no bitterness between them. It was this closeness that allowed Eden to accept Chiye's possible doubts now and she said, "Anyway, I wish to God I had the chance."

Andrea saw the piercing blue waters beyond the Moana Hotel and clamored to go wading. Eden was in the middle of promising Andrea her very own surfboard when she noticed the nervous pursing of Chiye's mouth.

"What's wrong? Is there something you haven't told me?"

Chiye swung inland leaving the close proximity of the rolling surf and dark, primeval-looking Diamond Head.

"I wrote you that I'm working at Tripler now. The hospital has all the nursing staff they need. Or so they say. They remember that I taught Japanese before the war. Anyway they need hands for scrubbing and cleaning up. I'm good for that, and it makes me feel useful."

"And a wonderful idea it was. Tony thought it was great. He said . . . never mind. What were you going to tell me?"

"That isn't my news. I know you're here to get away from things. But we have a visitor. He arrived last night, and he's turned the house inside out."

"Steve?"

Chiye glanced at her. "Not Steve. Are you and your father-in-law that close?"

What an idiotic thing to say, as though she and Steve had something going! "That did sound bad, didn't it? The truth is, I had a call from him just before I left for the airport yesterday afternoon. He wanted to know if I'd received Tony's things. He flew home to be with Randi, but he plans on returning to London. Says there's always a chance for Tony." She wrapped a strand of Andrea's hair over her fingers, then let it go. The curl sprang out. Andrea's hair would be like Tony's one day.

"Chiye, you won't believe it. I got to praying on

the plane. The selfish kind, you know. Please, don't let him be dead, please. Well, that kind of last-resort prayer." She came back to the present suddenly. "So who's visiting you?"

"Leo Prysing. He's been invited to Honolulu for a whole week of his film showings. The final night will be next Saturday. They're throwing a benefit for the USO."

Eden was angered by the timing. "He didn't say a word about it in the projection room day before yesterday. The bastard! What does he expect me to do? Attend in a fancy formal? Make a big splash?"

"He didn't mention that to me. He did say he was going to contribute the profits in Tony's name, since Tony was living here at the time the war started."

"Nice of him."

Hearing an edge in her voice, Chiye changed the subject quickly. "How are the Lombards taking this?"

"Steve still has hopes. Randi? Salt of the earth and all that. I feel sorry for poor old Brooke. She has no inner resources to fall back on."

"Very true."

Eden felt uncomfortable. There was never any love lost between Chiye Akina and Brooke, who had been her stepmother for a brief time. As a child, Chiye dreamed that her mother, Dr. Ware's housekeeper, would one day marry the doctor. Brooke's arrival had caused that dream to be postponed for a while.

Eden made a weak defense. "Brooke means well. Nobody in San Francisco takes her seriously. I think that's her problem. And Randi is a tough one to match — she's in everything, running hospital auxiliaries, the USO, and I suspect she writes a lot of that home-front propaganda we're getting these days. Probably a leftover from the time when she used to write B-pictures for Leo."

"Can your mother-in-law explain what has happened to the Japanese-American people along the Pacific Coast?"

Eden wished she hadn't mentioned the propaganda writing. She certainly didn't want to be in a position of defending the famous (or infamous) order excluding American citizens of Japanese ancestry from the Coast; yet, she remembered the terror in coastal cities during those first awful months after Pearl Harbor. Brooke's letters were filled with fears of the blackouts in San Francisco. Even Randi had spoken of the apprehension felt at the sight of an Oriental face.

As Randi said whenever Eden argued the matter, "When we saw Orientals wearing lapel buttons with two flags, we knew they were all right. They were Chinese. But Orientals wearing one flag — the Stars and Stripes — had to be Japanese. Who could forget the sneak attack on Pearl Harbor? And what they're doing to our men and our nurses now on Bataan and Corregidor? These people say they are loyal, but after Pearl Harbor, how can we trust them?"

Randi had added, "Steve hates the whole business. He's fighting the order."

But still it went into effect. It was war. They were the enemy, whether they were Japanese-American or not. Without further thought, all coastal citizens of Japanese descent were hastily uprooted and shipped off to concentration camps in Arizona and New Mexico.

Eden had been bitter. She was too closely allied to Chiye and the memory of Tamiko, her father's wife. She said now, "I saw one of the camps in the Owens Valley desert. It was horrible. Chiye, we despise it. My father-in-law and Mayor Rossi in San Francisco tried their best, but the order came from the White House."

Chiye made a grim little joke. "They would have a more difficult time if they decide to lock up all the Nisei in the Islands. Who would do all the work?"

It was a subject so embarrassing Eden put it aside as quickly as possible.

"As I was saying, Randi puts Brooke in the shade all the time, and it's hard for poor Brooke right now. She was very fond of Tony. I sometimes think Tony and Alec should have switched mothers at birth." She had to speak brusquely when she mentioned Tony. Otherwise, she would break down, remembering . . . remembering . . .

"I like Randi," Chiye said. "She's a woman of strength, like my mother was. But I have no sympathy for that Brooke that you're so fond of . . . no matter. Mr. Prysing is our problem for the moment. He wants to stay with us at the house. And he goes around asking everyone questions about Pearl Harbor. What happened, where everyone was at the time, the emotional details. I've no idea why. Most of the neighbors enjoy it, but it hurts some of them."

Like you, dear Chiye, Eden thought, but she merely said, "Oh Lord!"

181

Chiye recovered from her upset, or seemed to. "So, you are twice welcome. You are the only woman who can handle Mr. Prysing."

"Me and Randi Lombard. She handles him well." With a grimace Eden sank down in her seat. "I see it's going to be a busy time. Anyway, I'll do my best to help you. I haven't said much about your work and the way you've kept up under everything, but believe me, Tony and I, the whole family, are mighty proud of what you're doing at the hospital."

Chiye was looking ahead at the heavy jungle growth that still shrouded the road in spite of heavy navy and air corps traffic. When there was a lull in the rumbling wagons, jeeps, trucks and speeding VIP cars, Eden could almost imagine she was back in the prewar serenity of the Islands.

*. . . I must be getting old . . . I keep having fond memories of how it was before the war . . .*

She remembered just such talk between her father and his friends after the war of 1914–18. It had always seemed so irrelevant to her as a child. What had those ancient days to do with today? And here she was, feeling like an old lady. Without Tony. That must be it . . . he always made her feel so young . . . *Tony, the light goes out when you aren't here.*

They turned back and climbed to the Pali Road, still as narrow and dangerous as it had been in Eden's childhood. They passed the breathtaking cut in the Koolau Range where the sheer drop into thick green jungle growth also gave a first view of the distant windward shores and Eden's home coast. Andrea tried to jump up, pointing excitedly to the aqua-colored waters of the Pacific that seemed to roll back into infinity.

Chiye leaned around Eden and spoke to her goddaughter.

"Andrea, you may wade for practically miles here." She caught Eden's eye and added, "If someone is with you, naturally."

The Chevrolet rattled down over the narrow road to the coast. Andrea's excitement was contagious. That and the sight of the one-story Ware house which spread along between sand and hibiscus, parallel to the coastline, like an overgrown plantation bungalow. Eden had dreaded coming home. She was sure that without Tony she would only feel emptiness in the house where she was born. One by one they had been taken away — her father, Tamiko, Chiye's fiancé whom she had been so fond of, and now, worst of all, her own Tony with whom she had shared so much in this house.

Two soldiers in fatigues who proved to be convalescents from Territorial hospitals were busy with rakes and trowels under the huge, shimmering *Pandanus* fronds that joined the hibiscus in sheltering the west face of the house from the sun. The boys, out to earn a little beer money and enjoy the sun, wore coconut hats thumbed to the back of their close-cropped heads. Everyone seemed to be in excellent spirits. Leo Prysing's big head was sticking out the window, his grizzled, curly hair tangled by the sea breeze. He seemed to be giving orders. A natural habit for the producer, but his gardening experience was nil. The soldiers took his instructions good-naturedly but went right on raking and hacking.

Chiye gave Eden a look and Eden rolled her eyes.

"My God! I never thought I'd see the day Leo Prysing would take an interest in growing things."

"Wade, mommy. Wade," Andrea screamed. She was pointing to the long surf rolling in and out like green-veined lace.

The old bushes of what the mainland called Vanda orchids were still swaying gracefully over the sandy path around the house toward the long, screened lanai facing the ocean. Seeing the fragile stems with their fluttering mauve blossoms, Eden murmured, "Remember how Brooke felt about the orchids when she was married to dad?"

"How can I forget? To her they were commonplace — too easy to get."

Chiye pulled into the wooden breezeway whose roof was picturesquely covered with pili grass over a few beams of lehua wood alternating with bamboo. Much of the grass had blown away in spite of its anchoring, and the sunlight striped the car as the women got out with Andrea.

They greeted Chiye with an easy familiarity which surprised Eden, who had always known her to be somewhat reserved and cool with strangers. Occasionally she could even be downright rude. But today Chiye was calm and smiling as she asked them questions about their work.

Through the roar of the incoming tide Leo Prysing had heard the car's engine and jogged around the house with arms held out. Eden was the star he had personally discovered in Paris, created, and built up with considerable shrewdness to her present eminence as one of the most honored of the younger stars. He hadn't made her into a su-

184

perstar, but as Eden readily acknowledged, he did well with the material at hand. From the look on his face, he seemed about to make an entire speech welcoming her to a house that was half hers anyway. Eden decided to get in the first dig.

"Leo, are you following me? I thought I'd have at least a few days to myself before you started bombarding me with scripts."

He grinned, but she knew her sarcasm was well placed. You could insult him in any way and he would rise above it, getting his revenge professionally, but you didn't insult the quality of his films. Nobody quite dared that.

"And how's the little princess?" He bent to kiss Andrea's cheek.

Andrea tugged on Eden's sleeve. She whispered, "Mommy, he's funny-looking."

Shaken out of her annoyance and self-pity by this innocent cruelty, Eden shook her finger at her daughter.

"Andrea, behave yourself. Mr. Prysing is one of my dearest friends."

The child's whisper had given Prysing's lips an odd twist that *did* make him odd-looking, though Eden's quick reprimand seemed to lighten his heavy features. She saw once more the compelling and powerful face she had always admired, with no trace of the embittered man who had sought — and gained — a supreme and subtle revenge against the man responsible for the death of his brother and sister-in-law six years ago.

He probably slept every night with a good conscience. Judging by Steve's remarks, he didn't share that clear conscience, though Eden wasn't sure she understood why. They only did what they had to do at the time.

She and Prysing met belatedly, cheek to cheek, while Andrea, hurt by her mother's scolding, toddled over to join Chiye. The two soldiers immediately made a fuss over her and Andrea was happily in her element.

When Eden had settled in her old room that opened out on the south end of the lanai, Leo came in with the barest hint of a knock. Eden resolved that he would have to be trained like a blooded bulldog if he was going to move in on *her* property. Well, half her property, she amended, thinking of Chiye.

He began with a hint of apology. "My girl, I am not insensitive, an idea that may have crossed your mind. I simply want to keep you from dwelling on painful thoughts. This Prysing Festival wasn't my idea, but you must admit it comes as a happy coincidence that you're here at the same time."

"I don't believe you. It's too pat, but never mind. And don't go adding my name to any of those ego appearances of yours."

His heavy eyebrows shot up. "Why should I share my glory with you?"

It was probably a lie but she grinned widely, said "Good!" and shoved him out through the doorway. Probably to devil her, he kissed her knuckles, but she pretended not to notice. "Meet you on the beach. Get into your swim trunks."

All the same, when she and Andrea showed up on the white sand in matching black-and-white harlequin-patterned swimsuits and a photographer from the *Honolulu Advertiser* snapped a picture of them, she felt the old familiar call to what Prysing called "glory."

Leo Prysing dove into a wave, then rode it ashore to arrive at the feet of young Andrea. He shook off water like a shaggy dog, causing the child to giggle and scream with delight.

Eden was surprised at how vigorous and masculine he looked, half-naked in those dark trunks, though he held no attraction for her. A little coarse in his obvious masculinity, and besides, he was too old for Eden. Mid-fifties. Eden tried to be honest with herself. Sexually, she was aroused by younger men, but only those who wanted her. She had never gone after a man if his interest wasn't obvious, and she was careful to treat those men who did desire her with an amused, light touch. They were never large, domineering types like Leo Prysing, even though what she had supposed was Leo's fat body proved to be muscle and bone.

She could understand now what so many women saw in men like Prysing and probably Cecil B. deMille and David O. Selznick. It was more than their enormous professional power that was attractive. They had a sexual aura as well.

Leo offered to teach Andrea to swim but this was indignantly refused. The little girl replied, somewhat incoherently, that she *could* swim. What did he think she was, a baby? All the same, she allowed him to wade her through the surf, riding on his shoulders. As she watched Andrea and Leo frolicking in the water, she caught sight of several soldiers at a distant point to the north replacing barbed wire that had been broken down by the currents. The sight gave Eden a sudden chill. She couldn't help wondering if a Japanese sub might be hovering out there beneath the clear blue Pacific, waiting to make another sneak attack. She noticed that nobody else seemed worried, but they had lived with this fear for three years, and had learned to handle it. They had to, she reasoned.

Long after Eden had plunged into the water for a refreshing swim and come ashore to shower and get a sundress, Andrea was still being entertained by Prysing and the two young soldiers, who were acting as backup. When she was sent reluctantly to bed for her afternoon nap, Prysing came into the house, this time covered with drying sand, which he shed over the big kitchen, the young Chinese cook and Eden. Eden sat spooning out the bright, apricot-colored meat from half a papaya.

"Healthiest thing in the world, Leo. Puts hair on your chest."

"Not an ambition of mine. As for the papaya, I lean more to *Borkenschokolade* and any other *Süss-speisen.*"

"What a vile thing to say to me!"

"No. Just a Viennese mouthful. Dessert dishes. Josef and I grew up on *Borkenschokolade*. It's a form of chocolate. Very thin. Our mother made it as a topping. We Viennese were always long on sweets."

She concentrated on squeezing a lime into what remained of her papaya.

"You and Josef were very close, I guess."

To her relief he could speak easily of the brother he had lost because of Kurt Friedrich's treachery, back in '38. "Yes, we were close, until I got the Hollywood offer. That was 1922. By the way,

188

speaking of the Golden Oldies, they're running one of my UFA German silents Monday night. Won more awards than any of my talkies. Even *Journey*, which put you on the map, young lady. And speaking of *Journey*, that reminds me. That little bastard, Kurt Friedrich, had a juvenile lead in the silent film I made right here on Oahu, *Prince of the Golden Isles*. Ironic, isn't it, in view of Friedrich's later career."

As a child Eden remembered seeing the attractive young Austrian actor during those weeks when Prysing was filming on location near Dr. Ware's property. She had found Friedrich charming in his bright, arrogant, Aryan way. But his surface appeal had lessened by the time she saw him next.

"I don't think I ever told you, Leo, but I met Kurt Friedrich again in the Islands, in 1928. He was here with a silent film star, Olga Rey. I think she supported him until Brooke Lombard fell for him in Vienna later on. Anyway, I wanted to get in the movies so I went to see him at the Royal Hawaiian Hotel. He tried to rape me. Olga showed up just in time and raised the devil with him. She was a great girl."

Leo nodded. "Sounds like Kurt. And Olga, of course. She had a family somewhere. Used to rush back to Europe to be with them after every film. We never could pin her down. She was a trifle over the hill when talkies came along. I never did know what happened to her."

She hesitated, then blurted out, "Do you ever think about what happened to Friedrich?"

He took the last spoonful of papaya off her plate

189

and chewed it. Instead of being troubled by her question, he made her uneasy by the bland way he gazed at her.

"Not bad. For fruit, that is. But my teeth require something a little harder to crush. I'm really a very soft guy, at heart. But I still have good teeth. In spite of all the *Kaffee mit Schlag* when I was a boy, I can still bite."

"You're avoiding the subject, although I don't know why you should. Strictly speaking, it wasn't you who . . ." She hesitated for a moment . . . "brought on Kurt Friedrich's death."

This time, when he smiled, she was much more aware of his solid, strong teeth.

"That's right. I didn't actually spill the Friedrich blood. Still, there's no Kurt Friedrich left now. That's the joke of knowing how."

Behind Eden, the busy young cook began to chop vegetables for quick frying in his steep-sided pan. Eden had a feeling that Sunny Ching had understood the implications of their grisly subject and wanted them to know it. His big, sharply honed chopping knife made repeated hard cuts that threatened to drown out their conversation.

Prysing raised his voice.

"Anyway, I've got to go and contact Lana Turner."

"Lana Turner!"

He was all innocence. "I can't very well ask you to make an appearance next Saturday, but it *is* the climax of the Prysing Festival. I thought I'd make a tribute to Tony and the rest of the crew. But I've got to have a big name. They say Turner may be available for a USO tour, starting here."

"Saturday! That's when they're showing *Journey*. My movie!"

"There were five other stars in it, as I recall. And you had fourth billing."

"A special card — 'And Introducing Eden Ware.' Or have you for gotten?"

"Me forget? I've got a memory like an elephant."

She didn't doubt that. "If anybody's going to appear in tribute to my husband when they show *Journey*, it's going to be Eden Ware."

The minute after she agreed, she knew he had used a cruel but effective way to help bring her out of the depression she had fallen into when she heard Alec Huntington's public acknowledgment of Tony's death.

He shrugged. "If you insist."

But she saw the edge of a smile on his face as he left the kitchen.

She grabbed a handful of bamboo shoots, barely missing Sunny Ching's chopper, and threw them at Leo Prysing's broad back.

# Chapter Thirteen

Carl Friedrich was aware of a keen and unexpected disappointment. Against his best judgment he had begun to trust this friendly, uncomplaining Yank who was so cool under the daily threat of the Gestapo. It had seemed an act of providence that the son of a powerful figure in the free world should fall into Carl's hands. He had hoped that Lombard could act as a willing hostage for ammunition and weapons. Sten guns were desperately needed for the uprising — and above all, for the recognition by President Roosevelt of General de Gaulle as head of a provisional government after the Liberation.

If Roosevelt came around, Prime Minister Churchill would not be difficult to convince. Churchill certainly didn't want a Communist takeover of a free democratic country. But the enormous egos of the stubborn American president and the equally stubborn French general would need outside influence to bring them together. Even the four years of hard, dangerous work by the Free French with their mystic Cross of Lorraine symbol apparently could not move the American president. The word of a powerful man like Steve Lombard in the ear of the right men might possibly help.

Carl had built up a scenario in which Tony, whose fate was unknown, would show up in England safe and sound, thanks to the Gaullist Resistance in Paris. Surely, both Tony and his influential father would be grateful.

But Carl's plans did not include using Jany as an enticement to keep Tony on the Gaullist side, against Danielle's similar plans for him in her own Communist cell. He had found that sleeping with Danielle produced political dividends far beyond Danielle's own schemes. At strategic moments Carl fed her what he wanted her to know, and Danielle — clearly not as clever as she thought she was — repeated these lies where he wanted them repeated.

No matter how often he used these moments to gain information from her about the workings of her Communist friends, it never became less despicable an act to him. Were it not for the war, he would have stopped seeing Danielle when he first learned of her indiscretions with others.

During their years at the Lycée when they were both much younger, he had thought that making love to Danielle was the greatest thing in the world. How he would have hated any man who would seduce his voluptuous girl friend just to learn what her Communist friends were up to! But the years of Occupation by the enemy had done something to his moral fiber. He knew that. He now did what he had to, even if he despised himself for it.

Tonight's broadcast by Alec Huntington had put everything in a different light. Jany was probably brokenhearted now that her puppy-love dream had been shattered. And Carl himself felt the Yankee had deliberately deceived them. Not once had he mentioned his child, much less his wife.

Tony jumped up to help Jany rescue what remained of the broken cup and it was Carl who spoke first.

"So your wife is a famous cinema star! That is most interesting. Can we have seen her, do you think? The name is not familiar to me."

Tony hated his own casual response. Jany's feelings were surely of some account . . .

"I doubt if you'd have seen her. She made her big splash in 1939. A film called *Journey*. It was considered anti-Nazi propaganda. I don't think the French government allowed it to be shown here. They didn't want to rock the boat."

"Ah, yes. The Munich Pact, and all that. We must see Madame Lombard's film sometime, eh, Jany?"

Jany was busy hanging the remaining cups in the cupboard. Her voice was muffled by the cupboard doors.

"When the Boches are gone, I hope."

"Certainly. That was what I meant. Now, Tony, we must get you back to your wife and your little baby, isn't it so?" He saw Tony's quizzical look at his remark and said, "I know. You have spoken of your return for days upon days. But with a family waiting for you, it makes a difference. You should have told me." He amended without looking at his sister, "Us."

"I'm sorry. The subject didn't come up, did it?"

At least, thought Carl, the fellow should have realized the effect of his own despicable behavior. No matter. He could still be used as an emissary to his high and mighty friends in England. Luckily, he hadn't yet compromised Jany romantically. And he wasn't going to get the chance. Carl was fiercely determined that Jany should not follow his mother's trail, producing two children outside the marriage bed, quite as if it were the most proper thing in the world.

Carl watched his sister and Tony when they said good night. It worried him, that warmth in the Yankee's eyes. He should have more self-control. Poor Jany seemed pale and dispirited to Carl's anxious gaze, but at least she had pride and good sense. She avoided Tony's offered hand and after giving Carl a fast kiss on the cheek, she rushed into her room, carefully closing the door.

By morning, to his infinite relief, she seemed much more her normal self, although somewhat more mature. While he drank his bitter ersatz coffee, made of God knew what combination of straw and grain sweepings, she prevailed on him again.

"Carl, please do be nice to the Boche in the offices and hint about cooking fat. It's impossible to cook without any grease at all. I don't ask for butter. But just some fat."

"*Chèrie,* you know how dangerous the black market is these days. And our own people might inform on us."

Tony, who was carefully putting away all signs of bedding, stopped folding the mended sheet to ask, "What is the punishment?"

"Lately, with the Allies so close to Normandy and Brittany they have been putting black marketeers against the wall at Mont Valèrien."

"Shooting them?" The Yankee sounded incredulous.

"It's not a cocktail party, this war."

Carl swallowed the last of the coffee, made a face at the aftertaste, and got up. He had a lot to do today and if he wasn't careful, his nerves might betray him. It was supremely important that he hold on until Liberation. Only a matter of weeks, he told himself. Or even days.

Meanwhile, he didn't like to leave Jany with the Yankee. He gave Lombard credit for using some restraint. But he did have a way about him that even more experienced women than Jany would find irresistible.

Before Jany could mention her plans for the day Carl contributed to what she hoped would be her escape from Tony. She had to get away, at least for a while.

"Good luck in your class this morning. Be careful, *ma petite,* and remember to cross the street before you get to the SS. But don't let them think you are doing it deliberately."

"I know, don't keep telling me. Mother of God! If I could just once do and say what I feel!" She slammed her mother's chair under the table and went into her bedroom to dress for an imaginary shorthand class.

"*Au 'voir, chèrie,*" Carl called as he left. It made him uneasy when she didn't reply. These days every small variation from the usual routine was a bad omen and he wasn't looking forward to today's events, either. He had to see Madame de Souza, his contact.

His office in the Ministry of Education was a cubicle separated from three other similar "offices" by a plasterboard partition. The building had little to do with the official French Ministry of Education beyond the usurpation of the title by the SS for the purpose of manipulating the minds of those living in the Occupied Zone. Carl's surname and his quiet acceptance of the Occupation had gradually made him as free from suspicion as any Frenchman not directly acting as collaborator. Carl suspected they trusted him more because he did not play the eager collaborator. He did his work, helped the Germans think up slogans, even slanted the news, often more cleverly than his German cohort could do.

His advantage was obvious. He could report the original version of most news to Madame Adelaide de Souza, called the Old One, the only member of his Gaullist cell who was his immediate contact. It was Madame's job to send his and other reports to the Gaullist Free French headquarters, wherever they might be. Her skill with wireless communication and her ability to evade the touring Gestapo vans was legendary.

Madame acted as concierge for a huge, half-empty building on the rue de la Paix that had once been a hotel. She was typecast for the part, being crabbed, ugly, and curious about everything. The Gestapo knew her as an ornery old woman and most of them were afraid of her sharp tongue. They couldn't believe anyone that openly nasty to them could be a clandestine operator. Also, she had a habit of betraying petty criminals to the Gestapo. That these criminals were all collaborationists was "pure 'coincidence.' "

The weather was unexpectedly bad that day and Carl was soaked to the skin before he got into the foyer of the ministry's office building. All the way up the stairs to his first-floor cubicle, he wondered what the storm was doing to the Invasion forces in muddy, wartorn Normandy. If things had gone differently, if he had been quick enough to get out of the country in June of '40, he might be fighting back victoriously through those same muddy fields now.

But he couldn't have deserted Maman and Jany. Not even for the cause of a free France. Maybe it was better this way, after all. He edged into his tiny office whose chief benefit was its privacy, if a plasterboard wall could actually give privacy. On Jany's only visit she had covered that wall with postcards sent to them from their mother during her movie-star years. Something about their cheerful nonsense had always brightened his day.

There was a postcard from Grauman's Chinese Theater. Maman had been present at the premiere of *Trader Horn*, one of the last of the silents which she took Carl and Jany to see a year later in Paris. Carl considered the card. Grauman didn't sound like a Chinese name. He remembered how Maman seemed so happy that night, milling around with all the big shots who were there. But he wondered if she had also been worried. Shortly after she would lose both her career and the man she loved.

An even more glamorous postcard was tacked on above the scrawl from Grauman's Chinese. It showed a pink fairy-tale palace called the Royal Hawaiian Hotel. Somewhere in the tropics, obviously. It was dated in 1938, slightly earlier than the Grauman's Chinese card. Again she sounded happy, but Maman was always happy. She had given moviegoers much pleasure with her roles — flippant, voluptuous, sometimes vulgar, but they were real women she played, all the same. Did anyone remember Olga Rey now, in 1944? It just wasn't fair.

But nothing was fair about life, Carl reasoned. Look at that damnable Lombard, tempting little Jany, getting her excited about men and romance long before she could handle it. Then he would sail off to his baby and movie-star wife. Nothing would happen to the Eden Wares of the world. Their men wouldn't desert them. Their careers always went racing on. The lucky, lucky Lombards.

He pulled out the latest release "polished" by his SS superior. It went on at great length about the brutality of Allied troops, especially focusing on rape, toward the citizens of Normandy and Brittany. His attention was distracted by two Germans talking in low tones beyond the plasterboard partition.

"They say it must be in the house itself. The woman confessed as much before she died. They got nothing from Mercier, a tough old bird. Now he is worthless. The brain is gone. It is stupid, this method. What have they left? In a thousand places the records may be concealed."

"These French, they have no system. No order."

"A depraved mentality. I have always said so. My brother married a Frenchwoman."

Carl smiled sourly. He returned to his work but his thoughts were spinning. It was vital that he get word to Madame de Souza about the fate of the Merciers. The Gestapo was unlikely to leave the house until they found Maître Mercier's records and the equipment by which he had furnished fugitives and spies with their false papers. Mercier had been one of the few Resistance fighters who apparently operated both for the Gaullists and the Franc-Tireur Partisans. Danielle's friends from the Communist sector of the Maquis had used him, too.

Evidently, to some extent Mercier had been able to resist the Gestapo's methods. At what cost? Carl did not like to think of that. But the recovery of Mercier's materials and records by the Germans would be a total disaster. Even Danielle deserved to hear of this. She might have more immediate remedies.

He could hardly wait until his two-hour lunch period. Even the Occupation hadn't been able to shake that indelible French habit. Meanwhile, he rearranged the Nazi propaganda from the Normandy front, phrasing it better. He had no doubt it was true. All armies looted and raped; he knew he wasn't passing on an overwhelming secret.

One piece of good news came in before noon. His French superior, formerly an editor of the famed conservative newspaper *Figaro*, laid a sheet of close-typed paper on his desk.

"An explanation of German fallbacks in Normandy. It must be worded to appear that they have fallen back to draw the Allies into a trap."

"I understand, monsieur."

The editor winked.

Carl thought of Jany's complaint. She did remarkably well, cooking only during the one hour of the day they were allowed to use the gas stoves,

200

making do without sweets, butter or milk, and only occasional meat of the worst quality. Even rice was impossible to obtain. He said abruptly, "Monsieur, you know my little sister. She is an excellent cook. She does wonders, considering how tight they've made the rationing. But she had been begging me to get some shortening. You know. Fat for the cooking."

"Very difficult. Difficult, indeed. I'll do what I can. My respects to the little mademoiselle . . . fat. Yes. Our cook is forever complaining. Well, we must sacrifice until the world turns a few more times."

He left Carl after tapping the communiqué significantly. It was moments like this, when his own skill was called into play to give the German propaganda a double meaning, that he enjoyed his work. He reworded the communiqué so that it appeared to save face for the German army. At the same time, by the insistence that this and not retreat was the true explanation for the fallback, Carl knew his French readers, sensitive to the slightest nuance in wording, would say "he protests too much."

He left the building hard upon the noon hour, pulling up the worn collar of his summer jacket to protect his neck, if not his head, from the gray, afternoon drizzle.

He avoided the front of the Hôtel de Crillon where there were sure to be Wehrmacht officers going in and out. He took a little back street behind the rue St. Honore, reflecting at the same time that along this street, virtually an alley, his mother and Jany and their sometime hired cook had shopped at the open market, carefully picking and choosing, so easily discarding a slightly bruised apple or cherry, ignoring the courgettes and aubergines that were not perfect in color. Even the battered fruits and vegetables thrown away in the gutter would be treasures now.

He went the long way around to throw off anyone following him and to avoid the Hôtel Ritz with its German guards. They seemed to swarm around the reserved, almost secretive Vendôme and Capucines, thankful for the spurts of summer rain that helped to conceal at least half his face. No one seemed to be following him, although a German soldier loitered a block behind him, busy looking in shop windows.

Madame de Souza, like a typical concierge, sat in her little parlor with the main foyer door open. She barked at Carl, glowering at him over her spectacles.

"Eh, it's you, is it? You come to see the yardage company? Gone. No more imports from the captive countries, though the company has not picked up their samples yet. Troubled waters there. Or is it troubled mud?"

With the huge, double street doors closed he felt that he was in a hollow bathhouse. A staircase leading upward to four empty floors opened off the narrow foyer. At the far end of the foyer Carl could see the interior court, an eerie, shadowed green under the high glass roof. Nobody there. He had once walked in on a Boche corporal and a young French waitress making love in the desolate little garden where he noticed signs that a body or two had been buried under the drying ivy and drooping crimson amaranth.

"No yard goods, madame. So they have gone from the third floor. My sister will be sorry. May I see the samples? She might make something for herself. She is very slender."

Having informed each other that they were safe, they shook hands and she hobbled out into the foyer with the aide of a gnarled cane. Though well over sixty, Madame de Souza was as fleet-footed as Carl himself. She locked the door of her little room and hung an Out to Dinner sign on the knob in the middle of the door.

He followed her up the stairs. As they passed the first and second floors Carl scanned the open corridors. He wondered how she could live in this great barn of a building with its hundreds of empty rooms. They seemed to echo with the memory of all the tourists and Parisian men with their mistresses who had occupied these hundreds of rooms in the twenties and thirties. He wasn't even sure what had closed down the hotel. But closed it was. The rooms were no longer furnished, yet the beautiful cornices and the *trompe l'oeil* details on the public rooms had not been destroyed.

The Gestapo, accompanied by the *flics,* or Parisian police, had examined every room during the first months of the Occupation, at which time any remaining objects of value were "liberated" and sent back to the Reich homeland. Since then, except for sporadic searches when Resistance leaders were on the run, the building remained virtually deserted. The mechanics of Madame de Souza's operation were complicated, and succeeded on the maze theory.

"Do you ever get lost in all these rooms?" he asked. "They all look alike."

She snorted, which was her rather unappealing form of laughter. He was glad there was only the light from the central court sifting in. Her face was not pleasant to look at.

"An SS lost himself in here one night. When I heard him calling to me in his hideous French, he was frightened, I may tell you. He and two *flics* had chased an escaped RAF airman in here. The *flics* returned to me soon enough and we French enjoyed a pleasant Pernod I keep for these occasions, while the Boche wandered around above us."

"Did they find the prisoner?"

"What is this you ask me? How could they? The *flics* had an eye problem."

"Eye — ?"

"It must be. They looked directly at the prisoner in a water closet on the third floor and didn't see him. Eye trouble, what else?"

He laughed. "What will you do when this place is turned into an office building as they intend?"

"That will be after the Boches have gone. I do not think so far ahead."

He knew the hotel had gone broke during the Great Depression and had been leased piecemeal before the war to individual importers. The harassment of the Occupation authorities had combined with the failure of the importation markets from defeated or Allied countries. Since then, it had developed a reputation for bad luck and ended in Madame de Souza's hands. She befriended the Germans in her gruff way and consolidated her position. Carl did not envy her. He shared the general feeling that the building was bad luck.

All the same, Madame de Souza, with her watery dark eyes, her wrinkled mouth and sagging jowls, was the one person in Paris with whom he usually felt safe.

He found himself in a long salon on the third floor. Here several glass counters had been set up and bolts of cloth were thrown across them. The room was too large to conceal eavesdroppers, and the materials muffled their voices as they spoke in low tones. He told her what he had overheard at his office.

"So all of Maître Mercier's equipment and records must be destroyed, you see."

She nodded. "I have a Partisan boy, a Communist, in fact, who is fond of his old adoptive grandmother, as he calls me. I saved him from the police once. He has only one fault of the most minute kind. He loves nothing so much as a good fire, and you would not believe his skill at arson."

"Good God, madame! Let us hope he does not survive Liberation, or France will be the worse for it."

"He will not survive," she assured him in a voice so cheerful it made him shudder. "Next?"

"A guest staying in my apartment. He is the son of a highly regarded American named Stephen Lombard. I hoped we might persuade him to intercede for our cause. But if your arsonist fails, they will certainly find evidence of his papers. The Gestapo has his name on records as my cousin, under the name of Antoine Lenoir."

"Believe me, *mon ami,* the real Lenoir existed once, or Maître Mercier would not have used the name for your American. The Gestapo has certainly checked on him. Otherwise, they would not have let him in peace. But if he disappeared, if we lifted him to London, what would happen to you and your sister? And all our plans?"

"We cannot keep him. He poses a problem in the household."

"Trust me. We will reach London with the truth about your guest. We will ask in this man's name that his father use whatever influence he has to support General de Gaulle and the democratic system in France after the Liberation. That is all we can do, with Liberation so near. With Liberation, I remind you, will come a bloodbath from the Boches — and perhaps between the Communists and ourselves."

He knew but he wished she had not reminded him. He started to leave. Madame de Souza cleared her throat roughly. "You came for cloth to give to Mademoiselle Friedrich. I suggest you let me cut off now. You grow careless, *mon ami*."

He knew it was details like this that could cost him his life, and worse, Jany's life.

"*Pardon*, madame." He accepted the folds of flowered cloth and sleazy rayon which she cut off with gigantic shears.

"You have not mentioned your Boche friend, *cher* Carl."

He stared. "Those I work with?"

"No, no. The other. The Oberstlieutenant. Von Leidersdorf. Disgraced. Sent with the Gestapo vans to check radio transmissions."

Her knowledge increased his foreboding. "Why was he disgraced? For affairs with children like my sister?"

Madame de Souza stopped on the stairs causing him to collide with her. She scowled.

"Leidersdorf is of the old army. He resented the intrusion of SS battalions in his beloved Wehrmacht. He has said so. He spoke publicly against Himmler. You see the result. This Boche may be useful. More useful than the American. If he has a penchant for young females, encourage it. Your little sister may be of some help in this war, after all."

"Now, madame, I will not permit my sister to —"

She cut him off. "Be silent. This is for France. You must think of Jeanne d'Arc."

"Not this time, madame." He started out of the foyer but looked back once to ask, "May I count upon you? About the Mercier house?"

"Certainly. And may we count upon you, *mon ami?*"

Her crisp answer should have given him comfort, but her vaguely sinister grin was not reassuring.

To make matters worse, the minute he stepped out on the rainy sidewalk he saw the outline of a tall German army officer loitering across the street near the closed Schiaparelli salon. Carl hoisted the unwrapped bundle of cloth, keeping it well in sight of any passerby. Not for the first time, he was grateful to the Old One for reminding him about the yard goods.

He made a play of examining his watch which was running slow, as usual. Then he put on a display of haste and started off at a fast clip. Minutes later, he saw his reflection in a café window and behind it, at a distance, the long, lean German.

He knew if he were under suspicion he would be followed by the French police, Pierre Laval's Milice, or the Gestapo. But certainly not by a German officer. Could it be von Leidersdorf? He wondered.

The curious, unhurried pursuit did not end until Carl reached his office. Suddenly, the man was gone. He must have stopped at the far corner when Carl crossed the rue du Faubourg St. Honore. Carl wished, not for the first time, that telephones were more easily obtained. He might warn Jany. Then he remembered that she had promised to go to the typing school. That would help, for a couple of hours, at any rate.

Something had to be done. But he had neither the constitution nor the wish to murder the German officer. Besides, it would only result in terrible reprisals for hundreds of French citizens.

"Murder! So I've gone that far. I'm at the point where I can actually consider murder."

He was appalled at the changes that four years of war and Occupation had made in the mild-mannered boy he once was.

# Chapter Fourteen

Jany didn't need her brother's warnings. She was already terrified of anyone she saw wearing a German army uniform, always afraid she would find herself blundering through a conversation with someone like Lieutenant Colonel von Leidersdorf. The longer she avoided him, the more terrifying an image he became in her mind.

To make matters worse, Jany harbored an irrational fear that if she wasn't careful, all her pent-up feelings for Monsieur Tony would be directed to another man, the first one who showed her any attention. At the moment the colonel, with his questionable motives, was the nearest of them. It was horrible to think of being touched the way Tony had touched her by one of the Boches.

Another bouquet was threaded through the door latch when she came home from typing class two afternoons later. The sultry August air had wilted the anemones whose vivid purple, plum and lavender heads drooped below the latch. She tore the flowers out of the latch and threw them over the bannister. She felt sorry for the poor, helpless flowers. It wasn't their fault. Sentimentally, she had a sudden impulse to run downstairs and rescue them.

While she stood there considering this Madame Charpentier's door opened. Jany held her breath. She could see that there was a man in the concierge's room, probably Monsieur Tony. That dreadful, fat female spy was always after him. Then she saw the man's arm extended, the fingers holding the door open. A Wehrmacht officer's uniform. She pulled back from the bannister, but it was too late.

Lieutenant Colonel von Leidersdorf was settling his peaked hat securely. His hand remained in place on his forehead, making him look as if he were saluting as he stared up at Jany. He didn't smile. It was his solemnity more than anything that scared the young girl for the moment. Or was it something else — his obvious tension? But why should the Wehrmacht be tense?

Jany told herself that it was also his ugliness that repulsed her although, objectively speaking, he wasn't ugly. He was even rather distinguished looking, but it didn't help a bit. Besides, men who weren't typically handsome had a certain appeal for Jany. At least they didn't frighten her the way this one did. She couldn't decide why the little vein throbbing in his neck, or for that matter anything else about him, should terrify her so. Except, of course, his uniform.

"Ah," he exclaimed at last, giving it the throaty gargle. "Fraulein Friedrich is home at last. I am so glad."

"No, monsieur! I am not home. I am going to . . . to the market. I am very busy."

She knew it was absurd at this hour in the afternoon to be going off to the markets. Any Frenchwoman would tell him so, but she had to get him away from the flat. Either Tony or Carl would return and be sure to cause trouble and get hauled off to Fresnes Prison or Fort Valèrien, or be put on

210

one of those ghastly cattle cars whose prisoners were never heard from again. Anything was better than that.

She came down the stairs toward him, trying to avoid his fixed, unblinking gaze. He took her hand, gallantly helping her down the last two stairs. It felt bony against her fingers. He must be fifty years old if he was a day! Poor old man — no wonder he thought of her the way he thought of his daughter, Erika. He was homesick. With this realization Jany decided she would try to think of him in that way and overlook his excessive attentions.

"You must let me accompany you, fraulein. It is not safe for such a very young lady to be walking about these streets. This is not Berlin, you know."

"Is it safer in Berlin?"

Her voice held no sarcasm that might offend him. She tried to seem only naively inquisitive.

"*Naturlich.* But I offend your ears. I must speak in your soft language."

"It is a beautiful language, monsieur."

"*Natur— naturellement.* Soft and beautiful. France is a lovely female to be cherished . . . when she is obedient."

She wrinkled her nose at that and he chuckled. By this time it was clear that he planned to accompany her to the market. His hand planted firmly under her elbow, he pulled her body closer than was necessary to his. Jany, feeling more and more stifled, began to perspire. But it wasn't from the heat of the warm August day — it was the cold sweat of fear. As they left the stairwell, she asked herself where they were going. Would he let her return safely? How long must she be nice to him?

When they got out into the brick courtyard, she fell into her clumsy limping walk with her feet turned in. She knew it was ugly and produced in him a quick revulsion which she noted with interest. She kept on, even after they got out to the street, but it was enormously difficult. His hand propelled her along, sometimes almost lifting her off the sidewalk. He must have begun to realize that it was intentional, but he didn't mention it.

"Where is this market of yours? I assure you, it will be of great assistance to you, my presence. These old harridans who sat knitting around your guillotine during your revolution are very eager to sell to a German officer."

"It wasn't my guillotine, and the revolution belonged to my ancestors, monsieur."

"Now I have made you angry. It is not my desire, my poor little Erika."

She stiffened. He had kissed the top of her head. He seemed to think her revulsion came from his use of his daughter's name and he apologized quickly.

"*Pardon,* mademoiselle. Memories of my child. That is my excuse. You have lost your father, I believe."

"I never knew him."

There was even more activity than usual on the narrow, ancient street. A black car which she suspected was Gestapo had been parked in front of the Merciers' house. Many children gathered to watch as the Gestapo began to systematically tear the building's interior apart. Behind the porte cochère boards, bricks and furniture were piling up amid great clouds of choking dust.

Jany thought of the information about Monsieur Tony that might be uncovered. She tried to control her fears, reassuring herself that Carl would have done something about it before this. Carl always saved the day. He had been father, brother and, lately, mother to her. She knew that her enormous faith in him was justified, many times over.

"So, *Liebchen*, no father. A pity. You might have appreciated our German culture had you known Herr Friedrich. Tell me, little one, do you enjoy the pretty materials your brother brought home to you?"

"Materials?" She was confused but something told her it could be a trap. She said quickly, "Very much."

"Appropriate for your use. In the kitchen, and perhaps the parlor."

This gave her an idea. "I am a very good cook. It was good of Carl to buy them. Everything is so hard to get these days. Good utensils are impossible. And less than an hour's gas to cook an entire meal . . ."

His fingers tightened their grasp on her arm where he held her. A fleeting expression crossed his face, a frown that disappeared. Then he made an odd, disturbing remark, almost to himself.

"Well then, it does not concern you, after all. You know nothing of your brother's affairs."

They came to another narrow passage between two old buildings whose windows had seen the Revolutionary tumbrils pass by. The colonel stopped in the shadow of the passage, drawing her reluctant body to him. It was like the German long ago on the Ile de la Cité, the night she lit a candle for Maman.

"Please. Don't."

"My poor child." His hands were trembling but they were as hard as ever. "You must be your own sweet self to me. I can be very useful to you. And the day may come, soon enough, when only my protection can save you. Do you understand me?"

She licked her lips nervously.

"I think so." She looked up at him. "But not — I couldn't m-make love to you. Surely you wouldn't ask that. I mean, if a French soldier asked your daughter —"

"Certainly not!" He was so upset he shook her. The vein in his neck throbbed again, accentuating his intensity. "What is this you take me for? A common seducer? We do this with Jew whores. Not with pure young ladies of Aryan blood."

She longed to blurt out, "I am a Jew. My father, with your beloved Aryan blood, was half-Jewish."

But she was not a noble heroine. She wanted to avoid the hideous consequences to Carl and to herself. They might send her and Carl off to God knew where, in a sealed cattle car. Instead she murmured lamely, "Thank you, monsieur. Now could we go on to the markets? It's getting late."

"The markets. To be sure. Exactly as my daughter's attention to business."

He exhaled as if he were tired, or had just come through a major crisis. In a strange way she felt sorry for him. Maybe he didn't want her *that way* at all. Could she have imagined it? She must be getting too sensitive. And with Carl's work she must be especially careful.

The colonel seemed to feel that this understanding entitled him to bestow another fatherly kiss on the crown of her head. She took care not to react.

Unfortunately, their new "understanding" gave him the opportunity for even closer attention, very like the way she thought an enthusiastic father would behave, except that his knuckles under her elbow continued to rub against her right breast. She could almost imagine that his fingers belonged to Tony Lombard, but hastily reminded herself that that was a forbidden thought.

Thinking of the handsome young American, she felt the sudden sting of tears, remembering how hopeless any relationship with the American would be. All her dreams of their happiness together were gone. It was dreadful news, like a blow to her stomach that left her feeling weak and breathless. It had been bad enough to discover that he was married to a famous and undoubtedly beautiful actress. She knew she could never compete with a movie star. But at the very least he should have mentioned his daughter. As the daughter of a man who had never taken the slightest interest in her, she felt that Tony's biggest crime was his disregard for his little girl. It tarnished all her thoughts of the kind of man she'd thought him to be.

Even Colonel von Leidersdorf was better than that.

Shouts and running footsteps across the street caught their attention. Bicycle riders halted quickly in the street and traffic piled up behind them with angry shouts, mostly in German, to the delight of French passersby. Twists of black smoke spiraled out of the Mercier mansion's second floor.

But the factor that aroused so much interest was the panic of the Germans involved. Their work had been so important that they didn't employ any Frenchmen. Now there was trouble and they had no one to blame but each other.

It was the colonel, of all people, who gloated over their problem.

"That will teach them. Herr Himmler and his attempt to infiltrate the army! That is not enough for him. He must use his scum at every menial task. They have managed to set fire to their own work."

Jany too rejoiced. Holy Mother of God! Maybe their clumsiness would destroy the evidence against Monsieur Tony.

In much better spirits Jany and the colonel went on to the nearest fish market. Jany hadn't anticipated the awkward scene that followed. The fishmonger, a proud young veteran, was barely polite to Jany. But she got through the exchange with no unspoken apologies, too proud to show that she did not go willingly with her tall, arrogant companion.

Just as she and the colonel were leaving after his brisk "Heil Hitler!" to the fishmonger, who responded in kind with the flip of a limp wrist, a new customer walked in. Jany was adjusting in her string bag the choice fresh carp produced by the magic effect of a German uniform. When she looked up she hardly recognized Monsieur Binet, graying, with stooped shoulders and an air of hopelessness that touched her heart. The death of Georges, his only son, had broken him.

She stopped the colonel. "Wait. I must speak to

him. He just lost his son. Monsieur Binet, how is Madame?"

"Tolerable, mademoiselle. You are kind to ask. And your brother?"

"Excellent, *merci*. Working hard, as usual. My cousin is with us. He's still trying to find work."

"These are bad times for France."

"And for the world, Mein Herr," the colonel said.

Binet raised his head, saw that the German officer was with Jany and all the heavy lines in his face hardened.

"You collaborate with the creatures who shot my child?" To Jany's horror he spat at her. *"Boche putain!"*

The colonel was livid. He raised his arm and for one terrible instant Jany thought he would strike the Frenchman. She screamed and got between them.

"No! Don't hurt him."

The German recovered his dignity and calmed down. The fishmonger too, tried to intervene, holding back Monsieur Binet. "Come, *mon vieux*. We do not quarrel with the Boche. Not now."

"My boy is in his grave. And she, his friend, she can go with this *haricot vert*." It was an absurd insult, worthy of children, but he was obviously desperate. He struck the counter with his fist, hard enough to make everyone jump. "Give me the fish you promised yesterday, Jacques."

"None, my friend. No more today. I've got to hold it for *them*."

Jany looked at the colonel, her eyes full of meaning. The colonel stepped back into the shop.

"Give him the other carp." The fishmonger hesitated. "On my order."

"Yes, monsieur."

Before he could reach for the carp in its barrel of water, Binet thrust his arm aside.

"Not from the Boche. Many thanks." He pushed past Jany and stormed out.

Jany didn't blame him, she would have felt the same way. But she knew that, with the colonel at her side, her position was suddenly insecure with her own countrymen.

On the way back down the street she and von Leidersdorf saw that the fire in the old mansion had gotten headway, amid the frantic efforts of French firemen and Gestapo amateurs, whose efforts only seemed to fan the flames.

His excellent mood having returned, the colonel asked her what flowers were her favorites. When she said she had no idea, they all made her sneeze, he wanted to know whether she enjoyed bonbons. Jany hadn't eaten any sweets in two years, and although the temptation was great, she resisted acknowledging her fondness for them.

As he seemed ready to question her about other rationed items she might crave, he broke off suddenly and surprised her with a curiously unrelated remark.

"You make good use of the kitchen utensils your brother bought for you, no? I envy him those delicious meals. Your cousin, also, he enjoys the dishes you prepare from those so pleasant little pots and pans?"

He was jealous of Tony. That must be what this was about.

"When they are hungry, I expect they do enjoy my food. Most of the time we eat beans. Tony isn't used to flower bulbs, of course. That is all."

"They eat better, perhaps, in Gascony?"

Realizing her mistake, she became desperately cheerful, trying to cover up the remark that implied Tony wasn't used to scant food supplies. "Oh, yes. Being so near the Spanish border, they naturally have different tastes. May I go now?"

"You are not with a schoolmaster, mademoiselle. You may go when you like."

While she was saying a brief, hurried good-bye to the colonel, anxious that none of her other friends should find her with him, Madame Charpentier passed them on the sidewalk as she headed into the Café St. Just. Giving them a long, interested stare, she asked the German coyly, "Aren't you glad you waited, Monsieur le Colonel?" Addressing Jany she said, "He refused to leave until you came home from school. Ah, mademoiselle, do I sniff a romance?"

Things were getting worse and worse. The only saving grace was that if the woman were a Gestapo spy, she would hardly endanger a friend of the colonel's by indiscriminate gossiping. She added as an apparent afterthought, "You just missed your cousin, mademoiselle. He left not ten minutes ago with that deBrett woman."

Having done her damage, she was received on the terrasse of the café by the owner, who gave Jany a grimace behind the woman's back. He and Carl had suspected the concierge since she first appeared at the flats. Jany smiled shakily, still sick over the thought of Tony and Danielle in a tête-à-tête, but relieved that the café owner didn't seem to find the colonel an objectionable escort.

Jany waited until they were alone again. Bidding the colonel good-bye, Jany turned to leave when he said, "One moment. If you value your brother's life, give him this warning: 'The rue de la Paix is an expensive shopping area.' "

"I don't understand. What do you mean?"

"Do not concern yourself. Your brother will know."

His warning sounded so harmless that she didn't know why it scared her so much, except that it hinted cryptically at something quite different from its surface meaning.

Turning her key in the lock, a frown etched across her forehead, Jany almost, but not quite, forgot that at that very moment Monsieur Tony was out somewhere with a voluptuous Communist collaborator who would probably stop at nothing to win him to their side.

On this occasion Tony and Danielle were received at the Café au Coin with almost embarrassing enthusiasm. The patron waved them to a table near the kitchen, where he saw the little Maquis leader named Thibaud grinning broadly. The huge, inarticulate Breton seated beside him had an unaccustomed pallor, but looked belligerent nonetheless, even with his arm in a sling. He must have seen some heavy action for a man of his size to be hurt.

The men all shook hands. Danielle kissed both Maquis leaders. Thibaud revealed some special knowledge about London and Alec Huntington which immediately angered Tony.

"I don't give a damn what you saw my cousin about, or my father. If you two were in London since you stranded me here, surely you could have gotten me out with you."

"That is precisely what we wish to discuss with you, comrade. You see, it can be dangerous, as witness our friend here. Broke the arm on landing off the coast of Bretagne. The currents around the Ile de Sein are treacherous. What price are you prepared to pay?"

Taken by surprise, Tony was quick to reply in his American-idiom French. "Whatever the traffic will bear. I've got to get out of here."

Danielle leaned closer, touching her warm cheek against his. "Too much virginal adoration, Comrade Lombard?"

He played it lightly. "She is a child. Now, about my escape. I can make it worth your while as soon as I hit London. What do you want from me?"

"Recognition, comrade. We demand to be recognized as the true Liberation Party and future rulers of France."

Despite the pompous absurdity of this, Danielle and the Breton sat nodding their heads in agreement like little Japanese dolls. They had asked for the one thing he couldn't give them.

Stall for time, Tony thought to himself, it's the only answer. Above all, Carl Friedrich would have to make the decision about how to handle this.

"Even my father hasn't that kind of power. Is France so close to deliverance?"

The Breton and Thibaud glanced at each other. After a noticeable pause Thibaud said, "The new military governor, von Choltitz, has been ordered to plant explosives all over Paris. We have friends. We learn these things. It means that the Boche plan to make a stand."

"Paris will be the center of a holocaust," Danielle put in rapidly, "unless we can prevent it by our uprising. Surely you see that. The Gaullists, the Centrists, *Combat,* Liberation, all these are splinter movements. Each of them will be helpless without us — none can succeed on their own. Do you dare to chance that?"

"It isn't for me to say. Recognition of the postwar government in France isn't my decision," Tony said, trying to reason with them.

Thibaud shrugged. "Then you must remain here, become a part of that holocaust." He leaned toward Tony. "It is a bad thing to desert one's wife. Wives need a strong hand. If we let them think we are dead, they will not grieve for very long."

Tony opened his mouth, wondering what the fellow was getting at. "Was that meant for me?"

The little man looked around. No one else seemed to be listening. He abruptly pulled a many-folded square of slick paper from his wooden sabot and offered it to Tony who spread it out, wondering what could be so important in a page from what looked like *Life* magazine.

It didn't take long for Tony to spot the pictures, two of them featuring his wife. Or widow, in a manner of speaking. Evidently she had appeared as the "special surprise guest" at a Prysing Film Festival in Honolulu, held 'in memory of her late husband, Anthony Lombard, Prysing Films' talented director lost over the Normandy front."

She looked a trifle somber, though the pictures showed her waving to fans, still every inch the star. At least she'd worn black, a kind of flowing chiffon, from the look of it.

"Can I keep it?" Tony asked.

Thibaud got a nod and faint smile from Danielle.

"Most certainly. You see how important it is that you return to your wife as soon as possible? A little longer and on will be completely forgotten."

Tony took a deep breath. "On the contrary, I don't seem to be missed. In fact, I'd probably be doing her a big favor if I never showed up."

Danielle and the others suddenly seemed disgruntled. They had counted on his desire to return to his wife before he lost her, but he was behaving in reverse fashion.

"It's that damned little Friedrich girl," Thibaud muttered.

Danielle let out one of her guttural laughs, a sound that grated on Tony's nerves.

"Not for long. The Boche colonel has taken a fancy to her. Forget the virginal Jany. That is all changed now, or soon will be. You may be sure, comrade, that the Boche will take her with him back to the Fatherland."

He was furious but tried not to show it. "Impossible, comrade. The German has a daughter and probably an entire family."

"You are mistaken. Oberstlieutenant von Leidersdorf had a daughter once. Erika-Gertrude. She died in Berlin with the colonel's sister during an RAF bombing last winter. According to our information, she had been sent there from

Darmstadt by her father for safety. A joke, that. So little Jany is his substitute. You can be sure he will not let her go, nor will he leave her behind him."

It was becoming clear to Tony that, although he longed to return to his own family, he couldn't leave Paris while these dangers hung over her. Without knowing it, his comrades of the Maquis had ruined their own chance of using him as a pawn.

His decision made, Tony couldn't forget little Andrea, thinking her daddy would never come back, probably growing used to other men in the family who would surely take his place in her childish affections.

Facing his three unwilling "comrades," Tony realized he would have to rely exclusively on Carl Friedrich to get the news through that he was very much alive. For Andrea's sake. Glancing again at the page from *Life* magazine, he knew that whatever his relations with Eden would be after the war, Andrea had to be the most important thing in his life. Andrea, he amended, and Jany Friedrich. But he had no idea how he could ever reconcile the two lives.

# Chapter Fifteen

It was Heather Huntington who excitedly called her husband in his London office to tell him Mr. Broome had important information for Alec and his uncle Steve.

Broome was a high-ranking official in the British government who knew Mr. Churchill personally. The mere sound of his familiar, slightly stuttering voice always impressed Heather. There was an edge of humility to it, uncommon in a person of his rank. Something was going on. Heather reasoned that the more favors Alec could do for these people, the better position they would be in when it was over. Money was nice, but position in life was more important. Besides, position *made* money.

When this disgusting war was over, her mother pointed out repeatedly, Heather could return with Alec to San Francisco as mistress of the Lombard mansion.

"You'll be thinking about it if you've a brain, my girl," Stella Burkett would say. "You'll have my third part of it, and some day Brooke will be gone, so that's another third for you. That makes you twice as much a Lombard in that house as anyone else. Your old ma didn't twiddle her thumbs all them years. Workin' for you, I was."

"You were a common parlormaid, mama."

"Common, says you. I got to be old Red Lombard's wife for a couple of hours before he

225

died, didn't I? Long enough to be his heir."

All the same, nice as they tried to be, not one of the family had ever accepted Stella Burkett as a Lombard. She remained the former housekeeper even to herself, and privately admitted it to her daughter.

"That's as may be. But Randi Gallegher was no better. I rec'lect the day she come delivering tickets to the house for a War Bond rally. Armistice Day it was. Met Mr. Steve that day. But before that, the Galleghers and the Burketts all enjoyed a bucket of beer together, many's the night. Never you forget. Randi Gallegher is no more a born Lombard than you are."

When mama said that she looked almost hand-some, standing there in the Richmond Hill hotel room, straight-backed and boasting. "Your old Stell' is as good as any Lombard when it comes to that."

But it was nice to know that important men like Mr. Broome should seek out Alec and want him to call back — no, "ring down" as soon as possible. What was the big secret? Maybe the war was over. Maybe Alec was going to be president of the Universal Broadcasting Company. It could be any-thing, but it was sure to help Alec's position, and her own.

"Mama, get fixed up, quick. We're going into London to find Alec. Maybe I can meet Mr. Broome in person, too. You can drive that crazy old Austin of yours."

Stella sighed but changed to her best tweed suit, grumbling a little. "Sure, I never knew it to fail. I'm back to waiting on the gentry. Thought I'd got rid of maiding them fancy ladies."

Heather brushed her hair up into the dated hairdo the English favored. Then she swung around and hugged Stella.

"Now you're maiding me. And you love it, sweetie, you know you do. How do you like my hair? Sophisticated, wouldn't you say?"

Stella grunted. "You've always looked all right to me. You know that. Let's go. I sure don't want to run into any of them buzz bombs. Hasn't been any coming across for hours now. They're overdue."

"Then you'll just have to speed a little like the dear, loyal mama you are."

"Don't you be giving me any of your sass, young lady."

All the same, the two went down the old Tudor staircase arm in arm.

They were not pleased to run into Eden Ware on the ground floor. She had unexpectedly arrived in England two days ago against everyone's advice, immediately distracting Steve Lombard and even Alec from their attention to Heather. In spite of the war, the desperate slogging through Brittany and Normandy in the midst of unseasonal rains and the V-bombs exploding all over the parts of London that hadn't been destroyed during the Blitz, Steve and Alec still seemed to have time to dote on Eden.

Stella noted with satisfaction that the actress had never looked worse. Her hair was unkempt; looked like it was thinning, too. But then, it had always been thin. Her clothes were wrinkled as though she'd slept in them. To Stella's eyes it certainly wasn't the look of a respectable widow.

From what she'd overheard between the men talking, it appeared that Eden was still searching for contact with someone who had witnessed Tony's death.

Long ago, Stella had dreamed of Tony Lombard as the right husband for Heather. Her marriage to Tony did little to endear the actress to her. Nor did she believe Eden had come in search of her dead husband. Probably hoped to get publicity for her new movie, or something.

"Going into town?" Eden asked them with a desperate lightness. "Mind if I hitch a ride? It's so hard to get transport these days. Steve thinks he might get permission to accompany the French units up through France. They're getting so close they can almost smell those Paris odors. I wish I were going. I'd face a hundred Nazis . . . well, make that a dozen. I'm modest."

Stella looked at her daughter and rolled her eyes. Heather laughed politely.

"If you really think you can fit in, you're welcome. It's mama's Austin."

"Oh, Lord! Thanks. I'll risk it if you will. I've just got to see Steve before he goes. I've got a nibbling little hope that Tony is alive. It looks good. One of the RAF boys who got back tells me there are about five or six prominent Resistance groups, and they have reason to lie about these things. Alec says that the two Communists who talked to Steve were here to use some polite blackmail. Since the blackmail failed, we figured they very likely lied about Tony."

Stella was pessimistic. "What about the clothes and all?"

"Just part of their weapons for blackmail. They didn't actually tell Steve about Tony's death until they lost their deal. Makes sense to me that before it fell through they intended to tell him something else."

"Maybe."

Out on the knoll overlooking the green, serpentine Thames far below, Stella climbed in behind the wheel of the old car. There was a moment's polite discussion between Eden and Heather as to which girl was smaller and should sit on the other's lap. Eden was thinner but Heather was the smaller of the two. Eden insisted that since she was the intruder she should take the bottom place, to which Heather readily agreed.

Stella found Eden to be all wound up with hopeful excitement. Between the heavy military traffic and the jumble of lorries, and trying to drive on the left side of the road, she was in no mood for Eden Lombard's chatter, repeating again all that stuff about her husband's fate. Stella thought that the two Frenchies Steve and Leo spoke to were eyewitnesses. What more did anyone want? Stella squinted into the sky which was clouding up for another of the typical English summer showers.

"Hear anything, mama?" Heather asked nervously. "There haven't been any V-bombs around for nearly twelve hours. The desk clerk said at breakfast that's a good sign. Maybe they've run out of bombs."

Eden agreed. "They have to run out sooner or later. I was told last night at the Savoy that the Yanks had blown up another silo, one of those cement things the bombs are launched from near the

French coast. The Nazis can't keep on forever, especially when they're fighting on three fronts."

"We got your word for it, anyway," Stella mumbled sourly. She passed a lorry whose driver proved to be a woman, her hair streaming out from under her cap. The girl swung out around the little car, passing on a curve, making Eden and Heather even more jittery.

To Stella's amusement they didn't start talking again until Eden remarked on how odd it was to enter buildings in London that were almost buried in sandbags. The barriers made on both sides of each entrance were at once oppressive and comforting.

"And I still can't get used to the shelters," Eden went on, obviously wanting to talk. "Some of the tube stations open, some closed, some with sandbags and some all bombed out. I spent half an hour looking for Green Park yesterday. I never did get into the Strand station I was looking for."

Heather explained that the Streatham area always got the worst until the V-bombs moved their targets, following the people who were trying to evade them. The sandbags and other barriers helped against some of the blast.

"It's the silence before it hits that I can't stand," Eden said. "First that swirling sound, then a stream of fire like I saw yesterday, and then nothing. After that — blooey!"

"If you get a direct hit, you won't much care," Stella muttered.

"Thank you, mama. You're such a cheerful soul."

The two younger woman were silent as they

passed giant craters where, a few days ago, a solid building had stood. It seemed almost irreverent that Buckingham Palace should have been attacked, but only Eden was shocked by that.

As they continued to pass the debris of destroyed buildings, Heather grew quiet again and seemed to crawl down into her shell.

"Puts my girl in mind of the Strand earthquake back in '33," Stella explained calmly. "She was stuck in her room until we pried her out."

Heather offered no comment to this but Eden felt the shudder that coursed through the girl's body. Heather was much prettier than any of the young starlets Eden regularly saw around the movie sets, but as her mother had said before, there was an oddness about her. Even with her platinum hair rolled up in a sophisticated pompadour, Heather seemed childlike. In an eerie way, she didn't belong in the adult world, and somehow it seemed that she never would.

Eden had marveled that Alec's emotional life could be wrapped up in such an immature person, but she seemed to suit him. What was even stranger was the way he willingly fed that childish dependence of hers! Men were strange creatures. There were times when Eden suspected that even Tony would have been happier with a dependent wife. Maybe that explained his extreme attachment to Andrea. Maybe he was just as happy with a dependent daughter as he would have been with a dependent wife.

Soon they might all be together again, Tony and Andrea and Eden. She wondered what that would be like, after almost reconciling herself to his almost certain death.

"If you're going to stop off at the hotels later today for a schnapps," Stella advised Eden, "get there before dark. Every hotel we've tried is closed by nine."

"Thank you. I'll remember that."

Stella gave her a side glance to see if she was being sarcastic. It was hard to tell.

They pulled into the Strand and headed for the Savoy where Alec was due to have lunch with some BBC bigwigs. Stella drove as near as she could get to the huge hotel on the Thames embankment. Attempting to park, she was ordered out, being told that something official was going on involving the foreign ministers of several governments in exile. Evidently Alec had left for the other restaurant in Holborn he frequented. Stella found a spot to park in what had once been a mews behind an elegant Regency mansion. The devastation of the Blitz had long since been removed and replaced by temporary offices which, in their turn, had just received a direct hit from a buzz bomb.

Stella complained that her little car would be covered with dust by the time they returned, but it was hard not to borrow a little of her companions' nervous excitement. On foot the three women followed Alec's trail toward the Holborn district in the heart of the city.

Eden was shocked by the changes she noticed in the people on the streets since the early days of the war and even since the Blitz. Not unexpectedly, they were edgy, nervous and much more prone to flare-ups of anger. During the Blitz and the firebombing they had known what was coming — they'd heard their fate, and there was a brief, all too brief, time for running. But since the pilotless bombs began to rain down on them in June they jumped at even the slightest of noises — the crackle of paper, a dropped book, or even an unexpected footfall.

The three women had just reached the barrier of a blasted office building when the wail of a siren started up. Heather scrambled over the debris on the sidewalk crying "Mama!" and reached for the security of Stella's strong arm.

Eden panicked inside. Like Heather, she, too, wanted to fling herself into someone's arms. She thought that it would have pleased Tony to know she needed him at a time like this.

The crowded streets resembled disturbed anthills, crowded with people rushing for safety. Eden herself swung around in confusion, trying to remember where the nearest subway shelter was. Spotting Stella, she saw that the woman was having trouble controlling Heather, who had panicked with fright. Stella tried to drag her daughter along the sidewalk, but she dug her feet into the debris left from the bombing of the day before and latched onto every obstacle she could reach. Sweating and worn, Stella looked to Eden for help.

"She don't like all this noise and confusion."

By this time, they could hear the roar of the explosions near the east end of the city. Total confusion set in, and Eden found herself being pushed away from the two women by the running throng. She fell over a heavy office chair but managed to pick herself up, at the same time trying to close her ears to the metallic wail that cut through the murky air. The cacophony everywhere broke down into separate noises, dominated by a buzzing sound overhead.

Then came the dreaded silence.

She covered her head with her arms, cowering in the midst of broken furniture, chunks of plaster and lath. The acrid odor of burned, smoking wood stung her nostrils and eyes.

The explosion came at some distance. Maybe in the next block, but Eden didn't dare look up to find out. She burrowed like a mole under a large conference table beside her.

The explosion threw Stella to the sidewalk, tearing Heather away from her. Stella struggled to her knees, calling for her daughter. Though the blast was over, the earth still seemed to shake, and the smoky air made it hard to see anyone clearly.

"Earthquake! Mama, help me."

Slowly the world righted itself again. Figures emerged from the smoky gloom and Stella was able to make out Heather. Having been hurled against a broken wall that was in the process of being torn down, the girl looked around vaguely, then staggered into Stella's arms.

As the all clear sounded, Eden clawed her way through the debris of the previous bombing, marveling at the casual attitude of the British around her, in spite of their terror. Their faces looked drained. Most of them were dazed, but Eden caught their remarks as she looked around for her friends.

"Nasty one, that."

"I've seen 'em closer."

"Jerry's out early today. Couldn't wait for one of them nice foggy nights."

Pushing her way among them, she finally spotted Heather frantically hugging Stella, her tousled white-gold head tucked firmly under her mother's chin. Stella gazed over her head at Eden, her mouth quivering nervously.

"She's all right, my girl. Just a bit of a shake-up. She bumped her head. Now, now, mavourneen, mama's here."

Eden's legs were still wobbly but she got to Heather's other side.

"We'd better go on or we'll miss Alec."

Already fire wagons were clanging by on their way to the bomb site, signaling the bomb disposal units that would follow. A fire warden rushed past them on the sidewalk. Eden wasn't used to these everyday horrors of war and had the uneasy feeling that another unpiloted V-bomb just might follow the first at any minute. With this thought, she tried to hurry the two women along.

In the Charles House Restaurant some minutes after the all clear sounded, Alec finished his gin-and-it, set the glass aside and nudged Steve. "Here he comes now. Don't go by his looks. He's not very prepossessing, but Broome is a man who gets news right from the horse's mouth. And he says it's good. At the moment he's functioning as a kind of liaison between the Free French in London and the British government. He says he'll give you the straight stuff. I think it involves the Gaullist committee. Cross of Lorraine, and all that."

Steve nodded. His throat felt tight. "They're my

choice. I know they're only a part of the French Liberation group, but this Charles de Gaulle has some sound ideas. A lot more moderate than the Commies or the Monarchists. And the Socialists can't seem to pull themselves together. Each man has his own party."

"I'm inclined to agree with you. De Gaulle is a haughty bastard but the best of the lot. Too bad Roosevelt has it in for him. Thinks he's arrogant and stubborn, I hear." He grinned. "Well, it takes one to know one, I always say." He lowered his voice. "But only in whispers."

Steve laughed. Then both men got up to receive their pink-cheeked, diminutive guest. His handshake was soft, his mouth was soft, and when he spoke, his voice was soft. He stammered occasionally like a man unsure of himself. It didn't take long for Steve to see that the outer appearance didn't necessarily make the man.

Mr. Broome refused lunch but accepted a pot of tea. Steve waited on tenterhooks while the little man emptied his cup and dabbed carefully at his lips before bringing up the subject of their meeting.

"N-now then."

Steve's patience gave out. "My son?"

"Alive. And free, at the moment."

"My God, my God . . ." Steve wiped his forehead.

Sensing that his relief over his son's safety had left him momentarily speechless, Alec took over, hoping to get more details.

"How about it, Broome? What's your source?

There's not a chance that this is another ploy to gain our support, is there?"

"N-not at all, Alec. The Gaullist headquarters have received a transmission from an unimpeachable source. Paix Blanche, one of their P-Paris agents."

Steve started to get up, almost in a daze.

"It's really true then. Tony's alive. I've got to tell Randi and Eden. Where's a phone? I've got to get San Francisco on the line . . ."

Alec put out a hand. "Hold it, Uncle Steve. There's more, isn't there?" he asked, glancing back at Broome.

Mr. Broome poured more tea and reached for a lemon slice — this was one of the few places in the city where a sliver of citrus could be obtained. To Steve's astonishment and impatience he proceeded to suck the juice of the slice before discarding it. Wiping his fingers fastidiously, he sipped the plain tea before continuing with his remarks.

"Mr. Tony Lombard, as I believe is his correct name, has taken the identity of Antoine Lenoir. He is accepted, we believe, as the cousin of a family called F-Friedrich. They live in Paris in the First Arrondissement."

"Friedrich!" Steve cut in excitedly. "Is that a coincidence? My sister's late husband was named Friedrich. An Austrian."

"The Friedrichs, a young man and his sister, are French. Their mother was an actress in the f-films. Silents, you know."

"Is it possible they'll betray him?" Alec asked.

"Most unlikely. The young man is an active p-patriot."

Steve impatiently butted in. "How about . . . suppose I got permission to join the troops of, say, General Leclerc? Assuming we could get to Paris . . ."

Alec nervously waved his hand in front of Steve's face. "Don't discuss it so loudly." He turned to Broome, as if to take him in his confidence. "Mr. Broome," he said quietly, "is there any way we can help get my cousin out?"

Mr. Broome answered quickly, "P-Please, I'm not quite sure of what's possible yet. Your son, Mr. Lombard, is involved in something very serious to the cause of the FFI, the French, in fact. I'm referring to, as I'm sure you know, the liberation of Paris. A ticklish thing, if I may say so. Those people need ammunition, weapons, and above all, recognition as the legitimate government of a free France."

"I want my son out of France. I don't give a damn who likes it." Steve took another breath. "Maybe I can give money to buy them arms, if that's what they want. But I haven't any political influence — it has to be money or nothing."

"Excuse me, but it isn't the actual arms, sir. It's the d-delivery of them. If arms are dropped, they could be picked up by the Communists. Many of the Maquis are Communists. In any case, we don't want th-that."

"Regardless," Alec interrupted, "I'm afraid Steve is set on the idea of going into Paris with the liberating troops."

"And I'm going to do it," he said, "I've got credentials from the *San Francisco Chronicle*. It's a cover that I think will work."

Broome shook his head. "I'm sorry, Mr. Lombard, but the plan is to b-bypass Paris. They don't want another Warsaw."

"Then I'll attach myself to the French contingent. I doubt if even Eisenhower can stop this General LeClerc once he gets that close to Paris."

Before Broome could object the headwaiter appeared, looking flustered.

"Beg pardon, gentlemen. Mrs. Huntington is waiting in the lounge with two other ladies. They're a trifle disheveled and prefer not to join you here. They seem to have been caught in the recent V-bomb unpleasantness."

Alec and Steve got up, Alec moving so quickly he overturned his water glass. Despite the waiter's assurance that the ladies seemed quite all right, Alec and Steve hastily started between the tables, followed by the haughty stares and raised eyebrows of the other diners.

Huddled in a leather armchair with her head in her hands, Heather was surrounded by a nervous waiter, a badly shaken Eden, and her mother. Stella remained her usual tower of strength where Heather was concerned. She caressed her daughter's bowed head, though she was speaking to her in a stern voice.

"It's all over now. You behave yourself. You want Mr. Alec to see you carrying on like a baby?"

Stella was wrong about Alec. He moved her aside not too gently and took Heather in his arms, kneeling before her chair.

"Alec, don't let me be alone again, please," she sobbed.

"No, no, sweetheart. Never. Do you hurt any-where?"

"My head."

"I'll kiss away the hurt."

Steve and Eden had always been astonished at Heather's effect on the typically cool, self-contained Alec Huntington, but today Steve's thoughts were in a state of chaos and Heather's condition was the least of his concerns. He took Eden aside.

"Brace yourself, kid."

Eden was still a little shaky but she suspected at once what Steve was going to say. She read it in his eyes and hugged him.

"It's Tony, isn't it? He's alive. He's safe. Oh, Steve, thank you."

"Alive and safe, *so far.* And I mean to see that he stays that way."

"What are you going to do? Let me go with you."

Broome's gentle voice pricked through Eden's moment of elation.

"Afraid not, Miss Ware. Pardon, I mean, Mrs. Lombard. In point of fact, Mr. Lombard here will be in serious difficulties himself if he attempts any linkup with the French contingents."

But Eden was wrapped up in her own plans. She felt as if an enormous weight had been lifted. All the maybes were gone, the hopes followed by the painful prick of doubt. Tony was alive, and he would be coming home to her and Andrea, and life would soon be normal again.

"Thank you, dear Steve."

Full of nervous enthusiasm she kissed him, missing his cheek and meeting his lips. But she barely noticed the act, or the hint of excitement she found in his warm mouth. Seconds later she felt his arms holding her away from him as he looked at her.

"I'll bring him back to you, honey. You wait right here in London. Now, you'll have to excuse me. I've got to put in a call to San Francisco."

With that he turned abruptly and left, leaving Eden feeling somewhat amazed at her remarkable father-in-law.

# Chapter Sixteen

The Old One, Madame de Souza, called Carl at the Café St. Just. She was as abrupt and crabbed on the phone as she had been during their meeting on the rue de la Paix.

"Friedrich, there is news."

"I warned you. I can't make the Paix Blanche. The lieutenant colonel has been following me."

"Had you followed, you mean. Gestapo?"

"No. Himself. Von Leidersdorf."

"Not possible. You would be in Fresnes Prison, or on a trip in one of their nasty cattle cars. Those cattle cars, by the way, now end their journey in a Polish hellhole. The Boches call it Auschwitz."

He knew nothing about the German name and he did not find her black humor amusing.

"I told you von Leidersdorf's warning to Jany," he insisted. "And I'm sure it was he I saw following me."

"But nothing has happened to my little arrangements on the rue de la Paix. Is it that your oberstlieutenant is good-hearted? Pro-French, perhaps?"

"Unlikely." This was bad, almost as bad as falling into the hands of the Gestapo, because it meant that von Leidersdorf's motives were personal, involving Jany. Anything was better than that. "You said you had news for me." It was unlike the Old One to relay news to other agents unless it concerned their own assignments.

"But of course. Number one. Since the Gestapo associates your 'cousin' with your household, thanks in part to your friend von Leidersdorf, your cousin can only be removed under cover of the American advance. Number two. There is to be no advance by the Americans, or by our troops under the orders of this Eek."

"Eek?"

"Eek Eisenhower."

"Ike." Then, realizing what she had said, he was appalled. "You can't mean it! The Allies are within two days of the gates of Paris."

He had raised his voice. Always a mistake. Pierre St. Just, the café's proprietor, turned away from his zinc counter and asked quietly, "Bad?"

"The worst. They aren't coming."

"Mother of Christ!" Pierre muttered.

Carl returned to the phone. "What are my orders? What does *he* say?"

*He* was understood to be Charles de Gaulle. Pierre cocked his head to hear through the wall phone receiver.

"I am informed that his instructions are that if the Allies bypass Paris, he will take his own troops out of the Allied armies and order them into Paris alone."

Pierre and Carl reacted with shock. They both understood that de Gaulle's warning had been either a monumental bluff or a last-ditch act of desperation.

Carl covered the mouthpiece automatically. He whispered to Pierre, "Would an uprising have any chance under those circumstances?"

"Not if this Eisenhower fails to back our forces."

"I heard that," Madame de Souza cut in, her voice scratching at his ear.

"Is it true?"

"Probably. No uprising until we have backing from the Allies. Those are my instructions from Pleyel Violet."

"Codes, codes," Pierre complained. "Why can they not call their transmissions Jean or Jacques or Charles? Pleyel Violet and Paix Blanche and good God knows what others."

Carl held up his hand. Madame de Souza was issuing more orders. "Friedrich, you will wine and dine Mademoiselle deBrett. You will try to learn what the Communist plans are if the Allies bypass Paris. And Friedrich?"

"Yes."

"Encourage the *petite* Jany to befriend her Boche admirer. She may be useful."

"Impossible. I will not have —"

The line went dead.

Carl looked at the earpiece. Controlling his fury, he hung up. Pierre asked, "Why will they not come? It is because the Anglos and the Yankees have always hated us. That is why."

Carl had more sinister ideas. "On the contrary. It is because they fear the Boche will destroy Paris as they destroyed Stalingrad and Warsaw. The Boche may be laying their explosives at this minute."

"What!"

"Three *Pionierkompanies* have been busy for days, mining half of Paris. All our bridges, certainly. And, I should think, all the public monuments. The churches, Notre Dame. It would be more easy to guess where they are not placing their explosives."

"Mother of God!"

Carl's smile was grim. "Light a candle to Saint Genevieve instead. Paris is her city."

Carl straightened his shoulders and ran a hand over his hair, wondering if he would have to key himself up for Danielle. Not that he thought it would be much of a problem to do so. He had always been attracted to Danielle physically, and Danielle was especially receptive on warm afternoons.

"Pierre, I must go up to Montmartre in a hurry. May I borrow your bicycle?"

"Ah, the beauteous deBrett. I envy you. Take the bicycle before my wife gets it. She has an eye on a black marketeer with what he claims are materials stolen from La Chanel's salon."

On this Friday afternoon Jany Friedrich was ironing her two-year-old Sunday dress, a skimpy white crepe with puffed sleeves. She had waited all day for the hour when the rationed power was turned on. One small, wooden-handled flatiron stood heating on the stove while she moved the other systematically back and forth, up and down on the board propped between the sink and the cupboard. She was intensely aware that Tony Lombard stood in the doorway between the parlor and the little foyer, watching her from a distance.

Since the news of Tony's wife and child, he had been painfully proper in his dealings with her, and she knew she ought to be grateful, since it made it easier to resume the friendly, light relationship that marked their first acquaintance. But she couldn't help suspecting that in spite of his famous wife and the baby, he had feelings for her, too.

It was more than the common sexual desire of those German soldiers on the streets. Tony very subtly showed tenderness in every way. He was always ready to help her, yet he tried not to be intrusive. And she knew that he watched her at odd moments when she was trying to behave naturally. She had caught a new, gentle look in his eyes, quite unlike the flirtatious, casual air she first remembered. Sometimes she felt like the sad heroine in a romantic movie, a suffering partner in an impossible love. For at least a month she had dreamed of being involved in an "impossible" romance, and now it was hers. She wasn't sure it made her as happy as she thought it would, if only because she knew Monsieur Tony was unhappy.

She set the worn, time-darkened iron back on the stove and took up the hot one, carefully pressing the meager length of the skirt. Tony had moved up to the kitchen doorway. He could hardly go farther. Even she and Carl were a tight fit in the little kitchen.

"I love to watch you do that."

Gratified, she maneuvered the iron with an unconscious grace, making long, dreamy movements as she thought of Tony.

The dangerous mood they had allowed themselves to slip into was broken by Carl, who slammed the outer door shut, lacking his usual consideration. Tony moved casually away from the doorway, backing into the parlor, but Jany reacted nervously. She knew Carl's strict ideas about her conduct.

"I was pressing my dress for church day after to-morrow," Jany babbled, but Carl waved her aside.

"Never mind. I am going to Montmartre. It is important. But that accursed Boche von Leidersdorf may come before I return. Stay with her every minute, Tony. No excuses. Do you understand?"

Scared as much by his order as by his tone, Jany nodded. She was proud of Tony who reacted with quiet sincerity.

"You may trust me."

"Thank you." Carl turned away, then remembered a matter closely concerning Tony. "I received the answer. With Paris on the verge of boiling over, the Boches are ready to destroy the city. Any spark will set off the explosion. An attempt to rescue you and several RAF pilots hiding in Paris may be just the pretext they need. But patience, my friend, there will be action. You played the baseball in your boyhood?"

"Football in college. Sandlot baseball as a boy. Why? I didn't know you French were interested?"

"We may be interested in anyone with a good — I believe you call it a pitching arm. There is a thing called a Molotov cocktail." Tony's eyes widened slightly, while Jany stifled a gasp. She too had heard of it. "When the Allies enter Paris anything may happen. We must help them."

"When? Soon?" Tony asked.

"It may not be for weeks. But some time this fall. We cannot rise until we know they are coming."

Tony quickly glanced at Jany.

"I'll help you. If you need an extra pair of hands, you know where to find them. But I've got to get out of Paris. Soon."

Following his glance, Carl said tightly, "I agree, I'd find another place for you, but there is that damned Boche. I can't leave Jany alone." He offered his hand. "You said I might trust you. I hope we understand each other."

Tony accepted his hand. "We do."

Satisfied with his word, Carl left on the run. During the Occupation years, he had learned to walk from the Bois de Boulogne to the Bois de Vincennes, from Montparnasse to Montmartre. He stayed away from the Metro where, early in the Occupation, several murders of German soldiers had occurred. The resulting massacre of innocent bystanders also drew into the Gestapo dragnet the leaders of two Resistance cells. Carl had stayed alive and free because, in general, he was cautious and, more importantly, he behaved like any other Parisian who cooperated passively with the Occupation authorities.

Pierre's bicycle was a big improvement on walking. He had been so intent on completing his mission that the coming pleasure of an afternoon with Danielle didn't occur to him until he was peddling up the Butte above the crowded place Clichy.

He was not the kind of man who placed pleasure above responsibility, and he despised the ruttish woman Danielle had become. But she had useful information to leak out, and she made few demands on him except for her teasing efforts to entice him into her Communist cell.

He brought the bicycle into the dark, cool courtyard, parked it against a wall and climbed the five flights of sloping wooden stairs to Danielle's room beside the turkish toilet used by the four house-holds on that floor. Danielle was proud of her room with its window giving a southwesterly view of Paris and, more immediately, of the street below.

Carl tapped his knuckles lightly on the wooden door just above the printed cardboard notice; "Mlle. D. deBrett." From habit he walked in, got tangled as always in the heavy crimson drapery that formed an entrance foyer about two feet square. His entanglement provided a minute for Danielle to tumble off her couch, pull down her slip, the only thing she was wearing, and laugh at the terror of the young German soldier who was with her.

Carl recovered quickly enough to notice the boy's discomfiture. He looked eighteen and couldn't be over twenty. He pulled his green tunic together and tried to put his pants into some kind of order while stammering in German. Carl reassured him in the same language.

"You need not concern yourself. Mademoiselle has no husband."

The young German grinned shyly and offered to shake hands. Carl accepted. He could see that Danielle was enjoying the scene and felt a surprising urge to spare the boy's feelings.

In the doorway, having eluded the trap of the crimson drapery, the German clicked his heels, bowed stiffly, raised his arm with rapid "Heil Hitler!," and marched out.

Danielle strutted around Carl, mimicking her recent bedfellow.

"Heil 'itler! Heil 'itler, Herr Friedrich!" She

stopped behind him, clicked her bare heels, and tickled the nape of his neck. "Why aren't you jealous, you disgusting Gaullist? You bourgeois crypto-Fascist."

Usually her sexual exuberance overwhelmed him at first, and he pretended to ignore her prose-lytizing. Now and then, his sister Jany accused him of being shy, a trait he indignantly denied. He was a proud man, always afraid of being repulsed, or worse, laughed at. He could never forget that he had been born a bastard.

But such matters were easily mislaid when he and Danielle made love. He reached for her, held her body still, no easy job, and kissed her on the mouth. As always, it was like entering a warm, wet cave. A part of him enjoyed the sensation which quickly aroused his body, so that every visit to her couch was an event. She drew him over to the couch, with its disheveled green coverlet.

"Quick, quick! Do not let me wait, Carl *chèri*. I have work to do. Messages to run."

If she would only pretend. Just once, let him think it meant something to her besides a tempo-rary thrill, a cheap orgasm. He went down on her accommodating body, but just as he was working to a climax, aided by her skilled fingers, she mur-mured dreamily, "We make this special today, *mon amour*. Tomorrow, we may both be dead, isn't it so?"

It was not the way to guarantee an orgasm. At the same time his mind was alerted by the com-ment. Had her friends planned something for to-morrow? In his excitement he carried on, satisfying her, but aware that once this sexual mood left her, she would be more discreet in her talk.

They lay quietly together for a few moments before Carl caught her up and began to fondle her again, gazing into her dark eyes with what he hoped was a look of sincerity.

"Why must we die? Let the rest of them go. Your friends and mine. Must we care?"

Her wide lips parted in her cat-grin, but her voice still held the remnants of her sexual dream.

"Your friends are too late, *chèri*. You have not organized. My friends rise tomorrow. By nightfall the hammer and sickle will fly over half the public buildings of Paris. To the barricades! That's the cry you'll hear tomorrow. We are the true children of 1789 and 1830, and 1848 and 1871. Isn't it glorious? You will have a part in it, you know. All Frenchmen. But it is we who will win it for you — and our cause."

He couldn't prevent a slightly betraying breath of shock but managed to turn it to good account by bending over her body again, kissing each of her eyelids.

"Then you have beaten us to the prize. France will be yours. But you and I? Tomorrow night. Again."

"I know your people. The Gaullists are Frenchmen. They will fight beside us at the barricades, as we would have fought beside you if you had moved first. Come, *chèri*. Taste me."

Her own command aroused her. He did the most difficult acting of his life and remained with her another half hour, before he felt he could safely leave without arousing her suspicions.

Though he lay quietly beside her again, softly stroking her hair, he was frantic to go. He couldn't afford to wait until he got back to the telephone in the Café St. Just. He would have to get the information to the Old One from somewhere in the Montmartre district, and it had to be without Danielle's knowledge. This last was of supreme importance. If she guessed that there was still time to organize the democratic cells of the Resistance, he would be dead in minutes.

He looked down at her, aware that she was still somnolent, dreaming of their sexual moments. A pillow was near his hand. In seconds it could be all over for her and he could warn the Old One. The alternative? She had boasted that her comrades would repeat the violence of those bloody former times, the Great Revolution, the second of 1848, and third, the Commune of 1871.

All he could see of tomorrow's uprising by the Communists without the help of Allied troops was the final destruction of Paris. And if they won, they would rule France.

Either way promised disaster.

The knuckles of his right hand touched the pillow. Staring at her face, slightly bloated after their recent lovemaking, he became aware of his fingers curling up into his palm. Almost without his volition, they had revolted against his thoughts.

He kissed her once more, an attempt to wipe out the memory of these last few minutes when he had considered murder. He moved slowly. He didn't want to alert her if he could help it.

"What?" she said, stirring, "Going so soon?"

"I must. That damned Boche has his eye on my

252

sister. If I don't keep her in sight always, von Leidersdorf may try something."

"But yes. The little virgin."

She laughed, a raucous, coarse sound that set his teeth on edge. If she had made that noise a minute earlier, along with the taunt against Jany, the pillow might have been used.

He left her with great calm, promising "Tomorrow night." In the doorway he pretended to entangle himself in the crimson drapery and complained, "You have this accursed thing here to trap your lovers and make them more eager."

She was still laughing when he started down the stairs. With an effort he refrained from running.

There was a telephone in a *charcuterie* along the place de Clichy, and after having purchased two slices of ham he was allowed to make the call. There was no answer at Madame de Souza's office in the big, empty hotel. Now he didn't know what to do. The names of the top Gaullists were known to him. There was a rumor that the famous Chaban-Delmas, one of the general's few intimates, was in Paris, hiding out until he received permission from de Gaulle for the uprising. Something had to be done. He had heard talk about Alexandre Parodi as the top Gaullist representative in Paris, but there was no reason to believe he controlled more than a handful of men and women who happened to believe in de Gaulle.

Carl studied the telephone receiver, his mind whirling. The last colors of a clouded sunset poured in through the open front of the shop, and when he looked out the city seemed to be shrouded in a blood-red light. The heat of the day added a dusty veil to the evening. The sight depressed him. True, it was a typical August night, but to his overcharged imagination it was a foretaste of the days to come, no matter which Resistance organization rose against the Boches.

After devouring the fibrous grain of what they were selling as ham, he rushed out to Pierre's bicycle and pedaled back across town to the First Arrondissement. The rue de la Paix was crowded with German traffic, a few French bicycles, and German pedestrians, busy window-shopping. He rode by. The two big doors of the hotel were closed, and there was no sign of the Old One. He was afraid to wander around behind the building. There would be no legitimate reason for his presence, and if the building were watched, he might inadvertently lead the Gestapo to the Old One's transmission equipment. He knew she changed locations often but the huge, rambling building was her chief haven.

"Now what do I do?" he thought to himself.

He pedaled on through the place Vendome, past the limp, hanging swastika flags outside the Hôtel Ritz, and swung onto his own street. The Café St. Just was full of patrons, mostly men, sipping their aperitifs before wandering home, most of them on foot, to severely rationed meals.

Seeing Carl, Pierre wiped his hands on his wine-stained apron and came out to the curb. Carl cut in, "I've got to reach the Gaullist committee," he said quietly, but fervently. "At least Monsieur Parodi. Immediately."

"I'll contact Parodi. Give me the message.

Come back behind the bar. And be on the watch for lip readers."

Carl supposed he was joking but couldn't be sure. He blurted out the explosive news.

"The Communists are rising tomorrow."

"Name of God! And where are the Allied armies?"

"That isn't the worst of it. If things get too rough, the Boche will blow up the entire city."

"Didn't the Old One say de Gaulle would send French troops, no matter what the Allies do?"

"Saying and sending are two different things," Carl reminded him. "Can you get through to the Gaullist committee?"

"I have a friend in the police." Carl looked at him. Pierre smiled grimly. "Our police. They talk of taking over the Prefecture. I'll call Sebastiani. A Corsican. He's one of the organizers of something called *Honneur de la Police*. About thirteen or fourteen hundred members. They're ready and willing to act against the Boche, just waiting for the word."

"Thank God. I'll leave it to you. I've been on the edge for the last two hours. I'm going up to the flat to get a little rest."

"You'll have it, friend. There's no one home."

Carl stopped suddenly, with the cold sensation of something worse to come. "It's only minutes until curfew. Where did they go?"

Pierre shrugged, anxious to make his first phone call to the men who might save Paris. Individual problems were of little importance at such a time.

"They got a call here in the café. They whispered a bit, argued about it, and Mademoiselle left. I saw your cousin follow her."

"Followed!"

"Quiet . . . *merde*. I must be on duty. I'll try head-quarters now. Don't worry, your cousin will get Mademoiselle back before curfew. He's quick on his feet."

Carl went out on the now deserted street. He looked up and down past ancient, blacked-out buildings that had seen the tumbrils driven past long ago toward the rue Royale and the guillotine. No one was in sight.

In the distance a German patrol car turned onto the street across the place du Théâtre Français.

He took out his watch. What could have called Jany out at this hour?

Curfew started.

# Chapter Seventeen

While Carl was hurrying down the stairs on his way to Danielle deBrett, Tony examined his hand as if he had never seen it before. He caught Jany watching him and showed her his palm, whimsically.

"I guess I gave my word. He's the first fellow who ever cared enough about my honor to bet on it."

She smiled and went on ironing, moving her lovely young arm back and forth, unconsciously seductive. More graceful than she knew.

"Carl is trusting and honorable himself. I think at times he inspires it in others, when he wants to."

"You love him very much, don't you?" He was closer now, not touching her, but close enough so that the iron could become a lethal weapon. She ran it within half an inch of the heel of his hand, giggled, and brought the iron back to the stove, trading it for its heated twin.

"Of course I love Carl. I never had a father, and Maman died three years ago. Carl has been everything to me." She looked up and asked him a question so suddenly that he was taken by surprise. "Do you love that beautiful movie star you're married to?"

This made him uncomfortable, but he did her the justice of answering truthfully.

"I thought I did. My cousin Alec and I have always known, sometimes dated the same girls.

Eden and Alec have been friends since they were kids. Even the girl Alec eventually married . . ." He finished lamely, "Come to think of it, Alec also knew her first."

"But you both loved her? This girl your cousin married?"

Feeling more and more uncomfortable, he shrugged off his none-too-nice memories of Heather Burkett as a precocious young girl who had shamelessly invited him to make love to her. He had obliged. Luckily for him, she then went after the man who really adored her, his cousin Alec.

"I wouldn't call it love."

"And your wife?"

He *had* loved Eden. She was unconquerable, independent. He had always suspected she and his father had something going between them during the attempted rescue of Leo Prysing's relatives at the time of the Nazi takeover of Austria. Perhaps that, too, made the conquest of Eden important — to succeed where his father had failed.

But there were no ulterior motives in his passion for Eden after their marriage, especially following Andrea's birth. During his long weeks of recuperation after Pearl Harbor, something happened to the Tony Lombard who had lived and loved freely. He began to want different things from life, among them a wife who stayed home, took care of Andrea, and thought of Tony as the center of her life, at least emotionally.

"Of course I love my wife," he blurted out finally. "It's just that I'm *in* love with . . . never mind. I shouldn't have said anything. I have to straighten things out first."

She kept ironing the same dress panel over and over, not looking at him. They were both quiet for a few moments until finally their eyes met.

"I don't think we should talk about love. You belong to Miss Ware."

"I don't *belong* to anyone, except myself. Besides, there's always divorce."

"But divorce is a sin. Don't you know that?"

"Not in my religion. Besides, what do Catholics do when they find they've married the wrong person?"

"There are annulments occasionally. But divorce — never."

"Then what are we to do?"

"I don't know. I can't think of it. I mustn't."

He even loved this about her, her inflexibility and, to him, her old-fashioned religious scruples. Watching her being so earnest and vulnerable when she had so little to gain, he longed to take her in his arms. She seemed to be concentrating intently on a neatly ironed surface when he saw that it was gradually becoming spotted with her tears. Unable to hold himself back any longer, he reached for her.

"Don't cry, Jany, don't," he said, wrapping one of his arms tightly around her waist. He was keenly aware of her soft, warm flesh. How dear she was! Could he bear to live without her? His other hand moved slowly over her hair with long, tender strokes. "Don't cry, sweetheart. We'll work it out."

Belatedly, she protested, trying to free her arm from his embrace in order to continue her work. He suspected that she didn't mind his affection, but was looking for a diversion to avoid admitting her own — in her mind — forbidden feelings.

"We promised Carl."

Tony had to admit to himself that he wasn't used to being on his honor. In fact Tony had never thought of "honor" as anything more than a stuffy, dated notion practiced in the nineteenth century, like the Light Brigade or something. Resigned to being "honorable," he let her go. Dropping his hand to the improvised ironing board, his knuckles scraped against the iron, making him start slightly.

Jany, thinking she caused the burn, cried out and began to fuss over his hand. Tony thought that he'd never enjoyed pain so much. Feeling guilty over his own pleasure from her attention, he dismissed the burn casually.

"It's nothing, really."

"You are so strong."

She rubbed some of her precious cooking lard on the burn and then, to Tony's surprise, bent her head and kissed it.

At that moment someone knocked at the door. Though slightly disgruntled at the interruption, Tony thought that with all that business about honor, it was just as well. Jany started to the door but he stopped her.

"It may be that damned Hun. Let me answer it."

On seeing the door open Pierre St. Just bellowed from the stair landing, "Telephone for Mademoiselle."

Jany immediately assumed the worst. "Something's wrong — it must be Carl."

"I'll go with you."

"Yes, please do."

She ran down the stairs almost on the heels of St. Just. He waved her behind the bar to the telephone while Tony remained only a step or two away, aware that the few remaining patrons were watching the pretty blonde girl with interest. Two German soldiers at a table on the sidewalk drank as if they had all the time in the world, and perhaps they did. It was the French inside who kept checking the time with those who had watches — less than an hour until curfew.

Jany had a quizzical look on her face after answering the phone. "It's someone Carl knows," she whispered, glancing up at Tony. He could barely hear her. "Some woman called the Old One. She wants to give me a message for him."

"Resistance?"

She nodded, then turned back to the receiver. "Carl isn't here. Our cousin, Antoine Lenoir, is also one of you."

The harsh, rasping, aged voice surprised her with its cursing. "He must do, then. I've hurt my arm. It's broken, I think. There are messages. They are waiting to hear in London." The old woman groaned, obviously in pain, "You and Lenoir will have to do. Get here quickly. You understand?"

"Carl should be back any minute," Jany said, frightened.

"*Now*. Name of God! There is no time to waste. You are needed now, both of you." The harsh voice was broken by another groan as the woman tried to catch her breath. Jany's heart responded to the woman's misery.

"We will come at once. But we must get back by curfew."

"Devil take the curfew. I'll be waiting." The line went dead.

Jany motioned Tony out to the street, past the two young German soldiers who regarded them with curiosity.

"Better hurry, *Franzosen*," one of them called out. "You will be caught out after curfew, *nein?*"

Tony took her arm and tried to keep her from running. The street was already dark and beginning to look deserted.

"Where is it? How far?"

"An old hotel on the rue de la Paix. It's very large. They meant to remake it into a building of offices, but the war came and nothing was done. An old lady, Madame de Souza, is the concierge. Carl tells me she is a very courageous woman. Tony, she's hurt. We must help her in any way we can."

"Do we enter the street through the place Vendôme?"

"No. To do that we would have to pass the Hôtel Ritz. It is one of the Boche headquarters. I have a better way, behind the marché St. Honore and into a passage near the building. I used to play in all these courtyards and alleyways as a child."

He moved his arm to her waist, helping her up over a curb. "This Madame de Souza isn't the only brave woman in Paris," he said, with not a little pride in his voice.

Nervous and excited as she was, she smiled shyly at him. "I am Carl's sister. I owe it to him. My father was brave too. He was an anti-Nazi. Some SS men beat him up on the street in Berlin and killed him."

He began to feel uncomfortable whenever she or Carl mentioned their father's death. He tried to change the subject but she went on anyway. "He was once a movie actor. The great cinema producer, Leo Prysing, did a broadcast about how brave my father was." She cocked her head to one side reflectively. "I'm sorry now that I didn't like him. My father, I mean."

He couldn't help laughing at her sweet sincerity.

Jany grinned reluctantly. "Carl has always wanted to see the famous Prysing film about the attempt to rescue Mr. Prysing's family. He says there may be a character like father in it. *Journey*, it's called. But it couldn't be shown in Paris in 1939 because it was anti-Nazi and we were neutral then."

"You wouldn't have liked it."

She was leading the way through a tiny, foul-smelling court behind a vegetable store but the sharp way he bit off that absurd opinion made her stare up at him. She didn't bother to ask why, assuming it was for a reason he might not want to talk about . . . maybe because his wife was in it . . .

"Where to next?" he asked, breaking the momentarily awkward silence.

"Between the houses. That dark passage over there." She pulled him along until the passage brought them within half a block of Madame de Souza's building. No one seemed to be watching them, but it was hard to tell. Much of the street was lost in the deep shadows of dusk.

"Here we are," she whispered.

The enormous bulk of the building surprised him. It seemed to be a series of houses, all with the requisite mansard roofs and long, narrow windows opening out onto minuscule balconies. Not one light shone behind the entire facade. The double doors were impressive enough for it to house the president of the republic, or what passed for that position in Vichy France.

What father could do with this, he thought. He'd have it whipped into shape and sold as another Waldorf, or maybe convert it into a gigantic department store . . .

It annoyed him that he should automatically give his father credit for what had been his own idea, but it was the story of his life. Sooner or later, he would have to beat Steve Lombard at something.

Approaching the massive doors, Jany motioned him ahead to try them.

He pulled on the huge handles, both at once. To his surprise they opened with reasonable silence — no squeaking hinges. They opened inward onto a large foyer with the concierge's tiny office to the left side, along with the main staircase. Straight ahead, closing off an entrance and another lobby at the far end, was a desolate-looking garden, enclosed by the four walls of the building. Tony wondered why he could see the scrubby plants so clearly in one particular spot. The climbing flowers and vines seemed to be indirectly lighted.

Tony gave the concierge's office a quick once-over, but found nothing but one unexpected object, an English "torch." With the power cut off at this hour the Old One would surely need her flashlight. He flipped it on, but couldn't get it to work. Dead batteries, he decided.

"Perhaps we should look for her while there's still a little light," Jany suggested logically. She motioned to the garden and started toward the glass doors, spotting the first faint glow from the far corner. Obviously, it was a second flashlight that had been dropped — but by whom? Tony put his hand over hers as she reached for one of the doors.

"Don't."

"She needs help. I think I see her over there by the clematis vine. She must have dropped her torch." They quickly crossed over the small area for a closer look.

The flashlight had fallen into an herbaceous border, giving off an eerie green glow. Jany reached down for the light and was caught slightly off-balance when it was jerked suddenly out of its place in the weeds. Amaranth flowers growing against the wall drooped over the hand that held it like long, bloody chains. Tony made a grab for Jany, just in time.

The flashlight shone in her face, making her blink. Behind the light Tony made out the stocky figure and narrow, sinister-looking eyes of Unterofficier Hansherger, Colonel von Leidersdorf's aide. The light he held was powerful and blinding, probably twice as strong as the useless flashlight in Tony's pocket.

Tony found only one hopeful sign at this moment. Hansberger seemed to be alone. But his brown leather holster-flap was unfastened and there was no arguing with the heavy German pistol in his right hand. His grin was plastered on, and he was obviously intent on making the most of their predicament. Tony couldn't help but notice that he was far more interested in the girl's reaction than in his.

"You startled me, fraulein. You were much quicker than I thought. Such a German quality, promptness. An inheritance from your father, no doubt."

Tony felt his muscles tense as the realization swept over him that Madame de Souza's call was a trap. With a good deal of effort he forced himself to remain cool. "The phone call came from you, I take it."

"Not difficult. My colonel had his suspicions of the old hag. And of your brother, fraulein. I had a little idea while the colonel was detained and decided to come here. An excellent move, no? I heard the old hag making her transmission to London."

"What have you done with her?" Jany asked in a low voice.

"The hag will not again betray us. I left her body upstairs with her sending equipment. A nice touch, no?" He waved the flashlight, the glow briefly illuminating the garden. "I have located her codes, here under these vines. They mention you, *mein Herr.* And the Fraulein's brother. But I am not the Gestapo, for which you will thank me."

His remark gave Tony a glimmer of hope. There was in it the suggestion of a deal.

"They don't know about Carl and Monsieur Tony? You won't tell them?" Jany whispered.

"Not yet, fraulein. The dead woman was an important British agent. Killing her was my patriotic duty. Then I thought, maybe my colonel does a great favor for this lovely fraulein. From the Gestapo he saves her brother and this — cousin. Surely my colonel would be grateful to me for my little efforts, no, Herr Lombard?"

His smile broadened slowly as he saw how the sound of his name struck Tony. "The old woman transmitted the news of Herr Lombard to London. He is masquerading as a Frenchman, this American spy. As you know, a crime punishable by death."

It came at last. Tony had a creeping fear of just what this bargain would entail. Hansberger must be trying to ingratiate himself with the colonel by offering him Jany in some kind of trade for the safety of those she loved.

"Now, look here," he began, hoping to nip it in the bud before it was spelled out to Jany. "If you think —"

"You see, Herr Lombard, the colonel is being ordered home to the Reich on sick leave. He has difficulty accepting the fact that his only daughter is dead. She was his whole life. I'm sure you understand."

"Oh!" Jany murmured, sympathetic in spite of herself. "How did she die?"

"A firebombing in Berlin. Herr Himmler told the colonel of the loss. He did not put it in very kind terms. The colonel said things to Herr Himmler that were unwise, and he has been in disgrace since. Fraulein, he wishes to save you from what is coming to Paris. It is to save you that he wishes to take you home to the Reich."

Jany spoke before Tony could vent the anger she saw building in him.

"What will happen to my brother and my cousin, monsieur?"

The pistol wavered slightly. Evidently the German thought she was about to agree to his offer.

"My colonel is prepared to turn them over to the army for internment. A *stalag* — that is to say, a prisoner-of-war camp. He does not yet know of Herr Lombard's true identity. But I myself am prepared to forget what I learned tonight if the fraulein will leave tomorrow with the colonel."

"How can you leave, monsieur?" Jany asked in her sweetest, most innocent voice. "The Allies are blowing up the railroads and the French rail workers have gone on strike."

He waved this aside, though the pistol went dangerously close to Jany. "Fraulein, Fortress Europe is not to be penetrated by a few lucky hits, or by a hundred Frenchmen who will be shipped to Bergen-Belsen for their treason to the Reich. The colonel will be driven home to the Fatherland. That is understood."

"Where is he now?" Tony asked, playing for time and looking for a chance that might give him the upper hand.

"At the Hôtel Meurice. Awaiting an interview with the commander of Gross-Paris, General von Choltitz. The general is busy with matters of security. There is talk of an uprising among the Communist lice over the weekend. Before that happens we will blow up every stone of Paris, Herr Lombard."

To Jany he added, lowering his pistol an inch or two, "You will be safe in the Fatherland when Paris is destroyed. Even your brother and this one will be safe. It is better than to give them into the hands of the Gestapo. Think about it, fraulein."

"I wouldn't be so sure," Tony said harshly. "My hunch is he plans to turn Carl and me over to them no matter what you do, Jany. Don't you see that? There is no bargaining with him. You heard how he boasts of what he did to Madame de Souza."

"I must do what he says. It is your only chance, and Carl's. I must go."

Tony knew his obvious anger would only keep the bastard on guard. He tried to relax and made a pretense of giving up, but it went against his grain.

"If you really want to oblige Jany why not just give Carl and me twenty-four hours? No one needs to know what became of us."

"Not possible. I could not explain to my colonel. As I said, he has suspected you and the fraulein's brother for some time. It is his wish that you be transferred as prisoners of war. Nothing better is possible. And if I were to reveal your true identity, you would not do even so well. Come along." He motioned with the big flashlight.

"We're prisoners now," Tony muttered resignedly. "It won't get any better . . . I suppose it's out of your hands."

"You're a very sensible man," Hansberger said. Contempt curled his lips and Tony longed to smash that grin into his fat face.

Jany gave Tony a quick, furtive glance. She sensed that the crucial moment was at hand. He might have fooled Hansberger but she knew better. She moved closer to the German in a show of innocent acquiescence.

"It is sad about the daughter of the colonel. I had no idea. But suppose I do not like Germany?"

"You will, fraulein. One may obtain better food there. A better life. The oberstlieutenant comes from an excellent family. There is money." He abruptly turned to Tony with a sudden change of heart. "You, Lombard — go before me. The Gestapo will love your insolence."

Tony took another step to pass Hansberger. The German was watching his right hand with the pistol. Tony had the dead flashlight in his left pocket. His arm, casually bent at the elbow, brushed against his pocket while his fingers moved inside with what he considered to be agonizing slowness.

An instant later his lightning strike surprised even himself. With the edge of the flashlight he caught Hansberger across the head, just above the left ear. It carried with it every nervous ounce of his strength. The German's flashlight clattered to the floor. Hansberger stood there staring ahead, his head swaying on his thick neck, his fingers and palm working to position the pistol, as if his muscles reacted automatically.

For a few terrible seconds Tony and Jany thought he was unhurt. He must have a skull of marble. Jany's face, oddly illuminated by the fallen light, looked white and old. Tony swung Madame de Souza's flashlight again, landing another solid blow to the head. Jany cried out.

"Enough, Tony! Wait — no need."

Hansberger took two steps, then collapsed. Tony lowered his arm but kept the weapon handy as he knelt to pick up Hansberger's pistol. Jany leaned against the wall, staring at the unconscious man.

"Mother of God! I hope he's dead. He must be dead."

Tony knew that only unmitigated desperation would have drawn such a prayer from her. He felt for Hansberger's pulse, his neck, his heart. Jany took the light and flashed it on the body. A thread of blood trailed down behind the German's left ear.

It was several minutes before they could be sure he was dead. Beyond relief, Tony's reaction over the first man he had ever murdered was indifference. Moral questions failed to move him while his own life was at stake.

"Let's get out."

"But we must find Madame's body."

"We have no time." He saw her pained reaction and agreed, but there was a bothersome itch where the stitches had scarred his neck, and he rubbed the ridge of scars absently. Jany offered another, better idea with a calmness that impressed him.

"I'll take the transmission codes he stole. They mustn't find them."

Ashamed that he hadn't thought of this vital matter, he found the moldy tin cylinder in the dead man's pistol holster. It contained a tiny roll of paper, less than an inch wide. He gave it to Jany and hesitated about taking the pistol itself.

"No! They can trace it," she warned him.

He had just reached for it, still debating, when she pinched his arm. He looked up. Out on the sidewalk shadows moved past the doors.

Then a French voice was heard. "I tell you, it's never open. Not at this hour, after curfew. I know the old woman well."

Jany froze. "Police."

It was all over now. There would be no talking their way out of this. They stared at the door. First one, then a second *agent de police* stuck his head in.

The flashlight in Tony's hand illuminated the scene to its full effect: a man and woman kneeling over the body of a German soldier, apparently rifling his pockets.

What followed was the longest silence in Tony's memory. The shorter of the two *agents* spoke finally, in a conversational tone, to his comrade.

"Sebastiani says it's now or never. Why dawdle here? You want to give the Boches a chance to stop us? Where is your patriotism, man?"

The taller one took his stiff, billed cap off, ruffled up his grizzled hair, set his cap back on and, to Tony's amazement, looked straight at him and winked.

"One less for us to fight tomorrow, I see. Go home, you two. And avoid the patrols. We may need you in the fighting."

Tony was so tense he could barely raise his hand in a salute.

"Thank you, monsieur. We are not what it looks like. We were tricked. You see —"

The *agent* waved him aside. "You detain us. We have work to do. Good night. And take care, after this. We might have been Gestapo."

Jany clasped her hands, but her melodramatic gesture was from the heart. "I will pray for you, messieurs. With all my heart. May the good God be with you."

The short *agent* grinned. "When you see the *tricouleur* snapping above the Prefecture in ten hours . . ."

"Nine," his companion corrected him.

"Then you will know your prayers were answered, mademoiselle."

They both saluted casually and were on their way before Jany and Tony were able to fully recover from their good fortune.

They no longer considered looking for Madame de Souza's body, but took off as quietly as possible, remaining in the deep shadows of the blackout, along the back passages they'd followed only a short time before. Finally they were safely through the rear entrance to the court below the Friedrich flat.

Carl was frantic by this time. Not even the recovery of the transmission codes could soothe him, so upset was he by their close brush and news of the death of his old friend and collaborator. Aside from the friendship involved, Madame de Souza's loss would be a heavy blow to the Allied spy system in Paris. He persisted in repeatedly pointing out their idiocy in answering the plea for help in the first place — there was always a password or coded message to verify the identity of the caller. Madame de Souza, forced into making the call, used neither. He knew, of course, that they had no way of knowing this, but even that failed to dissipate his anger.

Carl refused to speak to Tony even after the two men finally lay down, Tony on the floor and Carl on the lumpy couch, his brief sleep disturbed by nightmarish images.

It was Pierre St. Just who gave them the news the next morning, waking both men out of their dreams of Gestapo agents hammering on the door.

Carl climbed over Tony and made his way across the room to let the café owner in.

"Go and see for yourself, friend," Pierre cried. "Our flag. Flying from the Prefecture de Police as

273

big as life and twice as beautiful. The Boches are shooting at the Prefecture but our boys are answering back. After four dirty years, we are in the fight again!"

Tony opened one eye, then the other, and got up off the floor with a groan. "Okay, *mon capitaine*. Give us your orders and we'll march to hell and back."

"Are the Commies involved?" Carl wanted to know.

"They'll go along with us. They must. But we got to the post first. The Cross of Lorraine beat the hammer and sickle, and I swear to God, we'll beat the swastika too. So it's out to the streets, men. *To the barricades!*"

Even Tony felt a tinge of excitement on hearing the ancient battle cry.

# Chapter Eighteen

As she knew she would, Eden had won out and accompanied Steve on his trip across the Channel, a hazardous undertaking despite the maneuverings of Broome and other top officials on both sides. With only a little irony, Steve and Eden called themselves the "army of Tony's liberation."

They were the only ones who did. As unwanted civilians (pretending to represent stateside newspapers) they were stuck at the tail end of the most dramatic race of their lives. Thanks to General de Gaulle's ultimatum, they were on their way with his troops to liberate Paris, even if it sparked a full-fledged holocaust by the enemy.

Eden tried to understand the annoyance their presence caused the Second Armored Division of the French and, even more so, the Fourth American Infantry.

Despite their success in finding a way across — in itself a miracle — Steve still had nagging doubts about the information furnished by Alec Huntington's mysterious friend, Mr. Broome. The diminutive man might be, as he claimed, a liaison between the Free French committee in London and the British government. But even the Gaullists might not have the latest information on the Friedrich family that Tony was supposed to be staying with.

Eden was simply counting on Steve's instincts, which had made him pull strings to get to France in the first place and then stick like a leech to General LeClerc's headquarters. If anybody got the word to march on Paris it would be LeClerc, a trusted soldier, loyal to the Free French cause. And Steve's instinct had proved right.

But now, closer to his goal, he was growing more and more impatient. "The hell with Paris!" he grumbled, "I'm on my way to save my son. And I don't give a damn if the whole place falls off into the Seine, as long as it doesn't fall on my family." A typical Lombard, Eden thought, bullheaded and single-minded.

Eden was at the wheel of a jeep which brought up the rear of the procession that had split off to enter Paris from the southeast. If the troops hadn't been speeding through the towns and villages of the countryside, they might have enjoyed a Roman triumph. The were saluted, hailed and cheered on by the French as they rumbled over the black Norman soil, then through forests, coppices and farmlands toward their rendezvous with the formidable Wehrmacht.

A cloudburst had soaked Eden's slacks, sweater and pea coat to her skin and sent her fine, flyaway hair crawling across her face. Still, she was immediately recognizable by the American troops. A correspondent in a camion rattled past, then slowed down beside the jeep. He leaned out to yell at her across the equally soaked and disgruntled Steve.

"You're Eden Ware, aren't you? I heard she's around here somewhere."

"Bet your life, pal. How'd you guess?"

He leaned farther out, looking her up and down

and waving both hands in the air while Steve gritted his teeth and watched the fellow's untended steering wheel.

"I'd know you anywhere, Eden," he said grinning and started to drive past.

"Wait!" Eden shouted, leaning on the horn. "Think we'll make it to Paris today? I heard the big guns a while ago."

"The French columns had a lot of action this afternoon. Germans were in solid off to the west of us, but the Frenchies got 'em. Captain Dronne should be pulling into the Paris outskirts in the next couple of hours. There's been a lot of street fighting in the city, but the Prefecture of Police is still holding out. The Jerries burned up the Grand Palais, though, and we got the word that every bridge in Paris is mined. That'll be something interesting, crossing those damned bridges."

She wondered where Tony was. What if he were lying somewhere hurt, without help . . . "Then our men will be hitting the center of the city in the dark."

"Sure thing. Might make it easier."

"Sure hope so. We'll be right behind you all the way," Eden shouted over the drone of the trucks. "I've got a wandering husband in Paris."

"How about that! Give me a call if you don't find him . . ." the soldier hollered back. She shooed him away, and with that he went driving off past the next stream of trucks, cars, tanks and jeeps.

The twosome bumped along behind the procession, each absorbed in special thoughts about Tony and how — and where — they would find him. But other thoughts played on Eden's mind, thoughts she couldn't easily dismiss.

"Steve? What about this family Tony's supposed to be staying with? It's the Friedrichs, isn't it? You don't suppose they could be related to Kurt . . ."

Steve Lombard shrugged. "I suppose it's possible, and if they are, I guess we'll just have to cross that bridge when we get to it."

Eden visibly cringed at his mention of bridges, remembering what the soldier had told them, but she meant to pursue the subject and asked him again what he thought they should do if the family was related to the Kurt Friedrich they had known in Vienna six years ago.

"Look, Eden," he said, resigned to discuss it for the last time with her, "if I had been in Leo's place, and my loved ones had been involved, I just don't know if I would have gone that far and manipulated things the way he did. Leo did what he felt he had to do, and I can't say I would have done the same or differently. Leo's a devious man; I think you know that. Still, I like him, but I've never fooled myself about his darker side. I'm just not one to hold grudges and I don't go in for revenge."

"Except against your father. You and Red were quite a pair."

"I don't see the connection. There was some competition, yes. There wasn't any hatred or real bitterness between my father and me. Any more than there is between Tony and me. You ought to know that."

She did know and was appalled at how little he understood his relationship with his own son. She avoided a Sherman tank that rumbled along with the great Napoleonic victory at Austerlitz painted on its flanks so that all Paris would know the French army had come home, even if they were using borrowed equipment.

"Besides," Steve added, "it's a pretty sure thing that these Friedrichs are French, not Austrian. Let's just try to put that business with Kurt behind us. It's part of an ugly time."

"Like the present."

She scowled ahead into the murky afternoon light, wondering just how soon she could make out the skyline of her beloved Paris. It would be a silhouette, black against a cloudy sky, which was an odd way to view what she thought of as her City of Light.

She wondered if Tony would be changed much after his experience here. He was used to the best. He had never enjoyed roughing it, and she couldn't imagine how he was getting by with very little food, only an hour a day to cook what there was of it, and above all, the company of insular, chauvinistic Parisians whose ways she thought must seem positively medieval to her liberal, easy-going husband. Poor Tony, she thought.

Eden hugged herself in her imagination, re-membering what it was like to have Tony's arms around her, his mouth on hers, his body pressed hard against hers. Wanting him this way suddenly, she speeded up, got a nasty warning from the horn of the jeep in front of her, and dropped back to the pace that seemed so maddeningly slow. These fellows were only going to a war. She was driving to her husband's arms.

Steve, who had handled the jeep most of the night, complained now that he wasn't going to be able to wind down until he saw "the kid" in Paris.

"So make room. I'm taking over again. If you insist, you can have the wheel when we mow 'em down in the Paris streets."

She grinned, wiped her streaked, dirty face and let him climb over her as she shifted to his seat. Bucketing along, the jeep felt hard as nails. Like Steve, she was sure she couldn't rest but she had to admit that Steve looked as handsome as ever sitting there, straight-backed, his still abundant gray hair ruffled in the damp air. General MacArthur's famous "I shall return" could not have been expressed more firmly than Stephen Lombard's vow to rescue his son. It was the very act Tony would hate most — one more time in which Steve was the hero and Tony the recipient of his father's largesse.

She hunched down in her seat, studying Steve's profile and wondering if she would ever have made love to him six years ago had Leo not been in her attic room on the Ile St. Louis that night . . .

She had bumped into Steve accidentally, and they ended up spending a friendly hour together over a cheap bistro supper. Then he walked her home along the quai to her room, where Leo had been waiting.

Her eyes closed tiredly, but she still seemed to see Steve the way he had looked that night. Only this time, Leo was also there in her thoughts.

It must have been — it was March 9, 1938. Leo was trying to explain something to the two of them with a quiet desperation. Evidently Brooke Lombard, then married to Kurt Friedrich, was in Vienna with Leo's brother, Josef, and his wife.

"I'd fly to Vienna myself with a fake passport, but with my face I'd never get out if the Nazis really are marching in. But Steve could go in to bring out his sister. She's Aryan, and it doesn't hurt having a Nazi husband. She could say she's coming to Paris for the spring fashions. I have passports for Josef and Sarah that say they're Mrs. Friedrich's servants, so they, too, must come along. If you can get out before the Germans march in and close the barriers, there should be no trouble. Nothing should happen before Sunday when the Austrian elections are held."

It had been simple as falling off a log. Again, Eden insisted on going along. It was an adventure, and she was an unknown young actress, making an uncertain salary dubbing English in foreign films. If she obliged Leo Prysing in this, she reasoned that he might give her a break in Hollywood.

It was even easier when she and Steve reached Vienna. Poor, addled Brooke Friedrich wanted to get out of Austria. She loved her young husband but she loved her own hide even more. Kurt's strutting around in the uniform of the Nazi party, his drinking bouts at the rallies, and his vehement talk of what they would do to their "enemies" terrified her. She was happy to go gallivanting off to Paris, convinced that her devoted husband would join her as soon as he discovered her absence.

The Nazi armies did not wait for the Sunday elections. They provoked riots and marched into Austria, joining it to the Third Reich, the night of March 10, the night Steve and Eden were to take the Preysings, as Leo's brother spelled his name, out of Austria with Brooke. It was the only time they could leave unnoticed by Kurt Friedrich, who was attending a rally celebrating the *Anschluss*.

At the last minute, with planes grounded, Steve decided they should take the Zurich night train, the last to leave the Greater Reich before all borders were closed.

Eden still had nightmares about that ride . . . the nerve-wracking tension they all shared, hoping they'd successfully eluded Brooke's frightening husband . . . The Swiss border was so tantalizingly close, shrouded in a kind of blue night light . . . but in the ten minutes it took for the Swiss train crew to take over, Josef and Sarah Preysing disappeared from the train.

They died together while being "questioned" in the presence of Hitler's personally appointed gauleiter, Seyss-Inquart.

In almost the same hour Leo and Steve traced the betrayal directly to Kurt Friedrich.

Using his own personal knowledge of Kurt Friedrich, his longtime actor and colleague, Leo Prysing began to devise an exquisite, long-distance revenge that culminated in his famous broadcast, praising Friedrich at a most inopportune time for the Nazi sympathizer. He died, and vengeance had been wrought.

The jeep leaped over a rocky stream bed and Eden was shaken back to the present, startled to find that night was all around them. She began to sit up, then straightened suddenly pointing at the distant skyline against the dark blue sky.

"Paris! We're coming in. Oh, Lord! We may not even find him tonight."

She rummaged in her pants pocket and brought

out the little black-and-white snapshot of Andrea that Randi Lombard had sent to her in London.

"This is a perfect snap — Randi caught her with that mischievous look that's so like Tony. She's her father's daughter, all right. He's going to love this. I can't wait to see him. God, Steve! Suppose those Friedrichs have moved, or he's been hurt, or something."

"We'll find him, all right. I didn't come this far through one hell of an obstacle course for nothing." He was peering ahead. "I thought I knew Paris but I can't make out a thing. It's all black to me."

"No, no! See those sprouting Byzantine domes in the distance? That's Montmartre. And over there's Sacre Coeur. Not my quarter. My haunts were around the Ile St. Louis, in the Seine, behind Notre Dame. Over to the left is the Eiffel Tower. Those damned Nazis! The monuments ought to be lit up."

"Maybe they will be," he reminded her grimly, pointing to the plumes of darkness that were not clouds, spiraling up above the Champs-Elysées. "Must be the Grand Palais, or some other pet monument of yours."

She gulped and was silent. Somewhere in the dark city Tony must be hidden by the family that took him in. She hoped to God they hadn't moved. The Gaullist committee in London had lost contact with their Paris agent, Paix Blanche, who furnished them with the Friedrich information. Paix Blanche was dead, the other Paris agent said. There were no more particulars. Neither Pleyel Violet nor Montpanasse Noir had ever heard of the Friedrichs.

Steve ploughed on, but Eden was aware of sounds that cut into the crackle of tank treads, the distant boom of the big guns and the individual snap and ricochet of rifle fire. It was hard to believe all this had been going on within the city itself for almost a week.

She began to listen carefully, then shook her head. To her surprise, Steve guessed what she was doing.

"If you're listening for the hum of city life, forget it, but try listening for the cheers. I'll bet you Captain Dronne and the French Second Armored are zipping into the city proper right now. Hear that?"

It was hard to tell, the bedraggled procession itself made such a noise. But in place of the familiar hum she associated with great cities, she seemed to hear the rise and fall of sound that was the cheering of the people of the suburb as they passed through.

They must have rushed out in the twilight, only half-believing, to see what had been forbidden for four years, the tanks with familiar French words painted on their flanks, and the *tricouleur,* everything roaring past, headed toward the Seine and the Hôtel de Ville, the city hall of Paris.

The French units manning American tanks, American units in jeeps, tanks, camions, staff cars, all ahead of the Lombard jeep, passed from the suburbs into the city of Paris. Those at the head of the procession roared ahead, hardly slowing before the delirious enthusiasm of the district's populace. It was not a rich district, not even bourgeois. It gave these inhabitants of the quarter a special pride that they were the first to see what they were sure would be the victors.

Other vehicles slowed to a crawl with men and women alike, but mostly women, hanging all over tanks and jeeps. Every visible part of the liberators seemed to be covered with lipstick or flowers in gratitude for their arrival.

In ordinary times Steve Lombard might have enjoyed the attention. But he was in a hurry now, and just ahead, between him and his son, were the mined bridges of the Seine where anything could happen.

Eden too, in her mannish outfit and with her boyish figure, got her share of attention from the happy young girls, waving and shouting. She took it all with a grin so as not to disappoint them, though she did urge Steve to push on faster.

Eden was torn by hopes and fears. By hopes because the enemy seemed to be resisting only in pockets, around the Austerlitz Station and the Luxembourg Palace where the Luftwaffe had its headquarters. Her fears were just beginning to surface. Who had gotten word of Tony's safety to London in the first place? If the Friedrichs were involved with the Resistance, they risked Tony's life as well as their own. It seemed unlikely, but who could be sure?

They pushed on through the streets of Paris, rattling through quarters long familiar to Eden. She was amazed that there were so few changes after four years of war and Occupation. The café in the middle of a block near the Jardin des Plantes was still open, with two tipsy tables and wicker chairs out on the terrasse. The patrons were inside, probably because of the gunfire at the gare d'Austerlitz, but Eden could picture in her mind the old gray cat that used to lie in the middle of the floor by the zinc bar. Everyone had to walk around him. There was never any question of his moving.

She wondered aloud if the fat old tomcat was still there.

Steve's reply shocked her. "I doubt it. It's probably been eaten by now."

It was an offhanded remark, but somehow his casual words brought the reality of the Paris Occupation home to her as nothing else had. She was so upset she felt only numbness when Steve pulled up on the quai and brought the jeep to a stop.

"Shall we test whether the bridge is going to blow?"

"We've got to get to the Right Bank somehow. I'm not that good a swimmer. Besides, no one crossing before us has hit anything . . yet," she added as an afterthought.

Sniper fire behind them at the gare d'Austerlitz gave the strongest inducement. The jeep leaped forward onto the pont d'Austerlitz.

Slowly making their way across, Steve muttered, "Maybe the German commander of Paris appreciates the finer things of life. It looks like we're going to make it."

But he got no answer from Eden, who sat tensely beside him. She was looking out at the dark waters of the Seine, sparkling and pure as they never looked by day, hoping he hadn't spoken too soon.

# Chapter Nineteen

While his wife bounced along in a jeep toward the gates of Paris and Jany tended to the café upstairs, Tony was learning how to make Molotov cocktails.

Not being mechanically inclined, he took it on himself to supervise the operations in Pierre St. Just's wine cellar.

"Carl, you take care of the acid. St. Just just handles the chloride."

"Chlorate," the café man corrected him.

"And I'll empty the wine bottles. Personally."

"No, you don't." Carl's sense of humor did not cover such ticklish moments as the making of a Molotov cocktail.

But St. Just grinned at Tony. "Good thing I've watered down some of these bottles I reserve for the Boches."

Carl lined up the stack of collaborationist newspapers which would envelop the bottles. "Well, then. We've all had our laugh. Now, in the name of God and all the saints, get on!"

Their high spirits slightly dampened, Tony and St. Just got back to work. "At last, a suitable use for these —" the café owner remarked as he handled sheets of the collaborationist paper and the potassium chlorate.

"Wipers?" Tony suggested in English, referring to the papers.

"Wipers? What is this word *wipers?*" A slow

smile crossed St. Just's face. "Oh, I think I understand." St. Just threw a bottle to Carl who caught it and was amused for the first time when he saw the look on Tony's face, who evidently thought the bottle was full of potential explosives.

"You played the American baseball," Carl said good-naturedly, "you should be very good for throwing the Molotov cocktail."

"No. I played the football. And I was a hell of a lot quicker at a sneak through center than I was as a pass receiver."

St. Just shook his head. "I will never comprehend this American-English . . . how many bottles do we fill?"

"How many Boches in Paris?" Carl replied.

Tony uncorked another wine bottle, tipped it up and drank from the dusty neck. He passed it to Carl who likewise took a long swig and handed it on to St. Just. The café owner drank, then spat out the beaujolais.

"Damnation to it! One of the watered ones."

They all laughed and then did not look at each other as they worked. They understood that the death they held in their hands cemented this odd comradeship. It was a moment in time that could never return.

The bottles containing the homemade explosives lined up rapidly. They were removed at intervals by half a dozen chunky, sinister-looking men in berets and blue smocks who merely grunted as each took one or two of them back up the stairs with great care. Tony did not ask what part of the city would be the recipient of their efforts, but even in the St. Just cellar he could hear the explosions that tore at streets, German tanks and patrols.

It was one thing to kill Unterofficier Hansberger out of desperation, but it chilled him to think of all the unknown French and German soldiers being blown up, many of whom had nothing to do with the horrors of the Occupation.

Whenever this remorse nibbled at him, he took another pull at a dusty bottle and his conscience was lulled to sleep.

Tony and his companions were not drunk when they made their way out of the wine cellar into the cloudy, humid daylight, but their spirits were buoyed enough that they felt they could personally conquer all Hitler's legions.

Rumors had been repeated for the last week that the Allies were on their way. By this time Tony was cheerfully cynical, and even Carl, with his passionate belief in the Gaullist cause, had begun to lose faith in outside rescue. The police in the Prefecture still held out, but only with enormous difficulty and losses. Sporadic fighting elsewhere had produced nothing but death and crowded hospital facilities for both the French and the Occupation forces. Carl and Tony had worked throughout the week getting weapons to St. Just's friend Sebastian for the Prefecture, even smuggling in every handgun that had been tucked away for future use by the thrifty citizens of Paris.

The Friedrichs' biggest handicap was the ubiquitous Lieutenant Colonel von Leidersdorf who appeared at least once a day between his own duties, pleading that Jany be allowed to leave the city with him at the next cease-fire.

He was not a man who found it easy to beg, and

he soon resorted to blackmail, reminding them that, due to the "uprising of terrorists," his sick leave had been temporarily canceled. He remained at the beck and call of Heinrich Himmler's SS, though his ultimate superior was still the German army commander of Paris.

"And you will remember, fraulein, the murder of my aide, Unterofficier Hansberger, has been constantly on my mind. A hint to the wise — it is also on the minds of the Gestapo. If I were to confide my suspicions, or the fact that I have personally seen your brother visit a treacherous British agent in the building in which my aide was murdered, the Gestapo would certainly be interested."

Both Tony and Carl were well aware that it wasn't the kindness of the colonel's heart which kept him from having Carl arrested. He was probably afraid Jany herself was involved, and didn't want to chance that.

The so-called uprising of terrorists which had kept the Occupation forces busy during the past six days was a little like needling a fierce dog. Very little had been won for the Resistance except for the temporary alliance of the Democratic and Communist leaders, who knew their constant bickering would help no one but the führer. The Prefecture still remained in the hands of the Resistance, and their constant action kept the German troops on the go.

General von Choltitz, the commander of Gross-Paris, in his headquarters at the Hôtel Meurice, did not seem worried. The Gestapo was still up to its old tricks on the rue des Saussies. But one interesting development had been noted.

Someone said that at SS headquarters, even in the Gestapo itself, papers were being burned.

Tony knew what that could mean. He remembered Chiye Akina's boyfriend coming home to the Ware house that last peaceful Saturday before Pearl Harbor, and remarking casually that a lot of burning was going on at the Japanese Consulate.

Maybe there was something the Gestapo knew that threatened them in Paris. Whether there was or not, Paris got a great deal of comfort out of the story.

Only a few like Madame Charpentier confided less comforting thoughts. "Does the Gestapo expect Paris to be bombed, do you think, monsieur?" she asked Tony one day. "Or is Paris to be blown up by the Boches themselves?"

Neither possibility was one Tony wanted to contemplate.

So he and Carl emerged from St. Just's wine cellar as lighthearted as a bottle of beaujolais could make them, just in time to see their friend going off in a green Wehrmacht uniform and helmet. They learned that he was headed for the distant place de la Republique where units of the German army were defending their barracks against Resistance fighters, chiefly Communist. St. Just's uniform would get him to Republique if he avoided some of his own Molotov cocktails, but he was in no mood to be shot as a Boche. He wore a wrinkled blue smock beneath his jacket.

"I'll make the big change before our friends see me," he said, obviously pleased with himself.

Tony needled Carl as St. Just straddled his bicycle.

"I thought you and the Reds were deadly enemies. Here is Pierre, racing off to join them."

It was St. Just who reminded him, "When we've kicked out the Boches, we'll get to them. Meanwhile, we're allies."

"See you at Republique."

St. Just rode away, pumping madly.

Tony and Carl were starting out on foot toward the fighting in front of the opera house when Jany called to them from the café. She had demanded to do her part and was taking St. Just's place behind the bar for the sparse afternoon trade. Her eyes looked anxious as she gave them a message in a low voice.

"An actor from the Comédie-Française called. He needs you. He said, 'You will play your roles for an appreciative audience.' Must you go? Both of you?"

Carl came back to her from the curb. He kissed her left temple. "Try not to worry, *chèrie*. It is a necessary thing."

Tony watched. He ached to follow Carl's lead, to try and reassure her gently. Instead, he gave her a big smile and tried to look encouraging. "Don't worry. I'll bring him back safe and sound." Then he joined Carl, who didn't look back as he started up the street toward the place du Théâtre-Français.

There was a point where the old rue St. Honore met the wide avenue de l'Opera and the celebrated Comédie-Française, and within a block, the vast expanse of the Louvre itself. Tony was surprised to see that members of the theater had taken to the streets, echoing Carl with the ancient cry, "*Aux barricades!*" and setting up their own barriers. Many Broadway stars were in the American war effort, one way or another, but entertaining or serving in one of the armed forces was not the same as facing German tanks from an absurd barricade of old furniture, stage sets, and even, in one case on the Left Bank, a rusty, stinking *pissoir*.

Pockets of fighting erupted in unexpected places as the made their way. A block from the Théâtre Français, Tony recognized, almost too late, the deadly snap, like a branch breaking, and the "splat" that followed. The sniper's bullet had missed him by a hair. Carl pulled him into a doorway.

"It came from across the street. Probably one of ours, aiming at the Boches in that café."

The three German soldiers came rushing out, unfastening holster-flaps and blazing away, for all the world like the sheriff's men in a B-western, Tony thought.

He and Carl huddled in the entrance of a jeweler's shop which had been closed and shuttered, though it wasn't yet dusk. In the big, littered square across from the Comédie-Française, street fighting had broken out again. Carl surveyed the scene carefully.

"We'll go through the court behind you. It will bring us inside that barricade down the street. How is your throw arm?"

"Pitching arm." Tony breathed deeply. "Say the word. You furnish the brain. I'll furnish the arm."

At Carl's signal they made a rush through an old courtyard scarcely bigger than a skylight, and after avoiding a staff car carrying two black-uniformed

SS officers, they came on the avenue de l'Opera. Danielle deBrett called to Tony from a barricade outside a shop selling souvenir picture postcards of Paris.

"We can use these two," she said as they joined her group. They immediately saw that they had fallen into an active nest. As Danielle yelled introductions a huge, bearded Breton glared at Tony.

"He is dead, this American. I told his papa."

With her long black hair streaming, Danielle raised up from her haunches, threw something at a truck that was trying to run down their barricade. The explosion knocked her into Tony's arms.

Behind her, an elderly woman handed him a bottle containing a soaked newspaper. Doing his duty, he hurled it as far as he could.

If he had intentionally aimed it at the approaching Mercedes maneuvering between the barricades of wood, plaster and cobblestones, he couldn't have done a better job. The smoke and fire from the explosion didn't obliterate the sight of screaming men blown out through the windows and roof. Danielle laughed at the revulsion she saw on Tony's face. She nudged Carl.

"*Mon coeur,* they are weak, your democratic friends."

But Carl was made of sterner stuff. Tony could see the implacable determination in his face when one of Danielle's comrades, a wiry little man, fell forward onto the barricade, hit by flying debris from the Mercedes. Tony grabbed him by the shoulder of his smock, drew him back and laid him down on the sidewalk behind the battle line. The little man still clutched a heavy German handgun.

It was Carl, however, who forced the Luger out of his fingers, took it up and aimed at one of two Germans trapped in the burning truck.

The sky was dark now. Tony found that the hellish scene was illuminated by the explosions, the fires and car lights, mostly German. His skin burned and itched where burning particles had settled, eating their way through his clothing. He dragged the elderly woman back when her sparse gray hair caught on fire. With his arms and smoking sleeves he smothered the fire but the old woman groaned as she lay in a pool of overturned Paris postcards.

A man wearing the Cross of Lorraine on his lapel had crawled near the barricades from the direction of the Paris Opéra, whose huge shadow hovered indifferently over the scene. Carl got him past the barrier.

Ammunition began to run short. The Germans who had been caught in the barrage, but who managed not to be hit stumbled away to be rescued by fellow comrades beyond the main theater of the fighting. Tony made out the dim light of battle up the wide avenue, where the Comédie-Française was giving its greatest performance. He was glad to see that there, too, the fight had boiled down to the sporadic crack of guns of a great many pistols that had probably been unused for years.

Was there anything accomplished in all this bloodshed? He heard himself mumble to no one in particular. Carl, running out of bullets and Molotov cocktails, had momentarily given up fighting and was eagerly questioning the man who wore the little enameled Cross of Lorraine. From his expression it looked like the news must be happy.

Somewhere, some brave idiot exploded a flash-bulb, undoubtedly photographing these blood-thirsty moments for posterity.

In his exuberance Carl ran over to Tony and rammed his fist into his seared right arm.

"Listen to this, friend. Our armies have come home. A contingent of our Second Armored under Captain Dronne is in the Hôtel de Ville at this very minute. Was it worth the fight? Well, we've held Paris for the Allies. And for France."

"Great," Tony congratulated them tiredly. "Now, let's go home, damn it."

Despite the fact she was surrounded by democratic Gaullists, Danielle began hugging and kissing everyone including Tony, kissing him wildly on both cheeks and waving a little red hammer-and-sickle flag just as the patriot with the camera flashed another bulb.

"We've done it. We've done it!" she yelled. *"Vive la France!"*

Carl leaned over and kissed her. They had fought beside each other, as Pierre St. Just had predicted they would.

But Tony could only think of that last desolate look in Jany's eyes as she watched her brother go off to what might be death at the end of a German rifle, or an unknown fate in one of the SS question rooms. He was in a hurry to keep his promise and get Carl back, and, incidentally, to see her smile again.

# Chapter Twenty

In the dusk Jany walked out to the sidewalk to see where the sounds of battle were coming from. They had been shifting during the last hour. She shuddered inwardly at the sound of every distant noise, thinking it might mean the death of Carl, or of Monsieur Tony. She marveled that though death surrounded them, there were still two men and a woman sitting in the café, calmly drinking the ersatz coffee and talking about the rice shortage.

She would have given a good deal to go and make her prayers in Notre Dame, or even St. Roch. It made her more anxious that she couldn't. Her prayers may have been half superstition, but they gave her hope. Tonight would be different, she thought miserably. She had made no offering, lighted no candles, and things were bound to go badly.

She started back into the café as a car drove past — a Citröen, the first in many hours. The streets had been full of German trucks, staff cars, tanks, and an official limousine of some kind, but now they made themselves scarce and now this once-familiar French car appeared.

Jany had her hand on the long, brass door latch when the Citröen stopped beyond the café and Lieutenant Colonel von Leidersdorf stepped out, ducking as he did so. His height seemed to dwarf the car. All of Jany's earlier fears crystallized. He was going to be difficult and insistent. It would be easier if he was a man she hated, but she couldn't help pitying him when she thought of his lost daughter.

He saw her at once, even in the dusk, so she couldn't duck into the café as she would like to have done. When he reached her, he saluted. His smile made his facial lines less austere, but there was still something unsettling about the smile. He seemed unconcerned — though he must have known — that within a few blocks of the café snipers were picking off other Wehrmacht officers. He didn't even look around; his mind was entirely occupied with Jany. The idea of it made the girl even more uncomfortable.

"Fraulein. Something of importance I must say to you. Where can we be alone?"

"I'm sorry, monsieur. I can't. My brother will not permit it."

"You don't understand. This is a life or death matter. You may not survive until this time to-morrow night. I cannot let this happen."

"If you mean I should go away, I can't leave my family. I've told you that."

For the first time he looked around, searching for some place of privacy. He took her arm. She tried to free herself, but his grip was cruelly tight. She wondered if he was aware of the force he was using on her.

"Inside, then. The table by the window. Is that all the light you have?"

"At this hour? Certainly, monsieur. Our precious hour of electricity has not come yet. The candles are all we have until then."

His free hand was on the latch. He nudged her in ahead of him. "At home it is very much the same," he said wryly, "I must remember. The Fatherland has endured much since I was last in Darmstadt or Berlin."

She bristled, about to add something about the suffering of her own people, but he continued.

"Be still. Any minute it may come — the city blown up. At headquarters I have heard the talk. The führer ordered the bridges, the monuments, the churches mined." She gasped, though it was not the first time she had heard this rumor. He silenced her by shaking the arm he still held.

She sat down at the table, unable to take her eyes off him. "How could the Boches be so savage?"

He seemed to feel a defense was necessary. "It may be that the commander of Paris will not give the order. Some say he will. Some say not. But we will be safely out of the area if we leave tonight. I have my own papers. I am on leave. And I have papers for you. See? Erika von Leidersdorf."

She barely looked at the pages he unfolded. It sickened her to see the great black swastika on the pages.

"My name is not Erika, monsieur."

He looked at the name as if he had never seen it before. She was afraid his mind had wandered again but he surprised her by saying in a querulous voice, "Certainly it is not. But it will be easier if I call you by my daughter's name. I am used to it, and the papers were easier to obtain."

"Monsieur, forgive me, but your daughter is dead."

If he was surprised that she knew, he didn't

react. "I am aware of that. I prefer that while I am responsible for you, you will take the name of my daughter." He was prepared for all objections. "Fraulein, or mademoiselle, if you choose, I consider myself a man of honor. I give you my word that you will, in all ways, be treated as my daughter was treated. From me you need fear nothing. The daughter of Walthur von Leidersdorf, it is not a bad position. My Darmstadt properties are extensive. And with the death of my brother I own some choice city property in Berlin."

Jany persisted in trying to be patient; she didn't want to upset him. "I have my family," she tried to explain again. "I can't leave Carl, and he would never go to Germany."

For the first time he mentioned what she dreaded he'd known all along. "It may be necessary. Of your brother's interest in the British spy on the rue de la Paix, I have said nothing, although I am convinced he is responsible for the death of my aide."

"But he isn't! I swear by the Holy Trinity, I swear it!"

His eyes avoided her. He feared that she knew too much, but still he couldn't admit it to himself. "Yes, it is possible. But if I give my information to the Gestapo, even of the one visit by young Friedrich which I personally witnessed . . . and Carl Friedrich has Jewish blood. One-quarter, is it not so?"

"I am also one-quarter Jewish."

"Be still." He looked around. The two Frenchmen and the woman were staring at them curiously. He showed her an envelope with a Hôtel

Ritz letterhead. "I have only to mail this to the rue des Saussies and within an hour your brother will be under questioning. His ancestry will not help. It is better to save his life, and yours."

She stiffened. Whatever he said, whatever arguments he used were of no use. None of his threats would make any difference. She couldn't go. Carl wouldn't let her. She had to keep remembering that.

She leaned toward him across the table, trying with one last desperate effort to make him understand.

"Please, monsieur. I believe all you tell me, and I know you are a man of honor. I never doubted it."

"Thank you."

"But it is not possible. If you could only think of your daughter . . . imagine she was pleading with some Frenchman to understand! I *must* stay with Carl. Even if you spared him and he remained free, he would never let me go to Germany. He knows they killed his father."

"Ah, so that's it. The Jew makes trouble again, even from the quicksand."

She was so shocked at this after his kind, reasonable tone, that she instinctively backed away from him. He managed to recover some of his suavity, but it cost him an effort.

"Dear Janine. Forgive the indelicacy of mentioning your father. You are tenderhearted and loyal. All those qualities one loves in you. But you do not wish to die in the holocaust of Paris. If you come with me, as my daughter, I swear I will do nothing to betray your brother. I swear this by my oath to the führer."

Dear God! she thought. It was plain that he would never understand. To live under the swastika would be another kind of death. She had seen its excesses for too long.

"I can't." It was inadequate but she was cold and tense with fear of what he would do next and even this response was forced out.

He stirred, then frowned at a noise somewhere. A grenade thrown, undoubtedly by a member of the Resistance.

"Do you realize what is happening out there?" he asked her. "Men like your brother are being used as shields on our tanks."

"Don't!"

"You must face it. I have seen five revolutionary flags hanging out of windows while I drove here. What are we to do? We are soldiers."

That sparked the wrong response. Her chin came up. "What you call a revolutionary flag is the *tricouleur* of France, monsieur."

"What are all these theatrics? You are not Jeanne d'Arc. You are only a little girl named —"

She blurted it out desperately. "I would rather be dead than Erika von Leidersdorf."

He got up. He had never seemed taller, leaner, more terrible. His face was rigid and gray in the dim candlelight. He reached across the table and slapped her hard, stingingly across the face. She flinched but watched him, her eyes big and questioning.

The two Frenchmen half-rose from their chairs. The colonel turned and looked at them. They sat down again, slowly.

"Now you have assured your brother's fate," he

said, pulling an envelope from his inside pocket. "I must report his work in the Resistance to my superiors. You have left me no choice, fraulein."

Regarding her harshly for one last time, the colonel moved stiffly away from the little table and opened the door. After he had gone she got up and went out on the sidewalk.

He would mail his letter. Carl would die, all because she had said something cruel and stupid. She watched him stride along the sidewalk to the beat-up Citröen. Hearing heavy footsteps, she looked around. A man passed her on the run. It was Monsieur Binet, whose son was killed when he ran across the street to the dentist's office. Monsieur Binet's short, stout legs worked rapidly, propelled by his hatred. Spotting the colonel, he swung an old bird rifle to his shoulder and fired at the instant Jany cried out.

Colonel von Leidersdorf had his hand on the car door. At the impact of the shot he stiffened, his long fingers clinging to the roof of the car. He slid down with agonizing slowness, his fingers smearing parallel sweat marks on the car window until he collapsed at the feet of the small Frenchman.

Jany ran over and knelt beside him. Binet stood over her with the rifle barrel hot against her cheek.

"Through the back of the head. The coup de grâce, eh?"

She couldn't bring herself to touch the mass of blood and bone that obscured the colonel's straight, graying hair.

"He is dead, the scum!" Monsieur Binet said with obvious satisfaction. "You mourn him? Will you mourn him when we parade you down the Champs-Elysées with all your pretty yellow hair shaved off? Collaborator! Nazi lover!"

The German must have died instantly. She was glad he hadn't suffered, but if only they could have parted in dignity! A white envelope in his left hand caught her eye — the letter that would condemn Carl.

She reached down, slipped the crumpled envelope out of his fingers and tucked it in her smock pocket. Monsieur Binet shouldered his rifle. With a vehemence she'd never before seen in a Frenchman, he spat at her. She didn't move, but held her breath, half expecting him to shoot her as well.

"Nazi lover!"

He turned and clattered on along the street. She had no doubt he would ultimately make trouble for her, once Liberation came.

Heads were beginning to appear in open windows. She got up, looked around, and cried out for help. She knew it was too late, but at least he would not be left all night on the sidewalk. She waited but when no one came she turned and walked slowly back to the café, to the three French customers who had seen the whole affair.

She went inside behind the zinc bar and opened the envelope. It was unsealed, but her nervous fingers had trouble getting out the single sheet of Hôtel Ritz paper. She held it up to the candle to read it.

The sheet was blank.

She examined the envelope. It, too, was blank. It had all been a bluff. The colonel had never intended to betray Carl, possibly because it might have incriminated her as well, but she would never really know why.

Only minutes later the café was empty. The cook in his overheated kitchen threw down his apron and hurried out by the rear door through the court. No one wanted to be around when the Gestapo came to question the neighbors. But the Gestapo must have been busy elsewhere, since only the French police showed up, examined the dead colonel, and called on the German army to remove their man.

Nothing further happened, except that the French themselves ended up removing the colonel's body. The Occupation forces were busy elsewhere. It seemed clear to the police that it was just one more murder by what the French referred to as the Resistance and the Germans called terrorists.

Half an hour later Jany went out to stack the table and chairs on the sidewalk and lock the front door. Two men passed her and disappeared into the dark entranceway that led to the inner court. One man was big and athletic-looking. The other was slender, with light red hair cut short. He carried himself with a careless, easy stride. Neither of the two looked French, nor were their clothes French.

Jany couldn't imagine whose flat they were headed for. She bolted the café door and went out the back way in time to see that they had been questioning Madame Charpentier. By the lamplight from the concierge's open door they made their way up the stairs to the Friedrich flat.

Though the evening was warm, Madame Charpentier shivered as she pointed them out to Jany, adding an explanation in a low voice.

"The thin, young one spoke French, but the larger one spoke in English. I could swear it. Has the invasion come? Are we now to take orders from the Allies?"

"You are sure they aren't Germans?"

"Certainly. These are strange ones."

Jany ran up the stairs. The two strangers were in the shadows but the big man spoke to her in English, his voice filled with tension and excitement.

"I hope to God you're Madame Friedrich."

Aware of Madame Charpentier's sharp ears, she unlocked the door and pushed both of them inside, ahead of her.

The young, slim one cut in. "Take it easy, Steve. You're scaring her. They're still under the Germans, you know."

But the big one spoke again, this time in careful French. "If you are one of the family named Friedrich, we are your friends."

"I . . . I . . ." Too much had happened this evening. Jany couldn't make it all out. "You are in great danger," she finally said, "there was a murder out on the sidewalk tonight. You must take care. Where have you been hiding? The Gestapo is sure to be questioning us at any moment."

The youthful one moved into the faint light provided when Jany lit one of their last remaining candles.

Jany stared. The young man grabbed his cap off, tousled his light red hair and grinned at her. It was impossible not to smile back.

"I know. You thought I was a he, and here I am nothing but a tired, aching she. We've been told that Tony Lombard, my husband, is staying with you. Is he safe?"

"Mademoiselle," the big man put in, seeing the bewildered look on Jany's face, "allow me to explain. I am Steve Lombard, Tony's father, and this is his wife, Eden Ware."

Jany wet her lips. Her head was spinning. Too much today, too many shocks. "Monsieur Tony's Eden?"

"That's right." It must be obvious that she mistrusted them. The man was big, handsome and sandy-haired. He didn't look much like Tony. He fumbled in his jacket and pulled out a card, which he showed her.

She glanced at the badly creased card that said "Press Pass" in English. The name was there, as he said. He added quickly, "Do you know where we can find Tony? By the way, you do speak English?"

"Monsieur Tony is with my brother," she said in English. Her pride recovered. "Yes, monsieur. To answer you, my mother spoke in English and French. She, too, was an actress — Olga Rey."

"Good God!" Monsieur Tony's wife gave her father-in-law a look. "She's Olga Rey's daughter. Small world."

So she has heard the fame of Maman in the early cinema, Jany thought with satisfaction.

"Please," Stephen Lombard said, looking at Eden with exasperation, "units of the French Second Armored Division are in Paris at this minute. Also, units of the U.S. Infantry. Together they're a token force, but they will give the Germans trouble, at least until the rest of the army gets here tomorrow. Where can I find my son?"

"Monsieur, I, too am concerned for the safety of your son and my brother. They are fighting in the place du Théâtre-Français, I think."

"Palais royal," Eden said crisply. "Steve, can you get some of the men in Captain Dronne's unit to help them out?"

"I'm sure as hell going to try," he said, already headed for the door. "It's kind of like the old days, with André and me fighting off the Krauts."

Jany ran to the door after him. "Take care, monsieur. Your son would never forgive me if I sent his father into trouble."

Steve waved her away, laughing at the idea of Tony going somewhere that was unsafe for his father, and then he was gone.

Tony's wife explained briefly, though Jany hadn't even noticed the reference to Steve's French friend.

"Our daughter is named for André. The comte de Grasse. He died at Dunkirk, trying to save his men." She frowned, looking Jany over with concern. "You poor child! You look completely beaten down. Let me get you something. I could use a little tea or coffee myself. God, I'm tired. That jeep was like a bucking bronco."

She started into the little kitchen, admiring all the tacky old furnishings, everything that Jany had gotten heartily sick of in the last four years.

"Makes me a little homesick, Miss Friedrich. I used to live in a place smaller than this, before I was married."

It was humiliating to have to reveal the poverty

of the Friedrich flat to Monsieur Tony's wife, of all people. Jany followed her, coloring a little.

"We have no tea. And, I'm afraid, not enough coffee. I have saved the last of it for my brother's breakfast."

"And very right, too." Eden Ware had a friendly, understanding way that made Jany forgive her for her tactlessness. "Well, you just wait. By this time tomorrow night, we'll all be dancing in the streets. What d'you bet?"

"Oh, do you think so? How good to hear such promising words, after four years under the Boche!"

Constantly watching the movie star, Jany knew why Tony had married her. She was everything Jany could never be, so sure of herself that she didn't even need to act proud. The strange thing was, she hadn't an ounce of beauty in the ordinary way, and yet, you couldn't stop watching her. Like her other fans, Jany succumbed to the actress's totally natural yet charismatic presence.

"We do have some wine. M-Monsieur Tony seemed to like our beaujolais." She fussed around the kitchen with nervous fingers, pushing aside a glass that was unwashed, looking for others.

Eden laughed. "Here, this will do." She pulled the glass toward her with two fingers, watched Jany pour and then drank half a glassful at one long swig, swallowing automatically. Over the glass she studied Jany with interest.

"You really are the prettiest child! When you're a little older, I'd like to have you see a friend of mine, Leo Prysing. My boss, in fact. He's a movie producer — the very best."

The name wasn't new to Jany. According to Carl it was Leo Prysing, the rich, powerful movie producer, whose radio broadcast back in 1938 informed them of their father's heroism. Jany was sure that Carl would love to meet Leo Prysing, and the fact that he was rich and powerful gave him an added appeal to Jany.

"Thank you, madame. I would love to meet Monsieur Prysing. But I wouldn't ever do anything like acting. I couldn't bear having everyone stare at me."

"To each his own," Eden said affably, "although I never met anyone who didn't want to get into the movies. The more credit to you that you don't. But you can certainly meet Leo, if you'd like."

"I would. My brother says he is a very great man."

"Well, I don't know about that. He's a great producer. And he has the knack for making films that put him high in the chips." She watched Jany take several sips of wine before she added softly, "I'm sorry. You must have gone through so much more than we can ever know."

She motioned Jany out to the living room and the couch with the bad springs.

"I'm really not as hard-boiled as I must seem. I've been trying to keep my mind occupied so I won't have to think about what's going on out there." She paused. "I don't hear any shooting now. I guess they've settled down for the night. But Tony is so unused to fending for himself. I'm glad your brother is with him."

Jany didn't contest this, feeling that most people must agree whenever Eden suggested something.

But she couldn't help remarking on Eden's odd notion of her husband.

"Monsieur Tony has been what you call fending very well in Paris, madame." She thought of the time in the deserted hotel on the rue de la Paix a week ago, but she couldn't mention that, ever.

"Good. Glad to hear it. He has a very strong father and needs everything he can muster inside to fight Steve's image. But Tony —" Eden resettled herself. She had run into the broken springs in the couch. "Well, Andrea's birth made him a new man. Andrea adored him, and I've never seen a more devoted father. I know he must seem like an older man to you, but sometimes he can be very boyish. He has enormous charm when things go his way."

Jany marveled at the blindness of this woman who appeared so wise and all-knowing. But Jany wanted to hear about Tony — anything, even the bad things. A thought crossed Jany's mind that almost offered some hope until she remembered her own fatherless childhood. This remarkable actress, with her talent and self-confidence and fans, might be able to go on after a sinful act like a divorce, but what about the little girl who adored her father?

"What is your daughter like, madame? Monsieur Tony said she was born around the time America came into the war. He said she is very grown-up for her age and can talk."

"Call me Eden, dear. After what your family has done for Tony, I feel you're part of the clan. Now about Andrea . . . she has a nickname for everyone and can make herself understood whenever she wants anything. Steve says Tony was the same way.

She has dark hair and is extremely pretty. Not at all like me. She has Tony's nice nose and those gorgeous smoky eyes. She's going to break a lot of hearts, that girl." She sat up straight, startling Jany. "But what am I saying? I brought a snapshot to show Tony how she's grown. Here."

Andrea Lombard was all that Jany had expected, a little beauty with a look of mischief in her eyes that was softened by her tender mouth. She wasn't just a cute little baby that looked like a million others. The picture showed real personality, and her resemblance to Tony made Jany love her at once.

Even if Tony asked for a divorce, Jany thought, even if she could bring herself to go against her church and all her beliefs, she could never take him away from this darling little girl who peered out at her from the snapshot.

"You can't see her coloring, of course," Eden pointed out, "but it really is extraordinary." Her pride in the girl was so like Olga Rey's pride in her own daughter! Jany's earliest memories were of Maman smiling with pride as strangers admired her on the street. Jany had dreaded those encounters. A shy child, she never knew what to say or how to behave except to hide behind her mother's skirts. In her young mind she was sure that since she had no father, those same strangers were only being nice to her to hide their contempt.

At least little Andrea wouldn't have to come into womanhood without a father. Not only did she have a father, but one who adored her. Jany envied the child for a brief moment. She tried to think of something appropriate to say besides the typical praise that all mothers must be used to, but Eden held up her hand, at once scaring and silencing her.

"Do you hear that?"

It was music. A radio. Radios were forbidden, and this one must be very loud. Jany had never heard someone else's radio played during the Occupation. She knelt on the couch and pushed the windows open, and saw that others along the street were doing the same. The dark, starless night was filled with the sound of a French voice saying something about "the final struggle. Tomorrow, we must be free . . ."

Surely the whole city was listening. She could hear other radios turned on in almost ever building. This caused the most peculiar repetition of the Resistance voices blaring over the National Radio Station.

Suddenly, the voices stopped and there was an eerie moment of silence. Paris seemed to be holding its breath. Eden reached over and grabbed Jany's hand, squeezing her fingers so hard that Jany winced, though she didn't pull away. Her emotions ran too deep for mere physical pain to distract them.

The first words of the French anthem broke slowly upon the night air. Echoed from every radio, the voices seemed to rise from the ancient stones as well:

*"Allons, enfants de la patrie!"*

Jany listened to it with pride that she was French, and that this most stirring of anthems belonged to her people. Like all the others, many of whom had hidden behind the warped shutters for

313

four years, she picked up the words now and joined in the chorus.

"*Aux armes, mes citoyens!*"

Exhausted by the excitement of it, and the triumph of having dared to sing the forbidden "Marseillaise" when the city was still under the guns of the Boches, Jany glanced at Eden. She was astonished to find tears running down the actress's cheeks.

Seeing her stare, Eden laughed and rubbed the tears away with her knuckles.

"What drama! I can't help it. I adore scenes like this."

It was very odd. Jany was glad she couldn't hate this woman who had everything in life that Jany wanted. It made things easier. Jany reminded herself that she had never expected to be Tony's wife. She had known how it would be when they heard his cousin broadcast the obituary of Eden Ware's husband.

It wasn't long after that that they heard footsteps on the stairs and Steve Lombard threw open the door into the tiny foyer.

"I've got them back safe and sound, just as I promised. Guess where I found them, Eden? Can't wait to tell Randi. Singing, by God! Marching along one of those alleys arm in arm, singing at the top of their lungs. This is Carl Friedrich, Eden. Nice fellow, all right. I'll step aside and let you at your hero."

Eden was still crying when she went into Tony's arms and Jany was sure the sight troubled Tony. He was glad to see his wife. He had to be. But the look he gave Jany over Eden's head both

314

warmed and shamed her.

Surely Eden Ware loved him. She had come through so much danger to meet him, and yet Jany had seen that twist of pain in Tony's face. The minute he and his wife stopped kissing, he asked how Andrea was. Jany tried not to listen.

She hugged her brother who was also looking at her searchingly. "Oh, Carl, it's such a relief to have you back. Were you in danger?" She babbled on, trying to reduce the awkwardness of the moment. "Guess what? Madame Lombard is going to present us to Leo Prysing. You know, the man who made the broadcast about father."

With his arms comfortably around his sister Carl turned to Steve, who was beaming as if the liberation had been his idea.

"Is it true, monsieur? You and Madame are acquainted with Leo Prysing, the producer? I know Tony says she appeared in his films."

"I ought to be familiar with him. I've got shares in Prysing Productions. Want to get into the business, do you, son?"

"No, monsieur. But I would like to thank him. If I had not heard his praise of my father on the radio years ago, I would never have known the kind of man Kurt Friedrich really was."

For a minute or two no one said anything. Jany looked at Steve and caught his quick glance at Eden. Steve ended the silence by making an offhanded remark that didn't sound quite like the friendly man she'd just met.

"Well, that's Eden's department. Can these two kids meet your boss?"

Eden looked a little rattled as well, maybe because she was still breathless after kissing her husband with so much enthusiasm.

"No problem. I've already promised Miss Friedrich. Leo is going to adore her."

Carl scowled but she laughed and waved away any objections he might have.

"In the nicest way, I can assure you. Don't worry, Leo's tastes run to rather mature women. But he does admire beauty. The least he'll do is invite the two of you to Hollywood for a visit. You being Olga Rey's children and all. Olga worked at his studio years ago."

Steve cleared his throat. "Eden . . ."

She shrugged. "Sooner or later it was bound to happen. Why not?" Neither Carl nor Jany understood this remark, but they assumed she spoke of something that didn't concern them.

"I would appreciate it if I might meet Monsieur Prysing, madame," Carl said eagerly.

Eden and Steve seemed to be discussing something between them, in code.

"I don't —" Steve began again.

"All out in the wash sooner or later," she said.

Meanwhile, Tony excused himself from his wife's arms and took the snapshot of Andrea over to Jany. While his wife discussed the producer with Steve and Carl, Tony seemed to feel comfortable in speaking quietly with Jany. She didn't share his feeling. She felt as guilty as if she had been taken in adultery with him.

"Your daughter is enchanting, Monsieur Tony. You must be very proud of her."

"Sweetheart, I would be if —"

She laughed, too loudly, to cover his endearment. "When you go home, you must give her my love. She will be so happy to see you. Madame says you are the little girl's whole life."

"Yes, but — listen to me."

Eden was watching them. She laughed about something Steve said, then put her hand easily on Carl's arm to emphasize that he would be welcome in the United States, but she had glanced over at her husband and Jany.

"Andrea's a dead-ringer for Tony, don't you think, Miss Friedrich?" she called out.

"Very like."

Tony pretended to study the snapshot. Jany put everything she could into a teasing comment. "You must get back to that young lady as soon as possible or she will divorce you as her father. And divorce is a sin we French will never permit."

She wondered if he understood and added more sternly, "Never!" All the same, she wanted to kiss away the hurt she saw in his face, but she felt Carl's light touch on her shoulder.

"Will we really go to America and see this great Mr. Prysing?" Jany asked her brother. "I'm sure he could do so much for you, Carl . . . You see, messieurs — madame, no one in the world has done so much for me as my Carl. He deserves that someone should help him."

"I do not need help, I only want to know more about our father," he said stiffly. "You see, Monsieur Lombard, as I'm sure you know this Prysing made a very famous film about the attempted rescue of his family from Vienna. My father's character is certain to be in it. It was called *Journey*, the one Madame Ware starred in."

"Yes, yes. That one. Came out in '39."

Eden leaped onto the subject hurriedly. "I doubt that you could see it now. Most old films are junked after five years."

"But not famous ones such as this, madame. I heard that they show them in theaters they call 'last-run.' Over and over."

"Not that one, though. I haven't heard of it playing anywhere in years."

"At all events," Carl persisted stubbornly, "I shall look for it if I must comb all of Europe and the United States."

There was a great deal of tension in the room. Jany could feel it. She supposed it must be what remained of the beautiful thing she and Tony had shared for a little while and would never share again. So much had happened today and she was so tired. She wished Tony would go away and she could begin to forget him. Then she could rest, and cry. At the same time, she wished he would never go away. Better to see him like this than not at all. In the meantime, there was the very rich Monsieur Prysing to consider. She thought that possibly she could win the good will of this man. He was the only rich person she knew of, and she had to do something to give back all Carl had sacrificed for her during the war. If the Boches were really forced out of Paris tomorrow, she knew she would be hounded by Tony, who would insist that he loved her and would give up that pretty child and his famous wife for her. But it was all wrong in every way. A sin against her beliefs, against the child, and she knew that he would one day be bitterly sorry.

One day. Maybe the world and life would be different. Maybe this deep anguish she felt would soften to mere sweet memories, like old songs and sentimental love stories. She wished that one day was now.

# BOOK TWO

# Chapter Twenty-One

Within weeks after the liberation of Paris Tony found himself home on Nob Hill, half a world from Jany Friedrich.

He still saw her everywhere, her sunny hair bouncing around the boulders of a Stanford girl coming out of the St. Francis Hotel, her shy smile on an Italian girl who served him at Sabella's on Fisherman's Wharf, her beautifully fringed blue eyes . . . no. He hadn't yet seen anyone with her gorgeous eyes.

Eden had made the homecoming easy. He owed her a great deal for that, and intended to pay her back with an unaccustomed fidelity. She asked no questions whose answers would hurt. She seemed to understand and even to share his hesitation when they made love, an act in which both of them had always been in perfect tune before his Paris experience.

Their first attempt had been a disaster in London the day after they returned from a Paris that was jubilantly celebrating the inglorious exit of the Wehrmacht.

Tony found London in the throes of ferocious V-bomb attacks so unpredictable that even the iron courage of seasoned Londoners was shaken. An air-raid warden on the Thames embankment explained, "It's the coming of the buggers with nobody at the wheel, so to speak. Not quite human, if you take my meaning, sir."

Tony did. But dutifully making love to Eden while unpiloted buzz bombs exploded around them was not conducive to success. For the first time in his life he found himself impotent.

Eden was sensitive enough to understand the problem and cast all the blame on the Germans.

"Damned Krauts! They're ruining my love life. I'm sorry, darling. I'm behaving badly. Stiff upper lip and all that. I'm shaky too . . . let's just lie here and not think about anything."

She had gone to sleep, or seemed to, against his shoulder and he could imagine her head as Jany's. He caressed her hair, trying to picture it long and curly and sunlit. Then something unexplained and disturbing happened. He murmured to himself, "Sweetheart," and heard Eden respond in her famous movie star voice with its hoarse, gutsy quality:

"Don't call me that."

Her eyes were still closed. He lifted his head to look at her. "Sweetheart?"

"Darling. I'll accept *darling.*"

They flew home to San Francisco when Steve and Leo Prysing were able to pull the right strings again. At the big, spiked iron gate enclosing the old Lombard house he saw his daughter Andrea, astonishingly grown-up, looking every inch her almost-three years. And calling him by name, instantly recognizing her father after the months he had spent away from her in London and Paris.

"Daddy! Daddy!"

Sweeping her up close, her warm, small arms went around his neck, threatening to choke him.

"She's learned to say daddy," Tony said excitedly

to Eden, "whatever happened to *dada?*"

He bounced Andrea up and down, pretending to toss her in the air as he moved up the walk between his wife and Brooke Lombard Friedrich. His aunt Brooke fluttered around him like a dear but persistent hummingbird. The old scars along his neck and jaw itched as they always did when he was going through an exhausting emotional ordeal, but the ordeal had ended and he couldn't figure out why he kept feeling the pressure.

Even his relationship with Eden was on an even keel. Their sex life hadn't quite returned to perfection, but it was satisfactory and in many ways he genuinely liked Eden more than before. He realized now that he had always liked her. It wasn't an emotion he had shared with any other woman except his dead grandmother, Bridget Gallegher.

"She'd love that," he thought wryly, "being compared to my grandmother." But Eden had no personal vanity — it was one of those likable things about her.

He met his mother in the doorway. Behind her, and beyond the dark, Victorian entry hall, he could make out the front staircase, heavy and depressing in spite of the shafts of early October sunlight. It appeared to be lined with the household staff, all eager to express their pleasure at his return. He appreciated the good will but wished he could have sneaked in without all the fanfare about a time he preferred to forget — with, of course, the exception of one person he couldn't even talk about.

Randi was her usual calm self, but her voice shook a little as she and Tony embraced.

"You certainly look — and feel — alive to me.

Oh, Tony. They said you were dead, but I never believed it for a minute."

Brooke interrupted gleefully, "We knew that was a lie. Nobody could get my nephew down. I told Alec so. I said —"

They didn't hear her. In one breath, Tony and Randi made a mutual discovery.

"You look older," he said.

His mother was still lovely in her own way, but there was signs of strain around her mouth. She had always had his respect, as a disciplinarian and as a woman who seldom showed her emotions; yet he knew she loved him. And he knew it now, even though she was making very little fuss over him.

"I *am* old," Randi reminded him. "Fort-six last birthday. Well, come in, and please be nice. They've all waited so long."

He knew they expected his old prewar act, the playboy with the good opinion of himself. Eden encouraged him with a slap on the back.

"Go to it, Errol Flynn!"

Tony decided to put on the act. It seemed to satisfy the housekeeper, Miss Thorgerson, and the cook, a stout little Korean woman that Chiye Akina had sent over from Hawaii, and several new young females. No male servants. He didn't have to ask. He was already tired of hearing the explanation that fit all ills: "There's a war on."

Oddly enough, all this fuss and attention from a half a dozen women put him in excellent spirits and he was able to enjoy his stay in San Francisco.

It was Eden, however, who told the family that the Friedrichs in Paris who gave Tony a temporary haven were the illegitimate children of Brooke's own beloved Kurt Friedrich.

"What a bastard he was," she said, thinking again of the abandoned Friedrichs.

"Not at all," Brooke insisted, leaping to defend the memory of her late husband. "What my Kurt did before he married me had nothing to do with his character. He was just naturally popular with women — like Tony here."

"Good God!" Tony said, and everyone laughed.

Eden smiled but her mind seemed to be on something else. Tony noted uncomfortably that Randi looked troubled as she watched her daughter-in-law. Randi seldom missed these little nuances. In his guilt, Tony thought his wife's reaction, or lack of it, was due to some knowledge of his secret passion for Jany. She did laugh at Brooke's insistence that Kurt's children must be handsome.

"I'd really be curious to see them. Do they speak of him at all?"

"Constantly. They adore him," Eden explained. "He's their dream father. You'd get along great with them."

Brooke insisted that the really sounded like two charming children. "And no matter what you say, I hope they're like Kurt."

Tony and Eden were strolling across the street and down the block one night in December after dinner at the Mark Hopkins, when Eden surprised him by bringing up the Friedrichs.

"What did you ever tell those poor children in Paris about their father?"

"Tell them? There wasn't much to tell. I know you never liked him. But what was all that business about *Journey*? It's only a movie. And if he really wants to, Carl could see it somewhere, especially if he comes to the States."

She stopped on a cable slot and stared at him. The humming cable vibrated in its slot and broke the uneasiness that still baffled him. Evidently, it had nothing to do with his relationship to Jany.

"You did see the picture. You were with me at Grauman's Chinese the night of the premiere. Of course, you were a little under the weather."

"Hangover, due to your cruelty. You kept me dangling with your damned indecision. I thought you'd never see the real, noble, many-sided me. So I slept through most of the movie. You were good, I remember. You didn't get nominated for an Oscar for nothing."

"Well, I did marry you. Remember the weekend in that little one-horse Nevada town? Vegas, wasn't it?"

"Talk about drunk. Remember how one of our witnesses, the guy in the plaid shirt, had to be propped up through the entire ceremony."

They walked along companionably, arm in arm. It was a crisp, clear pre-Christmas night after a breathtakingly beautiful day with no fog. At this time of night, and in his present mellow mood, Paris seemed far away, and Jany the heroine of a movie seen long ago, in the soft haze of nostalgia.

But she was still there in the haze, and it hurt. He didn't want to start up again. "I hope they don't come here," he murmured, thinking out loud.

"What?"

"I mean, because of Carl's obsession with his old man. He's bound to find out he wasn't a saint."

"Oh, that. Well, maybe they won't come. Leo

certainly isn't excited over the idea. Still, I wanted to do something for the kids and I've written to them." She avoided his eyes and concentrated on the distant skyline. "I hope you've written to them, too. You owe them a lot."

"Yes, I've written. They don't say much in return. Carl's had trouble getting a fellow named Binet to shut up. Seems he's been gossiping about Jany and a German officer who made a little trouble for them during the Occupation."

"What does Jany say?"

"I don't know. She's never written. Just Carl."

They reached the iron gates. She sniffed, and they stood together, studying the starry sky before they went in.

"There'll be fog by morning," Eden said, "look at Twin Peaks. Just remember. You heard it here first. A foggy Christmas." She paused again. "Oh, Tony, it's so good having you home."

She hugged him and, after he returned her embrace, they went up the walk together.

August of 1945 meant prospects of peace for most of the world, but for Brooke Lombard Friedrich it would always be the summer she became a surrogate mother.

Randi, who knew her sister-in-law better than anyone else did, guessed at once how it would be when Brooke received the snapshot of Carl and Jany Friedrich that she had requested. The girl failed to interest Brooke, but the boy was slim, light-haired, and rather serious-looking, much like her husband. It was this striking resemblance that seemed to interest Brooke most.

What surprised Randi was Brooke's maternal feeling toward the boy, which had hardly been in evidence during the childhood of her own son, Alec. But unless she was a remarkable actress, she was definitely showing signs of motherly interest — not at all what Randi had expected.

At first, she thought Brooke had the whole family fooled. But her plans for inviting the Friedrichs to Nob Hill for a visit were interlarded with such fussy details that Randi decided the feeling must have been inspired by Brooke's still-deep affection for her dead husband. Randi knew little about the Austrian actor. She had met him only twice when he and Brooke visited America, but her overriding impression was that he was shallow, arrogant, and lecherous.

"Poor children! When you think what they've been through," Brooke remarked to Miss Thorgerson, whose rough exterior concealed a good deal of sentiment. "The boy saved my nephew, you know. Gave him a home, shared their food with him, lied to the Nazis."

Randi put in drily, "The girl seems to have been pretty heroic, too. Don't forget her."

"Don't be silly. You know what I mean. Anyway, if Kurt and I had ever had children, they could have been mine."

"Undoubtedly they wouldn't have turned out the same. Olga Rey seems to have been a thoroughly nice person. If she hadn't been, she could have made your married life pretty uncomfortable, Brooke."

But Brooke's charitable feelings refused to stretch any further and include the woman who had preceded her into Kurt Friedrich's bed.

"She couldn't have been very bright. Imagine bringing not one but two innocent children into the world without any claim to legitimate names! You would never catch me doing that. However," she wound up magnanimously, "I'm going to tell them right off the bat that I've no objection to their borrowing my name."

"Your name?"

"Friedrich."

"Oh. How nice of you. But since that little matter seems to have been settled some time ago, it might be better if you didn't mention the name business at all."

Having given her okay to the bedroom Carl was to have, which had once belonged to her son Alec, Brooke considered Randi's advice.

"You may be right. From the snapshot he sent, the boy has a very sensitive mouth. It might upset him for me to bring it up again."

Randi shook her head over Brooke's one-track mind and went off to a meeting of the Letterman Hospital Special Committee. But her thoughts remained on the plight of Kurt Friedrich's illegitimate children.

Poor Jany — such a pretty girl, and a bit shy, if the snapshot was any indication. Maybe her looks were what turned Brooke off — she'd always regarded most women as her rivals. Randi knew well that she and Brooke had always been friends because Brooke, with her curly auburn hair, her voluptuous mouth and prominent curves, didn't recognize a rival in her elegant, self-contained sister-in-law.

The invitation to Kurt's children was accepted with conditions. Randi thought it was a little nervy of the Friedrichs, and reminiscent of their father's cheeky behavior, but she didn't really care that Carl "would most appreciate a brief interview with Monsieur Leo Prysing who is, I believe, a short distance away in Hollywood."

The letter came a few days before the newspapers and radio reported that a single bomb had been dropped in Japan and wiped out an entire city. It was hard to believe that while Europeans were making plans for the postwar trips, the horrors of war were still going on in other parts of the world.

To the great relief of the Lombard family, and especially Randi, Steve arrived home in San Francisco one August morning shortly after Tony and Eden, just in time to revive his flagging marriage to Randi. By some means unknown to her, he had managed the impossible. In spite of the war and the United Nations crowd gathered in San Francisco for the forming of that body, Steve had been able to get the very same Market Street suite at the Palace Hotel in which he and Randi had spent their wedding night almost twenty-seven years before. His memory failed him on the exact menu of the room-service dinner they'd ordered, but as Randi reminded him, there was a war on, and that left room for a few substitutions anyway. Because of the severe sugar rationing they hadn't the heart to order the superb Palace cinnamon toast for their second honeymoon breakfast, and the dinner steaks were not filets but tough sirloin.

Soon after they'd checked into their suite, Steve

teasingly began to undress her.

"Can you remember everything we did that first afternoon?" she wanted to know.

"You'll see. Stand still. And don't help me."

She stopped reaching back, straining to help him get the eighteen buttons undone. She stood very still but her thighs trembled with anticipation and when he said, "Oh, hell!" and stripped off her new moiré sheath, sending buttons flying, she was delighted. She turned in his arms, her busy fingers unzipping his fly, and in their excitement they fell back across the bed, just as they had before.

She drew him into her body with infinite care, caressing him while his warm, generous mouth covered hers.

Their enjoyment in rediscovering each other didn't end when they arrived at a burst of sexual fireworks together.

They lay back, still in each other's arms afterward. Running her forefingers across his groin, she murmured, "You waited for me."

"You hurried up, sweetheart." He sighed with pleasure. "Keep that up. It's been so — damned — long."

She continued her ministrations while she enjoyed his purring contentment.

"Don't tell me there weren't some pretty little English girls willing to do this for you."

"Sure."

He turned his head, licked her shoulder. "You're salty, you know that?"

"What?" she jerked away, not over this, but over his previous remark. But he quickly set about soothing her.

"There must have been, but I was so busy I never noticed. You should ask Tony. He's the Don Juan of the family. Or at least he used to be. I guess Eden's broken him to harness."

"I don't know. I have a funny feeling about him and Eden. I hope I'm wrong."

"Well, you *are* wrong. She's crazy about him."

She thought this over.

"Yes, I believe that. But he's different, somehow. Steve —" She looked into his eyes, reverting to her normal demeanor, which was usually serious. He sensed that there would be no teasing, no avoiding the matter.

"Steve, what is this French girl like? Tony didn't let her go too far with him, I hope."

"Tony? Let? If anything, it's the other way around. But there's nothing to worry about with little Jany. She's just a child. Prettiest little thing you ever saw but not much . . . well . . ." He frowned and looked as if he might be memorizing Randi's face. "Maybe you'd call it presence. You have it. The minute I laid eyes on you, I could see it. And mother had it."

"Yes, she did." Alicia Lombard had been gracious to the young Irish girl who married her only son. But curiously enough, no feeling of that gently bred Virginia lady remained in the dark, masculine halls of the Lombard house.

Steve chuckled suddenly. "Now, I'd never say that about Bridget." He felt Randi stiffen beside him, knowing how she'd always been sensitive about her own mother's rather crude, earthy personality.

"Mama didn't have your mother's advantages."

"Nope. You've got it all wrong. Bridget Gallegher had pizazz. People were always glad when she was around, and God knows you can't say that about everyone. Honey, I can't think of a finer epitaph for her."

She stretched a little and pressed closer, silencing him with a passionate kiss.

"Thank you," she said softly.

"Don't thank me. I mean it. Anyway, you can forget the French kid. She doesn't have presence and she doesn't have pizazz."

Still, there was something that puzzled Randi about Jany Friedrich. Her brother had written that he would probably come to San Francisco alone, but he also asked how Tony was doing and if he happened to be in San Francisco, too. When Brooke wrote that Tony and Eden were back in Hollywood, Carl replied saying that his sister had agreed to accompany him, and that they would be coming as soon as they could get space on a ship.

With the war in Europe over they were able to get two berths on a passenger vessel carrying wounded soldiers home to New York. Still, it seemed to Randi that the girl was avoiding Tony, and she couldn't help but wonder why. There were undercurrents. She could feel them, unlike Brooke, who was enthralled that she would soon be meeting her dear Kurt's children.

"And Randi," Brooke had begged her, "you must get that boss of yours up here to see Carl. At least once. The boy is dying to hear Leo repeat that tribute he paid Kurt on the radio back in '38."

Randi couldn't share in her enthusiasm. There was something not quite right about the whole

Kurt Friedrich business. Randi had always felt that the story of the aborted rescue of Josef and Sarah Preysing from Vienna never came out. She knew that the shooting script of the film had been changed several times by Leo, that certain aspects of the movie plot had been softened, but neither Leo, Steve nor Eden, the only ones involved, ever explained why. They had to be hiding something, Randi reasoned, but what? And whatever it was. they clearly didn't want Kurt Friedrich's son to know the truth. Why else would they all insist that the film *Journey* was gone, pulled off the circuits and unavailable? Randi knew that wasn't so.

She shivered.

Steve's clasp tightened around her shoulders.

"Cold, honey?"

"No." She laughed. "You know what they say. Somebody just walked over my grave."

The minute she said it, she wished she hadn't.

# Chapter Twenty-Two

Steve brought back Randi a pair of diamond-and-amethyst earrings that he had bought from a refugee family in London. The earrings were unusual in that the amethysts surrounded beautifully faceted diamonds, instead of the more common setting, with an amethyst in the center. They had been in the previous family since the days of Maria Theresa, and Steve gave Randi the letter the former owners had written. It spoke gratefully of Steve's purchase of the earrings having saved their pride and perhaps their lives. Randi felt less guilty about the gift — it was, after all, still wartime — and was especially grateful that Steve's buying them actually helped someone else.

Brooke's reactions at first seeing the earrings struck Randi as unusual. Acquiring jewelry was a hobby that had grown with Brooke since she stopped acquiring husbands. But she was bustling around so much, making plans and preparing things for the Friedrichs' visit that Randi's amethysts passed almost unnoticed.

"Those earrings do bring out that marble complexion of yours, Randi," she'd said after giving them a quick appraisal, "or do I mean alabaster? What do you think? Doesn't Heather's old room seem perfect for Jany? It's small but light and dainty, with those new curtains and venetian blinds."

"I think it's perfect. But remember, the Friedrichs don't intend to stay very long. Tony says young Friedrich is very proud and isn't going to want to take much from us. We must be careful not to treat them as poor relations."

"There's nothing for them in France," Brooke said, sweeping away an entire nation. "If things work out and the children fit in, maybe Carl can get a job here. You don't suppose Leo . . ."

"No. I'm sure of it. For some reason, he's playing the inaccessible producer with me over the Friedrichs."

Brooke rolled her eyes. "If he's inaccessible to you, that'll be one for the books. You've been like his right arm over the years."

"Don't be silly."

All the same, it was the first time Leo *had* come close to refusing Randi anything. and his conduct in the Friedrich affair was part of that mystery that she couldn't ask anything about. It was Leo, after all, who had paid public tribute to Friedrich on European radio after the failed mission to save his brother and sister-in-law.

Maybe the memories, though seven years old, were still too painful for Leo to face. Still . . . Randi mused . . . Leo *could* have a change of heart, if he would only meet them.

Carl Friedrich felt it necessary to pretend he wasn't moved by the enormity and lush riches of the United States, but Jany had no guile and little pride about expressing her awe as their train, suitably named The Forty-Niner, raced across the two thousand miles from Chicago to San Francisco.

New York had scared her a little. It was like

being locked in a swarm of pushing, rude people, a microcosm of the world. Jany found it too big, too foreign for her chauvinistic French nature.

They were riding in the stiff coach seats of a train, finding themselves almost the only civilians making the trip. The train was filled with servicemen bound for the bloody beaches of the Pacific, and though Carl held his reserve for the first few hours, even he found the GIs' friendly high spirits infectious.

Jany was a great hit among them. They loved the gentle lilt of her accent and kept making her repeat things, much to Carl's annoyance. At first he thought they were ridiculing her, but he could soon tell that their interest was real and that they genuinely respected her. He was amused when, one by one, they confided in him the fear that one of their "buddies" might take advantage of her innocence.

"You just keep a tight eye on her, Charlie," one of them remarked, adding offhandedly, "you got nothing to worry about here. I got a kid sister too. Just about her age."

At least, he thought, they meant well toward Jany, unlike some of her countrymen. Loyal Frenchman though he was, Carl found it hard to forgive Danielle deBrett for testifying that Jany had been "overly friendly" with a Boche named von Leidersdorf.

Only Carl's own involvement in the Resistance had saved Jany from having her head shaved by the vindictive Binet. Together, Carl and Pierre St. Just made a passionate defense on her behalf and won. But Carl felt it was just as well to get her out of the country for a few months until all the furor made by her accusers died down.

It was difficult at first to find himself universally addressed as "Charlie" instead of Monsieur Friedrich, but he liked even less hearing his sister referred to as "Janey." It was obvious to him that the informality was an American custom, of sorts, a mark of acceptance, in its way, though not one he approved of.

As Carl considered some of the few unescorted women on the train, he couldn't help thinking of his voluptuous ex-mistress . . .

What was she doing now, he wondered. As the GIs would say, she was probably "screwing" someone else. Though Carl had eventually abandoned all feeling for her and used her sexual prowess for his own purposes, in the end, with no conscience whatever, Danielle still got the last grim laugh by supporting Monsieur Binet in his wildly exaggerated testimony against Jany. In spite of this, on the night before Carl and Jany left Paris, Danielle had had the cool nerve to ask Carl why he abandoned her.

The new Fourth Republic had stepped in to save Jany from disgrace by testifying to Carl's war work. Still, he wasn't promoted above his minor clerical position in the Ministry of Education, possibly because of the problem created by Monsieur Binet and Danielle.

Disillusioned in both love and politics, Carl decided to take three months off to reconsider his priorities in life. Though disturbed at having to borrow on his life insurance — the only "estate" he could leave Jany if anything happened to him — he felt it would be worth it if he could make the trip to America and vindicate his father to his own satisfaction. The unexpected invitation from his father's widow, Brooke Friedrich, was providential, especially since she almost promised that he could meet the one man he felt could accomplish his purpose, Leo Prysing.

Jany was making the trip mainly on Brooke Friedrich's word that Tony Lombard would not be around during their visit, though Carl knew there was a chance that he could show up at his parent's San Francisco home. Jany seemed to be getting over Tony's parting, and especially the scene of his reunion with his wife, for which Carl had yet to forgive him.

The trip proved to be an exciting one for her, filled with new sights, and Carl felt that her heartbreak over the American was beginning to heal. Even more than that, though, Carl wanted his teenage sister to enjoy something special after having lived through the grueling years of the Occupation. He hoped that in some way this trip to see the wonders of America would give her that something special.

Just as he had hoped, Jany was awestruck by such things as the enormous American river between Illinois and Iowa. The Mississippi, he told her. Then the Missouri, between Council Bluffs and Omaha in a *departement*, or state, called Nebraska. She spent the night hours after Council Bluffs looking for Indians, but the name appeared to be a misnomer. She saw a man on a horse in the *departement* of Wyoming, and was the first to spot some deer that one of the GIs called "antelope."

Everything about the country thrilled her, and though Carl tried to hide it, he shared in most of her wonder.

Although he'd spent a good deal of time worrying about Jany's feelings for Tony, he was relieved by her reaction to the bright lights of Reno after he pointed out that that was where people went for quick divorces.

"But they glorify a sin," she had remarked and stopped admiring the pretty, tree-lined streets.

Thank *le bon Dieu* she hadn't grown too fond of Tony Lombard, Carl thought to himself.

In spite of all they had heard from their soldier and sailor traveling companions in praise of San Francisco, the city came as a glorious shock to them. They couldn't believe that, having traveled across the continent by rail, they had to take a boat to reach their final destination. Nonetheless, their train rolled up on the Oakland Mole and along with everyone else they hurried across what looked like an enormously wide gangplank, onto a white Southern Pacific ferryboat.

From there they saw a huge bridge nearby that spanned the same area, and another, the Golden Gate Bridge, off to their right.

"I love it! Oh, Carl, it's so romantic!" Jany whispered, holding tight to Carl's hand as the boat moved out onto the choppy bay. It was sunny and windy, with the late summer fog hovering off beyond the Golden Gate. Sharing in Jany's excitement, Carl found it difficult to maintain his normally cool, reserved exterior — the effects of four years of working in the Underground had yet to wear off.

There were hardly any skyscrapers on the horizon, but all the buildings seemed to be perched high on hills, or else running up and down hills in a symmetrical fashion. They could see no level ground at all from the Bay. No wonder people were killed in earthquakes, Jany thought; they must all be shaken out of their houses to roll down those terrifying hills.

When the boat pulled into its slip just south of the Ferry Building tower, the servicemen gave cheers for their favorite leave city. Jany and Carl, however, were too busy trying to keep their balance to cheer. The boat rammed into one side of the slip, then modified its rift, until at last the planks were down and the ropes pulled aside. The crowd poured forward into long, salt-smelling passage that led to the main waiting room, where the odor of roasting peanuts filled the air.

Carl walked proudly through the crowded area carrying their two old, battered suitcases, with Jany's arm tucked in his.

"Suppose Madame Friedrich isn't here," Jany whispered.

He would not for the world have let her know that he shared her same fear. "You are being very silly, *ma chèrie*. We can always take streetcar."

"A cable car?" she asked, hopefully.

"Well, perhaps." He wasn't at all sure. The city might not even have cable cars any more. Such transportation was long out of date elsewhere, Carl reasoned, but then, so were ferryboats. It seemed to be a very quaint city.

They didn't see a soul that they recognized on the long, smooth benches in the waiting room.

Jany clutched Carl's arm more tightly. In the hubbub, with foreign languages being spoken rapidly everywhere around them, they felt cut off from the world and more alone than ever.

Suddenly a cheerful male voice called to them.

"Hey! Over here. Carl. Jany. This way."

Carl had never dreamed he would be so glad to see the familiar face of Steve Lombard, who strode around the benches toward them. With him was a tall, beautiful, tawny-haired woman who looked somewhat reserved and formal, but not unfriendly. Steve hugged Jany, and to Carl's surprise, hugged him as well before introducing them to his wife, the elegant blonde lady. Mrs. Lombard shook hands with both of them. She wasn't nearly as gregarious as her husband, but all the same, one felt that she had a genuine interest in people outside of her own family. Carl relaxed a little.

"Madame Lombard," Carl said, "it is an honor. We've been admiring your very beautiful city."

Randi glanced around at the travelers coming and going, taking in the general air of decay in a building that had once been among the busiest in the nation.

"You will like it even more when we get out of here. Mrs. Friedrich — Brooke, that is — will meet us at the house."

Jany was obviously nervous. She murmured with almost too much enthusiasm, "I am most anxious to meet Madame."

With a glint in his eye, Steve said, "She wants to greet you as the lady of the mansion. That's my sister for you, but don't take her airs too seriously. She means well."

They walked out together, Randi with Jany and the two men slightly behind. Carl felt it was an opportune moment to assert his wish not to impose on the family.

"Monsieur — I mean, sir — my sister and I will stay at a local hotel. A *pension*, perhaps. We do not wish to become dependents of Madame — Mrs. Friedrich."

Randi turned and looked back at her husband as they made their way toward Brooke's car.

"Steve, please make it clear to these nice children that we owe them Tony's life."

Steve grinned, clapping Carl on the back. "True, we can't pay you back for that, but we expect you to be generous about it."

Carl was puzzled. "What do you mean, sir?"

"You must be generous and allow us to show you our gratitude in the form of crass materialism."

"*Pardon*, monsieur?"

"You are to be our guests, Carl and Jany. We insist. And later, we will look into your future. Possibly there is a position here worthy of your talents."

"I must return to Paris, monsieur. I would not be happy anywhere else."

"Later, Steve," Randi advised quietly.

But Steve continued on blithely. "You'll love it here, I know it. You just have to give it time. It'll grow on you. Europeans always feel at home in The City, as we call it." The group came to a halt in front of one of the biggest cars Jany had ever seen. Steve's high spirits prevailed. "Here we are. My sister's Caddy. Prewar. Even Brooke couldn't manage a Rolls in these times. You want to take the front seat with me, Carl? We'll chauffeur the ladies."

Jany was so busy looking around, awed by the curious vertical structures of the city that she hadn't said a word to Randi except an occasional, "*Ah, oui.* I mean to say, yes, Mrs. Lombard." The Embarcadero swarmed with military equipment and sailors in their sassy dinks and flapping pants. Jany's eyes opened wide at the sight of the American sailors — they looked so dashing. She was thrilled when she caught one of them winking at her when they stopped for a red light. Luckily, Carl didn't see it. She smiled back at the sailor as the big, sleek black car pulled away.

Carl soon saw that cable cars still rattled, clanged and hummed their way over the hills of the city. Steve Lombard followed one of the cable slots up California Street toward what Randi pointed out as Nob Hill. To Jany, the most fascinating part she'd seen in her brief introduction to the city was Chinatown. They crossed its main street, Grant Avenue, on the spur of the hill and Jany sat up, pressing her nose against the car window to stare at its wonders. Randi lowered the window for her so she could see better, touched at the young girl's eager fascination at the sights around her — the upturned roofs, the Oriental signs and faces were her first glimpse of a far distant world.

"Used to be full of Japanese shops," Steve remarked. "We had quite a fight to hold the property for them, but most of it went. War fever."

"These Japanese, are they not enemies?" Carl asked.

"*These* Japanese are perfectly good American

citizens. Born here, many of them, like the rest of us with foreign blood, and like my friend Gene Cortapassi. Or our doctor, Ulrich Schmidt. But nobody locked *them* up. I'm happy to say. Some of the Japanese properties here have gone to blacks who moved in to work in war production, so it's still going to be rough when the war is over and the Japanese return to claim what was theirs. Somebody's going to be hurt, one way or another."

"It's very confusing," Carl admitted. "I thought when we defeated the Boches it would all be over and good things would come."

"Our war was in the Pacific, my lad. Anyway, we'll see that good things do come to you."

"You are very kind, monsieur, but you see —"

"Call me Steve."

"But you see, I am here with one purpose. I wish to speak with Monsieur Prysing about my father. It is of great importance to me."

Jany became aware of a lull in the conversation in the front seat of the car. Steve was muttering something about two cable cars ahead of him that blocked traffic while a man high up in a little sentry box maneuvered the difficult crossing of cables at Powell and California streets.

Randi Lombard, sensing the awkwardness of the moment, took up the conversational slack.

"Leo is working on a new project just now, Carl, on postwar readjustment. The boys come home, that kind of thing. But I'm sure he would love to meet you. It's just a matter of finding time. Isn't that the case, Steve?"

"Oh, absolutely." He raised his hand briefly from the wheel, explaining to Carl (and changing the subject), "One thing you have to learn when you drive in San Francisco, Carl. The cable cars always have priority, even if it interferes with your leveling off as you climb a hill. Another rule: always level off before you stop, or you slide back." Carl started to ask how he could level off if a cable car had priority, but Steve interrupted him before he could finish. "You'll learn. And one other thing — always curb your wheels, or you'll slide downhill."

*"Curb the — ?"*

"Nothing to it," Steve said, leaving him more perplexed than ever. A short time later, the Friedrichs found themselves staring at the big, solid, stone house ahead of them, surrounded by a wrought-iron fence — the only two-story "house" in a neighborhood full of great hotels like the Mark Hopkins and the Fairmont.

At the end of the walk, standing outside the massive doorway, was Brooke Lombard Friedrich, affecting a pose of welcome. Jany found her presence far less formidable than that of Tony's elegant and reserved mother. Brooke's glistening auburn hair with its curly tendrils made her look younger than she was, and her expansive gesture of welcome with arms outstretched reminded Jany of her own mother. Carl hung back at first with his usual reserve, but Jany readily went into the arms of her father's widow.

While Steve rolled his eyes heavenward and grinned at Randi, Brooke gushed over her two guests.

*"Mes enfants, bienvenue! Mes chères enfants, si jolie, si beau; n'est-ce pas?* I would have known my Kurt's

children anywhere." She glimpsed Carl over Jany's shoulder, and the girl sensed that her mention of their father would win him over at once.

Carl beamed and even allowed his stepmother to embrace him on both cheeks in the French style. As she ushered them into the house, one on each side of her, she said, "We must talk about your dear papa. I will tell you my memories of Kurt and you must tell me yours."

"Yes, madame, indeed. We would love to know more about our father. He was a hero, you know. We heard Monsieur Prysing's broadcast."

"Yes, yes, my dear Kurt, always such a charmer. But whether he was a hero or not is neither here nor there, my dears. Do come in. It's such a dreary old house, but it's been in the family forever and we call it home."

Jany found it awe-inspiring, not only this warm, bubbling lady, but the enormous house. The entryway, or foyer, was dark, due in part to the heavy staircase beyond. In the right wing, separated from the left by the staircase and the wide, lower floor hallway, were the parlor and the ballroom beyond it. Jany caught glimpses of the formal dining room in the left wing. Seeing Jany's glance into the luxurious room made Brooke apologize.

"You see how the wallpaper pattern is carried out in the upholstery? Rather nice, I thought. Randi's idea, of course. But that was in 1941. Heaven knows, it's all a bit faded now."

"Exquisite, madame," Jany breathed. "Like Versailles. *Très magnifique;* isn't it so, Carl?"

"In very good taste, madame. All of the house. It looks very French. Did my father stay here often?"

"No, poor lamb. Only twice. It was not *simpatico* to him, you see. He was pretending to be a Nazi, I believe, and everyone thought badly of him."

"My poor father."

Jany tried to empathize with her brother, but, having never met her father, she found it best to kept quiet.

Jany reasoned that feelings of guilt probably accounted for Carl's intense need to glorify their father. He had spent his entire boyhood hating him after he deserted Carl and the rest of the family. Then, when it was too late, he discovered that his father had actually been an anti-Nazi hero whose cover must have kept him from acknowledging his illegitimate family.

Carl needed a heroic father. For him it helped wipe out the strain of illegitimacy. If he could only accept people as they were, Jany thought. It was painful, but simple — like having to acknowledge that Tony Lombard belonged to a glamorous wife and adorable child.

Having grown up under the Occupation, and learned to make much out of small moments, Jany was properly thrilled by her lovely bedroom with its feminine, pink hues, its view of cable-car tracks, roof-tops, and a fog-shrouded mountain top called Twin Peaks. She gingerly approached the four-poster bed, but soon got enough courage to climb up on the spring mattress and bounce several times.

She devoutly hoped that Carl, too, had a bed with just such a mattress. He deserved it after years of sleeping on the horrid, broken springs of their Paris couch. But he deserved more than a good bed, she thought. If she spent a lifetime paying him back it wouldn't be long enough, especially after what they'd just come through.

An elderly woman, homely and wrinkled, knocked and stuck her head in before Jany could get off the bed.

"Hello, Miss Jany. I'm Miss Thorgerson, the housekeeper. Anything you want, you pull that cord beside the bed there. Old-fashioned, but it works. The girl will come and get you whatever you want. Hard to get help these days with the war on, but we got two girls we're training."

Jany let herself down hurriedly. "If there is anything I may do to help, madame —"

The housekeeper was taken aback slightly but she graciously declined Jany's offer. "You enjoy yourself, honey. My, you're a pretty one!"

She left, leaving Jany in a pleasant confusion.

Things got a bit tense before dinner. Randi dropped in to ask how she was getting along and if she needed anything. Jany needed nothing except the woman's advice on which dress she should wear to dinner. Randi was very kind and never indicated in any way that neither dinner dress was adequate, but Jany, who had a Frenchwoman's eye for clothes, knew that Randi's simple, sleek, blue-gray crepe gown was worlds away from her own slightly wrinkled georgette dress. The dress was three years old. Even worse, it had been designed for a fifteen-year-old, and Jany was now past eighteen.

"Come down when you're ready," Randi told her. "We're much more informal than we sound. We will all have a cocktail — aperitif — first to break the ice."

"Thank you, madame . . . Randi."

Jany breathed easier when Tony's mother was gone. Though Randi Lombard was a kind woman, she felt that Brooke Friedrich would understand and be more sympathetic. She seemed so warm-hearted.

Jany sighed over the jonquil-yellow dress, made from material used in one of her mother's old gowns, but after a little experimentation and the use of some safety pins she found in the upper drawer of the French dresser, she hoped the georgette dress showed off her figure to advantage.

Straightening up and walking as tall as she could, Jany went down the heavy front staircase. She felt a little like a cinema star making her grand entrance. When she reached the archway opening of the lamplit parlor, she saw that not only was everyone there, but a new guest had arrived — a stranger. Her movie-star feeling quickly dissolved. Her shyness overcame her, and she felt more like Marie Antoinette stepping up to the guillotine.

The strange man had just been relieved of his topcoat and presented an imposing pair of shoulders on a body that was almost stocky, but this only added to the power the man exuded. He looked around, saw Jany, and his dark eyes devoured her from her shining head to her well-worn pumps. Her first impression was of a square, unattractive face, illuminated by those eyes, and heavy, sensual lips. When he smiled she was surprised to find herself smiling back, though she couldn't imagine who he was. In a rather frightening way he fascinated her.

Brooke moved toward Jany, her chiffon sleeves

and skirt fluttering around her. She seemed uneasy, so different from her usual, effervescent self, knowing that Leo didn't expect to see the Friedrichs there.

"And here is Kurt's little girl. What did I tell you, Leo? Isn't she a doll?"

The gentleman's face changed, the smile vanished almost instantly. "How odd that you didn't mention that the Friedrichs had arrived," he said drily, with what Jany thought was an edge to his voice.

Could that be why Madame Brooke was babbling and behaving in such an uncharacteristic way? Not only did the gentleman not expect them, he didn't seem to want to meet them, either. Jany hesitated, feeling awkward, and fought an impulse to run back up the stairs to the safety of her room.

Then, without warning, he moved toward her, his expression softening. It gave his face an odd, though pleasant charm.

"My dear, since no one will present me, I must present myself. I am Leo Prysing." He took her hand and kissed it.

Although she knew she was shaking, she tried to affect the cool, almost insolent confidence of the Lombards who observed the scene from behind the awesome man standing before her.

# Chapter Twenty-Three

Carl Friedrich would have liked to corner the producer and have a long talk with him, but it would have been shockingly bad manners to intrude on the family's lively, if trivial conversation. He waited with the patience that had served him well, especially in the last five years.

It began to grow interesting when they discussed things that Carl, and most of his countrymen, had never heard of before. He knew vaguely about the fall of the Philippines, the islands above — or were they below? — Japan in the Pacific. Pearl Harbor had entered into it somehow. But the attack had occured while Paris was under the Occupation, and it was difficult to know what to believe from any source. Hawaii, somewhat to his surprise, had turned out to be allied with the United States as a territory . . . neither state nor dependency. Very confusing.

The conversation at dinner was passionate, centering on the suffering of American and Filipino soldiers during the "Death March" and a place called Corregidor. Carl felt honor-bound to admit that he had newer heard of either event, but the group understood why.

He stopped eating the delicious cracked crab — what a wonderful meal at a time when these people were still fighting a war! — long enough to explain.

"Even in the Ministry of Education I am afraid what news we received was badly censored."

Steve at once filled him in, describing the long, agonizing retreat of men who believed to the last that they would be rescued, that they would not be abandoned by their government.

Leo took up the argument. "Expediency. It was necessary, Steve. Every ounce of material, every man had to be scraped together to save the European theater. Those kids had to be sacrificed."

"Why?" Randi asked in a clipped, hard voice.

Shocked by such a question, Carl forgot himself for a moment. "But to save humanity, madame. To save France. Europe. Civilization."

Randi smiled, though it wasn't an indulgent smile. "Most of my son's schoolmates were in the Pacific theater. That's all."

The woman had strong ideas, ideas that were strange to Carl. He flushed, begging her pardon. He was sure Randi wasn't angry with him, but he was still relieved when Brooke reached over to squeeze his arm and reassure him.

"We say what we like here, Carl. We all respect you for speaking up. Don't we, Randi?"

"Of course. But Leo, Carl isn't here to argue the merits of the Pacific versus the Atlantic theaters of war. I'm sure he would love to hear something about his father."

"I am most anxious, sir."

Leo helped himself to more cracked crab from the plate offered by the young Chinese girl at his elbow.

"Nothing to say, actually, aside from what was broadcast a long time ago. Remarkable that you can still get fresh crab, Randi. What with the submarine net and all the navy activity."

Just as Jany started to speak for the first time during the meal Brooke corrected him.

"Oh, no. The meal was mine, not Randi's. I have the right contacts."

"Black market, naturally."

Brooke acknowledged her brother's hit with a shrug, but Leo Prysing ignored her comments. He turned to Jany, who was seated between himself and Steve.

"You were about to say, Miss Friedrich?"

Carl was grateful to the producer, even though the subject had been changed. He knew it cost Jany something to interrupt all these self-confident chatterboxes. Jany gave Leo a shy smile, which obviously appealed to the producer.

"*Pardon.* It is only that my brother would like to hear more about our father. But perhaps you did not know him personally."

"Know Kurt Friedrich? God knows, I ought to. I brought him to this country for my first American film, back in the silent days. *Prince of the Golden Isles.* Remember, Randi? You and Steve were on a second honeymoon or something, in Hawaii. I brought my company over to Oahu for the shooting."

Randi and Steve exchanged glances. "I remember," she said.

"So, if you'd like to hear about the old silent days, I'm your man."

Leo briefly covered Jany's hand with his own, though she was holding a fish fork. Carl, catching the gesture, frowned and stirred uneasily, but Jany managed to release her hand by dextrously turning the tines upward. Leo grinned and drew his hand back, much to Carl's relief.

He admired the producer, first because of his public tribute that had changed his life, and second, because Carl had seen two of his recent films in Paris since the Liberation, and there was no mistaking the Prysing touch: half art, half commercial, and all entertainment.

Above all, Carl desperately wanted to hear tales about his father during those days when he and his mother received magical postcards from faraway places like Oahu and Hollywood. Olga Rey had been far less impressed by their postmarks than her young son. She claimed that Hollywood, the city of the twenties, was only full of desperate girls, drug-addicted stars, fast Dusenbergs and Isotta-Fraschinis — not much of what her dreams were made of. Maybe so. But the cards represented a validation of Carl's claim on his father.

They adjourned for coffee to a comfortable old room they called the sunporch at the back of the second floor. Everyone sat around on couches and rattan chairs with faded cushions. The producer settled on one of the couches, and in his genial but imperious manner, motioned to the Friedrichs to join him. Carl was watchful, but decided that the man's behavior with Jany remained avuncular, even fatherly. This was a relief to Carl, who was sophisticated enough to know that many producers permitted themselves a great deal of freedom with young ladies, especially ones as young and attractive as Jany. As long as she made no complaint — she even seemed to like the producer — Carl was happy not to have to antagonize the man.

Despite frequent interruptions and non sequiturs from Brooke, Leo Prysing entertained the family with descriptions of the days of silent movies. Carl was interested but realized later as he reflected on the evening in an incredibly comfortable bed that very little had actually been said about Kurt Friedrich. He remained a half-sketched portrait to his son.

During one of Leo's more long-winded accounts of some of his silent film stars, Brooke suddenly said, "Randi, you polished Leo's script that time in Hawaii. Wasn't Kurt just the most handsome creature? Tall and golden as a Viking. So — "

"Aryan?" Leo asked with a grin.

In the awkward confusion that followed Steve tried to pass over Leo's subtle suggestion that Friedrich was not, in fact, an anti-Nazi.

"Brooke talks like a press agent," Steve said, "But Friedrich was a good-looking guy, as I recall. Not unlike Carl here."

"Oh, no!" Brooke said. "Kurt was *much* lighter. I mean, no offense, dear, but Kurt was admired wherever we went."

"Personally, I think his son is far more attractive."

Randi's comment embarrassed Carl far more than Brooke's unintentional denigration. He was left tongue-tied while they all argued about it jokingly.

"And what does Kurt's little girl have to say about it?" Leo wanted to know.

Jany's chin went up. "I agree with Madame Randi. But I never knew my father. I only know Carl."

Brooke promptly reversed herself by agreeing. "My dear, you are so right. Our Carl must have broken a few hearts already. Just wait until we turn him loose in San Francisco."

Feeling more and more uncomfortable, Carl tried to get the conversation back on the track. "About my father, sir. You were telling us about the days when he worked for you. But could you tell us again about his attempt to save your brother and his wife? How long had he been a part of the Underground? How did you come to know of his involvement? You know, sir," he hurried on, "one of my main reasons for joining the Resistance was to be worthy of my father. He was my inspiration."

"And you certainly lived up to him, believe me," Stephen agreed. "You helped to save France. And you most certainly saved our boy. He'd never have made it without you."

Carl stared at Tony's father. It seemed an unfair and probably untrue dismissal of Tony Lombard.

"Do you think so, sir? I don't. Your son was just as courageous as . . . as my father, or people like Madame de Souza and Pierre St. Just, and all the others who risked their lives in Underground work."

Throughout Carl's passionate defense of Tony Lombard, Leo had been studying Jany. "I'm afraid we're boring the ladies," he remarked. "Miss Friedrich, you strike me as having some of your father's affinity for the camera. Have you ever thought about following in his footsteps?"

Carl was amused, knowing how his little sister felt about such exposure. As he expected, Jany was revolted.

"Monsieur, I would hate it!"

The producer seemed pleased. "Extraordinary. Carl, this is a rare young lady."

"I know it, sir."

"All the same, I imagine she would enjoy visiting a movie studio. Randi, if you or Steve are likely to be dropping in at the studio soon, bring along the Friedrichs. They could renew their friendship with Eden Ware and Tony. Tony is doing a polish job on a little script about the liberation of Paris. If it goes well, I've promised he can handle the film. You might add a few ideas of your own, Carl. It'll be Tony's first directing job, and I'm sure he'd be grateful — after all, you were there, too. It could be worth a nice bit of change to you. Think about it."

Before Jany could refuse this also, Carl leaped to the next obvious step. "At your studio, sir, would it be possible for me to view your film, *Journey*? I understand it includes my father's part in the attempt to rescue your family. I would be most grateful to see it."

"Yes, why not?" Randi said.

Her husband looked at her. Then he and Leo Prysing began to speak at the same time.

"As Randi says, why not? It's all water over the dam, anyway," Steve suggested. But Leo's voice was clipped and sounded vaguely disingenuous.

"Sorry, but the master print is gone now. The studio fire back in '42. Remember, Steve? I've tried to recover a print but they're all hacked up — censored. I was told it had to do with wartime security." He stopped, looked around for a cigarette. His fingers curled tightly around the pack. He said briskly, "It was a shame about Friedrich's death. The Nazis play rough." After another glance at Jany, he added, "I've often regretted the public praise I heaped on your father, but I naturally assumed he'd escape safely to London." His heavy lips twisted slightly. "It was a tragic miscalculation."

Steve added quickly, "As I recall, nothing happened until several months after the broadcast. He must have been imprisoned immediately after the Goebbels gang or the Himmler SS heard of it, though. Then they covered his death under the general holocast of what they called *Kristallnacht*. Wouldn't you say that's how it happened, Leo?"

"Well, given the time that passed between the broadcast and his death, I would say that's a strong possibility."

There was an uncomfortable silence as the Friedrichs sat, absorbing this new information.

"Well, folks, anyone want to walk me a block to the Mark? I've got some Scotch, the real McCoy, in my suite. Don't want to waste it on the U.N. The place is swarming with them, by the way."

Only Steve chose to return to the Mark Hopkins with him, to discuss the financing of a B-picture unit that, according to Steve, could be resold when television came in. They were already arguing the matter — Leo standing for quality, Steve for profits — when they left the house.

Brooke bustled around, offering her French guests a vermouth cassis. "Eden and I used to love the mixture back in those wonderful prewar days. Are you young people going to take Leo up on his offer of a studio tour?"

"I do not believe so," Carl said, but he was surprised when Jany disagreed.

"I think you should go, Carl. Monsieur Prysing says he can help you. And maybe you could help Tony with his script."

"But I thought —" He was afraid she wanted to see Tony again. Damn the Lombards! It would only lead to more pain for her.

"— I will stay here and see this beautiful city," she announced before he could finish. "Madame Brooke says two of the best *grand magasins* are owned by French families."

"Oh, yes, my dear. Paul Verdier founded the City of Paris, back in my grandfather's Gold Rush days. And Raphael Weill's family own The White House. They're two of our best department stores."

Carl grew anxious again, only this time over another matter — they had very little money. Jany, sensing what he might be thinking, reassured him.

"I shall buy a scarf, perhaps a belt. But I like best just to look."

His sister's instinctive frugality endeared her even more to him, and at the moment Carl resolved to let her spend as much as they could possibly afford. She deserved it. As for himself his prime concern would be to find a movie theater somewhere that was showing Leo Prysing's great prewar triumph, *Journey*.

# Chapter Twenty-Four

Jany could feel it in the air — for the first time in her life she was in a position to help Carl. She knew from the moment she met Leo Prysing that he had the power and the money to help anyone he chose up the success ladder. First, she had to convince him to let Carl see the film he was so excited about. But more importantly, Monsieur Prysing was willing to pay Carl for his firsthand knowledge about the liberation of Paris, and the history and efforts of the Resistance as he had known it.

Everything depended on Leo Prysing, and he seemed most willing to do anything he could. He might have had a ruthless reputation elsewhere, but it was clearly exaggerated in Jany's eyes. In her presence he had never been anything but generous and kind.

Leo strengthened his favorable first impression on Jany by escorting her and Brooke to some location shooting at the marina overlooking the Golden Gate where, he explained, they would run the scene behind Walter Pidgeon, borrowed from MGM, and Virginia Mayo, who belonged to Sam Goldwyn and Warner Brothers. People in Hollywood all seemed to "belong" to someone, or some corporation. The film also starred Fredric March, but to Jany's disappointment, he would only appear in the Hollywood scenes. Film making was odd and not very satisfactory to her, because much was illusion. The actors weren't really in San Francisco at all, half the time, though they were supposed to be.

On August 9, a second atomic bomb was dropped on Nagasaki in Japan, and the next day the rumors spread like San Francisco's summer fog. The Japanese Empire was suing for peace.

Leo insisted on flying the Friedrichs down to Hollywood with him during the interim while talks of signing the peace treaty were still going on. Steve Lombard seemed surprised that Leo wanted the Friedrichs to visit the studio, which only proved how little Steve understood the basic goodness of his friend and business partner. No one but Jany seemed to be aware of this side of Leo Prysing's nature. It made her feel rather important, secretly, to think that she had been the only one to discover these marvelous qualities about the man.

At the San Francisco airport down the peninsula, where an army general's wife and her entourage had been bumped to make room for the Friedrichs, Jany overheard Steve talking quietly to Leo.

"Are you sure this is wise, such close contact?"

Jany began to feel guilty, knowing that, although she genuinely liked the producer, she also had Carl's interests in mind. Leo's reply instantly reassured her.

"I know what I'm doing. I knew the minute I walked into your house. This is something special. I haven't felt this was in twenty years or more."

"Just remember. Not your garden variety."

"I know that too. I'm on a straight course this time. No detours."

"I hope so, pal."

Jany wondered if they were talking about her. The idea might have been alarming a year, or even a few days ago. But she had begun to like him. Besides, feeling like a wordly woman who had almost broken up another woman's home, she thought that Leo Prysing might prove a solid barrier between her and her illicit passion.

Jany was further relieved when Leo remarked regretfully that Tony had accompanied Eden and the baby to Lake Arrowhead for scenes representing the Italian Alps. Above all, Jany wanted to avoid meeting the man she loved.

Keeping to his word, Leo treated Jany with great respect. He had the European habit of kissing her on both cheeks when they met or parted, but Jany saw that he treated Randi and Brooke the same way, and after a first bristling reaction, Carl made no further objection. Leo was being especially kind to Carl, including him on several private screenings in the Bay Area, pointing out what Carl should look for if he took the job of advising Tony Lombard on the historical accuracy of the movie.

Carl went along with the screenings, although it was clear to Jany that he secretly hoped one of the projectionists would have access to a print of *Journey*. Meanwhile, being a quick study, he picked up a surprising amount of knowledge about filmmaking. He impressed Leo with his occasional quiet reminders of small matters that slipped by the producer. He even remembered the footage and one detail of a setup that both the camera crew and the script girl had missed. Clearly his gift was for detail. Steve Lombard, observing his ability, remarked to Prysing, "If you can't find a place for this boy, maybe I can."

The producer grinned. "Don't you worry, there's always room in the business end of Prysing Productions. The trouble is, most fellows with any talent like the glamor side. Your Tony is one. But this boy is different."

Brooke Friedrich, overhearing the conversation, was immediately indignant, thinking Carl had been slighted. "No, you don't. Carl told me only this morning that my stock in Pacific Shipping wasn't going to build. I should look into aircraft manufacturing and electricity."

"Electronics."

"Whatever. Sam Liversedge says he's right. I've a notion to make him my assistant. Give him a modest salary, and see how he handles all my ventures."

"Haven't Sam and I done well enough for you?" Steve asked.

"Yes, dear, but the boy is Kurt's son. I owe him something."

Steve and Leo looked at each other. Leo shrugged. "Maybe we all do," Steve said slowly. On a lighter note, he added, "Talk about nepotism. Leo, you won't be happy until every Lombard friend or relative is on your payroll."

But Carl Friedrich's future was temporarily left in abeyance when Randi remarked the "the boy might have his own ideas." Leo, used to being the mastermind behind everyone and everything around him, silently — yet begrudgingly — acknowledged this possibility.

Leo Prysing had an impressive black limousine

waiting at the Los Angeles Airport for them, and without stopping at a hotel, they were driven across an enormous, sprawling city with no conspicuous landmarks toward a town called Culver City that seemed to be encapsulated by Los Angeles. Jany's first reaction was disappointment. They had not yet seen any of Hollywood's palatial movie houses, at least none to compare with San Francisco's Fox Theater. As for Paris, she considered the cinemas on the Champs-Elysées infinitely superior to the neighborhood movies in this odd, rambling city. Leo could only laugh in reply.

"We don't claim to rival your Paris, my dear. We're just going to be bigger."

"My mother and father sent me cards from Hollywood when I was a child," Carl said. He looked at the streets with different eyes, remembering the silent film triumphs of his parents long ago.

Leo watched the brother and sister with hooded eyes. He surprised and touched Jany when he leaned his head back against the side window, still watching Carl in particular.

"Your mother was a wonderful woman. I don't know any actress who was better liked. That says a great deal in this town, believe me. I know you are interested in finding out more about your father. But your mother was the special one."

Jany smiled at him. Her fingers touched his heavy hand with feathery lightness.

"Thank you. We loved her very much. It wasn't her fault that he didn't marry her. She was a wonderful mother."

Carl became stern. You mustn't talk about that

to strangers, Jany. They wouldn't understand our father's political reasons."

She felt the rebuke but resented it on behalf of Monsieur Prysing, who had been kindness itself. When she looked at him with thanks and Leo took her hand, she let him hold it, thinking privately that he behaved far more like her father than Kurt Friedrich had ever done.

Leo's executive secretary, Miss Belle Sweete, a lean, capable brunette with her hair pulled back in the new style like a pony-tail, took the old suitcase in which Carl and Jany packed a change of under-wear, a shirt and blouse, and a nightgown for Jany. The woman was kind enough to Jany but inclined to flirt with Carl. Carl saw this and surprised Leo, though not Jany, by responding with a certain lightness. Jany was amused. She knew her brother very well. He must hope to learn more about the industry from Miss Sweete. It was true that he hoped to find the film of *Journey*, but apparently found the motion-picture business interesting as well.

Leo intended to show the Friedrichs around the lot, through the three big soundstages and the back acres where so many of his movies had been filmed. The fact that he offered to act as their personal guide seemed to throw Miss Sweete. She had to have the fact repeated by Leo himself before it registered. Then, after Jany was made to understand the significance of his gesture, Carl bowed out of the tour. Once again, the background of films intrigued him more than the glamor of movie sets.

"Would it be possible to inspect your stock of films, sir?"

Leo agreed with a promptness that surprised Miss Sweete again.

"Why not? Miss Sweete, show Mr. Friedrich our film library. You might demonstrate with the Moviola. Show him how we edit." He added in partial explanation, "Not like the big screen, but it's adequate. With the Moviola we cut out most of the ham and sometimes the genius of our stars. The ham is more expensive."

To Jany this talk was all very boring. She much preferred watching her movies unfold in all their splendor — without explanation — among the beautiful accoutrements of a movie house. But Carl seemed eager to look over all the dusty, tiresome reels of film and heaven knew, Miss Sweete was anxious to show off her Moviola, whatever that might be!

With Carl and Miss Sweete off to bury themselves among cans of film Jany felt free to enjoy the glamor of Leo Prysing's presence and the sights of a small but select independent studio. She was already learning, after only a few days in the United States, that the reputation of Prysing's films was among the highest in the industry.

There was much talk of the impending peace everywhere, on the two sets currently filming, and later in the commissary. Entering the crowded room, Jany started to climb onto a stool at the counter, but the producer guided her over to the other side of the room where the stars, directors and anyone else with influence sat at the round tables with their double damask cloths and thick, ornamental silverware.

Leo grinned at Jany's mistake. "Peasants at the

counter, my dear. You belong here at my table."

His table was situated in the far corner, seating eight, compared with the other tables which seated four. Sitting from that vantage point, especially in Leo's chair, the only one with arms, it was possible to see virtually everyone in the room, including the secretaries, readers, script clerks, grips, electricians and other "peasants" who climbed on the counter stools to order their lunch.

Jany knew that everyone in the room was watching her with covert looks, followed by whispers to their neighbors. She tried to sit straight with head up, smiling, just as her mother had taught her. She was deeply aware of her childish-looking, three-year-old dress, and the fact that she was wearing her hair free and curly to her shoulders, rather than rolled up stiffly back from her face as most of the other woman did. But Miss Mayo's lovely hair was unconfined, and an extremely attractive man at another table smiled at Jany in spite of her out-of-style look.

Leo saw her pink flush of pleasure and explained. "That's Joe Cotten. We have him here for our new film."

"An actor?" No wonder he had such sex appeal. But Jany understood instinctively that Prysing hadn't liked her acknowledgment of the star's friendly greeting. It was this protectiveness that both annoyed and made her feel at home with Leo — he behaved much like Carl when it came to the attention other men gave Jany.

"You mean to tell me you never saw *Citizen Kane* in France?"

Remembering Carl's brisk answer to many such

questions, Jany repeated it, but in a more friendly tone. "Monsieur Leo, we had a war."

"Of course. I'm sorry." He slapped her hand playfully. "I'm not very diplomatic, am I? You see, Jany, I'm used to giving a lot of orders and having everyone jump. But I don't mean to be that way with you. I hope you won't mind — I don't want to offend you — but even here, with all these beautiful women, you are still the freshest, loveliest thing I've ever seen since I left Vienna back in '22. Now, don't be offended."

"I am not, truly." She was touched by his humility. She owed much to him, the sparkle and excitement of those special screenings, the introductions to movie stars on the marina with Golden Gate Bridge providing a fog-shrouded, dramatic background. That night he had taken her and Carl and the Lombards to an elegant dinner at the Fairmont Hotel. With his invitation to visit Hollywood, Jany was given her first airplane ride. And now she sat eating real Mexican enchiladas in a room with world-famous stars all around her. Some of them even smiled at her as if they knew her!

Although he complained of heartburn and wouldn't take part in the meal, Leo enjoyed her excitement in spite of what she suspected was jealousy over her response to the handsome Mr. Cotten. He watched her eat, pretending to be amazed at her appetite, and then insisted she order a huge strawberry-cake-and-sweet-cream dessert.

"On Monday you'll have to try the gulyas. They use my sister-in-law Sarah's recipe, a Viennese variation of the Hungarian. You'll like it."

"Oh, yes. I know I will." She licked the cream off her lips. Such a satisfying luxury after years of near starvation. What a shame Carl couldn't be here to enjoy it with her, she thought. Suddenly she remembered that she was Cinderella, and midnight would soon be striking. "It is too bad, but I will not be here Monday."

Leo Prysing was clearly disappointed. "I thought we might introduce you to Barbara Stanwyck and Freddie March. They'll be on the set Monday."

Her pulse quickened at the idea. Maybe, somehow, Carl would extend their stay in America, and she could come back to Hollywood. Just as long as Tony Lombard remained away in Lake Arrowhead, wherever that was.

"Monsieur — I mean Leo —" she said, as he raised a hand, chiding her with a smile, "it would be a great honor. Do not tell Carl," she confided, "but I would rather meet them than President Roosevelt or even General de Gaulle."

He laughed out loud at that and leaning forward, kissed her cheek. She didn't mind, he was so kind and dear. She only minded that everyone in the room seemed to stop eating at the same time and stare at Leo's table.

Suddenly feeling self-conscious, Jany drew back and made a whimsical plea.

"Do you think they mind if I had a little more of the beaten cream on my strawberries?"

"Anything you like." He called the waitress, a gorgeous blonde who looked ready to step before any camera. "Rena, more whipped cream for the young lady. And tell Marcel that when he makes up the menus next week the shortcake is to be called 'Jany's Strawberry Shortcake.' "

Jany gasped. The waitress raised her carefully arched eyebrows. "Sure thing, Mr. Prysing. That's Janney? J-a-n-n-e-y?"

"J-a-n-y," Leo spelled out, raising his voice.

Jany didn't care how it was spelled. This was the greatest honor she had ever been paid in all her eighteen years.

Miss Sweete's lean hips made a slinking pass between Carl and the files of cans all labeled and stacked in their separate cubbyholes.

"Pretty narrow squeeze in here. And with these bad lights . . . I know Mr. Prysing is refinancing next year's product, but we could at least afford a hundred-watt light bulb."

The names of many famous films stuck to the cans didn't impress Carl. He wasn't a movie fan in the traditional sense, but was rather interested in how they were made.

"Mr. Prysing lives very well. He cannot be short of funds."

Miss Sweete let out a short spurt of laughter. "You don't know this industry. We live on a volcano. With any independent producer, bankruptcy is right around the corner. And as if that isn't bad enough, Mr. Prysing has what he calls indigestion, but I'll bet it's ulcers. And these studio crews keep yapping about five-day weeks and triple-time pay and I don't know what-all. They sure don't help Mr. Prysing's condition. They're going to break us yet."

"How can that be, Miss Sweete?"

"Nothing easier. He wins Oscars, New York Critics' Awards, a few dozen lesser trophies, dozens of individual actors' and directors' awards, but his pictures seldom top the most important list of all, the Big Box-Office Hits. His films are popular, for sure, but it takes real blockbusters to earn back what Mr. P. puts into his films. He's one classy gentleman."

Thinking of Prysing's long-ago tribute to his father, Carl agreed. Half his attention was focused on Belle Sweete and what she had to say about the industry, but the other half was busy reading off the film titles to himself always hoping to run across an extra print of the elusive *Journey*, accidentally lost among these epics.

"Are these all of the Prysing films?"

"Sure thing."

"It is strange that the fire destroyed only one film."

"The fire?"

"In 1942, I believe. The studio fire that destroyed the master of the film *Journey*." Perhaps she hadn't been here at the time, he reasoned.

"Oh, that fire. Well, no. It was only a small fire. You saw the little machine on the table outside the vault. You run the film through one of those Moviolas. Kind of a projector of sorts, only you look into the projector itself. You can feed in miles of film and stop it wherever you like, rerun, backward, forward. Anyway, there was a fire while *Journey* was in the Moviola. That's what Leo was talking about."

"But *Journey* was an old film by then. Why would they be looking at it in 1942?"

She dropped a can of film on the cement floor, making a loud clatter. Carl stooped to pick it up. Belle was still staring at him when he handed her the sealed can.

"You really are something," she said. "I suppose the editor wanted some film to use in another picture. Won't any other film satisfy you?"

"I'm afraid not. I would give a great deal to see that particular film."

She shook her head at his stubborn streak.

By the time she had pointed out various other film cans and was ready to lead him out, she decided to get confidential, thinking that would spark his interest in her.

"Look, Carl, why do you really want to see that old movie?"

"I believe it shows my father's heroism in the attempt to save Mr. Prysing's brother the night the Nazi troops entered Vienna. My father was forced to abandon our family for political reasons and I'd like to learn as much about him as possible."

"I see."

She locked the vault, took his arm and led him out into the sultry August sunlight. They made their way along the badly rutted main street between two long soundstages. Carl found himself in the company of American Indians, Indian Indians, longshoremen, two trapeze performers and the Chinese army. Miss Sweete overlooked all these distractions. She seemed to be deep in thought.

"Look here, Carl," she said at last, "if I give you a hint, can you keep your mouth shut about where you got it?"

"I can, Miss Sweete. But why?"

"Damned if I know. Let's just say I want to keep out of this, whatever it's all about. Do you know Berkeley at all?"

It was the last thing in the world he expected.

"I believe it is across the San Francisco Bay."

"Right. Where the Cal campus is. University of California. They go in for studying a lot of old films over there. Anyway, there's a theater, one of the Fox chain, just below the campus. Off Shattuck, one of the main streets. If anybody would know where to get your picture, they would. They called our film library a couple of weeks ago, inviting Mr. P. and one of our contract directors to the screening of several old silents. If they don't do *Journey*, I'll bet they know where you can get it."

"Miss Sweete, you're amazing." He hugged her in his excitement. "You're the first person who's offered me any help."

She squeezed his arm. "My pleasure, I'm sure. Just forget where you heard it."

Carl was figuring rapidly. They were supposed to return to San Francisco in two and a half days, but the sooner they got back the better. He was sure Jany would be ready to leave, especially since Tony Lombard might return to Hollywood at any moment, and she made it plain to Carl that she didn't want to encounter either Tony or Eden.

"We can leave tomorrow morning," he murmured to himself thinking of buses or of coach seats on an overnight sleeper.

"Better let us book your flight early," Miss Sweete reminded him. "I just heard on the radio that President Truman has proclaimed tomorrow as VJ Day. War's officially over. And Frisco's the place to be for that celebration, let me tell you."

For Carl, the war had ended months ago with the reported suicide of Hitler, but he did wonder uneasily if such an important day for the Pacific Coast might bring Tony and his wife back to the house on Nob Hill.

# Chapter Twenty-Five

Eden and Tony had chosen to stay in one of the rustic bungalows a mile around the lake from the mock-Tudor village of Arrowhead high in the San Bernardino mountains. It meant that Eden made a vigorous hike along the lakeshore path every morning to meet the camera crew in the village, but it also gave Tony the excuse for hours of hiking with his eager, dark pixie of a daughter.

While he arranged mentally the camera setups of the Liberation film that Leo Prysing had promised him, he could stride along over pine needles, sniffing the glorious, slightly acrid scent of the forest, always aware of Andrea's small, tight handclasp and her welcome dependence on him.

There were times when he was so content he didn't ask himself what Jany Friedrich was doing at this time of the day or night. He had imagined every step of her journey across the United States, her awe, perhaps her fear at the skyscrapers in New York, the fast, sleek train that must have carried her and Carl to San Francisco, the beauty of that city, and now, of course, the exciting movie industry in Hollywood's environs. Wistfully he thought of how he would love to have watched her reactions . . .

A small demon of temptation gripped him occasionally. What if he and Eden had to return to Hollywood suddenly, on legitimate business? How could they avoid meeting the Friedrichs? What harm would that do? A simple, friendly meeting, maybe with Tony and Carl reminiscing about the days of the Liberation. Nothing to it; no harm in that.

"Daddy, I'm tired."

His daughter's voice jolting him back to the present, he picked up Andrea in her dusty little sandals, middy and shorts, and swung her over his head while she shrieked with delight. Her happy young voice echoed through the sunny glade as he pretended to toss her up still higher, firmly holding her legs. Eden had shaken her head in amusement and disapproval when he tried this in front of her.

"You're going to make her bowlegged or knock-kneed, or something."

But his little Andrea had the prettiest legs he had ever seen. So had Eden, as a matter of fact. He used to be very much aware of those long, slim legs of hers.

Oddly enough, he never thought of Jany in those terms. He was selfish enough not to want her to possess those qualities which attracted sexual remarks from guys on the prowl. He wanted to protect Jany, draw a circle around her and let no other man enter.

No use thinking about that — it was over and done with. Eden had been wonderfully understanding about resuming their relationship slowly. He was sure she suspected something between him and Jany, but her life had been lived in such a broadminded atmosphere that she apparently could accept what she thought of as a natural lapse from fidelity during wartime. He winced when he thought of all the women he had known before he was able to persuade Eden Ware to marry him.

There had been men in Eden's life before their marriage, but her determination not to marry was pretty notorious, and for Tony Lombard she presented a challenge to meet and conquer. He knew, in his heart, that this conquest had been one of the chief reasons for his marriage to her. What he hadn't known was how he would change during the long hospital siege after Pearl Harbor.

*Me, a family man? Fat chance . . .*

Yet he had become one while Eden, not perceiving his slow change, remained the independent, self-centered, generous-natured woman she had always been. It wasn't Eden's fault that he had come to need another kind of wife.

Miserably, he knew the thing to do was to forget Jany. Concentrate on making a family life so attractive that Eden would find herself more interested in her role as wife and mother.

"Daddy, can I ride? Can I?"

"Sure thing." He let her ride on the back of his neck, her legs and scuffed sandals beating a tattoo on his chest. "Shall we hike up to the rim of the World Drive, or around to the dam?"

"Lets see mommy playact."

He turned around and strode down the road. A needling worry made him ask, "Would you like to playact some day the way mommy does?"

"Nope." Her sandals beat madly on his chest. He pretended to cave in, which made her giggle. "Now *you're* playacting, daddy."

"But you act all the time. You mean you don't want to be a big movie star?"

"I want lots of friends like mommy."

"Everyone can't be your friend, sweetheart. It isn't possible."

Her small feet beat against him again.

"Ever'body. Ever'body in the whole world. Well, not the meanies. Just ones that laugh."

"That's a tall order. People may not always feel in the mood to be happy around you."

She wrinkled her nose. "Then I don't like 'em."

"With that sweet smile of yours, you just might get everything you want."

"Oh, daddy!" She giggled again, hiding her face against his hair, delighted to have his attention so completely.

By the time they reached the Tudor village a group of tourists and locals had gathered near the lakeshore to watch Eden Ware, soaking wet, drag herself laboriously out of the water only to see the shiny boots of the Waffen-SS lined up waiting for her. Three actors, European refugees, played the part of the Nazis, and although Tony had seen them do brilliant work on the screen, the sight of the uniforms brought back all the terror of those Paris days when the black-uniformed Gestapo meant torture and death.

He shivered.

"What's the matter, daddy?"

"Sh! Nothing, sweetheart." But it was too late.

"There's mommy," she cried out, pointing to her mother in the water.

"Jesus H. Christ!" the director bellowed. "What now?" He called "cut" and looked over his shoulder. "Quiet, up there. I'm sorry, Eden. Take it from the top again, when you rise out of the water."

Eden grinned, waved to Tony and Andrea, then waded back into the chilly mountain water, her dress sodden and clinging to her slim figure, her light, unruly red hair more flattering than usual as the wet strands outlined the lovely shape of her head. In a second she again became the exhausted girl desperately trying to escape over the Italian Alps, only to find the Gestapo there to meet her.

Tony always marveled at the ease with which she could turn her emotions on and off for the camera. He felt it was unfair that she had never won an Oscar. Despite the fact that she was his wife, he considered her one of the most skillful actresses around, and he knew that he was not alone in his opinion. Well, maybe this film would do the trick. Still, he knew that Academy Awards usually went to the actress who made some startling switch in character, no matter how affected, or a newcomer to films repeating a Broadway success.

Poor Eden. It wasn't fair.

Tony's pity for his indomitable wife surprised him.

When the scene was wrapped up and her entourage consisting of a maid, makeup man and hairdresser surrounded her, she led them up into the village where she signed a few autographs before she kissed Andrea and Tony, and asked him if he had heard the news.

"VJ Day is tomorrow. It's over, honey, all over."

They must have been on the same wavelength. Before he could speak she added softly, "Sometimes I thought we'd never see it together. From that Sunday morning at home on Oahu when I kissed father and Tamiko good-bye, all the way to the end of it, we've come through it together, you and I."

"I know, sweetheart." He had a sudden mental image of the cocky Tony Lombard who, one Sunday morning four years ago, drove his father past Hickam Field and Schofield Barracks toward Pearl Harbor and a breakfast interview with Admiral Kimmel.

*The first wave of planes zooming toward them through Kolekole Pass . . . U.S. planes? On maneuvers, of course . . . Why maneuvers this early on a Sunday morning? Most of the Pacific Fleet's officers had been out late, dancing at Waikiki . . .*

*But they were Nakajima bombers and low-strafing Zeros. Ripping the driver's seat of the car. And the glass. And the blood. And the long blackout that followed . . .*

*That* cocky Tony Lombard had died on the highway to Pearl.

He tried to grin. "Well, where do we celebrate this bright new world they've been promising us over our ration stamps?"

She took a towel from the hairdresser and rubbed her scalp vigorously.

"I thought there's no point returning to L.A. for the big celebration." Besides, she thought, Jany Friedrich was there with her brother. "How about San Francisco? That's where the real celebration will be. Unless — would you rather return to Hollywood, honey?"

"Not me," he said promptly. Still it hurt him that she should be afraid of a meeting with Jany.

Eden didn't deserve that.

At noon on VJ Day Eden and Tony arrived at the Nob Hill house with Andrea. They were keyed up after the hurried drive down from the mountains following Eden's last location shot, and the flight up from Burbank to a city already going wild with joy. The airport swarmed with VIPs pouring into San Francisco, many hoping for belated comments from delegates concerning the newly formed United Nations.

Even a movie star like Eden Ware couldn't win a taxi in that mob, but the name of Stephen Lombard had its usual magic effect in the Bay City, this time from a foreigner. A British U.N. delegate found out who they were and, claiming he owed "old Steve" his rescue from a buzz bomb, had his chauffeur drive the family to the Lombard house.

While Tony and the newest of the endless maids in training saw to their baggage, Randi and Brooke talked to a chattering Andrea upstairs. Eden, hearing voices, wandered into the living room. She saw three people huddled around the radio console at one end of the room. She recognized Leo Prysing's big, grizzled head and his hearty laugh, but surprised herself by her inner shock when Jany Friedrich raised her head and the cool sunlight caught her hair, making it look like a halo.

A slightly out-of-place halo, Eden thought cynically. Eden was a direct woman by nature, but Jany Friedrich's reaction when she saw Eden in the hallway made that directness impossible. The girl must be a born actress, Eden thought. She blushed like a ten-year-old as she backed into her brother, a very attractive young man whose cool poise must be a challenge to any female. His fingers closed on his sister's shoulder, as if to protect her. He wasn't overly friendly, but Eden couldn't deny his courtesy.

"Mrs. Lombard, we meet again. Mr. Prysing was good enough to let us see one of your films. Tony often spoke of your great skill — what he says, it is very true."

Stilted speech, she thought, but coming from a foreigner, and one so attractive, it was acceptable. He took one of his hands off his sister's shoulder and extended it. She took it, reflecting on how different his manners were from the usual Hollywood "darlings" with their kisses on short acquaintance.

Eden was further surprised when he presented his sister before Leo Prysing could do so.

"You remember my sister Jany, madame. We met in Paris the night before Liberation. She was of much courage during the Occupation."

Leo seemed to find all of this highly diverting.

"Why didn't you tell me about her, Eden old girl? She's pretty enough to follow in your footsteps."

Everyone looked at him. After a perceptible pause, Jany swallowed and extended her hand. Her fingers were small and soft in Eden's firm hand. Eden could hardly hear her speak. Qualities like that always annoyed her. In her long experience with the movie world, she always found such manners to be inherently phony.

"How right you are, Leo. Such a pretty thing! I'd almost forgotten."

Jany fumbled a few words in reply, but it seemed obvious to Eden that she was nervous about the prospect of seeing Eden's husband. She kept glancing past Eden at the archway and the big front hall beyond. Doubtless, she hoped to catch her first sight of Tony as he came down the front stairs.

"A great day for us all," Eden remarked and crossed the room to the bar. "War's over. Officially."

"Amen to that." Leo offered to join her. "Shall I mix 'em for you?"

Eden hooted. "Since when have I needed help at the bar? Anybody seen the scotch?"

Leo pushed the chunky crystal decanter toward her. She saw that the Friedrichs were drinking vermouth. Eden was pleased to notice that Carl seemed torn between watching his sister and paying attention to her. In some way it lessened the effect of Jany's crush on Tony. Leo, however, seemed to have other things on his mind besides making mischief between the Lombards and the Friedrichs.

"Eden, how is the crew behaving on your film?"

Keeping one eye on Jany, Eden said indifferently, "Okay, why? Are you expecting labor problems?"

"The old story. Unionizing. Five-day week. They've been just waiting for VJ Day so they could explode all over the place. Warners and Paramount and Fox, even the mighty Metro, are trying to hang onto company unions. But I get the vibrations."

"You're an independent studio. It doesn't affect you. Make a separate deal with IATSE and the others."

"Easier said than done. I'd rather kick their asses from here to the border than deal with those Commie bastards."

"Commie? My God! Where've you been? Back in the Dark Ages? Unions are here to stay, Leo. You can't turn back the clock."

"I'd sure like to try. We can't get a week's shooting done without a six-day week — you know that. Ah," Leo exclaimed as Randi Lombard entered the room, "the rest of our beautiful party has arrived. Randi, I didn't get a chance to tell you before Eden and Tony arrived — you've never looked more handsome."

Randi Lombard wrinkled her nose. "Whenever he calls me handsome," she explained to Eden and Jany with a smile, "it's an insult, believe me. Only old women and gallant generals are referred to as 'handsome.' " She came forward and kissed Eden.

Eden felt it hard to guess from Randi's easy embrace and quick departure to the next guest just how much affection had gone into her greeting of her daughter-in-law. Sensitive to all the nuances of Randi's behavior, Eden found her warmer to Jany. Brooke was her usual exuberant self.

"Eden darling, sorry I ran out on you but I just can't resist that cunning little niece of mine. She gets cuter every day. She's exploring upstairs with Thorgerson right now."

She breezed on to Carl Friedrich, chiding him for not speaking up. "Your glass is empty, dear boy. You mustn't wait on ceremony here. This is your home, as it would have been your father's."

Eden noted how Carl's smile warmed his austere features as he responded to Brooke's perennial, if shallow, enthusiasm. Eden turned around just in time to see Tony coming down the stairs.

After Jany's shock at seeing Eden, she had evidently steeled herself for the meeting, but Tony was entirely unprepared. He stopped in the archway, blinked and stood there just a second too long. There was about his face a kind of arrested emotion, his smile frozen in marble. Another second and he came forward easily.

"Well, this is nice, Carl, you sneaked one over on Eden and me. You and Jany could have come up with us and gotten acquainted with our Andrea."

Jany astonished everyone, and perhaps herself, by taking Leo Prysing's arm and tilting her head against his shoulder.

"Many thanks, Tony, but it was not necessary. As you see, Leo has been kind. Most kind." She smiled into the producer's face, a dazzling young smile that Eden envied. She admired the girl for her gracious recovery from what must have been a bad moment.

Leo Prysing was clearly delighted with the French girl's warmth toward him. He refilled her glass, cupped his hand around her slender neck, and announced, "Never had a greater pleasure, my dear. How's the script breakdown coming, Tony?"

"Pretty good. I didn't know how far to go with the Communist cooperation during the Liberation. I mean, they did help a lot. Carl, whatever became of Danielle deBrett? She was really in her glory that night Eden and dad arrived."

Carl shrugged. "With Danielle, it's politics before pleasure. She calls herself secretary to that little cell she belonged to. You remember her friends . . . they're all as active as ever. And I believe they'll end by destroying the Republic if they're not stopped."

"You are a ruthless fellow," Tony said, playing it lightly. "I thought she was your girl friend."

Carl saw everyone looking at him with varying degrees of curiosity. He seemed embarrassed by the attention but, like his sister, he managed to handle it well.

"We do many things when we are young. I knew Danielle long ago in school. It was only a puppy love."

His sister, knowing what the real attraction between the two had been, added hurriedly, "She is very firm in her beliefs. We — have not seen her since the Liberation."

Carl, however, was more frank in the reason for their parting. "She did something I can never forgive. Tony, she spread the story that my sister had collaborated."

"What!" Eden and Leo echoed Tony's indignation.

"Because of the Boche oberstlieutenant. The charge was brought by a vengeful man who was once a friend and lost his only son to the Boches. He had seen Jany with the German soldier once, when she had no choice but to go. The man drew his own conclusions. Then Danielle testified that she, too, had seen Jany with von Leidersdorf."

Eden was sincerely disgusted. Such injustices always aroused her angry defenses.

"Couldn't you do something? Tony could have testified. Tony?"

"It's vile. You should have called me immediately to come back and testify," Tony said, clearly disturbed at the news. Carl held up a hand to halt all the excitement.

"Please. It is over and done with. I simply tell you this to explain our — my present relationship to Mademoiselle de Brett."

"It's a damned outrage," Leo said, his anger building, "to even suggest that this innocent girl would collaborate with those devils."

Ignoring the Lombards, Jany looked at him with gratitude. "Thank you for understanding. But you see, I did feel sorry for Monsieur von Leidersdorf. I don't believe he would have betrayed Carl and Tony. The letter in his hand was blank."

No one understood this cryptic remark and, afraid to discuss it any further, Randi saved the day by suggesting that they adjourn to the upstairs rooms where they could get a better view of the excitement spreading throughout the city.

They all trooped up, glad to be rid of such unpleasant war memories on the very day when the war was officially over.

Steve Lombard found them there, crowded into the big front bedroom that had once belonged to his mother and now was a part of Brooke's "suite," as she called it, having enlarged the room to include a dressing room and linen room. Since Steve had just been included in a conference with the mayor and the Sixth District commanding general, he had all the latest news. Eden watched with interest as even Leo Prysing kept quiet long enough to hear Steve's recounting of the official Armistice.

It took a while for it to dawn on Eden that Leo

and the French girl were thick as thieves. At any rate, the girl made no resistance to Leo's attentions and Eden had never seen the producer so besotted by a woman. Probably Jany Friedrich's innocence — whether real or assumed — was refreshing to him.

Even more interesting to Eden was Tony's reaction to what he, too, seemed to notice. He seemed determined not to watch the growing romance, making it a point not to look in their direction even once. As much as the idea of it hurt Eden, she sensed that he was suffering.

She tried to reassure herself, thinking that Tony had been reasonably contented, even happy with her before Brooke got her bright idea of inviting the Friedrichs to America. Well, Eden thought, once this Jany returned to Paris, Tony would find that life went on splendidly — she would be sure to make it so. True, their sex life had not yet become as uninhibited as it had been before the war, but they needed more time to adjust. And there was always Andrea whom he adored — surely he wouldn't give *her* up very easily.

Tony was sure to get wrapped up in his new career, moving upward from being a lowly assistant as he had been before his Paris experience, to the big break he was getting with his first directing job.

At the same time, Eden couldn't help being relieved by the French girl's attempt to avoid Tony. It might only be puppy love on her part, but Eden remembered well her own girlhood crushes and her first love, the Comte de Grasse, who had died near Dunkirk early in the war. Eden cursed her idiotic notion of coming to San Francisco to celebrate VJ

Day. She knew in her heart that she had made the suggestion in order to avoid the Friedrichs in Los Angeles.

Serves me right, she thought, and was relieved when Miss Thorgerson came in with young Andrea, breaking Eden's mood. Everyone made a fuss over the child, who glowed under their attention. Fortunately, she did not appear to have developed conceit yet, and Eden meant to see that she never did.

Eden's relief at the way things were going was short-lived — Andrea took to Jany Friedrich at once. There was a definite warmth, almost a motherly affection in the way the French girl gained Andrea's confidence, asking her how she did her pretty dark hair so cleverly and answering in detail when Andrea wanted to know how she made her "funny dress" with hand-sewn eyelets.

Tony became more voluble than usual with his father, proceeding from the VJ ceremonies to Steve's memory of his meetings with ex-Prime Minister Churchill. In no time they were discussing Tony's first directorial job. They even quarreled over Steve's influence in his getting it, always a sore point with Tony.

"Look," Stephen insisted, "it was all Leo's idea. I have nothing to do with it. My plans are for a kind of A-minus or B-plus unit whose films would be sold later to television. Television is coming into the home. It's only a matter of time."

Leo must have had exceptional hearing; at this remark he shouted across the room, "Not while movies are blasting away at the box offices. *The Hollywood Reporter* predicted yesterday that 1946 would be the biggest year in the history of films."

Everyone looked over at him, Tony included. Leo was sitting with his arm around Jany Friedrich's waist. Perhaps she didn't notice; she was listening intently to Andrea, who was describing their exciting time at Lake Arrowhead.

Out on the street a cable car rattled by, almost invisible under the crowd of hangers-on. Most of them were sailors. Steve opened the window and waved, then turned to the family. "Let's get going or we'll miss all the fun. When I came across Market Street they were tearing the place up."

Everyone rustled around, hoping the celebration would relieve the inexplicably tense atmosphere.

Only Brooke and Carl Friedrich refused. Brooke had a date with the family banker, Sam Liversedge, and Carl made his apologies as well.

"I am sorry. If it is permitted, I have a telephone call to make to Berkeley, over the Bay."

Everyone looked surprised, but no one went further into the matter. The young Frenchman with the German name had never quite fitted into the jovial group; they probably wouldn't miss him, Eden thought. But his behavior intrigued her.

Who on earth did he know in Berkeley? He had said he knew no one in California except the Lombards. It was all vaguely mysterious.

She shrugged off her misgivings.

"After all," she told herself, "it has nothing to do with me."

# Chapter Twenty-Six

Carl was baffled by the list of West Coast Fox theaters in the East Bay telephone book which Mrs. Trentini, the cook, loaned him, but the woman helped him narrow them down to those near the University of California campus. Soon they settled on one that seemed appropriate.

While he waited for the theater to answer, he watched Mrs. Trentini scrub the sinkboard.

"No dinner today for that crowd. They'll have to have a snifter with every sailor on Market Street. Not that I blame them, Lord knows. My own boy was with MacArthur when he landed in the Philippines. I guess he's all right. I offer a novena for him every night."

Carl was called to his own pressing business by a young woman's voice. It surprised him — he wasn't accustomed to female managers of movie houses.

"Miss Armitage speaking. Are you calling about tonight's schedule? Hold on. I'll give you the box office."

"No. If you please. I am told your theater exhibits old films of Prysing Productions."

"Last Monday night, yes. An early silent classic, *Time Before Man*, a semidocumentary. And one of the recent Prysing films, *Wings of the RAF.* Next Monday is Bob Hope night — *Big Broadcast*, and *Louisiana Purchase.*"

"May I ask, do you expect to show the film *Journey*?"

The young woman consulted her schedule.

"We don't have any more Prysing films until early next year. However, you might check with us after Christmas."

"You did not show *Journey* last week?"

"No, we haven't been able to get ahold of it recently. If I remember correctly, it had several Oscar nominations. We'll do our best, but so far, no dice."

"Is this the only theater that shows old films?"

"On a regular basis, yes. Try us around the first of the year."

That was that. Carl set down the kitchen phone as Mrs. Trentini looked around.

"No luck?"

He shook his head, thanked her for her help, and left the big, sunny kitchen.

Still, Carl wasn't completely discouraged. The film might be shown in the next few months.

It occurred to him then that in a few months he and Jany would be home again in Paris, if fate did not point them in another direction. He was intrigued by Leo's hints that there might be a job for him in the studio, a way in which he could actually contribute some special skill.

Still thinking about his own problems, he noticed Brooke Friedrich talking on the phone in the front hall with upsetting results.

She seemed to be in a cross mood. Someone was breaking a date with her, some fool or other who didn't appreciate her. He resented anyone's unkindness to Brooke Friedrich. He considered one of her greatest assets to be her loyalty to her late husband. Unlike Leo Prysing and the others, *she* kept Kurt Friedrich's memory alive. She deserved to be treated better, he thought.

She slammed the receiver down and swung around in a complaining mood. "Here I have a date with Sam Liversedge and *he's* in the hospital. His gall bladder. If it isn't one thing, it's another." She got a good look at Carl and her face broke into a perky smile. "At least, you haven't failed me. My boy, how about taking me to some nice quiet place with good food and drink, some place where they never heard of the damned war."

He hoped she would not pick too expensive a restaurant, but he had liked Brooke Friedrich from the first and was anxious to go. She reminded him sometimes of his own mother. Besides, it would be a perfect opportunity to talk about his father again.

"I would be honored, madame."

"Call me Aunt Brooke. I'm used to that from Tony."

"As you say, Aunt Brooke. I wonder if I may meet you in half an hour. I would like to change for the occasion." He wanted to look his best, but it was awkward. His other suit, besides being old and shabby, was of a European cut and he was convinced that everyone looked at him oddly when he wore it. These people in the Bay City seemed much more clothes-conscious than those in Los Angeles and Culver City.

"Of course, dear boy. Run along."

He changed rapidly but with some qualms about the suit. He kept wondering also how he would broach the subject of his father, and if Brooke would tell the entire truth about him. Did she know of Kurt's heroism? It was possible she had been kept out of what seemed to be a mystery about the circumstances of his death. She did not seem to be a discreet woman. Anyway, she was Carl's best hope.

Brooke proved to be his ally in what he thought of as the renewed emphasis on his father's reputation as a hero. He was still trying to broach the subject while she debated the best place for a "nice, old-fashioned chat about darling Kurt. You'd like that, wouldn't you?"

"I would indeed, madame — Aunt Brooke."

"Good. You're learning. I know, we'll go down to a restaurant in the financial district. Kurt loved it. He got the biggest kick out of all the paintings."

Paintings? It didn't sound like his father. Kurt and Olga had gone no further than calendars when it came to an admiration of art. Neither of them, so far as he knew, had ever even been inside the Louvre, or any other museum.

"If my father liked it, I am certain I shall."

She laughed. "Don't be so sure until you see it. This is going to be fun . . . I can hardly wait to see your face."

Whatever that meant, Carl thought. It was puzzling, but he began to enjoy the day. Some of his tension and secret dread was beginning to vanish, to his great relief. She called for a taxi and even on this busy day a cab responded to the Lombard name.

"Your weather, is it always so superb?" he asked, staring out of the cab window at the strange, narrow-faced Victorian buildings that she explained had been built just after the Fire, as San Franciscans always referred to their earthquake-and-fire holocaust.

Brooke thought this comment was hilarious. "When we don't have fog, we have wind. Sometimes both. And summertime is our worst season. But we love it. That is," she added, giving it some thought, "the family loves it. I was very happy in Vienna until — well, those dreadful Nazis took over."

He took his courage in his hands. He wanted only one answer. "Was my father one of them?"

She shrugged. "Only in a sense. Everyone was, you understand. It was necessary. He could never have gotten another role, or succeeded in any field if he hadn't joined the Austrian National Socialist Party."

"Perhaps he joined the party to work in the Underground, against the Nazis. That is possible."

"Yes, that could be it. Poor darling . . . what beasts my family were. They should have gone in to rescue him, too. They were quick enough to rescue Dr. Preysing. You know, of course, that Dr. Preysing and his wife hid in our wine cellar, Kurt's and mine. They insisted that their lives were in danger. Dr. Preysing was a bit of a radical — a Social Democrat, very much against the Nazis. All the same, I didn't want to get into trouble with the government. I thought if I went with them, Kurt would follow us, but he didn't."

"Aunt Brooke, you risked your life to help that unfortunate Dr. Preysing and his wife. I am sorry the attempt failed."

"So am I. You see, I suffered a great loss, too."

"You, Aunt Brooke? I am sorry."

"Of course, I lost your father. He must have been too proud to come after me. If he had come, he wouldn't have been in the Reich when Leo made his broadcast."

Why had his father stayed behind — was it really his pride, or was it for the sake of his work in the Underground?

"Here we are," Brooke said, slapping his knee playfully, "The Little Gallery. Wait 'til you see this."

In a very un-European fashion, she led the way through two old swinging saloon doors. These opened into a small passage, then the restaurant interior, which seemed dark after the bright sunlight outside. He felt his way between the tables, following Brooke, whom the headwaiter recognized at once, with suitable obeisance.

They were seated at a booth in the far corner. Not many diners remained. The lunch crowd had apparently gone to celebrate elsewhere, and the dinner crowd was just straggling in. Carl's sight began to adjust to the dim lighting.

Slowly he made out his partner across the table. She reminded him of his lively, chattering mother. She looked charming, her deep auburn hair done in a way he hadn't seen before, poufed out around her face. It was a relief from the stiff, upswept style he had seen so often during the war in Paris and now in the United States. Not only was she attractive, she was very charming — she must have bewitched father, he thought.

"Now," she said, hiding a giggle behind her fingers. "Look around you."

He did so and was momentarily tongue-tied with embarrassment. The first portrait he saw was several feet above Brooke's head, a voluptuous Rubenesque nude, vulgarly posed so that her vagina and pubic hair were clearly on display. Her body reminded him a little of Danielle deBrett, and he didn't like that unpleasant memory, especially after the way he left her in Paris.

He tried to recover his cool exterior, hoping Brooke hadn't noticed his initial reaction. When he looked around at the other nudes, most of them just as crude as the first, he managed to affect an indifference he was far from feeling.

"The one over the bar is rather charming," he said, "like something in one of your western films."

"How?" she teased.

"Well, lying on a couch, her elbow supporting her head. I've seen very similar paintings in the films."

"Of course . . . poor Carl, if you could see your face! Now, shall we order?"

They both selected the antipasto tray, linguini with clam sauce and a heavy California burgundy. He was surprised at the excellence of the food in America, and even more surprised at the quality of the wine. It was a respectable vintage. He waited until the sommelier had poured Brooke's third glass of wine before he asked, "How did you like Monsieur Prysing's film, *Journey*?"

She studied the candle through her deep ruby wine glass.

"I thought it was going to be the story of our journey with Josef and Sarah Preysing. You know, how we tried to cross the Austrian border with them and how the Nazis secretly took them off the train, which we found out too late."

"But that *is* the plot, isn't it?"

She twirled the wine glass rapidly, spilling drops on her knuckles and licking them off.

"Yes, but the characters are different. I'm not in it. I thought that pretty de Havilland girl was going to play me. Instead, she played a musician in love with my brother. And Steve's character wasn't in it, really. Just a silly combination of him and Leo Prysing. My dear boy, you know as well as I do — Tyrone Power is extremely handsome but he doesn't look a bit like either Steve or Leo. Tony, maybe. But not Steve."

He hid his impatience with an effort. "But what about my father? Did you like the way he was portrayed?"

He could see that the details of the picture had faded from her memory. She recalled them with an effort.

"Kurt wasn't in it, either. They had a different plot, involving a wicked Nazi in love with the de Havilland girl. He bribes the gardener to tell him about the Jewish doctor and his wife. He chases them to the Westbahnhof and gets there too late. None of that happened to us."

He considered. "The picture was made just before the war. I suppose Monsieur Prysing wanted to protect my father."

"But your poor father was dead by the time the film came out."

"You are right. They should have rescued him, somehow."

She finished her wine and began to wind linguini between fork and spoon. "My dear boy, I don't know why, but that is how it happened. When you think about it, what else could they have done? He had his chance to escape with us. Now, don't you get touchy about it. I want you to feel you are part of the family, not an enemy."

"I will never be your enemy, Aunt Brooke."

"Besides," Brooke went on reasonably. "You wouldn't want to get your brother-in-law mad at you, would you? He could be very helpful to you, if you'd let him be."

"My what?"

"I really don't believe you see what is going on under your nose. You are so naive, Carl. Leo is going to marry your sister. I'll bet you anything on it. And it won't be very long from now either. He's crazy about her! Something different, you know."

He couldn't get his breath for a minute.

"That old man?"

There was a slight edge to her musical voice. "Mature, perhaps, but he isn't much older than I am." She looked at him with an unexpected shrewdness. "You are very protective of your sister, aren't you?"

"I am all she has."

"Quite natural. And you didn't want her involved with my nephew, either. I could see that right away."

"He's married. Any feeling between them would be impossible."

Her smile made her look very young, almost enticing.

"Tony adores the impossible. He always did. My own boy, Alec, found that out long ago when they were both interested in the same girl. She chose Alec, but I always suspected it was because he could offer her a trip to England and the excitement of his radio job. I don't know whether Heather regretted her choice. I'm fairly sure Tony didn't."

"My sister would never permit a sordid affair," he told her stiffly, more upset than he wanted to be in public. "But I have heard of these Hollywood producers and their women. Is it merely an affair he wishes? Or marriage?"

"I have known Leo for over twenty years. He's serious this time. He wouldn't dare be otherwise with someone connected with the family. The Lombards' high opinion is important to him."

"I don't like it. I admire him but I want Jany to be happy. They are so different."

"You want to protect her. As a mother, I can understand that. But think, Carl, is there anything more safe for her than a mature man who adores her and will spoil her with every material blessing? Your little sister deserves better than the life she has had."

He had to admit she was right. "I have thought that myself many times. But so far, I haven't been able to give her all she deserves."

"Leo can. And he worships her. She is a little treasure to him — untouched. You couldn't ask for a better protector." Having finished her meal, she began to eat her spumoni, and raised her spoon, pointing to him. "As for you, think how free you will be, with all that responsibility off your shoulders. Free to live your own life for a change."

"Jany is no burden, madame. Believe me."

"Of course not. I would expect you to say that. But you've got to think of her, and all the wonderful things life has for Jany."

She was probably right. He had been selfish and perhaps even jealous that someone else might take better care of Jany than he could. But somehow,

Carl had always pictured Jany marrying an attractive French war hero. Maybe a friend like Pierre St. Just. Jany should have romance. He felt it a pity that Leo Prysing wasn't a more romantic figure of a man.

Still, Jany didn't seem to mind.

"She does hang on his every word," he admitted, "and she seems fascinated by all those stories about cinema stars and the old days of the films."

"You're so right, Carl. You just keep looking at it from that angle."

# Chapter Twenty-Seven

Tony Lombard's reaction was very like Carl's. He was repelled by the image of a middle-aged satyr like Leo Prysing possessing the lovely, virginal Jany Friedrich. But, unlike Carl, he didn't need someone else to warn him of the budding romance.

It became evident during the VJ Day celebrations, when Jany seemed to hang onto the producer as if her life depended on it. Things became even worse for Tony after she met little Andrea. The child's innocence ought to have reminded her of the difference between herself and Leo, who always had some girl friend in the wings. Instead, Jany became positively frigid toward Tony, though she made it a point to dote on his daughter.

During the celebration, Jany had mentioned that she didn't think it quite proper for Andrea to be out in all of the excitement and turmoil.

"This is history," Eden replied firmly, "I want my child to remember today as long as she lives. Then, if every child remembers, maybe there will never be another war."

Much abashed, Jany begged her pardon and tried not to interfere again. There was much pushing and shoving through the Market Street crowd, strangers kissing each other and people screaming until they were all hoarse. Jany found herself kissed any number of times by men in uniform, but it was Tony who shoved them away from her, though she insisted that it was "all in fun."

She wished several times that Carl had been with them, but otherwise he wasn't missed. Brooke's bubbling personality proved to be a bigger loss, but, as Steve reminded them, his sister always gave precedence to her dates, and this day was no exception.

When they were shoved along by the crowd into the bars on Market and then Powell Street, there was the problem of Jany being underage. While Tony tried to find an acceptable excuse to remain outside with Jany and Andrea (who insisted on clinging to Jany's hand), Leo Prysing took over the task of chaperoning the "younger set." Tony tried to protest that he ought to stay since Leo was their guest, but he caught Eden's quizzical little smile and was too ashamed to continue the argument.

At that the two parties separated, with Leo remaining behind. The Lombards let themselves be maneuvered by three jubilant sailors into a dark, narrow, crowded bar. Outside, Leo lifted Andrea and began to entertain Jany with gossip and scandal about all the famous movie stars she had seen on the screen.

Inside the bar Tony managed to wedge himself between the sailors and the door. To his anxious gaze it seemed clear that Jany — he couldn't help but think of her as his Jany — was enchanted by all his talk of glamorous stars, just as Desdemona had let herself be hypnotized by Othello's tales of exotic adventure. Surely she could see Leo for what he was — a delightful, somewhat intriguing charmer, but certainly not a suitor to be taken seriously. Surely she must know that he was a man famous for his brief amours.

Tony heard his father hail him from the far end of the bar. "Tony, your drink. Better grab it before this sailor gets his mitts on it."

Recalled to what he owed his wife and family, Tony returned to the bar and drank sullenly, returning with indifference the deafening toast to the "end of all wars."

Sauntering along the sidewalk, Leo ventured to Jany, "Do you want to go back to Hollywood soon? Seems like the future is there. This place always looked like an old movie set."

She hesitated. "If Carl wants to. I think we may have to return to Paris. We are not rich, you understand."

His big hand chopped away such objections. "I'm hiring your brother to beef up Tony Lombard's new project about the Liberation and postwar Paris. His salary should take care of your future. And his. For the moment, though, I'd like to put you on my payroll too. Any chance of your becoming the new Rita Hayworth or Betty Grable?"

"Never," she said vehemently, "I'm not good at very many things, but I know I would be a terrible actress. I couldn't bear having all those people staring at me."

"Good." Squeezing Andrea, to the child's delight, he managed also to hug Jany in his bearish, friendly way. "Girls like you two are rare in my world, you know that?"

Andrea piped up, "Daddy says people will like me when I'm grown-up."

Jany was shocked. "There is more to life than just being liked."

Leo would have protested but Andrea back-tracked anxiously. She wanted Jany's approval, too. "Don't you like me, Jany?"

"Of course I do. I love you."

The child was thrilled at this. "Oh! That's even better than being liked," she said.

Jany began to feel self-conscious over the little girl's wide-eyed interest and tried to edge away from Leo's embrace, but with Tony and Eden and the others coming out of the bar at that moment, she managed to smile up into Leo's face. The warmth of his protection against the cold indifference of the others and her own bodily craving for Tony made him more desirable than she'd ever thought possible.

At times like this Leo Prysing seemed to her more than a potential lover and patron for Carl's future. He was father and brother, even mother, in an odd sort of way. She knew that he had lived a very free life with women, and that he'd had many girl friends. But he never treated her in any way that she could find fault with. Whatever the kind hints from others — even Miss Thorgerson had asked if she thought she could "handle" Mr. Prysing — Jany only found tenderness in him and a constant desire to please her.

Leo could not be considered a handsome man, but his looks appealed to her — there was a manliness about him that was different from Tony's classical beauty. Besides, Leo had the added attraction of strength and confidence, and occasionally humor, although not like the lively humor that was so much a part of Tony's personality.

When the group emerged from the bar, Steve

Lombard laughingly warned Jany, when he saw Leo with his arm snugly around her waist.

"He's a ruthless fellow, Jany. Better watch out."

But Leo had never been ruthless or deceitful with her, and she was wise enough to figure that a good deal of the general feeling against him was based on his power. They were all jealous, and every one of them owed Leo something: a job, a position, influence. If he was truly a man to beware of, she reasoned, why would they all deal with him, accept him in their home, work for him?

Walking up the steep Powell Street hill, she turned her ankle on a bottle cap and felt Tony's hand under her elbow. It was a brief touch, but enough to inflame her. Glancing at him under her lashes, she knew that he, too, shared in that hot excitement. She must do something. Return to a Paris that didn't want her. Or . . . accept Leo Prysing's unmistakably growing interest.

Would that be so difficult? Except for Carl, no man had ever taken such good care of her. She liked his company, and she was enormously flattered to have the unflagging attention of such an important, busy man. She always felt comfortable and safe with him as she had never felt with Tony, who aroused in her all emotions that were forbidden, including a secret thought that she savored deep in her bed at night — what if Tony really committed adultery with her? What would it be like?

She despised her desire. She was even afraid to confess it when she and Carl went down the hill to old St. Mary's on Sundays.

By the time the group of celebrants returned to

Nob Hill late that evening with Andrea sleeping on her father's shoulder and Leo complaining that he had laughed too hard, shouted too much and wanted some Alka-Seltzer quickly, Jany felt that of all the Lombards and their allies, her favorite was Leo Prysing. Unlike Tony, he had never lied to her. He was entirely what he seemed. She thought she would rather return to his Hollywood than remain in Tony's San Francisco or return to a Paris that had branded her "collaborationist."

Carl was in a strange mood when they reached home. He kept insisting that he had to talk to her alone. She was tired, and even the small amount of wine she had been permitted to drink in the Lombard house was more than she was used to.

But she was used to deferring to Carl, and when she went to her room that night she allowed him to follow her. She thought that he wanted to see her after watching Leo Prysing kiss her good night. It was an innocent kiss, on her forehead, the way Carl often kissed her, and she had returned it with a hug and the warning to take care of his indigestion. She often worried about that, since she knew that Leo didn't eat or drink as he ought to. He needed someone to look after him, not like Carl, who seemed always to be angry at the world and certainly not in need of her ministrations.

Turning to face him, she tried to put on a little of the worldly manner used by the Lombard women.

"Carl, please don't be so cross. You're the one who behaved badly today by not coming with us. Don't you care that the war has ended? Soon the Japanese peace treaty will be signed. Think of it!

410

You didn't even go with us to celebrate. It looked very bad . . . people wondered."

Carl waved his arms around in an uncharacteristic fashion. He appeared either speechless or so mixed up in what he wanted to say that he couldn't get it out.

"You are behaving like a cheap — an American woman. Have you no pride? Letting that man touch you like that, and you're not even betrothed."

"Engaged."

"Just so. Even then, it wouldn't be proper for a young woman who isn't married."

"But we're not in France now, Carl. You continue to forget."

He was extremely agitated, and seeing this, she stopped acting the part of a "modern" Lombard woman. Her heart was touched by this excitement that was so unlike him.

"You must remember, *chèri*," she said, caressing his arm tenderly, "I am not a child now, and I am very fond of Monsieur Prysing. Sometimes he behaves exactly like you. In fact, if I were to go to his bedroom right now . . ." His eyes widened in disbelief. "Even then, he would tell me I was behaving in a shocking manner, just as you would. I know and admire the fine, decent side of Leo Prysing."

"But he is so old. Older than our own father," Carl objected. "And there have been so many other women . . ."

It was an old argument and Carl made a mistake when he brought their father into it. She wondered what Carl would think if she poured out her real feelings about him. Had he ever considered how she felt, abandoned at birth and never having known him?

She heard voices in the hall, the voices of her new friends. They were not easily intimidated by life, and she found herself taking courage from them.

"*Chèri,* I never knew father. He despised me so much he deserted dear Maman and you, just to be free of me. I do not forget these things about our father. Remember, too, Carl — you taught me to hate him when I was very little. Your attitude changed only when you discovered he was a hero."

"Yes, but I —"

"You think of him as a hero. But I cannot love him. To me, he is a dead stranger. I would as soon cry over Monsieur Leo's brother and his wife. They are dead strangers, too."

Confused and hurt, he backed against one of the bedposts — honesty obliged him to confess that the truth was on her side.

"You're right. It is my fault. I resented father's desertion, the way Maman had to work in those trash films to support us. But I know now that he did it for a reason. He was only pretending to be something despicable . . . only pretending. He must have suffered, too."

She didn't look convinced, but she jumped up to put her arms around him, instilling in him some of her own warm optimism.

"Don't be angry, Carl, please. Whatever I may do, please be happy for me."

Gradually, she felt him relax. He kissed her ear and smiled faintly. "I will be happy if you are," he promised her.

"And promise not to be angry, whatever I do."

He kissed her again, quickly, reminding her, "When you need me, *chèrie,* I'll be here."

Jany was inwardly thankful that he hadn't insisted on her returning to Paris with him in order to separate her from Leo Prysing.

"If only you could see that Leo is everything our father should have been . . . he almost makes me forget how much I loved Tony."

He answered her in his usual normal, low tones but his eyes were anxious and his hand on her wrist made her wince, though she made no protest. She knew he didn't mean it. He had never knowingly been cruel to her.

"Always these people. These Lombards. It is because of Tony that you sell yourself. To be free of him."

Again she heard voices in a doorway at the other end of the hall and knew she had to control her feelings.

"If you knew how I feel when I see his adorable child and wish that she were my own. But I know it is not possible. And Leo will be good to us both. You and me."

"Bribes."

"He is kind. He does little things to make me happy. He stayed with me today to keep me company when I couldn't go into the bars to drink with the others. He even named a dessert for me in his studio restaurant."

"Mother of God!" he whispered. But then he laughed and freed her hand, adding tenderly, "I don't blame you. It is the fault of these Lombards. Without them you would never have met Leo

413

Prysing. And if it weren't for Tony you wouldn't be driven to him."

She was more dignified than he had ever seen her. "You must never say that again, Carl. Leo wants to be your friend. And I love him. Not as it was with Tony, but in other ways."

He only hesitated an instant before agreeing.

"If it weren't for his interest in you, I could like Prysing easily. I do admire him for his work. But if he makes you happy, that is all I need to hear. *Bon soir,* little sister."

He kissed her good night and went to his room, passing Randi and Miss Thorgerson. The women were talking to Leo Prysing, who was protesting whatever they were suggesting in his usual aggressive manner. "Don't give it a thought, ladies. Seltzer fixes me up every time. It's been a great day, hasn't it? After four rough years, the war's finally over."

Six rough years, where I come from, Carl thought, and went on to bed.

Leo Prysing moved so carefully to consolidate his position with Jany that he didn't propose until nearly Christmas. During this time of suspense on every hand, including the studio's stockholders, Carl Friedrich allowed himself to be coerced into temporarily handling Brooke's secretarial duties. His advice on her stock investments proved sound, based on the thinking of his conservative French ancestors and his usual attention to details. He found himself caught up in the ironic pleasure of adding to riches of the Lombard family. Brooke had been especially kind to him and he was pleased, even proud, to help her in any way possible.

Meanwhile, Jany continued to lead an exciting life, thanks to Leo, who was always persistent in her joining him. She was his date at the Grauman's Chinese premiere of his latest war film, *London Yankee*, starring Eden Ware, Robert Walker and Samuel Goldwyn's latest find, Dana Andrews. Jany hoped Tony Lombard wouldn't be there, but since the film was a triumph for his wife, they both showed up, looking especially glamorous to Jany.

It was awkward for her, being constantly thrown in Tony's company, but she was learning to accept it and play a part. She pretended not to notice the way Tony laughed, which she loved to hear. Or the way his eyes were often shadowed mysteriously by his dark lashes when he was thoughtful. Even his quick temper made her heart beat faster, and in many ways she found her love for him stimulated by his jealousy. She was ashamed of the fact, but she recognized it as the truth.

His presence near her was a constant temptation and since she had begun to accept Leo as part of her life, she was terrified that Leo would somehow get a hint of her real feelings. She didn't want to hurt Leo, not after all he'd done for her and Carl. Even worse, she couldn't bear the deep shame, the disgrace of causing the breakup of Tony's family as well, especially knowing how it would affect Andrea. Jany knew too well what it was like to grow up without a father, and resolved that it must never happen to Andrea.

All these thoughts were beginning to disturb her, but they were soon washed away by that terrifying walk from the limousine across the footprints in the forecourt, to the Hollywood-Manchu lobby and the best seats in the house. Millions of eyes seemed to be watching them and Jany was sure that every one of the cheering, gawking fans was secretly critical of her dress.

It was her only evening gown, purchased at a small shop near Hollywood and Vine, and she had altered the pale blue crepe herself to give it a fit she considered more Parisian. Leo wanted to "lend" her the money for a gown, and when she refused him, he offered to let her pick out one of the elaborate, rarely used gowns in Wardrobe. Jany knew that to accept either offer could set a bad precedent — Leo might think she was merely a gold digger, after all.

All the noisy, eager fans in the bleachers called out after them as they passed by.

"Who's the dame in the corny blue?"

"Prysing's girl friend."

"That kid? Wow!"

"Cute, but no Grable. Here comes Eden Ware. God! That husband of hers is gorgeous. What's he do?"

"Nothing, dummy. He's her husband."

This comment aroused Jany's indignation, but Tony didn't seem to have heard it. He was laughing at something Eden apparently had said. Then he saw Jany looking at him as the two couples approached the master of ceremonies at the microphone. Catching her glance, Tony's laughter stopped suddenly. Jany raised her chin defiantly. Just let Leo ask her to marry him! She would put up a barrier between herself and Tony that even Tony couldn't break through —

a marriage, in the Church.

When Leo's clasp tightened around her waist, she was relieved, partly because her decision had been made. If the noisy bleacher fans hadn't been present she would have returned his embrace with warm gratitude.

By the time they reached the MC at the microphone, they were directly in front of Eden who wore a sparkling rust-gold evening gown that matched her artfully careless coiffure. The ordinary citizen couldn't get such materials yet, but to the crowd, she represented a bright, postwar future.

Though she tried to be fair to Eden, Jany couldn't help wondering who was looking after little Andrea tonight. She remembered her own childhood when Carl was at school and their mother was off working in Hollywood or elsewhere. Jany's only companion in those days was an elderly spinster whose lack of interest in children was exceeded only by her deafness and tendency to fall asleep while Jany was chattering to her.

The MC smiled in greeting as Leo Prysing stepped up to the mike.

"And here he is, ladies and gentlemen, the man behind tonight's film, the executive producer himself: Leo Prysing and his — and this lovely young lady is your latest discovery?"

The intimation was clear, but Leo corrected him, playing the genial, expansive film mogul. Jany felt that he was a trifle nervous, unlike his usually confident self.

"Miss Friedrich's father was the leading man in several of my silent films. And I hope to make Miss Friedrich my own leading lady. Mrs. Leo Prysing."

In spite of their relationship, it was like a bolt of lightning to Jany. She longed for a place to hide. This public proposal seemed to excite everyone but her. Her flesh felt as if it were burning from head to foot with her embarrassment.

"Well," said the MC, "this *is* news! And Miss — er — Frederick, you haven't given Mr. Prysing your answer yet?" He tried to maneuver her over to his standing mike. "Any possibility of an exclusive tonight before all these thousands of your future husband's fans?"

"I — d-don't — I haven't —" Jany fumbled, hoping the earth would swallow her. On the other side of the mike Eden Ware came to the rescue, obviously ignoring her husband, whose face had been drained of color under the shock of Leo's announcement.

"Darling," she said cornering the MC, "proposals are more romantic in private. Aren't you going to say hello to me?"

Jany breathed a silent thanks while Leo swept her into the lobby of the theater, leaving Eden to take over the interview. Once they were seated, Leo took Jany's hand, squeezed it, and in the dim lighting of the theater, kissed her knuckles. She looked away, hoping no one had seen this, but her fingers tried to respond to his as they had effortlessly responded to Tony in Paris. Only the degree of excitement wasn't the same.

He felt that her fingers had given him the reply to his question, and he leaned over to whisper, "Thank you, sweetheart. I'll see to it that you're never sorry."

She smiled at him. "I know."

This encouraged him to kiss her. She drew back instinctively, then remembered who he was and turned her face to his. She returned his kiss shyly. The touch of his heavy, powerful lips had surprised her by his gentleness, as if he weren't sure of how she would react.

Eden and Tony were seated on the other side of Leo, which was a relief to Jany, who preferred to see anyone in the world but Tony that night. But she worried about the reaction of someone even more important in her life.

"I must tell Carl," she said, leaning over to whisper to Leo, "I should call him tonight. But don't worry, he'll be happy for me. He told me so."

She waited for his response to this reassurance and was puzzled by the time it took him to agree.

"Don't you think so?" she asked anxiously.

"Sure. You ask your brother's permission. I'll ask McDevlin. He's my butler, chief cook and bottle washer. Got to go right to the top with these things."

"But you do like Carl, don't you?"

Now his response came too quick, too heartily.

"Smart boy, your brother. Not much like his father. You remember your dad?"

"I never knew him."

"Well — let's not borrow trouble."

He probably thought that Carl would disapprove because of the difference in their ages. Poor Leo, he didn't really understand. But she really did love him, in a very special way.

# Chapter Twenty-Eight

Leo Prysing made a gesture of requesting a wedding at the Temple Emanu-El, officiated by Rabbi Magnin, but he was so relieved by Carl Friedrich's calm reception of the engagement news that he felt he could even face a Catholic wedding and all it entailed.

Leo had one plaintive remark on the subject.

"My brother was Orthodox, but I'm just country-heathen. I only wanted to mention a fact in passing. Your grandfather, a man my family revered, was a rabbi. You don't think you owe him anything?"

Carl was apologetic. "I'm afraid my father was reared in a Protestant household. Our Austrian grandmother was Lutheran."

The whole discussion horrified Jany. Although she wasn't strictly religious, her beliefs played an important role in her life. Without the Church and its teachings, she might have urged Tony to leave his wife, or she might have slept with Tony — committing grave carnal sins. She became so frantic at the mere suggestion of a Jewish wedding that Leo gave it up at once.

"A Catholic wedding always makes good publicity anyway," he said happily. "And Louella Parsons will love it."

He had strange priorities. Jany pretended to be amused, but Carl wanted to know why a Hollywood gossip columnist would have anything to say about the marriage of the industry's top independent producer.

"Louella is Catholic," Leo explained. "She's interviewing Jany tomorrow over lunch at the Derby."

Both Carl and Jany had objections.

"That is a very expensive place, the Brown Derby," Carl said.

"I just couldn't," Jany added. "What would I say?"

Leo got up, paced the worn carpet of Jany's living room in the small Wilshire Boulevard hotel that Carl insisted was suitable to his budget.

"Now look, you two, you can't expect to bring Louella to this dump. She's a good kid. There's nothing snooty about her. But a frame is important to any portrait, don't forget. The wedding will help to sell Prysing Productions. And with so much labor trouble coming up on all sides, we're going to need all the favorable publicity we can get."

This same reasoning convinced Jany to allow Leo to pay for her wedding gown and the elaborate reception at the Ambassador Hotel.

A warm, hazy sun shone on the bride that April day, and it seemed to Tony Lombard that all of Los Angeles had turned out to watch the bride float down the steps of the Spanish baroque Church of St. Vincent de Paul. An enthusiastic crowd from the Adams Boulevard neighborhood had gathered, yelling and pointing at all the stars who had turned out for the ceremony.

Few in the excited throng had any idea of the scenes that had taken place beforehand. The show had been so perfectly directed that no one could have anticipated what happened between Tony Lombard and his wife in her dressing room three weeks before, when Eden told him that their daughter had a part in the wedding procession.

"It's obscene!" Tony insisted. "That old man was after my mother for years. Now, he wants to marry a girl young enough to be his grand-daughter."

"Don't exaggerate, darling. She's been growing up remarkably fast since Leo fell for her. Besides, Andrea is dying to be in it. It would be cruel to keep her away from it; you know how she adores your little friend."

Tony corrected her stiffly. "She isn't *my* little friend. But I might remind you that if it weren't for Jany, I probably wouldn't be alive today."

They were interrupted by a knock on Eden's dressing room door.

"We're ready for you, Miss Ware."

"That's my set call." In the doorway she looked back at Tony who was still scowling. "By the way," she added lightly, "let me remind you that her brother had something to do with your rescue, too. Not to mention that brunette you fell for."

The memory of Danielle deBrett in comparison with Jany made him laugh.

"Yes, there's always the heroic Danielle," he agreed. "A walking brothel, all by herself. We've got a Directors' Guild meeting tonight but you and I can get together for dinner first."

"No chance, honey. We're shooting late. Those damned rooftop shots downtown. I'm being chased by George Sanders."

"Chaste?" he wanted to know.

He was relieved when she laughed, too.

"Anyway, Andrea will play hostess to you in my place."

"After the Guild meeting I might have a few of the boys in from the Carpenters. They're talking strike. God knows they can't continue under prewar conditions. We had a depression going then."

She called, "Give 'em my love, but don't get involved. They're saying some of those union and guild members may be parlor pinks."

With this sage advice she disappeared.

Nothing had been settled. Andrea was still going to walk in the procession before the bridal party, carrying the bride's ring on a lace-covered pillow. Everything was perfectly cast except the groom. Steve Lombard, a three-million-dollar investor in Prysing Productions, was the logical — and diplomatic — choice for best man.

Tony had refused to be an usher, pleading the pressure of Guild problems. The question of possible Guild participation in any future union trouble was only a tiny mote in the eyes of prosperous studio heads whose 1946 products were breaking all previous records.

Tony wasn't by nature a do-gooder, and only his personal friendships with studio crews had aroused his interest in the union problems that poured in from all sides. He knew that some of his more intellectual friends were what Eden called "pinks." Tony had gone to college with men and women whose educational struggles during the Great Depression left them committed to the Soviet "experiment." The courageous Russian defense during the war had crystallized their views.

Unfortunately for these friends that Tony thought of as misguided do-gooders, an Iron Curtain now descended on half of the world. The Soviet armies were everywhere, breathing down Scandinavia's long back, and over Greece's borders, standing as an implacable barrier between the West and such formerly independent countries as Austria, Hungary, Yugoslavia, Czechoslovakia, and the ever-fermenting Balkans. Their allies, the Chinese Communists, had just opened new hostilities against the Nationalists.

Tony hinted to these passionate radicals that this was no time to talk down the capitalist system, since such talk immediately conjured up pictures of the dubious alternatives.

Nobody resented Tony for his casual advice. But nobody took it seriously, either.

Whenever he was notified of some new prewedding event, like bachelor parties, discussions of wedding wardrobes, catering, his civic pride sent him off to yet another labor meeting. The unionizers were passionate, but still capitalistic. They had the support of many Guild members, but there were always a few who turned the meeting into Party harangues.

Deluded, of course, he thought. To him they were all hopeless romantics, yet better company at the moment than all those wedding nuts.

Tony would have liked to go London to be with Alec and Stella Burkett during Heather's illness, and even suggested taking Andrea with him, but since he was halfway through the cutting of his second B-plus film, he was reminded by a jovial Leo that if he went galloping off before the wedding he would never work again in Hollywood.

"I've got my own little blacklist," he warned Tony.

Eden and Belle Sweet laughed dutifully. Didn't everyone know there was no such thing as a blacklist among the Hollywood studios?

It was Eden's direct approach that shook up Tony and made him accept the inevitability of the event. He thought he had been disguising his true animus towards the wedding until one evening when he snapped at Andrea, who wanted to go visit Jany.

"Well, you're not, so just go back to your doll house. That's an expensive toy and you've hardly touched it."

"Oh, daddy!" Andrea complained.

"I mean it."

Eden had been lying on the floor, memorizing the next day's lines, her eyes covered by a sleep mask. She raised the mask long enough to peer out at her family across the long room. They were staying in an apartment that Tony had insisted on leasing, without relying on Eden's considerably larger salary. She said nothing, but Tony was aware that her attention had shifted from tomorrow's script to tonight's drama between her husband and daughter. Tony, aware that his overreaction had caught his wife's attention, quickly got hold of himself.

"Sweetheart, we can't always do what we want in life. We have our work and our duties. And I think your duty, young lady, is to go to bed. Where's Miss — Eden, what's her new nanny's name again?"

"Miss Hadley," Eden said, "Larue Hadley."

"God knows I can't remember their names. We seem to have a revolving door with these people. She ought to have one of us with her all the time — someone she loves."

Pretending to ignore their discussion, Andrea gave a sigh worthy of a tragedienne and reached for her tiny father doll. "You're bad," she muttered to herself. "I hate you!" She threw the doll down the stairs of the little doll house, clearly making her point.

"What's all that about, young lady?" Tony said, rolling up his copy of *The Hollywood Reporter* in a sinister fashion.

Andrea's eyes opened wide. Fascinated more than scared, she watched her father raise the rolled sheets. Scrambling to her feet, she ran around the room, hotly pursued by her father. Sneaking a look back at him, she saw his grin and immediately began to scream with laughter, letting herself be caught up in his arms.

"Spoiled rotten, both of them," Eden remarked, covered her eyes again, and returned to memorizing her lines.

Hours later, lying in bed next to Tony, Eden remembered what had precipitated the scene with Andrea. Tony looked tired now as she thoughtfully studied his profile. The moonlight sifting through the dusty palm trees outside the windows gave him a pallor that reminded her of those first weeks after Pearl Harbor. Looking more closely, she saw that he was staring at the ceiling.

"Honey, are you unhappy?" she asked softly.

It took a few seconds for him to turn his head and answer.

"No, why?"

"You aren't having any trouble with headaches again, or those scars, are you? Remember, the doctors said they might itch and bother you."

"That was a long time ago, wasn't it? We were mighty young, those days before Pearl."

That hit her, although she knew it was unintentional. "You might have been. I sure as hell was not."

He propped his chin on his palm and looked at her a long time. Whether there was love or not, there was an unmistakable tenderness in his expression.

"Honey, you know age was never a problem with us. You never worried about it before, so don't start now. You don't have to."

She ran her finger along his arm to his wrist.

"Would you like a divorce?"

"What use would that be?"

She laughed without humor. "You mean, now that your little French savior is being married?"

"No, I mean, we've made it so far. Let's not rock the boat. Besides, there's Andrea . . ."

"Yep." She rolled over, turned her back on him and closed her eyes. There was always Andrea.

He reached out, gently stroking her shoulder. Eden didn't respond, but concentrated on a complicated bit of dialogue coming up tomorrow. Tony's hand retreated, and he fell into a deep, dreamless sleep.

At eleven o'clock on the morning of the wedding, Steve Lombard was driven up into the Hollywood hills to pick up the groom at his newly purchased home, a cozy twenty-six rooms situated high in one of its older sections. As Steve was ushered through several hallways and up two staircases to Leo's bedroom, he wondered just how the simple, bourgeois French girl would adapt herself to the Oriental splendor around Leo. Like the older part of Hollywood Boulevard, which wandered along a couple of miles below the estate, the place was something out of the movies of the twenties. It was filled with elaborate, heavy stucco, and corners and alcoves out of the *Arabian Nights*; yet, in some odd way, it was rather amusing. Steve wished happiness for the couple, but he wasn't at all sure the bride would fit in.

Leo's large, stocky form didn't appear to its best advantage in a formal swallowtail, and he was the first to notice it. Getting a good look at Steve, whose six-foot frame still looked much as it had in his football days at Cal across the Bay, Leo said, "I'm an idiot to let you stand beside me at my own wedding. I don't know what I was thinking about."

Steve laughed, slapping him on the back. "Mayer and Zanuck and Selznick will be green with envy when they get a glimpse of you with little Jany," he said.

This gave Leo some comfort.

"True." He finished dressing and they went out together, passing several servants who received no indication from Leo that he knew they existed. In former days he had always been proud of living without help, saying he couldn't be bothered with servants "cluttering up his life."

Steve had grown up surrounded by servants, although, on looking back, most of his childhood memories were filled with the sound of his mother's well-modulated Virginia accent serenely overpowering the indignant protests of his father, whenever she announced that the servants had departed en masse because they hadn't been paid for weeks. The family fluctuated between enjoying a feast or weathering a famine, due mainly to the ups and downs of Red Lombard's stock and land manipulations.

The problem of maintaining servants quickly changed when Steve brought Randi Gallegher into the family. Things became more organized, starting with salaries that were paid on time. Curiously enough, the household was put on a steady keel by a young woman who had never had servants in her life.

Reflecting on the early years of their marriage, Steve reminded himself of just how special Randi was. He had almost lost her once, but never again — he knew he had the best. Unlike Leo, he couldn't imagine getting involved with a child of Jany Friedrich's age. He hoped that Tony had finally gotten over his ridiculous crush on the little French girl. He couldn't afford to lose Andrea or a promising career with Prysing on Jany's account.

As for Eden, Steve doubted that she would ever belong to Tony or anyone else except herself. But it was just like Tony to reach for what he couldn't have.

"Pretty good-looking bunch of bridesmaids I picked, wouldn't you say?" Leo asked as his studio limousine drove them into Los Angeles proper.

"You bet," Steve replied. Why not? Every one of them was employed by Prysing Productions.

"How do you like the house? Signed the papers only last Friday. My little girl's going to love it, don't you think?"

"You mean she hasn't seen it yet?"

"Hasn't seen it. Doesn't suspect a thing. She thinks we'll go back to that old apartment of mine. She loved the 'castle' look of the building. Now, she's got a whole castle to herself."

"She certainly has."

Leo, usually astute, missed the irony in Steve's remark.

He tapped a cigarette on his cigarette case, a shabby old metal box. Seeing Steve's surprised glance he said, "Belonged to my brother. Just never had the heart to buy a new one. Don't know if I ever told you, but your French friend, de Grasse, managed to get me a few of Josef's things."

"I'm sure André did even more than that trying to help them before it was too late. He had a lot of Underground connections."

"Too late, all right, thanks to that Nazi son of a bitch."

"And yet, you're marrying his daughter."

"I don't believe Jany had any connection with Kurt Friedrich. From what she tells me, she never even met him."

"Have you told her anything about her father?"

"Indirectly. But to tell the truth, I don't think she gives a damn about him. Of course, the brother is something else again."

"I thought you liked him."

"I do. I'd like to get him solidly into Prysing Pro-

430

ductions. I think he'd be a real asset, so long as he doesn't go nosing around about his father."

"Do you think he could be dangerous? I mean, if he were to find out the truth?"

"He's his father's son, true. But there's still a lot of Olga in him. He's been loyal and faithful to his sister, and he's a decent boy — not like Kurt. Would he change if he were to know the truth about his father? That I don't know."

"I've wondered that myself," Steve said. Sensing that he was depressing the bridegroom, he changed the subject. "Sometimes I think this is the first woman you've ever loved. I hope she deserves you."

Leo laughed shortly. "I was married once to a woman who didn't love me. Remember Irita Vallman? Had to marry me to get into America when I first came over. She's been dead now almost twenty-five years. But I'll tell you something, Steve. Jany loves me. I know she does. And that's a hell of a lot better than having a woman marry me to get into the movies, or get into the country. Jany and I are going to do all right. Just so long as outside influences don't get in the way."

"Outside influences?"

"Well, sure, like her brother. But I know how to handle him . . . once I get him working for me he isn't going to raise a lot of trouble."

Relieved that Leo hadn't mentioned Tony as a possible source of trouble, Steve felt he could relax and enjoy the wedding, hoping that Leo was right about Carl, and that he was wrong about Tony.

# Chapter Twenty-Nine

Stopping to look back from the church steps shortly before noon, Carl Friedrich was stunned by the number of people who had come to witness the marriage of his little sister.

The last time Carl remembered seeing that many people was on Liberation Day over a year ago when the American opera star, Grace Moore, sang the "Marseillaise" before thousands who had gathered in the streets from the place de l'Opera to the Louvre. He recalled how the people had stared up at her, the same way they were staring today at his little sister, whose appearance stunned him as he came to take her arm for the procession. She looked taller than usual because of the high heels she wore, and the silk and chiffon of her wedding gown revealed more of her throat and bosom than he thought his sister should display, especially for such a solemn occasion.

Created by Sirene, the Oscar-winning designer, the gown had a long, low waistline whose V-point vanished in the draping of scalloped chiffon over her hips, the pattern repeated in layers to the floor. Her veil and fifteen-yard train were of tulle, descending from a small tiara of pearls borrowed from the prop department. She wore her hair free to her shoulders, cascading down in shimmering waves, a coiffure that startled many of the style-conscious guests.

Carl knew that Jany had wanted to wear her hair

properly confined, perhaps at the nape of her neck, but the bridegroom had pleaded that she wear her hair down, and Jany didn't want to disappoint him. Regardless of her outward appearance, though, Carl felt that she radiated a quiet confidence, a sureness that he had never seen in her before.

"How do I look?" Jany whispered as the processional music started.

"Very nice," Carl said, placing her hand in the crook of his arm.

Reassured, she concentrated on the procession moving ahead of her, the stunning young women in spring pastels, led by little Andrea Lombard in a grass-green miniature of Jany's gown. Jany carried her mother's Bible, newly bound in white, using her favorite *muguets*, lilies of the valley, as a placemark for the passage she had chosen: "Whither thou goest, I will go; and where thou lodgest, I will lodge. . . ."

The procession moved in lockstep toward the altar, where Father Roderiques waited with Leo Prysing and Steve. Leo looked uncomfortable to her. She was sure he was nervous and the idea made her like him even more. If only she could avoid Tony, she thought. After today, as Leo's wife, she hoped Tony would mean nothing to her. Moving down the main aisle of the church, she spotted his dark head, which she knew so well. He was everything she had ever dreamed of in a man. Sacred vows — his, and now hers — would separate them forever.

He and Eden exchanged whispers as Andrea passed them with a side glance and a hesitant smile in their direction.

Heads turned in one concerted move, following the bride and her brother down the aisle. Eden, watching along with the others, was wearing a funny little hat perched over one ear, with a green feather that kept falling over her face and under her nose like a mustache. She nudged Tony, who kept looking resolutely forward. Passing them, Jany gazed straight ahead also, saving her nervous, flickering smile for the first time her eyes met the bridegroom's.

As the group of bridesmaids parted, Jany tried to remember her vows, but her mind would only run in odd channels. She thought of the days when she and her mother had gone to the High Mass at Notre Dame, and how all of eternity seemed to be enclosed in those lofty transepts. What would Maman think of her husband-to-be? She knew only too well, the thoughts having crossed her own mind many times.

Feeling guilty for not concentrating on Leo, she glanced at him lovingly as he stood straight and proud beside her.

She couldn't remember afterward what she had said, or how her voice sounded, but there was no wavering in Leo's rumbling bass voice as he made his vows. He had sworn earlier to raise any children they had in her faith, knowing there would be no wedding without that vow, and he seemed anxious now to show her that he meant it.

Jany looked around once at Carl, who was watching her very seriously. She hoped that he had no doubts about her decision, and wished that she'd had time to convince him that she knew what she was doing, to make him understand that the

434

little girl he had helped raise was gone forever. It was about time.

There was a small contretemps when it was time for Andrea to present the ring. Raising it up to Steve, the little girl had forgotten it had to be blessed first. A slight confusion followed, and after handing it to Steve, she retreated a step, bumping into her grandfather. Putting both hands on her shoulders, he whispered something to her, which seemed to pacify her for the moment, although Jany longed to hug away the anguish the child felt at her mistake.

It was for this reason that Leo Prysing was not the first but the third person to kiss his bride. Immediately following the ceremony, Jany swung around to kiss her brother, stooped to plant a kiss on Andrea's forehead and finally turned to her husband to seal their vows.

No cameramen had been permitted inside the church, but on the steps outside Jany was dazzled by the crowd of newspaper columnists and photographers that had come to cover the event. Louella Parsons, who had been seated in the section reserved for family members, approached Jany like a friendly aunt, wanting to know what Jany's first thoughts were as Mrs. Leo Prysing.

Slightly embarrassed, Jany asked, "My very first?"

"Yes, dear, do tell."

"I wondered — I'm sorry, Leo — I wondered when I could take these high heels off."

She couldn't have said anything more winning to charm the crowd, although reporters from the New York magazines later commented on her remark as being "gauche" and "obvious."

By the time the limousines and other studio cars had carried the reception guests to the Hotel Ambassador grounds, Jany was a trifle more used to her new role as Mrs. Leo Prysing. Riding alone in the first limousine together, Leo fumbled to undo his new bride's veil and train from her tiara.

"It's all right," she said, "I can fix it. Or Aunt Brooke will. Didn't she look beautiful today? She told me Carl has been a great help in her affairs."

"Good old Brooke!" Leo had gotten the tulle train loose, but gave up on the veil, which dropped stiffly down her back. "I remember her second wedding. It was in Hawaii, while I was working on *Prince of the Golden Isles.*"

"My father was in that, wasn't he?"

"Yes he was, sweetheart." Not wishing to pursue that subject, he said, "You do look good enough to eat." He enveloped her in a bear hug and she responded willingly, without shyness. At that moment she felt that next to Carl, Leo was the dearest person in the world. She was sure of it. He was so kind and generous and considerate, and most importantly, he would be good to Carl, give him a future. This meant more to Jany than her own happiness, especially after all he'd done for her since their mother died.

In the biggest suite she'd ever seen, Jany let Brooke and the bridesmaids flutter around her, removing her veil and freshening the eve shadow and mascara she wore for the first time. When they considered her ready, she was escorted to the reception room, a long, palatial room with a lavish buffet spread along one side.

Throughout the time she and Leo spent in the receiving line, she couldn't keep herself from occasionally glancing at the incredible spread of food. *How awful, to be thinking of food at a time like this . . . I should be feeling such passion for my husband that my appetite is gone . . .*

Her self-incriminating thoughts were interrupted when Eden Ware and her husband, arm in arm, approached them in the receiving line.

"We didn't mean to be so late, but I'm afraid Andrea has been a little upset. She thinks she ruined the wedding," Eden said.

"Nothing of the sort," Leo boomed out, "she played her part splendidly, didn't she, sweetheart?"

"Of course," Jany answered quickly, trying to keep her mind off the man in front of her.

Tony took Jany's hand and congratulated her, just as all the previous guests had done. His smile was easy and his manner relaxed, reminding her of the time they had spent in the Paris apartment.

Lucky, lucky Eden Ware! She would be going home with Tony Lombard. *Her* husband.

To make up for her earlier lapse into mental adultery, Jany was especially anxious to show Leo how much she appreciated all he had done for her, and was prepared for what she thought would be his sexual aggression. Even from their few kisses before she learned he was married, she knew from Tony how exciting sex could be. Sensing Leo's eagerness, she had prepared herself for what was to come from the moment they got inside the doors of the huge old house they were pulling up to — evidently borrowed from another screen mogul for their first night together.

The limousine stopped in the semicircular drive before the mansion, with its tile roofs at various levels, and numerous balconies with wrought-iron railings. Leo leaped out and lifted his bride from the car, insisting on carrying her across the threshold.

The doors seemed to open by themselves, but then Jany caught sight of McDevlin, a hard-drinking character actor who was currently running Leo's Hollywood suite. McDevlin accompanied Leo everywhere, even on his wedding night.

"There's my butler, doorman and wine steward," Leo waved to him. "That's old Mac. He can play any part."

The huge foyer was lined with Moorish archways that opened into exotic-looking, but sparsely furnished rooms. The tile floor was slippery beneath her feet as she walked around, admiring the rooms.

"You borrowed this for me," she said, turning to Leo, "you thought I wanted something like the old movies that we've talked about so often — how dear of you!"

"Then you like it?"

She knew that she could put up with anything for the short time a honeymoon lasted. Then she remembered that the honeymoon destination was a secret. What if he planned on their staying at this Spanish atrocity the entire time?

"It is most . . . unusual," she said, managing a false enthusiasm.

"I knew you would feel right at home here. This

is McDevlin's doing — he's the one who found it. Built by early Hollywood royalty, then it was in the hands of bootleggers. After that, nothing — it was left to become an eyesore. McDevlin worked like a dog to fix it up. He even hired the staff. Anything you don't like, you just see Mac. He runs it."

When he's sober, Jany thought.

"The new owners, they have hired Monsieur McDevlin?"

He took her arm. "You could say that. Up these steps, sweetheart."

Jany took care not to let her husband know her real feelings about the house, but with every step away from the front doors, she felt more and more depressed — it was so gloomy, especially with the heavy Spanish decor.

The master bedroom also had an alcove shaped like a Moorish keyhole, but it was large enough to accommodate the bed. Jany caught Leo's uneasy side glance and beamed at him, finding it amusing that it was she reassuring him, a man of experience, on their wedding night.

"Do you like it, sweetheart? Look, there's even a balcony. There's another one outside of the music room, and I don't know how many others. Three, Mac says."

Leo fumbled to remove the little violet toque from her head until she reached up to help him get it off. Turning her around, he undid the clasp at the neckline of her Jacques Fath silk-crepe suit, with its fashionable fringed sash.

Jany thought her husband would enjoy undressing her without help, and let herself be maneuvered about like a doll. She wanted to get it over with, this first experience, and wished he'd hurry.

"You're so young, sweetheart. So — tender, like a flower bud." He pinched her in his attempt to hurry. "I'm sorry . . . you mustn't be frightened."

"I'm not. Maman told me all about sex."

"All?"

"Everything."

"Dear Olga."

He lifted her nude body onto the quilted satin bed coverlet and knelt over her. She knew the sight of her pale body excited him and she was pleased, though she vaguely felt that something was missing. She had always thought she would be deliriously happy on her wedding night.

After Leo undressed, Jany closed her eyes and held her arms out to him. From his powerful build she thought that he would be very aggressive and that his lovemaking might be painful.

Jany was pleasantly surprised when she felt his flesh enter hers. The sensation was wonderful, and Leo's movements were almost gentle. He was whispering all sorts of things, half of which she didn't understand. She murmured endearments in French, thinking they would please him.

As his hands moved over her breasts, her mind wandered to the time Tony passionately embraced her in the Paris flat, the sheer ecstasy she'd felt at his touch, his hands, his lips. If only they could have made love just once before she found out that he was married, before it became the greater sin.

Leo lay heavily beside her now, still caressing her nipples.

"I'll always love this place," he finally said, "thanks to you, sweetheart. You *do* like it?"

"Yes."

"It's yours, you know. I bought it for you. You're going to spend the rest of your long, happy life here. And after I'm gone, it'll be yours to do whatever you want with. What do you think of that?"

She found it difficult to respond honestly without hurting his feelings. After a long pause, she said only, "*Merci*, Leo."

He leaned over to kiss her and was surprised to find that she was crying. "Now, sweetheart, now, now. Why the hell do women always cry when they're happy?"

# Chapter Thirty

Movie-gossip columns throughout the country found good headline copy in the way Leo Prysing and his bride had spent their honeymoon — hidden away in their new mountainside castle. It was Louella Parsons' rival, Hedda Hopper, who revealed that Jany Prysing spent most of her time in the kitchen, preparing goodies for her husband and his studio cronies. While they played poker until dawn and Leo slept in his limousine on the way to the studio, Jany found her delight shopping in well-stocked American supermarkets.

Ah, these romantic French, wrote Hedda, with tongue in cheek. But six months went by with no sign of a divorce. It was beginning to look like a successful marriage.

Every month on the anniversary of their wedding, the Prysings — at Leo's insistence — held a highly publicized dinner, demonstrating their happy relationship to Hollywood, the only world that counted.

Louella Parsons was delighted to report that the Prysings' Christmas party would be the most lavish since before the war. In her column covering the upcoming bash, she advised all guests to have their chauffeurs fill up the gas tanks, since it was quite a trip up into the hills to the "lovebirds' nest."

Eden insisted that it would look odd if she and Tony didn't go. "Besides," she argued, "my contract is up for renewal and if we cross Leo now, he's not going to put out for the trade ads when Oscar time rolls around."

"Then you go, I'll stay home and play Santa Claus for Andrea. That new baby-sitter is hardly the type."

Eden's smile was a bit wry. "Tell her to slip her falsies down a few inches. They'll make a nice stomach padding for Santa."

"I wish mother hadn't gone off to Hawaii," he grumbled. "She would have kept Andrea company. But no, she has to play the perfect wife, waiting on the tarmac to welcome father back from Japan . . . as if MacArthur couldn't run the country without him. And us up to our necks in labor strikes."

Eden finished fastening on the small emerald earclips he had given her for her birthday. She was careful not to look at him. She didn't want to over-emphasize what she had always known was his deep jealousy of his father's accomplishments.

"If I know Steve, he's probably making deals to acquire half of Tokyo for a housing development."

He shrugged into his dinner jacket, gave his own reflection in her mirror a quick, contemptuous glance, then studied her profile.

"You look marvelous, Eden. You'll dazzle everyone there."

"Thank you, darling. I won't really, but thanks for saying so."

"A big-league star like you ought to learn to take compliments," he said, leaning towards her. She thought he was going to kiss her but her remark was out before she could stop herself.

"All eyes will be on the hostess and you know it."

He turned away so she couldn't see his face.

"I thought she looked tired at that preview of mine," he said. It had been Tony's first A-film and it hadn't gone well. Leo had decided it should be recut and some stock footage added.

"You'd be tired too, darling, if you went to as many previews as she does. She and Leo never seem to spend any time at home."

"Like us."

She glanced at his reflection. He was in one of his sarcastic moods, but she decided not to rise to the bait.

"Darling, you knew what I was when you married me. I never pretended to be anything else."

"Eden, do me a favor, will you?"

She knew the zinger was coming. "Depends."

"Don't call me darling. You call every male in Hollywood *darling*. It makes me feel like I'm one of the pack."

"Well, well, well. We *are* in a foul mood tonight."

"Carpenters are striking and there's a long trail following them. It's going to close down the sets if we don't do something."

"Damn! I work a six-day week and half the time it's sixty hours."

He became defensive at once. "Look, maybe they aren't as married to their jobs as you are."

"They say there's Communist influence in some of these unions. And the guilds, too. I had a line in my script yesterday: 'One for all. All for one.' I made them change it."

He loved that. It wasn't often that he got one over on her.

" 'All for one and one for all' is not Karl Marx, honey. It's Dumas — *The Three Musketeers*, as a matter of fact."

She grinned and made a face at him. "Your highbrow reading will get you in trouble yet. Just don't start quoting from Marx or — God forbid — Stalin."

"Some of my best friends are Communists," he said to annoy her. "At least, they're well-read."

"Just see that you don't go around making jokes like that at your precious Guild meetings."

"Too late now. And if the strikes spread, we may be eating our jokes."

After an uncomfortable silence he went to her bedroom, picked up the white mink jacket that Leo had given her as a bonus for her third — losing — Oscar nomination, and threw it around her shoulders. She raised her hands to touch his but he had already moved away, glancing at his wrist-watch.

"We'd better hurry. I've got to pick up Carl and it takes an hour to get through that Wilshire traffic. Not to mention those damned hills."

They started out having settled on an unspoken truce. They could both agree on the impossible traffic and the question of whether Carl would work out in the studio manager's office at Prysing Productions.

"If he can just get away from Aunt Brooke's apron strings. She claims he's made her a rich — make that richer — woman in the last three or four months just by a little advice here and there."

"Probably told her to sell out livery stables and buy up aircraft plants. I'm sorry," she said after a

445

pause, "I'm not making fun of him. But he does have that hangup on *Journey*. I hope to God he gets over it pretty soon."

Tony shook his head. "He even went out to Pomona one night last week, thinking they were showing it there, but ended up watching one of Leo's early talkies."

"Poor Carl. I can't help feeling sorry for him. It wasn't his fault. That he had such a father, I mean."

Tony pulled into the narrow driveway beside Carl's hotel.

"I don't see what the hell is so important about *Journey*. I suppose he needs to glorify his father. But all the characters were composites. Somebody ought to tell him he's not going to find anything in that old film. Everybody and his brother has made a B-minus version."

Eden said nothing. Tony hadn't been there when the original tragedy occurred, and it was something Steve, Leo and Eden kept to themselves. Brooke might have guessed what really happened — the true circumstances of the broadcast — had she not been so besotted with her husband.

Carl met Tony in the doorway carrying a worn European overnight case of splintering straw.

"I'm sorry. I telephoned but you'd already left. Your aunt Brooke just called me. She must leave San Francisco for London at once. Her son's wife is very ill. She tells me she can't travel all the way to England alone."

"Oh?" Tony thought of Aunt Brooke's peregrinations around the globe throughout the years. But Carl didn't know how capable a woman she actually was. In some ways, there was a naiveté about him.

"She needs an escort, naturally, to take care of the details. My mother was the same way. Very competent, but a man was necessary to her."

"Well, good luck, old man. I'll call Alec tomorrow. But Heather was always delicate — let's hope it's just another false alarm. Can we give you a lift to the airport?"

Carl refused, not wishing to be beholden to anyone.

"I've already phoned my sister. She won't be expecting me."

The two went back to the car where, on seeing Eden, he shook her hand. Eden regarded with amusement his refusal to follow the Hollywood habit of kissing. He surprised her by asking abruptly, "Do you think Jany is happy?"

"Of course. She's had to grow up fast, but she has everything under the sun. Leo is practically bankrupting himself to please her."

"I know she dresses richly and lives in all that elegance. She's out practically every night. I see her name often in the columns."

"She's happy, Carl. Take my word for it."

Convinced by Eden's word, Carl was on his way, but her remarks had sent her husband into another cool silence that lasted until they were greeted almost an hour later at the Prysings' mansion by McDevlin, who seemed already to have sampled the Prysing bar.

They were late, but Eden refused to take the full blame for it. "Leave it to me to make a late entrance. But your friend Carl did slow us up a bit."

"At least he's doing something out of kindness and concern. We're attending this thing out of pure selfishness."

"Business, dar — honey."

On this note they met their hostess, who had spotted them from one of the archways. The party sounded as if it were in full swing behind her.

Jany Prysing looked painfully sophisticated, unlike his little Jany of Paris, Tony thought. The sight of her always gave his heart a painful wrench. But she just wasn't tall enough to wear those black sequins, and her hair, gathered in a jewelled snood at the nape of her neck, made her look tired and worn. She smiled constantly, but behind that smile, Tony thought, was the shy girl he loved. It seemed that Leo Prysing was determined to make her into one of those damned Hollywood hostess-wives.

Tony took the hand she extended in greeting them. Then, under an irresistible impulse, he leaned over their joined hands and kissed her lips. At least her mouth hadn't changed. It was warm, tender, trembling, and she didn't draw back from him.

It was not a long kiss, and certainly acceptable by Hollywood standards, but Tony was still somewhat startled when Leo Prysing's muscular hand fell on his shoulder.

"Whoa, boy. That's my wife you're manhandling. Come and meet the others, Eden! You're looking Academy caliber, as usual."

"Liar. I never look Academy caliber and you know it. I'm strictly nomination caliber. How are you, darling?" She relieved the awkwardness of the moment by throwing her arms around Leo and giving him so resounding a kiss that the whole room cheered.

After their initial greeting Tony and Jany avoided looking at each other. He was ashamed of his own behavior and any gossip it might have generated about them. Only Eden had helped detract from the scene by adding to it in her typical, flamboyant way.

Still, as they stood together he was aware of Jany's hand next to his. The light touch of her slim fingers inflamed him. At the same time he was aware of Leo Prysing's hard gray eyes regarding him coolly. They were the only features in his expressive face that didn't seem to be smiling.

Coming out of the London hospital and into the dull light of a December day, Alcc Huntington looked around him for the first time since Heather had been admitted with what had proved to be a brain aneurysm.

The war might be over but the shattered city remained, still rationed, still hungry after a year of peace. It was a city of strength, and Heather had always been weak, but in some ways its remains were like his wife, beautiful in their final endurance.

There was one crucial difference, however — the city would live again.

He waited out on the rutted street for Heather's mother, Stella Burkett. A nursing sister who looked like a nun offered him a cigarette.

"Was it bad, sir?" the nurse asked in her quiet, unimpassioned voice.

"She died."

"How tragic, to survive a war and have it happen now. It seems especially unjust this way."

"Yes. But the war did it. She got concussion

449

from a V-bomb two years ago. It was her second shock. The other happened a long time ago, during an earthquake."

"I'm very sorry, I'm sure, sir."

"Thank you."

He didn't know for a fact that it was the V-bomb that caused his wife's brain hemorrhage two years later, but he preferred to think so. Otherwise, her death would seem even more pointless at the age of twenty-four. It had all happened so quickly that even the family hadn't been able to get there in time.

He knew he ought to loosen up, maybe cry. But he felt nothing except numbness and a pervading feeling of emptiness.

He wondered whether he had a broadcast that night.

Yes. He'd planned something about the anniversary of Pearl Harbor. It was five years ago, on a December day just like this one. Only five years? Incredible.

And, he reasoned, because he'd chosen this job long ago, Heather was dead today. It was time to move on, get back to the States. They had been after him to move into a prime-time nightspot in UBC's New York flagship station, but Heather enjoyed London and being treated like the wife of a VIP, and she had a chance to hobnob with titles. She'd even met a member of royalty once.

How young and eager he and Heather had been when they had first arrived in London, thrilled by his position as second only to the senior announcer for the new Universal Broadcasting Company. The onset of war in Europe brought Alec even more money and prestige.

At this development, Heather and her mother insisted that he was a full-fledged war correspondent. It sounded very impressive, and Alec always tended to talk his position down, anyway. It didn't seem as though he would ever overcome his fear of his mother's earlier rejection.

Reflecting on his past, he knew he wasn't as easygoing and gregarious as his cousin Tony, whom everyone seemed to like instantly. Still, he thought, in the long run it was he who had done better, at least as far as his career was concerned. Tony had gone nowhere, and rumor had it that he couldn't turn out a really big picture, that he was suited to the minor second features. More important than Alec's professional achievements, though, was the fact that he had won Heather from his cousin. By default, he suspected, since Tony hadn't wanted her any more than he wanted anything else he knew he could have.

Mutual friends of the two cousins kept saying that Tony had changed, although it didn't really make a difference if he had. They were blood kin and that's what counted. If Tony were ever in trouble, Alec would close ranks. That was just how it was.

Stella Burkett came down the hospital steps, walking stiffly as she always did, her dark head held high. Considering the fact that her entire life had been wrapped up in Heather, she looked surprisingly calm and pulled-together. In spite of the tears he knew she had shed, her eyes still looked very much alive, but with what — vengeance? Did she blame the Nazis for their V-bombs? Why the muted look of hatred, except at life, or God, or fate

. . . Alex never fully understood his mother-in-law, and didn't think this was the time to try . . .

"The car is around the corner in that lot where the chemist's shop used to be," she said without emotion. "I'll get it."

"No, I'll go with you." He took her arm. Neither of them was demonstrative, but she accepted this gesture as a common link. She was a rugged, though good-looking woman whose waterfront background and her years as the Lombard parlormaid had apparently given her that look of iron strength.

"Where to?" she asked when they got into the tiny car.

"Better make it Richmond. I've got to work on my war anniversary piece."

"Here's a surprise. When you called your ma and told her about my Heather being in the hospital again, you told me she wouldn't care. Well, she's gotten somebody to look after her and she's on her way over here. There's a cablegram waiting for you at home. How d'you figure that?"

Of course his mother was too late, but she always had been. In spite of it, though, he felt an unaccustomed warmth from the belated gesture. Had it finally come? He'd spent a lifetime hoping his mother would someday show that she cared a little. Not even knowing whether or not it was a serious illness, she was rushing over to be with him. Surely, he thought, that was a sign of maternal love . . .

"Well," he answered, "she *is* my mother, after all."

"Ha."

"Stella, you're a born cynic."

"My baby's dead, and them Lombards go marching on."

He wondered why he resented her saying aloud what he had thought himself.

"Mother encouraged our marriage. She always liked Heather."

"Who wouldn't like my baby? Prettiest little thing . . ."

He saw her brush tears off the wheel impatiently. Moved by the woman's obvious anguish, he found himself unable to speak. He tried to concentrate on that evening's broadcast but Heather was everywhere. He closed his eyes but couldn't blot out her lovely face.

He knew what others in the family had thought of Heather, that she was completely self-centered and shallow, demanding. Not unlike his own mother in many ways. But this gorgeous young girl had come not only to depend on him, but to love him. For Alec this was an unprecedented development.

Stella parked opposite the rambling Tudor hotel, high above the green valley of the Thames. Again Alec took her arm as they crossed the road and stepped into the dark, paneled downstairs hall of the hotel.

"You needn't worry," she said, pulling away from him, "I'm not going to faint. We're tough, too, us Burketts. Tough as your beloved aunt Randi. We come from the same stock, whether she likes it or not. The Burketts and Galleghers, they worked the docks together in the days of the deep-water ships. And if it hadn't been for that damned earthquake, Heather would've been as tough as the rest of us."

"I know," he said, though he doubted it.

She sniffed hard, ran a finger under her nose and went on, as if he hadn't spoken.

"Randi and young Tony and me, we was in the dining room that day in '33. The china closet fell over on us. While we fussed around trying to get out from under it, my baby was in the bedroom with the door jammed so's she couldn't get out. Ten years old, she was, and scared to death. When we finally got her out, she wasn't even bawling. Just making little sounds like a kitten. My . . . little . . . kitten . . ."

He cleared his throat. "I know."

She recovered quickly.

"Sure you do, boy. You're the only one a that Nob Hill bunch ever did. Well, here we are."

They were both reluctant to enter the rooms alone. By mutual consent they went in together, so that Stella could pick out her daughter's burial dress.

Whatever their personal feelings, both Alec and Stella were relieved when Brooke Friedrich and Carl arrived late that evening.

Returning Brooke's embrace, Alec told himself for the thousandth time, She must care a little. I knew if I waited long enough, she would be there when I needed her.

# Chapter Thirty-One

It all seemed to have happened a long time ago, and it was strangely unfamiliar to Carl Friedrich. All he knew was that Pearl Harbor was somewhere in the South Seas. But it must have been of supreme importance for Alec Huntington to take time away from his mourning in order to make an anniversary broadcast. As a result, Carl found himself acting as buffer between "Aunt Brooke" and the dead girl's mother.

Stella Burkett was a tall, impressive woman with dark hair going gray in odd strands that added to her formidable appearance. She struck Carl as being very angry and bitter — probably her way of dealing with her grief.

Brooke herself was shocked by the news of her daughter-in-law's death. She had always been fond of Heather, but the death of a beautiful woman always brought to mind other things as well — it was like the Grim Reaper breathing down her own neck.

Carl was sorry for the tragedy, but he couldn't help but wish he were a thousand miles away. He'd never met Heather Burkett's mother or Alec, and it was awkward to be surrounded by people mourning a stranger. He'd only agreed to make the trip with Brooke because he thought she needed him. He left his work, but reluctantly, wondering if Leo would fire him for taking time off so soon. And although Carl understood why Brooke wanted to make the trip, he found it curious that while she chattered incessantly throughout the flight, she had very little to say about Alec or Heather.

He knew almost from the time they left San Francisco that it was a mistake to go with her. He thought that it might look bad, accompanying a woman old enough to be his mother, but while he had wavered when she first asked him, she found a way to make the trip seem worth his while.

"We can talk about your father on the flight," she'd said, and later lived up to her promise. "The last time I saw him was at dinner the night of the *Anschluss*. Kurt had to leave the house for a while, about a rally, I seem to recall. Steve and Eden insisted we leave Vienna that very night. They said the Preysings weren't safe in our wine cellar. Well, we went all right, and that was the last time I ever saw your father."

"It was strange that Leo Prysing made your brother and Miss Ware do his — I believe it is called 'dirty work.' "

"Don't be naive. Leo couldn't enter Austria. He's Jewish."

Carl hadn't thought of that, and to do so only brought back the hideous fear he lived with in Paris. Would the Nazis ever discover that he and Jany had Jewish blood? In the days when many of their Jewish friends were rounded up only to disappear, the threat had been very real.

In addition to their talk about his father, Brooke was a lively companion. He wouldn't have had any reservations about the trip had she been an actual blood relation. As it was, he kept wondering if

456

people were gossiping about them, mistaking them for a couple.

Painful decisions were made early the next morning in Richmond after Alec returned from making his broadcast. He insisted that a memorial service be held in London, and that afterward the body be flown to the Lombard plot outside San Francisco for the funeral.

Listening as an outsider, Carl detected that Heather's mother was the mastermind behind the idea of the burial in the Lombard plot. Evidently, she wanted to be sure her daughter remained a Lombard, even in death. Carl thought her an interesting woman, though her dislike of the Lombards was slightly sinister. She seemed to harbor a deep grudge against the family, yet she went to great efforts to see that her daughter got her due as one of its members.

Carl found the relationship between Brooke and her son especially intriguing. The woman used all her charms on her son, who seemed to Carl a cold, superior fellow, probably in his late thirties. But the fellow treated his mother with a warmth that he found admirable. Alec didn't seem overly fond of Carl, but that was probably because he suspected Carl was out to get something from his mother. In an odd way Carl respected the man for his suspicions, and for the devotion he clearly felt for his dead wife.

It wasn't a feeling Alex Huntington extended to the rest of the Lombards. Carl couldn't miss the man's faintly sarcastic tone whenever Tony Lombard, in particular, was mentioned.

Before the memorial service, Carl found himself

alone with Stella Burkett while Alec arranged for the transportation of the body, and Brooke was dressing for the occasion.

The woman aired her hostile feelings with astonishing directness. "I guess you've figured out how to work your way into the family, Mr. Friedrich. Miss Brooke — I mean, my girl's mother-in-law, always had an eye for a good-looking man."

At this remark all of Carl's worst fears were realized. The woman *did* think he was one of those gigolos. He regretted that his fair complexion made his blush easy to see.

Remembering how the woman was feeling at the moment, he replied as gently as he could. "Madame Brooke was my father's wife. She is very devoted to his memory, and I admire her for that. She was also very kind to my sister when we visited San Francisco." Her dark eyes drilled into him.

"Sure. That's the Lombard way. I'm kind of surprised, though, that you've gotten so friendly with the Lombards — after that movie they made, and all."

She instantly saw that she'd succeeded in gaining his interest. "Which movie? *Journey*? That's the film about my father's part in trying to rescue Monsieur Prysing's family before the war."

"Well, yes, in a way. Haven't you seen it yourself?"

"Not yet."

She settled back, smiling. There was something about her look that he didn't like.

"That explains a lot. So you and the Lombards are real buddies. You must be quite an innocent . . .

458

or is it Christian charity?"

The woman really was vindictive, and speaking in riddles.

"They've been most kind to my sister and myself."

"Conscience, I suppose."

That was an odd way to put it, he thought.

"Perhaps so. My sister and I sheltered Tony while the Germans were looking for him."

Again that sardonic smile. This time he was sure — there *was* something sinister about it. What was she trying to tell him?

"Madame Burkett, if there's something you want to tell me I wish you would do so."

"Some other time," she said, as she heard Brooke open her bedroom door.

When Carl questioned Brooke later he had little more satisfaction. She, too, seemed utterly confused.

"My dear, I can't imagine what she's driving at. But you mustn't take her seriously. She used to be our parlormaid, and a clever one at that. If you can believe it, she convinced my father to eventually marry her. It was on the day of the Strand earthquake. Daddy was killed, so the marriage only lasted about two hours. We thought about suing her if she claimed his name, since we thought he was pushed into it anyway. It wasn't possible to have it annulled, so strictly speaking, Stella is a Lombard with daddy's third interest in the Nob Hill house."

He could see that they were getting to the root of Stella's hatred.

"Forgive me, Aunt Brooke, but I've noticed that she does go by the name 'Burkett.' Were things made uncomfortable for her?"

Brooke threw up her hands.

"On the contrary, she made life unbearable for *us*. She managed to take over the entire house and almost forced the rest of us out. Steve threatened to sue and make a lot of trouble for her. Then Alec married Heather, and Steve paid Stella to stay in London with them."

"Paid her? But it seems she wanted to be with her daughter."

"Certainly. I told Steve she'd go with Heather whether we paid her or not. But Steve knew Stella was always getting in Randi's hair, so he set Stella up with fifty thousand and it suited everyone. She's always hated the Lombards, you know. And I think she'd do just about anything to hurt us. She's probably already convinced herself that we're somehow responsible for Heather's death. I just hope she doesn't decide to come home now. Alec is talking about taking a UBC job in New York."

"Perhaps there are too many memories here."

She shrugged. "Alec is the only member of the family who likes Stella, mostly because of Heather. I just hope he keeps her in New York or there's going to be real trouble."

Brooke's gossip helped explain Stella's efforts to cause trouble between Carl and the family. Still, he couldn't help but wonder about what she was hinting at. He tried on several occasions to get the woman alone, but Brooke kept him busy escorting her to the Savoy Grill or Claridge's or some night-club.

Carl was becoming increasingly restless to return to work in the Prysing studio manager's office. There were endless problems he felt guilty about leaving behind: deciding which movie budget was entitled to certain props or soundstages or sets, who got the use of the back lot's thirty acres of sagebrush and ant hills . . . these decisions, though made behind the scenes, were still all-important to the success of a film.

After an endless four days Brooke saw that she would have to return to America with Alec if she was going to join the family funeral in San Francisco. Stella Burkett also escorted her daughter's casket by ship. The woman then planned to return to London with Alec as his housekeeper, while Alec decided whether to remain overseas or take a stateside job. Carl gave Huntington full credit. Apparently, he understood his mother-in-law in a way that no one else could.

A few hours after the service he ran into Alec, whom he spotted huddled over a pint of lager in a corner of the little Tudor bar downstairs. Not knowing him very well, Carl would have turned away, but on seeing him Alec waved him over to his table. Carl accepted, grateful for the friendly gesture.

He was a good deal surprised when Alec's first words were almost an accusation. The man was definitely not his normally careful, reserved self. It must be the beer, on top of the painful circumstances he'd endured for the past few days.

"Tell me," he said expansively, "you're a smart guy. Why don't these things ever happen to the Lombards?"

"I don't understand. Do you mean Madame Huntington's death?"

"For starters, yes. My Heather is dead while Tony's wife lives merrily on. My mother despises me, Tony has a wonderful mother. Tony got clobbered by the Japs and then the Nazis, yet he comes out smelling like a rose."

"I — I don't think I —" Carl stammered, not wanting to get involved in what began to sound like maudlin self-pity.

Alec waved the tankard in his face.

"Doesn't it annoy you, just a little?"

"Well —"

"All right. Don't answer that. But his time is coming. Has to." He looked Carl in the eye and suddenly laughed. It was a sharp sound, without humor.

"Don't get me wrong. I don't want any thing to happen to old Tony. He's my cousin. You know, same blood and all. I was just rambling. Thinking about — things."

"I know."

Alec blinked. "You like old Tony, don't you?"

"We fought the Boches together."

"Blood brothers. I know. All I complain about is that they've got things too easy. Uncle Steve and Tony and Leo. Things just fall into their laps. They don't really know pain. Never did."

"Mr. Prysing is not a Lombard."

"True. I got carried away for a minute. But look at Leo. He won a girl young enough to be his granddaughter."

"My sister loves Mr. Prysing very much," Carl said stiffly.

"Your sister. I forgot."

Alec looked into his tankard and set it down.

"Empty. I wonder how many that makes. I don't do this often."

Carl couldn't think of anything to say to that. He sympathized with Alec Huntington, but Leo Prysing had been his father's friend, and the Lombards had been very good to him personally — especially Alec's mother.

After a few more beers and more congenial talk, he helped Alec up to his room, feeling that he'd seen the humanity beneath Alec's chilly exterior.

The night before the sailing of the *Queen Mary*, Stella bumped into Carl as he walked down Richmond Hill to pick out one last souvenir for Jany. In politeness he could hardly refuse her company, but he wished she would stop dropping her obvious hints. They disturbed him more than he would admit, even to himself.

"Hello, Mr. Friedrich. I guess I can call you Carl, since we're all kind of connected, right?"

His reply was polite, though obviously lacking enthusiasm.

"By the way, are you free this evening?"

She must have known that they were all leaving on the boat train early the next morning. He explained his errand, thinking she might enjoy helping him pick out something for Jany. But she had something quite different in mind.

"Well now, you could buy a doodad and still have time for the movies."

"Tonight? I think not. We have an early train to catch."

"Not even for *Journey*?"

He stopped in his tracks.

"Do you mean you know where it's playing? Right now?"

"Sure. Europeans always have prints of old American films somewhere. Deep in Yorkshire's West Riding, or in Outer Warsaw, or Inner Amsterdam. A million places. I called the United Artists London exchange. They distribute Prysing films. They traced a print for me to Manchester."

"Manchester? But that's many kilometers . . . many miles from here. I couldn't possibly make it tonight, with the boat train leaving tomorrow morning."

"Not necessarily."

She hooked her arm in his. It was an oddly flirtatious gesture, odd because he was sure she had no interest in him whatever.

"Just come along. The Gaumont-Richmond has a Prysing double feature tonight, too. I've arranged everything. I have a small income."

"But you are a genius, and a generous one at that."

How right you are, Stella Burkett thought to herself.

Not until he saw the double bill advertised outside the old-fashioned movie house they were approaching could Carl believe it was really happening. But there it was.

"They were going to change bills tomorrow anyway," Stella explained. "You can see that the so-called Prysing classics are getting a good audience."

It was true. The line of patrons in well-worn coats and uniforms extended to the corner and was moving in fast. After the general prosperity Carl had noticed in California the shabbiness of these people touched him. They had fought the good fight, but so far their rewards had been meager. Getting into line, he was glad his own suit was not new. He recalled how much it annoyed Leo that he didn't dress up to his position, but Carl knew that would inevitably involve accepting unwanted gifts from Leo.

He and Stella found two aisle seats in the darkened theater, halfway from the front. By the time the British newsreel started the theater was nearly full. The news mainly reported on the movements of the Russian colossus, the doings of the new Communist states of Albania and Bulgaria, and the United Nations location donated by the Rockefellers in New York.

An early silent film was the first of the two features. Carl had settled into the uncomfortable seat, prepared to wait through the movie without paying much attention, until the title and names of the stars flashed on the screen.

FAMOUS PLAYERS — LASKY PRESENTS
A LEO PRYSING PRODUCTION
*PRINCE OF THE GOLDEN ISLES*
with
IRITA VALLMAN and KURT FRIEDRICH
Produced and directed by
LEO PRYSING

Carl sat straight up.

This was more than he had hoped for. He figured that it must have been one of the first films in which his father had a leading role. He wished Jany was there to see how their father looked during the time he was with their mother.

The film's plot was simple, but the setting was photographed with genuine art. It appeared to take place somewhere in the South Seas. No — Tony had said Prysing's earliest American film had been made in Hawaii, on the estate belonging to Eden Ware's father. It was pretty country, and Kurt Friedrich looked like some golden god playing — fittingly enough — a ruling Hawaiian prince. Seeing his father on the screen brought back all of Carl's cherished memories of the days spent with both of his parents.

By the time the film ended, with its predictable tragedy, Carl sat back, awed by what he considered to be his father's splendid performance. As the second feature began, he knew that nothing could have better prepared him for watching his father's last and most heroic role.

The screening of *Journey* began.

The film was loaded with stars, and as their names flashed on the screen, Carl tried to place them in their roles, according to the bits and pieces he'd learned about the true story. Tyrone Power was the hero and Olivia de Havilland the heroine. Prysing seemed to have combined his own role in the affair with that of the real rescuer, Steve Lombard.

The ingenue lead was Eden Ware, in what was to become her breakthrough performance. There were also several character actors, including Albert Basserman, Anton Walbrook and Conrad Veidt. Walbrook, a onetime star in German-language musicals, usually played sympathetic characters in English-language films. In *Journey* he was the betrayed Josef Preysing character. Veidt was cast in the role of a Nazi villain, which he acted with an aura of dangerous sexuality.

Carl was able to follow the story to some extent. A war correspondent and a young actress agreed to escort a brilliant Jewish political leader and his wife out of Vienna. Eventually the heroine, an American musician in Vienna, joined the war correspondent and actress in the dangerous attempt to smuggle out the political leader.

As the story unfolded, Carl tried to figure out how much of it had actually happened, and which character portrayed his father. There were several supporting characters and a few atrocious ones, the worst of which was Conrad Veidt's character. He played a Count von Frieden, a German admirer of de Havilland who betrayed the two escapees at the last moment. Carl continued to search the film for his father's part in the attempted escape, but couldn't make any direct associations.

His efforts seemed to have been parceled out among three or four minor characters, like an Austrian parlormaid and a ticket-seller at Vienna's Westbahnhof, the train station.

Two Yankee servicemen sat behind Carl, commenting throughout the movie. From the sound of their remarks, Carl figured them to be film experts. Despite admonitions from the audience, the pair spoke in loud whispers.

"That's sharp, the way he moves in his cameras, just catching that little shed on the Swiss border —"

"I'll say, then slides it away. Like nobody on the train gives a damn, and all the time, in that shed —"

"I love de Havilland's face when she finally realizes her Nazi boyfriend was behind the betrayal. It kind of crumples."

"Eden Ware's terrific — the way she moves like a lively colt."

"Cliché, boy. Cliché."

As they went on arguing, agreeing and analyzing, Carl felt more and more deflated. He had counted so much on seeing his father vindicated . . . Could Prysing have grown jealous of the real hero, and left him out entirely? Or did he feel it bad timing to make a hero out of an Austrian?

"The revenge is magnificent," the boy behind him whispered as the film came to the end. "It's cold-blooded and ruthless, but worthy of the crime. The first time I saw it I wanted to cheer."

Carl was aware of an inner trembling. It seemed he was so close to solving the mystery of his father's heroism . . .

The plot moved forward, showing how de Havilland's Nazi suitor, Count von Frieden, employed the Viennese household as spies. On the night of the *Anschluss*, de Havilland was shown fleeing from Vienna with her lover, Tyrone Power, and the two Jewish refugees. At the same time von Frieden was seen attending a Nazi rally, though he'd already arranged to have the movements of de Havilland and the two Preysing characters followed.

Carl felt himself breaking out in a cold sweat. He kept telling himself that de Havilland's Nazi boyfriend was only a fictitious character, used to em-

468

phasize the atrocity of the Austrians' crime in betraying their country to the Germans. Still, he had a pervasive feeling he was being forced into recognizing something he didn't want to see.

The climactic journey from Vienna to the Swiss border began. The Preysing couple seemed doomed from the start, having been fingered by a warning description sent ahead by von Frieden. The Preysings were removed secretly from the train at the Swiss border as a direct result of a phone call by von Frieden that sealed their fate.

When the other characters reached Zurich there was a ghastly wait. Hopes died slowly. The Tyrone Power character, acting out Steve Lombard's part, tried to buy the refugees from the Nazis, but it was too late. Word later came that they died in a suicide pact during "questioning" by Hitler's new gauleiter of Austria, Seyss-Inquart.

Carl tensed with frustration. Surely, nothing remained now but for someone in the movie to thank the anti-Nazi who maneuvered the attempted escape in the first place. And where was Leo's famous broadcast that went from Zurich via London to the entire Continent, including that part of Europe living under the swastika?

There was a scene showing the survivors listening to Josef Goebbels' powerful state-run broadcasting station, glorifying the character of the Nazi villain, Count von Frieden, for his success in destroying the Preysing pair, "a cancer that ate at the vitals of the Third Reich."

Next the Tyrone Power hero, along with Eden and the others, gathered when he made a Zurich radio broadcast in reply. Having been introduced by a British announcer from the BBC, he made his speech, regretting the betrayal and death of the Jewish refugees. Then he thanked those who tried vainly to save the couple. "First and foremost is Sigurd von Frieden, now safely in London, the brains behind the attempted escape, this brave man of Jewish origins . . ."

The words were almost exactly those spoken by Leo Prysing himself in 1938.

It was all wrong, Carl thought in confusion. Count von Frieden was the villain. The script was uniting his own brave father, who had secret Jewish origins, with the monstrous von Frieden. It was all a horrible mistake.

To further complicate things the script had shown Leo's famous speech about Kurt Friedrich being made about the villain of the film. It was a supreme irony Carl could make little sense of, nor did he understand why the others in the scene reacted with such a curious combination of horror and satisfaction after the fact.

Even the explanation of it puzzled him, under the circumstances. The BBC correspondent, apparently not aware of von Frieden's guilt, remarked to the hero after the broadcast, "Isn't your tribute somewhat dangerous, old man? Suppose von Frieden hasn't left the Reich yet. If he hasn't, you've just made him a target for every Gestapo bully in Germany and Austria."

"Yes," the hero readily agreed. "Unfortunately, von Frieden *is* still in the Reich. And his father was a rabbi. My family's rabbi, as a matter of fact."

"But — but this information will destroy him."

The camera moved in on a tight close-up of the

hero, who smiled. "Probably."

With that, his revenge against the betrayer of his family was complete.

The audience seemed to hold its breath until the Prysing logo appeared on the screen with the words, "The End."

Stunned by the ironic ending, Carl sat in his seat, unmoving.

*But they have made my father the villain,* his mind reeled over and over again.

Slowly he looked around. The house lights caught his face, pale and set, his eyes revealing his bewildered state. Everything was turned around. According to this film, Leo Prysing's speech was a deliberate attempt to destroy Kurt Friedrich. It hadn't been a deplorable accident of timing, after all. Prysing knew all along that Kurt was inside the Third Reich when his broadcast was made, knew very well that the Nazis would hear it.

Confused and sick, Carl thought of ways to justify Leo's portrayal of his father. Perhaps Prysing decided the truth was less melodramatic than this vile, contrived plot. Also, the picture had been made around the time World War II was ready to break out. To show a heroic Nazi helping Prysing's family probably wouldn't have been good politics, so Prysing twisted the truth to give Americans what they wanted: the black-and-white of a war movie, showing the enemy, represented by one man, getting his just deserts.

Yes, he thought, that must be the answer.

Stella Burkett gave the young Frenchman a few moments to digest what he'd just seen before she spoke. "I take it you got the gist of that — your father wasn't honored as a hero; he was set up to be murdered."

*"But why?"*

"Who knows? Maybe they heard a rumor and figured your father was guilty. They put their heads together and came up with that broadcast. It took a while, but eventually your father was killed as a result of it."

His mind was whirling. Like a kaleidoscope, it revolved around three images: Leo Prysing, Stephen Lombard and Eden Ware. The three of them in the Zurich broadcasting studio, Leo making his speech of praise and cloying thanks, knowing that Kurt Friedrich was still inside the Third Reich. Steve Lombard and Eden Ware finding out after the broadcast that Leo had sentenced Kurt Friedrich to death, and doing nothing to try to stop it.

Carl didn't say a word until he and Stella were out on the sidewalk in the murky night.

"A penny for your thoughts, my boy," she said in her harsh, deep voice.

He shook his head but couldn't contain his fury any longer. "It was deliberate. Prysing and the others knew my father was still in Vienna, and what would happen when the Nazis heard that Kurt Friedrich's father was a Jew. Once they checked and found it true, they murdered him. But they would never have found him out if Leo and the Lombards hadn't made that speech. To think of what he must have gone through . . . It was the most vicious revenge possible. A revenge for nothing. They surely had no proof that he was guilty."

Stella peered into his face. "How are you going to get back at them — those Lombards?"

Carl said nothing. He hardly knew she had spoken. His mind was too full of bitterness and confusion.

Leo Prysing and the Lombards liked to play at revenge. But they were mere children, Carl thought silently. Revenge was an art for adults, practiced in a civilization older than America's. Carl could bide his time. At that moment he decided he would find the appropriate and subtle weapons to destroy them as they had destroyed his father. But to do so it would be necessary to stay close to the Lombards. He didn't want to use Brooke, the only one he trusted, but if he had to use her, he would do so. He would use everyone.

Except Jany.

What about Jany, married to the ringleader of those monsters? How could he avoid hurting her?

There was no answer, but into his seething brain came a picture of Kurt Friedrich, the prince of the golden isles, noble and true. A secret patriot. Done to death by the lowest, foulest means.

He remembered those days when his father came to visit him and his mother in Paris. The companionship he felt, the closeness he had with his father. He had belonged to someone in those days. Once they were over, that feeling of security was gone. It was he who had to care for and work for and finally do battle for Maman and Jany.

Someday, Jany would understand. But nothing must stop him in the meantime, until their father was avenged.

"One thing you'd better remember," Stella said as they walked up Richmond Hill, "you're taking on a mess of snakes, believe me. You know the word subtle? Be subtle."

That made him smile. "I will be subtle. I promise you, Madame Burkett."

She rubbed her hands. They were workworn, yet shapely. Carl sensed that there was a great deal behind the impenetrable facade of this woman.

"Did you watch the newsreel tonight?" she asked. It seemed to be a complete non sequitur.

"Not particularly." His mind had been preoccupied with the coming films and the hope that his high expectations would be realized.

"Maybe you should've. Those Commies are raising old Ned. Infiltrating, they call it. Alec says during the war we got a lot of Commie propaganda into our stuff. Of course, it was okay then. Us being Allies and all. But it isn't going to go over too good now. In radio and movies and books. Stuff like that. Movies especially, that's what Alec says."

He looked at her. They had passed the dim street lamps so he couldn't read her face. He stopped.

"What do you mean to say, madame?"

"Me? Nothing at all. Just mulling over how the Lombards are all mixed up in your friend Prysing's movies. Look at the movies Prysing made that Tony and Eden worked on. A Russian pilot saves an American woman — he's a big hero. And one that Randi mentioned in a letter to Alec not long ago. Just finished. She said Tony had worked on it under Prysing's supervision. Troops meeting on that river in Germany, and all that buddy-buddy stuff between some Reds and the Yankee hero's platoon."

They reached Stella's hotel room, and she thanked him as he opened the door for her. But when he returned to his room her insidious voice trailed after him.

"Didn't somebody say Tony Lombard was mixed up with a Commie girl in Paris? Her friends visited Alec and Steve and Mr. Prysing right here in London. That was the summer of '44. I heard 'em in the hotel."

My war isn't with Tony, Carl thought, or if it is, it's only on the periphery. But Madame Burkett is right. Danielle deBrett would know what to do with Leo Prysing. And Leo Prysing was the culprit . . .

Carl didn't sleep much that night. He awoke twice from nightmares of his father's suffering during those months after Prysing's Zurich broadcast, the months when Kurt Friedrich remained in Nazi hands before they found a good enough cover to murder him.

In the dark-blue hour just before dawn he imagined again the faces of Tony's wife and Steve Lombard as they listened to the broadcast that condemned his father, perhaps to torture, certainly to death. To make Eden Lombard suffer he might have to hurt Tony.

But why not? Tony Lombard had ruined Jany's life, misleading her from the start . . .

By the time the group was ready to leave for the boat train the next day, Carl had worked out his plan for revenge. He began by writing a letter to Danielle deBrett.

The first problem was Danielle's testimony

475

against Jany — he had to find an acceptable way to "forgive" her before presenting his plan.

Danielle, *chèrie,*
How angry I was when we last said good-bye.

But I must confess that I've missed you more than I can say —

My poor sister Jany is now married to a famous film producer, who is notoriously unfaithful. Nothing would please me more than if a beautiful woman such as yourself could win him from her. Then Jany could be relieved of her burden, and receive a very comfortable alimony besides.

As you see, I am being frank with you, Danielle. You might be that woman who breaks them up, at my expense. And if you play this part well, who knows how far you might go? He would be the perfect vehicle for a girl wishing to break into the Hollywood cinema.

This man prefers impetuosity. He has made stars of women who merely kissed him in public. You see, it makes him appear irresistible.

If you feel you can part from your comrades for this occasion, cable me at once with a simple *oui* or *non.* I enclose my Hollywood address. Next time, perhaps it will include the money you will need . . .

If only I could embrace you tenderly and kiss you in all those special places . . .

Yours,
Carl

Stella Burkett knocked on the door. For the first time since he had seen *Journey,* Carl felt a great relief. The deep and terrible debt was in the process of payment. He opened the door to find her dressed for departure in a neat black suit with white gloves and a black-and-white veiled hat.

"Have you made any plans? I can't talk long. Brooke is coming for you in a minute."

Because he was so proud of it, he showed her the letter, then recalled the last lines and withdrew it before she could finish reading. But as he had expected, she was pleased with the idea.

"Let me know when she leaves Paris. If you get her on the next crossing that Alec and I make in a couple of months, I could see her on the sly and put her wise to what she should and shouldn't do."

"That won't be necessary."

"Well, when she tries to get a visa, suppose she boasts about her Commie contacts?"

That would certainly ruin the plan. His entire objective was to tar Leo with Danielle's Communist ties. The United States was getting more and more touchy about associations, no matter how innocuous — with "Reds" and "parlor pinks."

"You're right. I must settle that with her."

"How do you figure you can hit the Lombards with this? The Commie angle."

"It's a beginning. Only a beginning."

"Suit yourself. Let me know if there's anything I can do to help."

"Help with what?" Brooke Lombard asked from the hall behind her. She broke off the question to yawn. "Lord, how I hate these early risings for the boat train. Well, are we all set?"

"All set, Aunt Brooke. Just this letter I have to leave at the desk for the mail."

He pretended not to notice Stella Burkett's dry smile. For some reason, her participation in his revenge cheapened it a little. He wasn't sure why.

# Chapter Thirty-Two

Since Olga Rey's talk with her about sex, Jany had always imagined that the greatest problem in a marriage would be adjusting to her husband's sexual preferences, but in Jany's marriage such matters were of small moment. Sex had proved unexciting, unimaginative and ultimately boring. Regardless, she felt it her duty, and went to her husband willingly, especially since she'd taken a vow to obey.

What her mother had failed to tell her was of the hours of boredom that marriage would mean for her. She was alone by day, except for the servants who were strangers to her and resented her well-meant supervision. She was even frustrated in her friendly visits to the kitchen, with its long, bright tile counters and wide windows that looked east over Hollywood's rooftops and palm trees, and north to the dusty mountainside, covered with desert scrub.

The cooks always seemed to be changing. Most of them drank, and all of them proved temperamental.

"It goes with the territory," McDevlin explained, trying to pacify her.

Since the cooks insisted on rigid working hours, Jany was able to find herself useful. Her delicate, fluffy omelets and quiches prepared for Leo's poker crowd got a fast shuffle, but when she learned to make thick steak sandwiches for men who chewed and devoured them while concentrating on five cards and a cigar, she was voted a hit.

In her heart Jany knew that she had married Leo Prysing in order to help Carl, and though she'd never actually said anything about it, he certainly *had* helped Carl, who seemed happy in his job at the studio manager's office. As for her own happiness, she used every excuse possible to get out of the house with Leo and relieve her boredom. She looked forward from one preview to the next, and grew to welcome every premiere, even if it meant an appearance before the dreaded microphone.

Her false contentment came to an end the night of the Christmas party when Tony Lombard kissed her as he first walked into the house. Nothing had changed. Her marriage hadn't quenched the aching, yearning passion she felt for the only man she would ever love. Worse, she sensed a subtle change in Leo.

She didn't mind and was even touched when he asked her to repeat things like "Leo, *mon amour*" or "*je t'aime,*" as if they sounded more erotic in her own language. But he seemed always to be watching her; she would often catch him at it just before his gaze shifted.

When he was away at the studio, his alter ego, McDevlin, hung around, rarely letting her out of his sight. She suspected that he reported her every move to Leo, and as a result she began to develop nervous traits she'd never had before.

Leo first noticed it when her hand trembled as she held her cocktail before dinner.

"Better go easy, little girl. How many have you had?"

It was her second — some awful concoction called a Manhattan — but she knew she wasn't drunk. They were at Mike Romanoff's restaurant and she knew exactly what was happening. She simply couldn't explain to Leo that she had just spotted Eden and Tony across the floor from where they sat. They appeared to be quarreling in a rather civilized manner as people sometimes do — Eden was laughing and Tony was scowling.

Jany reassured herself that things would go better once Carl returned from London. Leo insisted that Alec Huntington was being put through "another phony death scene" by his wife.

"But why should she do that?" Jany asked.

"To get attention. She's pretty enough, but she always seemed to be lacking something. Of course, she's no competition for my little girl."

Jany wondered whether he would have dismissed her, too, if she'd had movie ambitions. His chief concern in possessing Jany seemed to be the pleasure of showing her off, whether in public or to his poker and drinking cronies. He was delighted by the spreads they — and particularly she — received in the press, even in the fan magazines.

He concentrated on making her live up to the headlines written about her: "The Beauteous Mrs. Prysing," "The Gorgeous Blonde Wife of the Screen's Top Producer," "The Best-Dressed Hollywood Wife" and "The New Hostess Supreme of the Movie Industry." Sometimes he even had her dressed from the costume department at the studio. Her "Juliet" at the Prysings' Gold Ball was a great hit. More frequently, though, a big-name studio designer was drafted to dress her. And heaven help the actress who happened, by chance, to be wearing a gown that copied or eclipsed that of the "shy and lovely Jany Prysing." After only a few months of marriage to Leo and being constantly in the limelight, Jany no longer felt shy. She saw how her position gave her power in others' eyes, and though she didn't use it, the knowledge was reassuring.

When they later were told that Alec's wife had died unexpectedly, Jany, remembering Leo's dismissal of the unfortunate girl, felt guilty for him.

Her guilt grew when she heard from Leo that the family was returning to San Francisco for the funeral, and that Carl would be with them. But she was hurt, too, that he hadn't notified her as soon as he was back in the States. Perhaps they had returned on short notice . . . Leo said "Aunt Brooke" always decided everything in a hurry.

The Prysings didn't attend the funeral. Leo had an important meeting with other independent producers to discuss strike defense, but all the Lombards gathered at Colma, on the peninsula below San Francisco. Brooke Friedrich had insisted that her stepson accompany her, so Jany didn't have a chance to see her brother until two days later.

She had missed him terribly. The only time they had been apart for so long previously was while he was in the army, before the French Armistice in June of 1940. During those months she and her mother had burned candles every night and prayed for his safe return.

When Carl finally did return to Hollywood, he surprised her by driving up to their hillside mansion in a secondhand Ford he had bought. What shocked her even more was the change in his looks. He seemed older and thinner, and somehow different inside — there seemed to be a false sophistication about him that especially came out when he dealt with Leo. When he lavishly praised her new hairstyle she was sure of it. She had seen him flippant with Danielle deBrett in that same manner, and it disturbed her greatly.

Once, when Leo was playing poker and losing an incredible sum of money, Carl asked Jany if she liked the way things were going. Since she never lied to Carl, she admitted, "We don't live dream lives. But this is my world, and I must make the best of it." She added with a little laugh that sounded hollow even in her own ears, "Isn't it an elegant world? And you haven't said a word about my new Dior. You see how long it is? And with the waist nipped in too tight . . . *très chère*. You wouldn't believe what Leo paid for it."

"I don't see how he can when he plays this poker every night. Does he lose twenty thousand dollars each time?"

Her eyes avoided his. "No, no. He wins sometimes, though not often."

He walked up and down, looking strangely excited. "This isn't a happy life for you, that I can see. But it will be better. You must be patient."

"If you mean Tony, that's impossible. You know it."

"The hell with Tony Lombard! You must forget

these Lombards." He had burst forth suddenly in English. His curse sounded more terrifying in the language they had never used to each other in private, as if it were done to purposely create a brutal barrier between them.

To her relief Carl gradually seemed to get over his obsession with her unhappiness, and began to take over more and more responsibility in the studio manager's office. While Leo hadn't yet fired Carl's superior, who was currently drying out after another alcoholic binge, he raised Carl's salary. Jany imagined Carl would be grateful, but she was troubled by his grim humor when he told her about it privately.

"I will use the money to good effect. Father would have been proud of me."

"I hope you will buy a new car. Leo is embarrassed by that old one. He says it looks as if he does not pay you enough."

But Carl had other ideas, ideas that startled her.

"There is someone in Paris who could do very well in Hollywood. I have already sent the money, and certain instructions."

"Who?" she asked, pleased. "Pierre St. Just? How wonderful! He won't stay, but he'll love the boat trip."

Carl smiled and tapped his knuckle under her chin.

"No, not Pierre. There is something to be done first. Madame Burkett is making the trip with Alec Huntington. She will see that my guest arrives safely. Alec has taken a job broadcasting the evening news from New York on UBC."

She had no particular interest in Alec Huntington, except that he was Tony's cousin and had suffered the loss of his wife. Leo said the man was talented and was preparing for a job on television when it became more widespread. But what baffled Jany now was Carl's connection with Huntington and the Burkett woman. Evidently he had seen her several times during his recent visit to England, but for what purpose?

Was it possible that he was having an affair with her? It seemed unlikely — the woman was old enough to be his mother.

But if it wasn't sex, Jany wondered, what could be the connection between Carl and Stella Burkett?

The thing Jany had most dreaded, but at the same time dreamed about, was a private encounter with Tony Lombard, which came about as a result of the turmoil among the Hollywood guilds and unions. The jurisdictional strife had begun long before, with an attempt by certain left-wing factions to break up the monopoly of the powerful union that included theater and movie employees in most of the crafts. Jany heard Leo and his department heads discussing "Yatsee" versus "those parlor pinks and Commies" in the new union, without quite knowing what it was all about. "Yatsee" turned out to be their code name for the monopolistic IATSE union. To go against them, he explained, would make the studio, its employees, union members and guild members "scabs," or strikebreakers.

The major studios now faced double jeopardy when the new union threatened to strike and put out a picket line. Leo, as the executive producer of an independent studio, had expected to go along with the decisions of the majors, but suddenly the danger was at hand. With three films in the works at various stages of production, Leo was driven down to his offices one morning to find that he was no longer in control of the situation. Pickets appeared in the parking lot outside and those already inside the studio refused to cross the picket line.

"Nothing to it," Leo announced, inviting the local press and trade papers in on the excitement. "We'll camp inside here until the thing is settled. I'll have it catered. It'll be like a picnic. We'll see then how long these two unions are going to hold out. I'd like to bust their heads together."

Before noon he called home. Jany answered the phone as she often did. As much as he liked to hear her voice, it annoyed him that she didn't allow one of the servants to do it.

"I need a few things," he said, after she apologized for taking the call, "couple of changes, and my razor. I'm certainly not going to let Gus here at the barber shop shave me. He's been needling me over my last two films. Claims that damned thing of Tony Lombard's glorified the Reds. How the hell can you show the meeting of two armies without having Russians in it is beyond me . . . Anyway, that's no concern of yours, honey."

"Is the strike very bad? You're not hurt, are you? Please be careful."

"Don't you worry about me, kid. We're just getting the overflow. It's the majors that have the real battle on their hands. Either way they turn for jurisdiction there's going to be trouble. There are some rough boys out there on both sides."

"Who else is in the studio with you? Some of your friends, I hope."

He laughed. He seemed to be enjoying himself through all the excitement. "Well, Eden is here, and some of the cast from her new film. And Carl says to tell you he's all right. He's been talking to the craft unions, giving management's side. He's helping a lot. Making up for Tony, I guess."

"Isn't Tony with you?"

"No, he was out working with some of the guild members. When the pickets showed up, he couldn't get through, and I doubt that he'd ever get involved with strikebreaking anyway. He's been talking too damned much lately about IATSE being a monopoly. Doesn't he know the other bunch is all Commie?"

She knew very little about either union, but suspected that any one who disagreed with Leo would probably be labeled a Red, a parlor pink, or just plain radical. She decided not to argue or try to defend Tony — it might be too obvious.

"Will McDevlin be able to get through the picket line?"

"Sure. Just tell him to give the stuff to old man Walbridge. He's working the gate. Here's a kiss, honey," he said, anxious to end the conversation. "Be a good girl. And don't forget to tell Mac to get hold of the gateman. Love me?"

"Of course."

"Of course, who?"

"Of course, *mon amour.*"

"That's the girl."

"Please, Leo, do not be brave. Take care of . . ."

But he had hung up.

Jany went through the halls, in and out of all the rooms that were still somehow unfamiliar, and finally found McDevlin's bedroom, which was locked. She was about to knock when the older of the two maids called to her from the back stairs.

"Excuse me, Mrs. Prysing. May I see you a minute?"

Puzzled, Jany followed her to the stairs. "Is McDevlin in his room? Mr. Prysing needs him."

The woman lowered her voice. "He's there. With Coral, the new parlormaid he hired last month."

Jany's first reaction was embarrassment, but remembering Leo's urgency, she became annoyed. McDevlin knew how Leo relied on him, and that he would be needed. Then it slowly dawned on Jany that this was a perfect excuse for her to get outside these walls.

"Hilda, please help me. I must get Mr. Prysing's shaving kit and pack a case for him. He's staying the weekend at the studio."

The maid was shocked. "Oh, no, madame! You have not quarreled?"

Jany laughed and shook her head. She was beginning to find the situation exciting, a relief from the long, lonely hours in Leo's castle.

She caught the chauffeur as he was about to drive down into Hollywood on some errand of his own. Like the other servants, he gave her the distinct impression that he would only take orders from Leo. She told him about the situation, and he finally agreed to take her across town to the studio, though he reminded her that he was on overtime.

"I thought that was what Mr. Prysing was fighting against in these strikes," she said, "that and the quarrel between unions."

"That's right, ma'am. Overtime, double time, golden time. Mr. Prysing always gets around it at the studio. A steno works until three A.M., he sends her home and expects her to be back on the job at nine A.M., with no extra pay."

"But that isn't right . . ."

He glanced around at her. "Sure it is. He gives them the next Thursday afternoon off. It works all right that way inside those big Prysing gates. But folks like me, being a man with a family, I have to have the money. Of course, I like to do him a favor occasionally, like now."

"I will remember."

"Thanks, Mrs. Prysing. Your word is all I need."

There was a traffic jam in front of the studio gates. Washington Boulevard was blocked by a studio trailer called the "honey wagon" because it had been constructed for use as a urinal during location trips. The driver wanted to pull into the lot. Although the gateman was willing to let him pass, the picket line wasn't.

Two other studios were also on the boulevard, and traffic from them slowly zigzagged around the trailer, tempers flaring as hot as the idling car engines.

Once the honey wagon backed out and rumbled down the boulevard, Leo Prysing's black limousine drove up to the closed gates. Its arrival was not greeted with cheers.

"Hey, Mac! Doin' the boss's dirty work?"

"Well, if it ain't a scab all duded up!"

"Hold it, boys," the gateman called. "It's little Mrs. Prysing. She's just being the loyal wife."

Many of those she saw on the picket line were men she'd met on the lot. In the present situation she didn't know quite how to act toward them. If she was to remain loyal to her husband, she'd have to regard them as enemies. But she felt sorry for the men, caught in a jurisdictional fight in which neither side was entirely right or wrong. She smiled at several faces she recognized, and some of them grinned back. The chauffeur unloaded the suitcases, a box of Leo's cigars and a hamper of Leo's favorite pâtés and other canned gourmet foods. He set them in the little sentry box that served as a gatehouse.

A groan went up as the smell of hot chili from Chasen's reached the line. Jany looked at the big container and then at her friends. She had an idea and lifted it up on the gateman's counter.

"Can you get large spoons from the commissary? Some of the — gentlemen might enjoy the chili. There's more than enough here . . ."

"That's mighty nice of you, ma'am." The gateman reached for his studio phone.

The chauffeur began to get impatient, but Jany only waved him away. Deliberately mistaking her, he drove out into the boulevard and pulled away. It would mean getting a taxicab for the long drive home. She hated making a call from an American phone, and then dealing with the driver. She never knew what to pay or whether she was being cheated, or how to tip them.

Feeling uneasy in the crowd of men, Jany resolved to find out how Leo and Carl were doing before returning to her lonely but safe home.

Suddenly she heard her name called out and, swinging around, saw a group of newsreel cameramen working busily inside the gates. They had been filming an interview with Tony Lombard and now began to shoot the parade of homemade picket signs. It was Tony who had seen Jany and called to her. Stopping the interview, he came over to her at the gate.

Seeing the troubled look in her face, he briefly took her hands. "It's going to be all right, Jany, don't worry. I've been trying to act as go-between. I've got friends on both sides of this mess. But things are going to change and Leo has to face that."

He looked wonderful to her, like a savior who could take her away from so much unhappiness. Still, there was someone else inside those walls whose well-being was even more important to her than her husband's.

"Yes, yes. But do you know how Carl is?"

Tony's laughter was good to hear. It reminded her of the days when he had seemed to her a single man, with no ties to a glamorous movie star or anyone else.

"Carl is fine. But he seems to have turned into quite a company man. The *L.A. Times* was here to interview Leo, and he put Carl on the line right away. Said Carl could testify to his good-faith intentions, or something. Carl really went all out to present the studio's side of it."

The news puzzled her. "I can't believe it. Carl was never interested in labor problems, and the only group he ever joined was the Free French."

"Well, he's changed, then. He talked up Leo so much that you'd have thought Leo was among the downtrodden, one of the oppressed masses."

"But that makes Leo sound like a Communist or something."

"Don't worry. Nobody will believe it. Carl meant well. Anyway, they're all locked up in Soundstage Three. I tried again to get Eden out, but she's so damned stubborn. Thinks she's standing up for the rights of the individual."

One of the pickets, switching his sign, knocked it against Jany's shoulders. The picketer apologized, but it was clear that this was no place for Jany, and Tony volunteered to escort her off the grounds.

They walked up the boulevard togther, Jany treasuring every minute in his company. They said nothing as they walked along but Jany couldn't ignore the excitement she felt at the touch of his fingers brushing against hers. She was so unnerved she heard herself babbling criticism of his wife which, under the circumstances, she knew wasn't appropriate.

"Andrea will miss her mother. It is very cruel, this strike. How can Eden prefer to stay in that dreadful studio?"

"Because Eden isn't you. Sweetheart —" He broke off.

She looked up at him. Her heart was in her eyes.

# Chapter Thirty-Three

The next steps were logical. Leo's limousine was gone. Tony had his car and was kind enough to offer her a ride home. They had to cross Holly- wood. Why not drop in and cheer up Andrea, who would love to see her? Tony asked.

Jany told herself that she was making this visit entirely for Andrea's sake. What harm could there be in briefly seeing the child? She would take care not to stay too long.

Driving back to Hollywood, Tony assured her of the same thing.

"Seems like a good idea, and I bet seeing you will really raise Andrea's spirits. Poor kid. She isn't too crazy about our new babysitter. Andrea will be going to kindergarten soon, so that should help. She'll have a ready-made audience, and you know how Andrea loves to perform."

"Perhaps she'll be a movie star, like her mother."

"God forbid . . . I want her to have a happy life."

"But Eden seems happy. Leo says she actually screamed with joy when one of the newspaper col- umnists the other day predicted she would win the Oscar next spring."

"My darling, you would never understand a woman like Eden. She has a man's ambition. I want my daughter to live like a lady, the way you do."

"But if a beautiful child like Andrea has talent, it would be a shame not to encourage her to use it."

"Most girls wind up on some casting couch because they lack the drive of a plain woman like Eden."

She was surprised to hear him describe his glamorous wife as plain. Eden Ware sparkled. She captured the attention of a crowd no matter where she went. Tony seemed to read Jany's thoughts.

"I know. She has something more valuable than beauty — there's something charismatic about her personality that's hard to ignore. Andrea, on the other hand, would be driven to compete in a battle she couldn't win. I ought to know."

"You? Oh, no! You have everything."

He turned his head slightly. "Thank you, my poor darling, but you couldn't be more wrong." His lips touched her hair and then, when Jany started guiltily, he explained. "I've tried all my life to become the man my father is. From what he says, he had the same struggle with my grandfather. The Lombards are caught in a competitive race that I don't want Andrea to be a part of."

Jany glanced at him. A nerve throbbed over his cheekbone, and she longed to stroke his olive flesh, to instill in him some of her own love and belief in him. Surely, she thought, he could do anything in the world if he had the proper encouragement. He needed a woman who made him her first priority. It was wicked and all wrong in the nature of things that Tony's wife should care more about her silly career as an actress than about this wonderful man.

He and Eden still lived in the older district a block above Hollywood Boulevard. Jany envied the warmth and coziness of their home. The big stucco building was almost across the street from Leo's spacious, comfortable apartment. Jany looked over at the other building wistfully.

"I thought we would live there after we were married. The people in the lobby were very kind to me, and the maids, too."

"Anyone would be kind to you." Tony opened the door, letting Jany pass under his arm and into the big lobby.

She spotted Andrea at once. The child had been lifted up onto the counter by the receptionist, a blowzy, yet well-liked ex-vaudevillian. Andrea sat keeping time against the counter with the heels of her new patent-leather shoes while the receptionist, Miss Honey Peck, demonstrated the Charleston.

On seeing Jany, Andrea stopped banging her heels, climbed down and ran over to her excitedly. "Jany! Jany! Honey, look who's here."

"See? I told you she'd be glad to see you," Tony whispered. He pushed Jany ahead of him so that Andrea could go into the French girl's arms.

"And where, may I ask, is Miss Cavanaugh?" Tony wanted to know, seeing no sign of the baby-sitter.

Miss Peck pulled her skirt down and shrugged.

"Had a studio call, I guess."

"Is she going through the pickets, or over their heads, or tunneling in?" Tony asked, obviously angry. He had chosen their latest babysitter because she'd sworn she had no movie aspirations.

"Private audition, I think. With some director at his house in Bel Air. But look, kids, Dree and I have been doing great here. No problem at all, is there, sweetie?"

"Daddy, I like Honey better'n Miss Cavanaugh."

Tony laughed. "Don't we all?"

Andrea, finally breaking away from Jany, snuggled up to her father before the threesome climbed up the wide staircase to the Lombard's second-floor apartment.

Long afterward, Jany looked back on that day as the happiest she'd known in a long time. She knew it was dangerous to pretend, although she did allow herself to imagine that they were a family together. From Tony's behavior, it seemed that he, too, was thinking along the same lines.

Since it was too late for lunch and too early for dinner, they decided to have a picnic meal together, French-style, catered by Tony.

"It was wartime, you see," he explained to his daughter, "and there was hardly anything to eat but beans. I never ate so many beans in my life. But Jany made them taste like ambrosia."

"What's ambrosia?"

"Jany's cooking."

"Stop, Tony," Jany said, blushing with pleasure. "You may do the same thing, *ma petite*, with what you call catsup."

They spread a tablecloth on the thick living room carpet and brought from the kitchen sliced ham, a round of Brie, a jar of red caviar, fruit and a bottle of wine. Jany was surprised when Tony refused to let his daughter sip a little watered wine, and they had their first "domestic quarrel" when he insisted Andrea drink milk.

496

And even this was done in fun.

Their joy in being together was interrupted by only one awkward moment when Tony absent-mindedly mentioned that the wine they were drinking was a favorite of Eden's.

"It's a cheap little Sancerre, but she used to get it at some one-horse café in Paris and now she's trying to get it imported. However, since we've gone this far . . ."

He filled their glasses again.

It was dark before the picnic broke up. Honey Peck went off-duty at six and insisted on staying with Andrea, while Tony gave Jany a ride home.

Winding their way up the narrow roads, they left behind the lights of Hollywood, spreading outward into Los Angeles and west toward Beverly Hills, West Hollywood and the beaches. Jany didn't look back. She sat next to Tony, his free arm wrapped tightly around her.

They had both drunk too much wine, and were acting in a way that their normal inhibitions would never have permitted. It was a moment, an opportunity, that neither wanted to let slip away.

When they pulled up in front of the wide, low steps and Jany looked up at the heavy doors of Leo's castle, she found herself feeling seductive and daring.

"It is early, *mon amour.* May I offer you an aperitif for the trip back?"

"Why not?" It was too easy, a throwaway line and she knew it.

They went in together, the only time she'd ever entered the mansion with a feeling of happy expectation. Aware that any display of affection could be reported to Leo, they were careful to keep their distance. Jany led Tony into the bar, a cubbyhole beyond Leo's spartan-bare poker room, only to find McDevlin sprawled out, snoring heavily on the leather sofa.

Tony was immediately on the warpath. "Does this jerk give you any trouble when he's like this?"

"No. He wouldn't dare. He's afraid of Leo."

Tony kicked the soles of McDevlin's shoes, but the big man only shifted his position, licked his lips, and went on snoring. Jany laughed. She stepped around to the back of the three-stool bar with its padded leather surface and brought out bottles of Cinzano, St. Raphael and Dubonnet. Tony was about to ask for brandy, but old memories of Paris got in the way and he allowed her to pour a dry Cinzano into the two bistro glasses. They lovingly toasted to "old times," and Jany wished that the moment would last forever. Tony glanced impatiently over at McDevlin's form on the couch.

"We can't relax — or talk — with that hulk around."

"I know." Taking his glass, she started out of the bar, letting Tony follow her. She didn't understand how she could be so bold, but she knew that for the first time in her life she was allowing her body to take control, forgetting all moral sense.

They went up the tiled steps to the master bedroom on the second floor. Closing the door behind them, Jany stopped and put her glass to her lips nervously. He took both drinks from her hands and set them down on the dresser. Returning to her, he bent his head and eagerly covered her mouth with his. Her knees wavered but she wanted to rise to great heights, pressing, drawing him into her body. She had never known such hunger before.

Embracing him, she dug her fingers into his jacket between his shoulders, clinging to his body. They kissed slowly and passionately, their bodies moving in rhythm as they stood pressed against each other.

"*Mon amour,* I've waited so long . . ."

". . . Adorable . . . my adorable darling . . ."

Their fear of being found out only added to the excitement of the moment. They undressed each other hastily, Jany hungering for the trim, beautiful body before her that she'd imagined for so long. In the huge bed she caressed him wondering at the smooth texture of his olive skin and the masculine strength of his body. Though wanting the moment to last forever, she couldn't wait for fulfillment any longer. When he took her it was a burning possession, filling her body as a tight sheath. It was as she'd always known it would be as they possessed each other completely, pressing, twisting, thrusting, with a sensation that sent exquisite tremors through her body.

She found ways of using her fingers to please Tony, things that had always made Leo draw away from her. Unlike her husband, Tony seemed to enjoy her taking the initiative, and they tossed about on the bed with a freedom Jany had never known, caressing, luring and sometimes twisting the flesh of his back and thighs until he grunted, but she knew the same erotic excitement she'd experienced caused his own body to quiver and twist in orgasm.

As they lay in each others' arms, they slowly became aware of the time passing, and with it the ultimate danger of discovery. Somewhere in the house a door closed. Jany sat up abruptly, reaching for her dress. There was no time for her underthings. While Tony dressed, she went to the dresser, took up her glass and sipped what remained of the vermouth, the tremors of desire still within her. Neither she nor Tony spoke for a few minutes, nor did she look around to watch him while he dressed, though she longed to. She thought to herself that surely it would be the most wonderful thing in the world, to know that for the rest of her life she might lie with him and then watch him dress afterward, as he had watched her.

Casting a glance about the room, she noted that everything there was Leo's. Still, there were other concerns, things she'd rather forget — like Carl's job that he liked so much, and the unbreakable bond between Tony and Eden. Which was the greater sin, she wondered, to meet like this, deceiving people they cared about, or to break up two families and leave a young child without her father?

Both alternatives were terrible.

Tony came up behind her as she stood deep in thought, raising her tousled hair to kiss the nape of her neck.

"Sweetheart, I know what you're thinking. Sin and lust, hellfire and damnation. All that self-condemnation, merely because you and I were born for each other. Because we've both made mistakes."

She let her head fall back against his shoulder,

wishing to preserve their last moments together.

"We must not. Ever again."

"But we love each other," he said, shaking her gently, "what more proof could you want? We belong —" He stopped abruptly. "I'm sorry. Everything I say sounds like a cliché." This time he shook her harder. "But it's true. Admit it."

She took a long breath, turned her head and brushed his fingers with her lips. Her thoughts jumped about, but they always included Tony.

"We have committed so many sins together. You killed that Boche for me, remember?"

"My darling, that was to protect ourselves."

She swung around abruptly, startling him. "It is always you and me. Our happiness. Oh, Tony! What do you say about the happiness of all the others? Leo, and Eden, and —"

"Andrea. I know. But sweetheart, we aren't making anyone happy this way. How can we go on like this? Would you prefer that we sneak around like criminals?" He tilted her head up and looked into her eyes. She was crying and felt miserable that their beautiful hour was ending in such a manner.

"We have lived before today without each other. We can live again. Dear Tony, God will punish us for this. I can bear that. But we can't punish my little Andrea."

He was beginning to lose his temper.

"This is crazy talk. If anybody punishes us, it's ourselves. These old-fashioned ideas of yours are going to end up ruining everybody's life. Wake up to the truth, Jany."

She heard footsteps in the hall only a second before the door opened.

"Mrs. Prysing, did you call me?" the maid asked, glancing quickly at the disheveled bedspread. Jany wondered if she had heard any of Tony's argument.

Jany cleared her throat. "Yes, Hilda. Mr. McDevlin is in the bar. He's been drinking. It was impossible for Monsieur Lombard and me to discuss the — a personal matter that's come up with that man snoring." To further her pretense she went on, "Will you take our glasses?"

Tony stared at her.

She tried not to notice his disbelief at her abrupt change in personality. "And Hilda, Monsieur Lombard is leaving now. Will you show him out, please." Before Tony could gather his wits about him, she continued with the pretense almost effortlessly. "Tony, your striking comrades have my sympathy. But I have no power to help you . . . forgive me," she said, lightly touching his shoulder.

He thrust her hand aside and started to the door. She followed him, unable to help herself. "Please . . . forgive me," she repeated.

But he paid no attention, nor did he look back when he left the room. After hearing the front door slam, she opened the long bedroom windows and stepped out onto the tiny balcony to watch him walk to his car. He must know she was watching, she thought, but still he refused to look back.

Suddenly she felt very old. The time with him had been both glorious and terrible. Their memories of it would have to last them for the rest of their lives. Guiltily she told herself that she was more to blame than Tony, that she never should have encouraged him. But she had never before known such a passionate temptation.

# Chapter Thirty-Four

Looking back on the time of the strike, Eden, in one of her rare self-reflective moments, wondered if she had made a mistake when she placed her career before her family. She knew they only had three more days of shooting before her own part in the script was wrapped up, and her sense of professionalism told her that she should remain inside to finish the job, especially since, as a member of the actor's union, she couldn't in good conscience cross the picket line.

Luckily, Tony wasn't involved in a film at the moment and was able to look after Andrea.

The moment the strike was settled she hurried home, making a fuss over Tony for having delivered everything she'd needed, and taking over the household responsibilities, but she felt a difference in his attitude. They hadn't made love in weeks. Tony was wrapped up in Directors' Guild problems, particularly in trying to find a way to counter the rising interest in "investigating" Hollywood.

When he came home from meetings full of angry shouting matches, she knew she'd handled herself badly, lightly warning him that free speech could be dangerous at a time when it was easily interpreted as a defense of Communism.

By the time he'd exhausted his argument that free speech was the opposite of Communism, the evening had ended on a bitter note. Their sexual compatability no longer solved the day's problems, and their sense of companionship was all but lost in their union quarrels.

To make matters worse, Eden suspected that Leo was beginning to find Tony a liability. He played down any of Tony's attempts to save his latest B-film, and even talked of shelving it, a sure sign that it was dead. When Tony brought up his ideas for future films he was fobbed off by Leo and, curiously enough, even by Carl Friedrich, the new studio manager, who had a million reasons why every one of Tony's ideas required props, sets and other equipment that would go over budget.

As with most strikes, the ending satisfied no one completely. Even Leo's studio, for the first time in its twenty-two-year history, was forced to join the unions, causing a sudden drop in six-day weeks and twelve-hour days. Even Leo was surprised at how many pages of script could be shot in a regular work day.

Although Jany was pleased for him, she was also aware of Carl's warning that the strike wars had precipitated investigations by Congress of radical influence in the industry. During all the discussions she'd heard about the strike, Jany had never heard anyone mention Communists. Carl only bewildered her with his explanations. For the first time in their lives he did not seem entirely candid with her.

"I do not understand, *chèri,*" she said, "is it not legal to bring people into a union? Why do these men of the government question such matters?"

"Monsieur Rankin is a representative from California to the Congress in Washington. He is investigating what he calls 'treason' — those who join organizations against the United States. But there are more powerful men in Washington who are also investigating these things. An Un-American Activities Committee of the House. That's one side of the Congress. Do you understand?"

She didn't, but it interested her only tangentially — none of it concerned Leo. She knew Leo was not a Communist, nor did he speak in favor of the liberals in the various guilds. She thought that Carl had praised him so highly to the newspapers and columnists, especially mentioning Leo's understanding of the liberals and his personal interest in "the people," in order to thank Leo for the job he'd given him.

When she questioned Leo about it, he only laughed.

"Carl means well. He thinks he's building me up. But I'd more likely be condemned as a Fascist if they were to analyze my work habits and the way I'm said to dictate to the poor peons."

Jany was determined to be a good wife and defend her husband.

"This is stupid. Imagine, comparing you with Adolf Hitler or Josef Stalin."

He pinched her cheek, touched by her loyalty, and sent her off to get the refreshments for his poker crowd, due to arrive soon. She returned in time to hear Tony Lombard's name being mentioned by an executive from Twentieth-Century Fox. She stopped with the glass tray balanced on one knee while she attempted to open the doors.

"A lot of them showed their colors in the strike. I've been at Guild meetings where I thought I was in the Kremlin. Some of these jokers have even spouted propaganda from the picket lines. Like one of your directors, Leo, young Lombard. Spilling his guts about the poor, suffering picketers. And I can guarantee you I'm not the only one who heard him. I'm sure some of the newsreel shots haven't gone unnoticed by the FBI and the Un-American Activities Committee."

"Don't look at me, I haven't seen them," Leo said. "Play cards."

Jany listened anxiously, remembering with clarity the day the cameras were at the picket line. She knew Leo would defend Tony sooner or later.

The argument went on. Finally, Leo said, "Put up or shut up, kid. Do you throw in?"

Another player, a supervisor from Metro, spoke up. "That guy Lombard sounds like a pink. You show me a writer like that, I'll show you a guy who takes his orders from Moscow."

Leo finally said something about Tony, though it wasn't what Jany had hoped to hear. "Lombard is a director. At the moment."

"Same thing," snapped the supervisor. "My God! You raising again? That does me in."

Jany was more troubled by their negative attitude than their casual remarks. But most of all, she was disappointed in Leo, that he hadn't risen to Tony's defense — he knew Tony was a loyal American and a good director.

Jany was startled by a touch on her shoulder. McDevlin reached around Jany. "I'll take that, ma'am. Too heavy for you."

She wondered if he knew how long she'd stood there listening. It made her uncomfortable, especially not knowing whether Hilda had mentioned anything to him about her evening with Tony. After all, she'd seen nothing more incriminating than a disheveled bedspread.

She and Tony seldom saw each other since their last time together. It was painful but also a relief. She wondered if Eden Ware could read her face, especially her eyes, when she looked at Tony. Jany often turned away, made excuses for not going over to talk when she and Leo would see the Lombards at Hollywood parties or previews. People supposed that she and Tony disliked each other; Tony at least behaved as if they did.

Perhaps he would never forgive her for making love to him and then turning him out in that terrible way. Her conscience told her it was just as well — if he hated her, they could never betray their spouses again.

She began to beg Leo for some kind of trip, a long sea voyage, anything to prevent these awful meetings between the Prysings and the Lombards. Leo soothed her with vague promises.

"We'll see. Shouldn't be too far off. That brother of yours is taking hold of his department nicely, but I ought to be around just in case. Loyal man, your brother." He studied his steak. Was it well-done enough to suit him, Jany wondered. It was difficult to persuade the new French chef to broil a filet that pleased Leo. He looked up blandly after chewing.

"Yes. Carl's a loyal one . . . like you, baby."

She looked at him with gratitude, but her guilt was always there, beneath the surface.

Eden Ware drove up through the gates of the

Prysing lot in time to witness the conflict between the gateman and a voluptous, dark-haired woman whose English, if inadequate, was more than compensated for by her sex appeal. She was denied entry onto the lot, but seemed persistent.

Eden had a ten o'clock makeup call, and set her palm on the horn as a hint. The gateman turned to her.

"Sorry, Miss Ware. A little problem here. The — ah — lady insists on going on the lot. Says she has an appointment with Mr. Prysing but Miss Sweete says she never heard of her."

It was an old story. But the girl was gorgeous. True, in a few years she would probably run to fat. Right now, though, she was certainly photogenic.

"Who is she?"

"DeBrett, she says." He glanced at his clipboard. "But she's not on my list. Claims one of Mr. Prysing's friends in Paris sent her."

Eden laughed. "Good luck to her. I'll bet Leo will be surprised." She drove around to her own parking space, next to Tony's prewar Packard convertible. Tony had driven in early, hoping to catch Leo before he got wrapped up in conferences.

Most mornings before she left Eden had recently found herself spending more and more time soothing Tony over his dimming prospects at the studio. Privately, though, she was worried. It wasn't like Leo to keep anyone hanging around without work, running out their contracts. For some reason, he was behaving oddly toward Tony. Surely he didn't blame Tony for the failure of his film. It wasn't Tony's fault that the war-film market had collapsed. Afterwards, Leo canceled Tony's latest film, a clever suspense story.

Inside the studio, between the long facade of the Administration Building and Soundstage Three, Eden saw the Frenchwoman again. Somehow she'd gotten that far, anyway. Surrounded by half a dozen grips and carpenters who'd been working in the area, she explained with a smile, "I have a dear friend — we met in Paris, of course. He told me to see *mon chèr* Leo."

As Eden approached the crowd shifted its glance toward her. Overhearing the woman's remark, Eden's curiosity got the better of her.

"Your dear Leo? Sounds as though you know him well."

The woman fluffed the ends of her hair and gave an upward yank to her sweetheart-shaped neckline, though it still allowed a full view of her heavy breasts. Whoever had sent her here didn't allow for Leo's new taste in women, Eden thought. She was the antithesis of Leo's young wife.

"I am Danielle deBrett. I am personally not acquainted with Monsieur Prysing. But a dear friend advised me that through him I could meet this famous producer. My friend and I were also political allies, you see."

Her name came as a jolt to Eden, who recalled hearing Tony joke about the sexual politics of the woman. Eden guessed at once that the "dear friend" in Paris had to have been Carl Friedrich — who else? And who would have guessed that someone as reserved as Carl would pursue so flamboyant a woman? . . .

Eden wondered what would happen when the

Frenchwoman met Leo. On the spur of the moment she decided to take over the situation.

"Let's see if we can locate Leo. Come along, Miss deBrett."

Leo's outer office was only a few steps away in the Administration Building. Eden introduced the Frenchwoman to Belle Sweete, who looked overwhelmed at meeting the unexpected visitor.

"Mademoiselle deBrett is an old friend, of Carl's. He recommended that she see Mr. Prysing."

"Is that so?" Miss Sweete answered coolly. She hadn't yet given up on Carl for herself.

Danielle rolled her eyes. "*Mon Dieu!* Not Carl. He would never suggest such a thing. It is my friend Monsieur Tony Lombard who sends me to your fine studio."

Eden was further jolted at this, but to protect her pride, she decided to play along. Eden reasoned that the Frenchwoman must want to use Tony in some way, since she had undoubtedly discovered that her ex-boyfriend, Carl Friedrich, had lost interest.

"Well, Miss Sweete, I'm sure you can handle this for my husband. I must go now. They're waiting for me in makeup."

All the way across the lot to wardrobe and makeup, Eden was torn by mixed emotions. Although she longed to see Leo's reaction when this voluptuous dish greeted him like a long-lost lover, she also wondered just how much Tony had been involved with her — it was one of the rare times when Eden's jealousy was piqued by her husband and not a role or an Oscar.

Could Tony have been involved with her in Paris? She'd heard him joke about the woman with Carl — was it just a coverup? Until the recent strike, Eden had always suspected that if there had been a romance in Paris, it was between Tony and Jany Prysing. But according to Andrea, who talked endlessly about the picnic with Aunt Jany, that was the only time the two had been together.

With considerable relief Eden was finally able to rule out Tony's involvement with Jany. Danielle deBrett, however, was quite another kettle of fish.

Eden seldom spent much time in makeup, even though she was on her way to a shooting session for stills to be used by the fan magazines and for publicizing her new films. Once the session was over, she headed towards the commissary for an early lunch, where she met a photographer with a young reporter who worked for Hedda Hopper, a lady of strongly conservative politics.

"How's it going, boys?" Eden asked, teasing. "Having any luck finding any fellow travelers on the lot? I know Hedda is hell-bent to throw a token force of Reds to the lions."

"Christ, don't joke about it," the photographer said nervously. "We got an anonymous tip that a Commie cell is being organized right here. With Senator Tenney and that Washington committee on the lookout, Hedda wants to be first one in at the kill."

To Eden it all seemed a ridiculous joke, to think of a Communist cell forming at Prysing Productions. She left laughing to herself when a typist from the steno pool ran across the studio lot with a message.

"Miss Ware! Mr. Lombard wanted me to find you and tell you that he's gone to Hollywood. He wants to present the script breakdown to Mr. Prysing, who's over at Musso-Frank's restaurant. He said to say that he'd be home in time to dress for the Zanuck affair tonight."

It occurred to Eden that Tony should be warned that Danielle deBrett was in the studio. He might want to avoid her.

Then again, he might not.

She went around the corner of the main office complex, built to resemble an antebellum mansion. The photographer followed her around the corner toward the front steps.

From there everything seemed to happen at once. Eden first saw Hedda Hopper, impeccably dressed and wearing one of her famous hats, a cartwheel decorated with the most elegant feathers she'd ever seen. The columnist stood by the gateman's box, watching as Tony Lombard came out of the mansion with his long, easy stride, obviously headed for his car.

Eden started across the gravel drive to give him the news of their "visitor," but she was too late. Danielle deBrett came trotting out of the mansion's main doors behind him, calling his name.

"Tony love, the wrong way. Wait for me." She burst out with a torrent of French so rapid even Eden couldn't understand her.

At this Carl Friedrich emerged from the same door of the executive offices. He appeared to be agitated, which was unusual, Eden thought, for someone so coolly reserved. Tony glanced behind him just as the Frenchwoman threw her arms around his neck. Eden moved up to Carl Friedrich, who looked more pale than usual. Eden, aware of who was taking in the scene, tried to laugh it off.

"How nice for old friends to meet again — you used to know her pretty well yourself, didn't you, Carl?"

"Yes, but she was to — she said she was here to see Mr. Prysing. What is she doing with Tony?"

Could he be jealous of Tony? He certainly seemed upset about something. "Leo is in Hollywood having lunch," Eden said, "perhaps she couldn't find him in time."

"But he was to have lunch here, in the commissary," Carl insisted. Seeing that his stubbornness puzzled her, he explained rather hurriedly, "I was to meet Mr. Prysing for a luncheon conference. And I am not too fond of that woman. She caused my sister a great deal of trouble. She accused her of collaborating."

In the meantime, Tony and Danielle became the center of Hedda Hopper's attention; the columnist observed the reunion from a distance. Tony clearly recognized the woman, but was trying to release himself from her octopus clutch while he fumbled to greet her politely. In the midst of Tony's confusion Hedda Hopper's legman shot out questions while a cameraman took pictures. None of this troubled Eden, but the presence of the columnist did. Hedda Hopper, evidently deciding not to stay on the fringes, moved up to the group with some speed, the brim and feathers of her hat gently fluttering in the wind.

What was Hedda doing here, anyway? Eden

wondered. Had Danielle deBrett become an international star, unknown to Eden?

"Who's your friend, Tony?" Miss Hopper asked in a sharp, metallic voice with a hint of amused arrogance.

Though still trying to extricate himself from Danielle's embrace as graciously as possible, he was quick to recognize the importance of the lady with the hat. Eden and Carl stood unnoticed behind him, thinking he might best handle the predicament himself.

"An acquaintance from my days in Paris, Hedda. Miss deBrett."

"Well, now," Miss Hopper said, acknowledging the Frenchwoman, but she didn't take the hand Danielle offered.

Eden found something disquieting in the fact that the cameraman was still snapping pictures as fast as he could, and Miss Hopper's reporter was filling his notebook as fast as he could write.

Why was it so important to cover this accidental meeting with Danielle? Eden wondered. She could have sworn it came as a complete surprise to Tony, but he appeared to be the only one unprepared.

"Active in the war, Miss deBrett?" Hedda inquired. "Could you be one of those brave Gaullists who helped save the Republic?" Her voice was filled with the acrid sweetness she often used before coming in for the kill.

*"Nom de Dieu!"* Danielle answered, "I? A Gaullist? Madame, I beg your pardon, I was *Danielle le Chat.* My cell of the Partisans led in the fight for the Liberation. All the political parties in the Resistance."

"And most of those parties were Communist, weren't they," the reporter asked.

"Some. See here, Miss deBrett contributed her part to the Liberation by fighting against the Nazis. Her party affiliations had nothing to do with it."

Eden watched anxiously. *For God's sake, don't lose your temper now, Tony.*

"So you were just all good comrades together, right?" Hedda asked craftily. "A matter of free speech, I take it."

"Exactly. There were dozens of parties, many of which were controlled by the Communists. At the time of the Liberation, all the groups banded together, fighting the Nazis. It's a well-known fact."

No longer able to contain herself Eden rushed into the quagmire. "Tony, Hedda misunderstands. When we say *comrades* in wartime . . ."

Miss Hopper's pale eyebrows rose. "Miss deBrett, you're a secretary to the Communist Party in the Montmartre district of Paris, aren't you? That is a high responsibility for one so young." Before the Frenchwoman could reply, Miss Hopper motioned to her assistant, who snapped shut his spiral notebook and pulled a rolled photograph out of the straps on his briefcase. He unrolled it. Everyone rushed forward to see what was contained in the enlarged picture.

Eden made out a sharply contrasting night scene, with excited, laughing white faces silhouetted against blazing fires behind them. Locked in an esctatic embrace were Tony and Danielle, who held in her free hand a flag with the hammer and sickle plainly in sight.

Carl Friedrich looked at it, then glanced at Tony.

"It was the night before Liberation. In the place de l'Opera." He turned to the columnist. "Madame, practically everyone in Paris was there, Communist or not. Monsieur Lombard and Mademoiselle deBrett had just blown up a Boche truck of reinforcements. There is nothing Communist about that scene. I might add that Mademoiselle deBrett's here to see Monsieur — Mr. Prysing, not Mr. Lombard."

"Both, *mon chèr*," Danielle said with a grin.

Hedda Hopper, looking coolly contemptuous, chose to ignore this explanation, and quickly signaled to her assistants to close up shop. As she was turning away to her limousine, she decided she had one piece of advice for Eden Ware before she left.

"I don't imagine you knew anything about your husband's . . . friends. But Eden, my dear, sooner or later you will have to ask yourself why your husband invited one of his old "comrades" to visit him in the United States, especially at a time when the Communists are trying to take over our industry."

Eden opened her mouth, trying to think of something deadly to say in response, but Miss Hopper added one parting blow. "Believe me, Eden, I do understand your position. Come and lunch with me in the next day or so. I don't see any reason why you should suffer for that man's involvements."

"Now, look here, Hedda —" Eden started to protest.

"Don't! She's not listening to anybody." Tony was furious, but he pulled her back while Carl tried to quiet Danielle deBrett.

"Madame 'Opper, we Communists saved Paris. Without us, the Boches would be talking to you in Washington. Madame 'Opper —"

"Shut up," Carl commanded, shaking her. "You said you were to see Monsieur Prysing."

"But how did I know it would be my beloved Tony I would meet first?"

She went on speaking in a rapid French while Carl jerked her back into the Prysing executive offices. Eden wondered over the scene between Carl and Danielle, but was more concerned with Tony to care much.

She clutched Tony's hand. "Don't look like that, honey. It was just a rotten coincidence. You didn't invite her here, for God's sake . . . did you?"

"Are you kidding?" he said, grimacing.

They linked arms and slowly walked to his car together, both deep in thought over an encounter that seemed anything but a coincidence. Sensing Eden's deep concern over the situation, Tony tried to humor his wife.

"Know any good lawyers?" he asked, grinning faintly. "I think I'm going to need one . . ."

# Chapter Thirty-Five

"Fred Troupe is the man for you," Leo advised Tony. "Not that you need a lawyer, for Christ's sake. All it boils down to is an old picture somebody made during the war."

"But Troupe is only the studio lawyer," Tony objected. "Contracts are his specialty. Shouldn't I have somebody like Jerry Geisler? He's the best."

"Why? You're not guilty of anything, are you?"

"I wish people wouldn't keep asking me in quite that way. No, I'm not a Communist, if that's what you mean. Never was and never will be. To me it's just Fascism spelled backwards."

Eden looked hopeful, but Tony wasn't as easily soothed by the producer's manner. He got up and paced the carpet at the far end of Leo's huge desk.

"You know my mother is in the Screen Writers' Guild. Somebody from Washington called her who would only identify himself as 'a friend.' He told her that I'm being investigated by the Un-American Activities Committee. They've already questioned some of mother's friends but they couldn't get hold of the only woman who counts in this matter — Danielle deBrett."

"I don't know why Carl can't find her," Eden said. "He's supposed to be your buddy. Besides, he knew her at least as well as you did, didn't he?"

As always, Tony was defensive about the Friedrichs.

"He's doing all he can. But she disappeared as

suddenly as she came here and he doesn't know what friends she might have in the United States any more than I do. Don't ask me why the congressional committee just doesn't talk to him. He's ready and willing to explain how we all worked with Communist groups in the end to free Paris."

"They probably figure he'd be prejudiced in your favor," Leo suggested.

"Well, good God! Some friends of mine had better come forward. They're asking everyone else how long I've been a Commie . . ."

Eden laughed abruptly. "Sounds like the old joke, 'When did you stop beating your wife?' They've called up any number of Guild members by now, asking whether they were, or are Communists. If this deBrett woman has run out, doesn't that make her evidence phony? It should be easy for Tony. He isn't a Communist and nobody can prove he ever was."

Leo glanced at his wristwatch, rather obviously, Tony thought.

"Look, suppose we let this ride for a few days," he said, "I promised Jany I'd make it home early tonight. Poor thing. She was almost in tears last evening when I had to go off to that damned conference over the Commie writers. At least one thing was accomplished, though. Johnston, of the Motion Picture Association, agreed that there shouldn't be a full purge. He's already talked with Congressman Rankin of the House committee. Rankin claims if we don't clean house, Congress will. Not a pleasant prospect."

This was far from reassuring to Tony, partly because he resented Leo's constant flaunting of his relationship with Jany. But it was also ominous that the executives were already having conferences, discussing what to do about "Commies, parlor pinks, and ultra-liberals" among them. His name was constantly associated with these elements, and the way the twisted evidence kept piling up, he began to wonder if he had a deadly enemy somewhere . . .

"Hell, I'm not even that important to anyone high up," he later complained to Eden.

But as far as Hollywood was concerned, the writers, directors and actors who were even mentioned were already through. Tony shuddered inwardly. To make matters worse, he didn't believe for a minute that his own damaged reputation could be saved by the hard-drinking studio lawyer who'd never even handled a case like his. It wasn't like Leo Prysing to be so obtuse in such a potentially dangerous situation, and Tony couldn't understand why he was willing to take a risk on him.

That evening Randi called to give him what she considered to be good news.

"Your father is coming back from Tokyo, dear. He's going directly to Washington. Believe me, he'll quash these ridiculous rumors. Too many congressmen owe him favors."

"No! For God's sake, mother, no . . . I don't want father mixed up in this, galloping to the rescue again in his big white hat."

Randi was taken aback by his violent reaction. She asked to talk to Eden, but Eden was on a night location. Tony was secretly glad — he knew that even though Randi and Eden weren't very close, when it came to Steve Lombard they thought alike. Good old Steve could solve anything.

Early the next morning Tony went out on his own to contact a supervisor at Metro who had been hounding him to come over from Prysing when his contract ended. Leo had been putting him off about renewing his contract anyway, so Tony considered himself a free agent.

Much to his surprise, he had some difficulty getting onto the huge Metro-Goldwyn-Mayer lot. First he had to spell out his name, then he endured the humiliation of having the supervisor's senior assistant gush over with excitement at learning who he was.

"Why, you're Eden Ware's husband, lucky man. The boss says she's a cinch to get the Oscar this Year. He adores her, you know."

"Yes, I know. Mel and I were discussing a property I've got in mind. I have it optioned," he said, hoping he would spark some interest in it.

"Great. Tell me, Mr. Ware, confidentially, is there any chance of our getting your wife over here for a picture? We'd even consider doing a trade. A Bob Taylor for an Eden Ware, or whatever Prysing needs. Could you put in a word for us, Mr. Ware?"

"Lombard. I'm afraid my wife makes her own decisions. She and Leo, that is. Now, about seeing your boss."

"Oh, Lord! Didn't I tell you? He's in conference with L.B. To tell you the truth, this is a rotten day for all of us. We're absolutely swamped. Suppose you give us a call when —"

He had started for the outer office but something made him stop.

"When what?" he asked.

She was unconvincingly vague. "You know. When — I mean — well, you're up to your neck in problems right now, aren't you?"

"You mean Hopper's column and the way the *Times* spread that picture all over the page?"

"Yes. It's disgusting, especially the way that congressional committee has been questioning everyone. I mean, Mel hardly knows you. I don't mean that the way it sounds, but he couldn't possibly know what your politics *are*." She giggled. "Is, are, whatever. Oh. You're going? I know this sounds awful but I wonder if you'd do me a big favor. Could you ask Eden to sign a photo for me? I'd appreciate that."

"Sure," he said dejectedly, letting the door slam behind him. "Why not?"

He drove over to Paramount in Hollywood. It was much the same case there, except that the assistant he talked to there wasn't a fan of Eden's. But he, too, had seen the recent spread about Tony in the *L.A. Times*, and read the more subtle comments that showed up in *Variety* and *The Hollywood Reporter*.

Tony sauntered out of the Marathon Gate of Paramount waving to the gateman, hoping to give the impression to anyone watching of a carefree young man without a problem in the world.

"Eden never gave a performance like this," he told himself as he forced another jaunty grin and crossed the street.

He stopped for coffee at the counter in Oblath's, the luncheon hangout for two of the major studios. It was with considerable relief that he found himself surrounded by friends, for a change. They were players of a lesser rank, all people who looked to him for jobs, plus a Paramount reader and two typists from the RKO script department. A few of those who greeted Tony were people who had never worked with him, but he liked their easy way of approaching his trouble.

"Hey there, Lombard, don't you forget me when you're rolling your next."

"Say, Tony, remember how you bragged that plane would never land you anywhere near the Krauts? You owe me fifty bucks on that."

He laughed. "You sure it wasn't the other way around, Gene?" Thank God he had enough with him to cover the bet. He slapped it into Gene's palm, and the man offered to treat him to a cup of coffee.

He spent a good hour with his less powerful, yet obviously more faithful friends, and when he left he felt encouraged.

Tony returned home to find Andrea crying. The baby-sitter and Honey Peck hadn't been able to console her. "Mrs. Prysing just called," Honey explained, "she and her husband are off on a cruise to the South Pacific, coming back by Hawaii. Andrea wants to go too."

It was bad enough to know that Jany and Leo were going off on a second honeymoon whose intimate details he didn't want to think about, but the timing of the trip seemed suspiciously apt: Leo didn't want to be around Hollywood to stand by Tony in the coming battle.

Early one afternoon a short time later, Tony had been out in the San Fernando Valley vainly trying his luck at Universal-International Studios, when he learned something from an actor who had appeared in his last film at Prysing. The actor, like Tony, was returning to Hollywood by way of a Big Red Train, of the Pacific Electric System. Tony found that one of the advantages of traveling this way was that he seldom ran a chance of being cut by his previous associates.

"You sure must have tweaked old Leo's ear. He's got his claws out for you."

Tony considered this a confirmation of his own private thoughts. "Why? Do you mean to say he called the *Times* and Hedda to set me up? He didn't even know Danielle deBrett. And God knows he didn't want that kind of publicity."

"Did he know anybody else who knew the dame? How about your father, or Miss Ware? That's gotta be it. Old Leo's got a yen for your wife, right? Who wouldn't?"

This struck Tony as the funniest reasoning of all. He laughed. "Bill, you're no Sherlock Holmes. You're not even Charlie Chan. Leo and Eden have been friends since she was born, practically. Besides, they've had plenty of time to produce this great amour. And now with Leo married to the most beautiful girl in —" He broke off abruptly before he could betray his feelings for Jany.

"My stop," he said, as they approached the Highland-Hollywood Boulevard corner. "Bill, leave your phone number with casting. I'll look you up when I get the final word on my new project."

Bill Meyers had done him a big favor, inadvertently reminding him that he had taken Carl

Friedrich for granted during the whole fracas. Tony had regarded him as a close friend, a man who had made Molotov cocktails beside him, and defended him when the Germans searched the flat. There were a hundred times when Carl might have betrayed him. Carl said repeatedly that he stood ready to testify for Tony, but the committee didn't seem interested, so far.

In spite of all this, was it possible that Carl had invited the Frenchwoman to visit America? Possibly he did, and when she caused so much trouble, he became afraid or ashamed to admit it.

Tony stopped in the drugstore across the street and called Carl Friedrich's office at the studio.

"Mr. Friedrich has a late luncheon date," one of the operators told him. "Could he see you about — say 4:45? It's with the agent for the carpenters and painters. He says it'll take forever."

Tony knew that when Carl wasn't grabbing a bite at the counter in the commissary he ate at a restaurant across the boulevard. He had been poor for so long that his frugal habits persisted. But "luncheon date" sounded like a female.

What if I catch Carl and Danielle together? What do I do next? Tony wondered.

He got back to the operator to ask if she knew whom his lunch was with.

"I wouldn't know, Mr. Lombard. He didn't say."

Tony thanked her and hung up. But he had an overwhelming curiosity to find out if, in fact, his career had been destroyed by his onetime good friend, Carl Friedrich.

He hailed a taxi and crossed town toward the studio.

Feeling like a spy, he dismissed the cab a block from the restaurant in order to make his arrival less conspicuous. He spotted through the large windows of the restaurant Carl, seated at a table for two, drinking something yellow — probably a Manhattan, he thought. Tony studied his companion's back and knew at once that it wasn't Danielle deBrett, but a middle-aged woman with graying black hair.

Tony was surprised at his own relief. He had liked Carl, even admired him. And, of course, he was Jany's brother. It was awful to have thought of him as an enemy, no matter how briefly.

Entering the restaurant, the headwaitress came up from behind him, startling him. "Hi there, Mr. L. We're all full-up right now, but we'll have your favorite table any minute."

"No, thanks, Cecy. I'm in kind of a hurry." He started out, then stopped as he caught the reflection of Carl's companion in the window.

*My God — not Stella Burkett. What the hell was she doing with Carl Friedrich?* They weren't even acquainted. And it certainly didn't appear to be a romantic assignation. Carl was frowning, his lips set stubbornly as the woman talked to him with great animation. Tony sized up the situation. Carl clearly was too busy concentrating on Stella Burkett to notice passersby, but Stella's sharp eyes would undoubtedly notice Tony.

He edged over behind a latticework barrier that separated two of the tables, but he was too late. Carl began to rise, along with Stella. She continued to talk as if she were trying to persuade him of something.

"I still say it can be done. You and your respect for the law — they won't touch her. It takes forever for them to move, anyway. Your precious pa respected the law, too. Nazi law!"

Tony backed against the window as Carl got up, but Carl paid the check and passed Tony at a distance of ten feet without glancing his way. The Frenchman was obviously angry, but said nothing to Stella's caustic remark.

Stella followed him out to the boulevard where she touched his sleeve, trying to make her pitch again. This time he ignored her. While Tony was making up his mind about what to do, a bus pulled up and she got on it.

Considering the options, he decided not to tackle Carl until he had first checked out a few things with Alec. For starters, why would Stella leave Alec just when he was getting settled in New York, and undoubtedly still grieving over his wife's death?

Maybe Stella and Carl had business connected with Alec and his new broadcasting job in New York. Tony earnestly hoped so, but he couldn't help doubting it.

He thought of going back to the studio and bumming a ride home with Eden, but he hated to be driven by a woman, and Eden always had reasons why she should get behind the wheel. She didn't have to point out that she'd bought their new Cadillac convertible coupe that replaced the Chrysler Imperial he had bought her last year.

Oh well, can't win 'em all, he thought, almost cheerfully.

He walked across the street, caught the next bus

to Hollywood and returned home to make a phone call to New York.

He didn't catch his cousin Alec at his UBC office, but did reach him in his apartment on Central Park West, getting ready for dinner with a UBC vice-president and his wife. He was surprised, as well he might be, to hear from Tony. They hadn't seen or spoken to each other since Heather's funeral.

Tony began in some confusion.

"How are things going? Think you'll like New York?"

"It's a challenge. I've got my eye on the company's television plans. We may be going national with a news hookup pretty soon."

"Great. They couldn't pick a better standard-bearer. Mother tells me you're getting a lot of publicity."

Alec chuckled. "You're not doing so bad yourself in that department." He caught himself then. "Sorry. I didn't mean that the way it sounded. How are things going for you?"

"*Comme çi, comme ça.* I'll get straightened around as soon as Washington gets off my back. I'm about as likely a Communist as dad is, or you."

"Stupid business. But Uncle Steve will get it all sorted out. And that reminds me. I had dinner with him the other night. I was down in Washington on a radio interview he helped me get. He's really burned up about the attacks on you — he thinks they're trying to get at him through you."

"Good old dad. He would think that. He figures I can't even create a national scandal that's all my own."

"He didn't mean it that way."

"Well, you always were his fair-haired boy."

Alec laughed shortly. "Remember when mother told Aunt Randi that you ought to have been her boy and I should belong to Aunt Randi? I guess we all have our cross to bear . . . look, Tony, I do have this damned dinner I've got to make on time. If it goes right, who knows? I may get that news job on UBC's TV expansion."

"Sure. Good luck. Just one thing, though. Have you any idea what Stella Burkett is doing here in Hollywood?"

Given the surprised tone of Alec's voice, the news must have astonished Alec as much as it had Tony. "I thought she's in San Francisco visiting her brother and his wife. In fact she called me yesterday from a rooming house off Columbus Avenue in North Beach."

"What would you say if I told you I saw her not an hour ago in Culver City, thick as thieves with Carl Friedrich?"

"You're kidding! They don't even know —" Alec thought it over. "Yes. They did get together in London. Went to a movie together one night. No romance, for God's sake. Just something to take Stella's mind off — what happened. Being Heather's mother, Stella is something special in my life. In fact, she's going to stay on with me — you know, take care of things in the apartment."

"I understand. Well, maybe it is a romance, after all. But I just wondered if their meeting could have anything to do with my problems. Stella never was crazy about the family, you know."

"I don't see how it fits. She doesn't even know

the deBrett woman." Even over the miles between them Tony could hear Alec catch his breath at a memory. "Unless . . . there were several French immigrants married to GIs traveling on the *Mary*. Got on at Cherbourg. They were in tourist class. I met one of the women once with Stella. Stella said she was related to a French family in San Francisco. They arranged to have cocktails together, and the woman evidently went back to tourist class at dinnertime. Funny but when I saw that ridiculous picture of you and the Frenchwoman in the *Times*, I thought the woman looked familiar. I couldn't place her, but she might have been the one I met on the *Mary*. I never got a really good look at her, but it seems there was a resemblance."

Tony felt shaken by the implications here. "Danielle deBrett, of course. Remarkable coincidence, you two on the same sailing with deBrett."

"No —" Alec began slowly. "Not from my end of it. Stella arranged our sailing date. She told me the previous sailing was booked up. But how could she have known your French friend was on board?"

"She must have corresponded with her, gotten her address somehow. My God . . . from Carl Friedrich, of course. They must have put their heads together in London. Stella, for obvious reasons."

They were both silent for several seconds before Alec said what Tony was asking himself: "But why, Tony? Why would they want to destroy your career? That's what it amounts to. How could the woman have mixed Stella up in it? Or this fellow Friedrich? I thought he was a friend of yours. He saved your life, didn't he?"

Tony was beginning to put two and two together. "You know how Stella feels about the family. And she's never been one of our favorites, either, the way she connived to get grandfather to marry her. She made life pretty miserable for mother when she took over the Nob Hill house. No use in going back to the beginning, but when you add it up, Stella most certainly could be in on this."

"Christ, I sure hope not. Stella and I go back a long time, too. She's always been straight as an arrow with me."

Tony considered for a moment, and knew deep down that for Alec family would come first — he could be counted on.

"Okay, Tony," Alec said, "I'll go to work from this end. But I hope to God we're both wrong in what you — what we suspect."

"I'm sorry I delayed your dinner. Maybe you could say an emergency came up."

"Never mind that," Alec said, slightly provoked, "I was dreading it anyway. One of those times when you have to pour on the charm. That's more your line."

"Not these days. Charm's running thin. My brand, anyway."

"I'll get back to you. Can I reach you at the studio?"

Tony hated to make the awkward confession. "No. Better try me at the apartment for now."

"Give me a couple of days," Alec said, and hung up.

Tony stood looking at the phone. He pushed it

back and went to relieve the baby-sitter, sending her home early to dress for an important date.

"I'd give a lot if I had an important *anything* coming up in my life," he told Andrea. She gave him her best smile but clearly didn't understand what he was talking about. She had gotten dressed up in one of her mother's dresses and a ten-year-old hat. She was having trouble maneuvering around in Eden's old high heels, and fell forward into his arms as she staggered across the room.

"Daddy, tell me Aunt Jany's letter."

"You had a letter? What did it say?" he asked, feeling something stir inside at the sound of her name.

"Miss Fish told it to me."

"Finch."

"She told it. But now you tell it to me, daddy."

He didn't want to read Jany's letter. He didn't even want to think about her. It was too painful. Still, he wanted to please his daughter.

"All right, sweetheart. Where is it?"

She went to the top drawer of the miniature ebony cabinet her mother had given her for her last birthday. She took out the letter with Jany's handwriting and, clutching it to her chest, stumbled across the room, falling into her father's arms again. He took her up on his knee with one hand while his other hand unfolded the long, flimsy page.

"Shall I read first, or call Chasen's to order our dinner?"

"Oh, daddy, you cook. I love it when you cook."

"Your mother's going to get sick of steaks, sweetheart. And that's all I know how to cook."

"Then can we have chili, daddy?"

"We'll see. All right, here goes."

At least the letter took his mind off the problems that haunted most of his waking hours.

*Ma chère amie* Andrea:

The islands of Hawaii are so beautiful it is no surprise to me that you were born here. Your uncle Leo has taken me to see the house of your grandfather Ware. It is where Leo says he made his first American film.

The sea here is lovely. To swim far, very far out, that would be the cure if one were unhappy.

Your uncle Leo is a very good swimmer, but he has trouble with what is called heart-burn, especially when he is angry with the servants. I ask him to permit that I speak with them, and then it is easier for everyone, I think.

I know you are a good girl as always and obey your dear mama and papa. I will bring you a silk muu-muu, and a pair of pretty sandals. You will be a Hawaiian princess. The prettiest of all.

Your godmother, Chiye Akina, asks me to send you her love. And me, I say,

*Je vous embrasse trés affecteusement,*
TANTE JANY

At two in the morning Tony was still wide awake and full of black fears. He worried partly about Jany, and her curious remark about swimming out to sea. But mostly he restlessly pondered over his

534

own future, or what there was left of it. What plagued him most, though, were the unseen, faceless enemies who were behind it all.

He got up quietly and went out of the bedroom. Eden's voice behind him gave him a start. Considering his occasionally adulterous thoughts for the past few hours, he wanted to be especially kind to her.

"Anything wrong?" she asked softly.

"I'm sorry, honey. I didn't mean to wake you."

"Worried about the hearings in Washington?"

"Damn the hearings. I just can't figure out why Carl is involved with Stella Burkett. What are they trying to do?"

Eden raised up, leaning back on her elbows. "Don't forget, Tony. His father *was* Kurt Friedrich. I suppose anything is possible."

His hackles rose at that. He couldn't forget that Jany, too, was the product of what Eden considered to be a vicious, Nazi father.

"Nobody can help what their parents do," he said evenly.

"Tony, does Carl *know* what his father did? And more to the point what we did to him?"

"How do I know? I wasn't there when it happened. And the film seemed pretty farfetched to me. Look," he said desperately, "he's a friend of mine. A man can sense these things."

She changed her position and plumped up her pillows.

"Come to bed, honey. You're worn out with all this studio trouble. You need your rest."

"I never felt better."

"You never looked worse . . . It's something else,

isn't it? Was there something in Jany's letter that bothered you?"

He was angered by her shrewd guess. "Certainly not. The woman is unhappy, but we could have predicted that. What did she expect, marrying a man old enough to be her grandfather?"

Then, out of left field, she came up with another mind-reading comment.

"Have you ever asked yourself why Leo ran out on you? He's not usually disloyal like that." Tony said nothing. He had gone to the nearest window and was peering out between the slats of the venetian blind. He stared at the lean, dusty date palms on the avenue without really seeing them. "I think we ought to confront him," she said, raising her voice. "As soon as my final scenes are in the can, I want to hotfoot it back home."

"Home?" He was thinking of San Francisco.

"Home. Hawaii. I'll call Chiye, tell her to expect us."

"I don't think that's such a great idea. We'll be practically next door to the place Leo has taken."

"I know, but I believe in facing things. Nobody is happy this way. And by God, if he's using this to destroy your career, he's going to pay for it."

"Eden, you're getting mixed up in things you know nothing about. Stay out of it. Nothing can be done."

She sat up with a violent movement.

"Ever hear of divorce?"

"Jany is a Catholic." He regretted it the instant he'd said it. The implication was clear that that was the one obstacle between him and Jany. He snapped the blind shut. "I mean —"

536

"I know." She looked around the room as if to fasten her mind on something tangible. Then she yawned elaborately. "Come to bed, for God's sake. I've got to get my beauty sleep. Seven o'clock call tomorrow."

He came over to her side of the bed, bent over and kissed her cheek.

"I do love you, Eden. But you don't need me. You don't need anybody."

She was brisk. "I'll take that as a compliment, darling. 'Night."

# Chapter Thirty-Six

Stella Burkett had an armful of Alec Hunting-ton's suits for the cleaners. She held up a dress shirt.

"Did you wear this one while I was gone?"

"For about half an hour one night. Then I changed my mind and stayed in."

"Didn't go to that big to-do with a vice-president of UBC? Holy Mary! I thought you were counting on that."

"Something came up. I had to make a few phone calls and take care of another matter. I'll get the job yet. Sorry I had to rush you back here like that, but I have a little problem and you might be able to help."

"Me? That's nice. Shall I take these?"

"Have a good time in California?"

"Sure. Glad to get back, though."

"I know. I can't seem to breath in mañana-land. Too full of smoke and haze all the time."

She had her mind on the pile of clothes. "Not always. It was pretty clear. Not like the Bay Area." She stopped, stood there with her arms loaded. Her strong features betrayed nothing. "I mean — I went with my folks to visit some in-laws down in Fresno. Sultry and hazy, you know."

"And some more in-laws in Culver City?"

"That?" She had gotten hold of herself. "That man Mr. Friedrich, he called and asked me to see him. Wanted to give me a job. Guess he was sorry for me. Anyway, I said no. I'm happy to be in New York with the man who loved my girl."

Alec motioned to her. "Drop those anywhere. Come back in. I want to talk to you." She obeyed but she had her courage back.

"Sure, Alec. But there's nothing I can tell you about Mr. Friedrich. Just what I said. I turned him down."

"How long have you known Danielle deBrett?"

"I never —" She licked her lips. "You mean the Frenchie on the boat? I had a couple of drinks with her, remember? She sent me a postcard. Got it this morning. She's on her way back to Paris."

"Just another casual friend, right? Like Carl Friedrich." He studied her until she shifted her weight uneasily. "Stella, it goes back before that Culver City meeting. You and Friedrich. What did you two have in common in Richmond Hill?"

Though pushed into a corner, she fought back. "If you want the truth, we happen to feel the same way about those damned Lombards. Not you, Alec. You always did right by my girl. But from the day I went to service with the Lombards and saw Randi worm her way in where I might've been, let me tell you, boy, I've hated their guts. And then, they were so glad to get rid of me when I went to London with you and my little girl. Okay. I didn't mind. Made me feel like we was getting even with them when Heather got to meet all those bigwigs."

"I remember." He wished she hadn't brought up the memory of sweet Heather, who was so afraid of being alone. She was alone now. God, she was so young, too. He forced the memory back into the deep recesses of his mind, to bring it out again at night. Alone.

"All right, Stella. You've wanted to get back at the Lombards all along. To make them suffer the way you suffered over Heather. Well, believe me, they are. Randi and Steve are frantic. Tony and Eden — their lives are ruined. Tony's career destroyed."

"Too damned bad."

He continued, unmoved by her cold sarcasm. "Don't tell me Carl Friedrich hates the Lombards because they've been unkind to you."

"They're only a side item to him. He wanted to get that Leo Prysing. But it just didn't work out that way, thanks to the French dame. She saw Tony Lombard first and let go."

Alec sat down slowly. "So that's how it came about. Friedrich found out that Leo Prysing's broadcast deliberately betrayed his father. What is Friedrich? A Fascist? Neo-Nazi? If he knows that much, he's got to know what a monster his father was."

She didn't say anything.

He stared at the leather insets in his desk top and ran his fingers over the joins. Like a jigsaw puzzle. The Friedrich-deBrett thing was a jigsaw and the tiniest little details were beginning to fit in. Carl Friedrich actually had been Tony's friend; he'd saved his life dozens of times in Paris. What happened to them? Obviously, Carl had discovered bits and pieces of the broadcast story and set out to destroy Leo in a filial rage. It seemed Stella was right about that much.

"By the way," he asked, "what was the movie you

and Friedrich saw that night in England?"

Her lips curled back in a smile. "What else? *Journey*."

"So if Friedrich wanted to destroy Prysing, how did Hedda Hopper's people get hold of that picture of Tony and Danielle?"

She had been caught unawares. To Alec, her wavering gaze gave her away. She started to shake her head, then shrugged.

"I figured to set up Tony Lombard too, while Friedrich was at it. Tony never done right by my girl."

"How did you contact the deBrett woman?"

"I saw her address on a letter Friedrich sent her from London. I wrote and told her Tony was a producer, too, and she could just as easily work one sucker against the other. I asked her how well she knew Tony, and she said she had a picture — very lovey-dovey. Then we talked our plans over on the ship. I got the picture from her and sent it to that Hopper woman. I figured if anyone could give it publicity, she could."

She leaned across the desk. "Look, Alec . . . I wanted to give the Lombards a little of the trouble they've given me. What the hell do I care about Leo Prysing? He never threw my girl over. He's nothing to me. Well, it worked out the way I hoped. But Friedrich quit after things started to go wrong for him. When I came to Culver City — I guess you know about that lunch — I wanted him to try and keep the Frenchwoman here just a week or two longer. She could've gotten Prysing after all, and put the final crusher on our fine Tony for me. But Friedrich said the Frenchie had to leave or she'd be deported. He gave me a hell of a bawling out."

"So you wanted to keep on with it and he didn't."

"Well, hell, you've always said yourself those Lombards deserved a little hard luck."

Guiltily, he knew she was right. But it didn't matter now. Tony, of all people, had come to him for help. Tony was kinfolk, and he couldn't let him down.

Carl Friedrich probably didn't know the full story of his father's treachery. Everything depended on whatever sense of decency and honor Carl Friedrich had in him. Alec wasn't at all certain he could count on Stella to repeat this story, if necessary.

He sat at the desk, jotting down notes of things that had to be done. Did he have enough clout to wheedle information through the Vienna Four Powers Pact? Maybe not. Especially if the witnesses now lived in the Soviet zone of the divided city. Very probably, though, Uncle Steve could be counted on to call in a few markers where they were most important.

Alec thought of one other possibility: his own mother, who could give him the names of the witnesses he needed. But he couldn't afford to tell her what he planned. Brooke Friedrich still regarded her handsome Nazi husband as a martyr. Steve and Eden had always understood the lay of the land, and never seemed inclined to reveal to her the full details of his treachery.

All of this must wait upon the witnesses, he thought, or at least their sworn affidavits. In the meantime, the House committee was moving ahead, receiving all the expected publicity.

He became aware of Stella, picking up his clothes again, about to go on with her business as if nothing had happened.

"Will you repeat your story in an affidavit when we need it?" he asked.

She gave a short, harsh laugh. "Ask that Friedrich fool. Don't ask me. I told you the truth because I respect you. You've been good to me. But I'd be crazy to get myself involved with lawyers and Washington, D.C., and all."

Looking at her iron countenance he suspected she might simply refuse to testify. At least there were others.

"Don't bother with those clothes," he said, as she was leaving. "That will be all."

"Sure." She started away, then stopped.

"You having your dinner catered again tonight?"

"No. I may fix something. I have to learn to fend for myself, it seems."

He wanted the painful scene over and done with.

Nothing he had previously said, none of his questions had shocked her as this simple statement did.

"You getting rid of me?"

"I'll have a check delivered to you as soon as you let me know what your plans are."

"Alec, you don't mean that." For the first time in their long acquaintance she was afraid. He suspected she had no one she cared about. She was alone. He felt sorry for the woman, but he knew he could never trust her again.

543

"Good luck, Stella," he said, holding out his hand. "We both loved her. But she's gone now."

Stella Burkett was speechless. She did not take his hand, but swung around and stalked out with her head held high.

He wished for his wife's sake that he could call her back. Instead he reached for the phone to call Uncle Steve in Washington.

Carl Friedrich had stuck the two morning Hollywood trade papers in his old snap valise for his short flight to San Francisco. On the plane he read the columnists who predicted that Tony Lombard was in hot water: "Red hot, to be exact," one of them wrote.

A Los Angeles newspaper that same day also reported that "the French Communist leader, Danielle deBrett, is now back on her own soil, having failed in her mission to pick up more than a pitiful smattering of fresh blood for her cause." She had evidently just missed being expelled as an undesirable alien. Among the "pitiful smattering," they implied, was Tony Lombard, maverick son of one of the nation's best-known capitalists, friend of generals and presidents alike, Steve Lombard.

"A real wheeler-dealer," Carl mumbled to himself. He had been curious to know how Lombard had acquired his great wealth. He discovered that it had come from real estate, stocks and bonds, investments of all sorts, and the ability to be in the right place at the right time. He also seemed to have the knack for getting along with foreign business powers, though he had never been appointed to any official capacity.

"Wheeler-dealer," Carl repeated to himself, disliking the sound of it; yet he hadn't disliked Steve Lombard. The trouble was he had liked most of the Lombards. His father's widow was his favorite, because of her loyalty to his memory and her generosity to Carl himself. Many a woman might have resented her husband's children by a former mistress. She was unlike the other Lombards, who had connived at his father's death.

And it had all backfired. He did his best to involve the real culprit, Leo Prysing, but what he thought was a foolproof plan fell through, thanks to the Burkett woman's meddling and Danielle's idiocy.

He had to admit that the sight and feel of Danielle when he dragged her away from Hedda Hopper brought back many pulse-pounding memories. Her flesh was still pliant. And exciting to his touch. It had taken everything he could muster to order her out of town, even though she was the woman who had betrayed Jany in Paris, the woman who took his money to set up Leo Prysing and then ruined the vengeance he'd worked out so carefully. All of this, yet he still wanted her in bed. He despised the urge that weakened him.

Meanwhile, Carl's own efforts to show Leo as a leftist sympathizer had been laughed at — the producer's basic nature made it too hard a story for the Hollywood community to swallow. Carl felt he would have done better to hint at Leo's dictatorial characteristics. At least it would have been more believable.

Despite all his efforts Jany remained chained to Leo with no hope of a separation. Closing his eyes,

Carl remembered Jany's uncustomary listlessness as they said good-bye at the Wilmington docks before sailing for the Hawaiian Islands. She persisted in her act as a loving wife, but her blue eyes were dull, and she seemed merely resigned to her life.

Damned murderer . . . if Leo were anyone else, Carl would have encouraged Jany to make the best of it and keep her marriage vows. Before he learned the truth, Carl himself had admired Prysing. Now, it took all his willful determination to remain polite and respectful while they worked together at the studio.

He liked his job better than anything he had ever done in his life, but he knew it would be difficult when Leo and Jany returned from the Islands. Sooner or later, Carl knew he would explode, let his real feelings show. It was maddening that the real culprit, Leo Prysing, had not suffered.

*What will I do if Tony Lombard doesn't get out of this trap?*

Tony's dilemma perplexed him — he wasn't as happy as he thought he would be at the Lombards' suffering. True, Carl had achieved that much, but there was very little joy in knowing he'd betrayed his former friend. He also felt a sense of shame, knowing that sooner or later Tony would figure out Carl's part in the scheme.

He slapped the newspapers into his valise and watched the approach to the Bay City. He still didn't know what to do about Leo, or, for different reasons, Tony. Once anyone suspected what he had done, he would be deported as an undesirable alien. He would lose his beloved sister and his chance at a career forever . . .

Brooke Friedrich had offered to have one of the family cars ready to pick him up at the San Francisco airport, but he decided to take the bus into the city instead. He didn't like to be indebted to anyone. Still, he couldn't imagine why Brooke had asked him to come, although she'd mentioned in passing something about his father.

Arriving at the Nob Hill house, Carl was shocked by Randi Lombard's cool greeting. She had always been kind to him and made him feel welcome on his previous visits.

With a sinking feeling he wondered if they suspected something already. He felt sorry for the loss of one more friend — he had nothing against her personally, except that she was Steve Lombard's wife and Steve was second only to Prysing in the conspiracy against his father.

Carl found the vibrations unpleasant everywhere in the house except with Brooke, who seemed indignant. If the family was suspicious of him, she obviously was not on their side. He was grateful for her warm welcome as she led him into the upstairs sunroom. A butler with a Caribbean accent was ordered to take Carl's valise. After assuring her there was nothing he needed, she motioned him to a wicker chair which was placed by itself at the far end of the room.

Noticing the setup, he saw that he had no choice but to accept it, and sat down rather stiffly. Carl never liked the idea of being the center of attention, and it was clear that that would be the case today. His foreboding grew.

Steve Lombard came in with his arm around his wife. Though he smiled, it did little to soften his tough exterior. He sat on the couch, his long legs sprawled out before him, crossed at the ankles. But even he didn't bother Carl as much as the man who came in last. For some inexplicable reason, it was the quiet, unobtrusive look of Alec Huntington that disturbed Carl most. He wondered briefly if it was because his conscience had been bothering him — still, he had done Alec no harm.

With an enormous effort Carl forced himself not to speak or even clear his throat, but instead studied a design on the wallpaper across the room. It was peeling in a spot just above Huntington's head. Huntington had chosen to sit on the hassock.

Brooke squirmed nervously in her armchair and, reaching over, patted Carl's arm.

"Don't let this disturb you, Carl. This is all some more nonsense about my dear Kurt. It doesn't sway me one little bit and it shouldn't you, either." She sat back with her fingers closing around the chair arms, looking a little like a queen presiding over an unpleasant trial. "All right, Alec. Do your worst. We're ready now."

Curious, thought Carl. She seemed to have no motherly affection for her son, though she had warmed to Carl at their first meeting.

Steve Lombard uncrossed his legs and sat up. Alec nodded. "Carl, you believe that we deliberately warned the Nazis of your father's ancestry, among other things. Is that true?" Steve asked.

"Yes," he said with forced restraint, "I do. I thought for many years that you and Monsieur Prysing were sincere in your praise for my father's heroism." They all stared at him, very much his judges. "I thought it had been a terrible mistake that my father was still in the Reich when the broadcast was made. I know now that Leo Prysing and you, Monsieur Lombard, and your daughter-in-law, intended to punish my father for some unproven crime."

Steve cut in. "On the contrary. Goebbels' own state radio described in detail how Kurt Friedrich betrayed Prysing's brother and his wife. They boasted of it."

"And you believed that Nazi broadcast?" Carl replied, impetuously. "Not only are you murderers, you are fools as well."

Brooke caught her breath but Steve was unruffled.

"It's clear to us now that after Stella Burkett arranged for you to see *Journey*, you found it necessary to avenge your father's death. In Stella you found a willing accomplice. Your modus operandi was to use my son's wartime relationship with a French Resistance worker who was, in fact, your own mistress, to accomplish this. I assume this is correct."

"I willingly admit to that. I am not a coward. But my intention was for Monsieur Prysing to suffer chiefly." Carl shrugged dejectedly. "Unfortunately, he did not."

"And you said nothing?"

"You did nothing to save my father, did you?" Carl snapped back.

Randi moved restlessly beside her husband. "This is getting us nowhere. Give him proof, for God's sake. Let him know how it really was — the uncertainty, the torn feelings you all had."

For the first time Alec spoke. The light from the windows caught his glasses, accentuating his cold, unemotional expression.

"Yes. It's time. I'll get them." He went out of the room.

No one said anything while he was gone, and they all avoided looking at Carl. He felt like a pariah and resented being placed on trial by his father's murderers. He supposed Huntington would march back in with Stella Burkett — maybe even Danielle deBrett. One never knew how much power these rich Americans could summon up when necessary.

Alec returned with a middle-aged man and woman, ushering them in as if they were prospective servants arrived for an interview. The woman, a typical Middle European, stoutish and motherly-looking, wore her cornsilk hair braided around her head. Her smile was tentative and uncertain.

The male was less prepossessing, with a large head on a scrawny neck and watery little eyes whose gaze jumped back and forth at the faces before him.

Brooke greeted them in her normal, breezy manner. "Frau Becker, don't be afraid. Do come in. And was your trip over satisfactory?"

"Very satisfactory, as you say, Frau Friedrich," the man replied in German with a stiff bow. Carl had seen many men like him in the lower echelons of the Occupation troops in Paris.

"*Ja*, it is so," the woman put in.

Carl figured the two ex-servants were rehearsed, that it would turn out to be a Lombard plot.

"Hans was our gardener," Brooke explained to Carl, "Frau Becker was the housekeeper. She reared Kurt from childhood. She loved him." The Austrian woman nodded.

"Such a pretty baby he was, Frau Friedrich."

"And you would do anything he asked you to, correct?" Alec asked quietly.

*"Naturlich, mein Herr."*

Anxious for them to get on with their "testimony," Steve urged Alec, "Tell them again that they will not be punished, that this has nothing to do with war crimes."

Frau Becker nodded, but she kept staring at Brooke.

"Otto Weiss, the butler, he went to the cellar for wine. He told us two Jews were hidden there. He reported to Herr Kurt who said 'Wait. We may catch others when they try to escape the cellar. We will catch all the foul *Jüden'* — his words, *mein Herren.* His mother had despised the Jews." She added eagerly, with a kind, motherly smile, "Many good folk believed it was the Jews who caused us to lose our empire in the Great War. They came out rich, owning the country . . . so it was said."

Carl felt the cold foggy San Francisco day pushing in at the windows behind his back. He remembered the awful fear that gripped him every day in Paris when he saw the yellow Star of David on the breast pockets of his Jewish friends. He himself had hidden several of them until they could be smuggled out of Paris and into the unoccupied countryside. God only knew what had happened to them when the Germans took over Vichy France as well . . .

But the fear had always been just as real for Jany and himself. Now he was learning that his own half-Jewish father was among the persecutors. He glanced at Brooke, expecting to see her revulsion at the housekeeper's story. Her expression was almost as shocking as the story being told. Brooke looked merely impatient, even cross. There was nothing in her smooth, pretty face to suggest her outrage at the lies these two servants were relating or, even more horrifying, the possibility that they could be telling the truth.

"All of this is irrelevant, Frau Becker," Brooke said. "This young man isn't interested in Kurt's childhood ideas. He was a friend of Dr. Josef and Sarah. You remember, Stephen. When you visited us in Vienna the Preysings were often invited to dinner."

"The fact that I was Leo's friend might have influenced that invitation," Steve said tightly. "From the time Hitler's party won the German elections Kurt changed. Brooke herself knows he joined the Austrian National Socialists. In short — the Nazi party."

"Don't be silly, Steve. He had to. Everyone did, who had any sense. And it also helped him get jobs."

"He deliberately betrayed our escape with the Preysings that night in March of '38."

"Is that true?" Carl asked Hans Becker in German. "Or was it an accidental discovery? He betrayed the Preysings as some sort of patriotic gesture. No?"

"Well then, *mein Herr,* I would not say an accident. Herr Friedrich was a man most loyal to the

Party. Naturally, today we feel this was a bad thing. But in those days, one did not know. There was a new order."

"I have heard of the new order. I ask of you only the truth. My father did not plan the betrayal of the Preysings. If he betrayed them it was because he discovered they were being smuggled out against the Austrian laws. Isn't this so?"

Frau Becker covered her mouth but was unable to conceal her irritating giggle. They all stared at her, incredulous that she could behave in such poor taste.

"Excuse, please," she said, apologizing. "But you do not know how clever Kurt was. When he knew these traitors were hidden behind his back in his own cellar, he planned very cleverly. He had them watched. Otto Weiss reported to him and to us. And Hans here. He watched. We were afraid for Frau Friedrich, but we later learned that she was to be left alone. The same for Herr Lombard and Fraulein Ware."

"So this is why the Preysings and my family were permitted to get on the train in the first place —" Alec said.

"Just so. The two traitors were removed at the Swiss border. The Americans did not know of it until they were beyond our reach. Beyond the borders of Austria, I mean to say," she amended with a furtive glance at Alec and Steve.

Carl sat listening to her in confusion, remembering the Kurt Friedrich of his childhood — selfish, superficial, a shallow charmer who, as even Jany said, produced two illegitimate children and then deserted his mistress to marry a wealthy

American. His own admiration for his father had come only after hearing the fake broadcast by Leo Prysing.

Carl looked over at Alec Huntington, remembering their evening together in London, hearing Alec once again as he shared his deepest feelings about his cousin Tony and the others. Carl, aware of the bitterness Alec carried with him, marveled that he didn't wish to cover up the truth, let his cousin suffer and sweat a little.

But here was that same Alec, unearthing the truth, knowing that once again his cousin would be saved.

Alec was not lying. Instinctively, Carl knew it.

The lies had been on the other side — his side, and he inwardly groaned at his own blind refusal to see what was always there. His Father was a dedicated Nazi.

Half of my life has been lived inside lies, he thought in despair.

He was aware of words being spoken around him, illuminating the full story of his father's treachery. He stared straight ahead, occasionally unaware that someone had glanced at him. There was pity in Steve Lombard's expression, but he could see that Alec Huntington, as cool and reserved as he, Carl, had once been, was not a forgiving man. He had lost a good friend in Stella Burkett and quite rightly blamed Carl for it.

"Do you want to ask them any further questions?" Alec said.

"Are there any others? What about his butler, this Otto Weiss they mentioned?"

"He died on the eastern front. The Beckers were

fortunate enough to come through unharmed, as you see. They live in the British zone of Vienna. According to their story, they are innocent in every respect."

Frau Becker nodded vigorously.

"Naturally," Carl agreed, with an edge to his voice.

"Anything else?"

Carl shook his head. The two Austrians told him nothing he hadn't known since the Prysing film. He had only drawn false conclusions based on a desperate, absurd hope. He had always known what his real-life father was like, but he hadn't been able to face it. He had needed to believe in Kurt Friedrich's secret courage, his martyrdom. And as the son of Kurt Friedrich, Carl wanted to believe that his own heritage was derived from a man of courage and strength. Instead, the image of the selfish, hateful man who was his father flooded his mind, blotting out all those dreams of a noble heritage.

*He would approve of what I have done to these people.*

It was a terrible thought; suddenly he felt his life crumbling around him.

His one last hope was to confront Brooke Friedrich. She had loved the man, and he knew she wouldn't lie.

"Are they telling the truth, madame?"

She seemed anxious that he should understand "the real Kurt," and not the black picture that was being painted of him.

"Kurt can't have known his father was Jewish," Brooke said, compassionately. "I'm sure his mother concealed it from him. *I* certainly didn't know he was Jewish."

Carl pursued what he read in those inflections.

"You helped Monsieur Lombard get the Preysings out of the country secretly. You must have suspected your husband was a threat to them."

She opened her hands and arms wide. Her big eyes widened as well.

"But Josef and Sarah were our friends," she said, opening her hands and arms wide. "There are Jews. And then again, *there are Jews*. We all know that."

Carl looked at each of the others, one by one. They all appeared stricken, staring at Brooke in disbelief. Her son, Alec, was pale in the foggy light.

"It seems that anti-Semitism wasn't confined to your father, Mr. Friedrich," he finally said.

Brooke started to speak. She was clearly perplexed by the silence that had followed her remark. Seeing the sly little twitch of Frau Becker's mouth, Brooke changed her mind, arose and ushered her two Austrian servants out of the room, down the back stairs and out to the waiting car.

Apparently, the Lombards and Alec Huntington were waiting for Carl's reaction. He got up, still silent, and made his way to the hall. Someone put a hand on his arm. He turned, his face almost brushing Randi's. There was an unmistakable silent plea in her eyes, and for an instant he saw Jany pleading through the eyes of Tony's mother.

He stopped. "Tell me what I must do."

Steve, joining them in the hall, was surprisingly sympathetic.

"It's rough, I'm afraid. You'll have to make an affidavit, which means you'll probably lose your visitor's permit. And your job," he added. Carl winced, though the news wasn't surprising to him. Carl abruptly became very businesslike, forcing down his personal feelings.

"Will Madame Burkett testify?"

Steve shrugged. "Alec isn't sure. Maybe. If you name her."

"That's inevitable. There are people in Paris who also can testify that Danielle was my . . . friend, rather than Tony's. I know Tony has claimed this before, but maybe my word will help in the matter."

"It was a tragedy for everyone," Randi said, "from the very beginning."

"And the beginning was with my father. I thought he was only pretending to work with the Nazis. I didn't know. I never dreamed he was a Nazi at heart. I mean, how could he be, with his Jewish heritage?"

"As Brooke said," Steve reminded him, "Kurt didn't know about his own father. Leo knew because the Prysing family remembered your father's birth. This revenge business — it never pays. First Leo. And . . ."

"Then me."

No one said anything.

Carl was surprised when Randi Lombard took his hand and held it momentarily.

"Thank you, for my son. We do know what this means to you, what you are sacrificing."

His demeanor didn't change.

"It must be done. You will tell me how I make

the confession, the proper channels to go through."

"Of course."

"And tell Tony that —" He faltered, and waved away the rest of what he started to say.

The two Lombards went down the stairs together, leaving Carl alone in the hallway. Leaning against the doorway of the sunroom, Carl closed his eyes. His mind whirled with images of all the losses that this would mean in his life. And at the bottom, there remained a pinch of regret that Leo Prysing would never have to account for what virtually had been murder.

But life was never perfectly balanced, he thought.

Was it?

# Chapter Thirty-Seven

"I've done it again," Eden confessed, as Tony drove the family across Oahu to the Ware estate. "Me and my bossiness. Coming here like this, upsetting Tony's life. And yours, Chiye."

Chiye was holding her goddaughter on her lap, and Andrea, almost suffocating under her six flower leis, was playing with Chiye's more simple one. Chiye laughed, removed the lei and dropped it, too, over Andrea's head.

"You don't upset me when you bring this little princess." She added quickly, "Nor otherwise, Eden. I've missed all of you."

Tony said nothing. He was in a dark mood. But it had been necessary to get him out of Hollywood where it seemed every day he lost another friend, another business acquaintance. Referring to several writers who refused to answer the House committee on their political affiliations, he said, "The Hollywood Ten are at least public heroes in some quarters. Even the ultras and the pinks despise me. If I go to prison, I'll be lucky if my fellow convicts don't knife me. It seems the only thing that's going to keep me out is to say I'm a Communist. And if I deny it, they get me on perjury. It's a no-win situation."

Though the Hawaii trip was meant to provide a respite from Tony's Hollywood troubles, he suspected that Eden had other reasons for wanting to return home. She was convinced that Leo wanted to ruin Tony, and she intended to confront him and find out why. Even more important, she wanted to know, once and for all, whether Jany and Tony were in love.

"I don't think you will be bored here," Chiye said, trying to liven up the conversation. "Mrs. Prysing walks along the beach every day. We've talked often. She is lovely, I think. And Mr. Prysing has invited me to their house for cocktails several times, when I'm not on duty."

"How is she looking these days?" It was the first time Tony had spoken since they got into Chiye's car.

Slightly confused, Chiye looked up from playing with Andrea. "Who?"

"Jany Prysing." It was Eden who gave her the name.

"She looked tired. Maybe our food doesn't agree with her. Paris is a long way from the Windward Coast. I prepared *lomi-lomi* salmon for her one day. She really seemed to enjoy it. I think she is lonely, poor girl. So far from home."

"Very likely." Eden glanced at Tony, but he was busy watching the road and didn't react to Chiye's remarks.

Things got a little better once the group was inside the Ware bungalow. The long sweep of the Pacific shoreline had never been more inviting. Tony immediately got into his swim trunks and went for a swim. He remained in the water for some time, seemingly cleansing himself of his bleak memories of Hollywood.

Sitting on the beach with Andrea, Eden watched her stepsister with the first real pleasure she'd

560

known in a long time.

"Chiye, you look so contented and happy. How do you do it?"

"Good Lord! Grief and guilt can't last forever. I moped around for years. But I'm over that now. Remember when Steve got me to Japan for the translating job?"

"I do. Don't tell me — you met a wonderful man —"

Chiye's slanting eyes crinkled with her smile.

"Many of them. But I finally got my self-respect back. I discovered I hadn't been wrong about my ancestors, after all. They were fine people, and so is the culture that's been passed down to me. I was able to love it again, as I had before the war."

Eden knew that Chiye blamed herself for the deaths of her mother, her fiancé and her stepfather during the Pearl Harbor raid. Chiye felt that it had been a punishment for her passionate defense of her Japanese culture before the war broke out. It was an enormous relief now to find that Chiye was again her feisty, opinionated, passionate self. Eden hugged her spontaneously.

Her enthusiasm proved contagious. Andrea insisted on climbing all over her godmother so she could embrace her, as well.

Andrea, decked out in the wardrobe Chiye had brought back from Tokyo, a bright hibiscus-red kimono with its long, matching obi, charmed the two women with her antics.

Chiye asked Andrea to officially model her new costume, including the delicate ivory fan that had been Grandpa Steve's present from the Orient. Andrea obliged with enormous excitement. There was nothing she liked better than having the rapt attention of those who loved her. Andrea was a unique little girl who'd inherited an intriguing bundle of her parents' more outstanding characteristics.

About the time Tony climbed out of the surf and strode in through the long shallows to take his daughter for a swim, Eden returned to the house to make her call to the estate leased by Leo Prysing, which was a short walk away around Crouching Tiger Point. A young Filipino woman took Eden's name and Leo came on the line. He seemed glad to hear from her.

"What's new, kid? Guess you're pretty excited about the Oscars coming up. Going to attend and fly the Prysing colors, I hope."

"Think for a minute I'd miss that, Leo? I'll be there with bells on. Suppose I've got a chance?"

"According to the *Variety* scuttlebutt, you're a shoo-in. How's the old town these days?"

She chuckled. "I wouldn't know. I'm here in Hawaii."

"What?" He must have swallowed his cigar, at the very least. "You damned fool — you should be there to supervise the ads, the publicity, making appearances."

"Don't worry. I'll be in Hollywood on Oscar night. But right now, I'd rather be relaxing here and trying to get my life back together with Tony."

He was off again. She had never known him to be so explosive. "You mean you brought that bastard here? Practically on my doorstep?"

"Don't forget I'm Mrs. Bastard, Leo. Besides, it was you who chose to lease that white elephant only a few steps from my family's estate."

"Why shouldn't I? I've always leased it." He backed down. "Sorry, I guess I got carried away. I didn't mean that the way it sounded. I've been feeling like hell this morning. Goddamned cocktail parties. All that coconut gook and nuts and liquor, just to get a little new money into next year's schedule."

Knowing the answer, she suggested innocently, "Can't you touch my father-in-law again? He ought to be good for another million or two."

"Not while the damned Un-American Activities bunch in Washington is sniffing around his son."

"Running away wasn't the answer."

He was up in arms over that. "Nobody ran away. Jany's been pleading for a real honeymoon. I'm doing this for her. She's getting a big kick out of this banana-land. But you'd be smart if you took my advice and got that husband of yours away from here. Far away."

To further torment him, she teased, "Every single thing you say makes me more anxious for Tony to stay here. He's had so much trouble lately, he needs a little Hawaiian hula."

"You don't understand, damn it! I don't want them to meet."

Her heart was beating faster than usual, but she managed to respond with commendable assurance. "I understand perfectly. But you're going about it all wrong."

"Well, you may be willing to chance it, but I'm a little older. I'm not so free with my time."

"You're an idiot, Leo, but I love you anyway. Chiye tells me you're having an open house tonight. We'll be over for cocktails, sevenish."

"Eden, for God's sake —"

She hung up.

Jany Prysing had borrowed the caretaker's field glasses again and stood at the rocky tip of Crouching Tiger Point, staring at the awesome expanse of the Pacific before her.

She was not an "ocean" person. Until her trip to the United States, she had never been further from Paris than the city of Rouen on a childhood visit. She was accustomed to the city, and felt most comfortable in one. But somewhere at the far end of all that deceptively smooth water were the two men she loved, Tony Lombard and Carl. She cared for her husband, out of gratitude and in remembrance of her vows, but that was quite a different emotion. She tried never to let him know what an act of will it was to be happy with him.

She wondered at times if she tried too hard. She knew he wasn't well, in spite of all his bellowing, and he was so like a child, always wanting his own way. She tried to acquiesce in everything, his opinions and plans. She even pretended to agree that it was better for him to be away from Hollywood while Tony and so many of his other colleagues were being questioned about their politics. She didn't understand what Tony might have done, but she believed Leo when he said his testimony would only hurt Tony more.

It was dusk when she turned the glasses to the north to examine the beach front of the house Leo had leased.

There was a long balcony that extended over the beach, which the local staff called a lanai. She often stood there late in the evening while Leo played poker with his Honolulu friends. Jany, on the other hand, spent an inordinate amount of time mentally listing all the reasons why she had married Leo Prysing.

She had helped Carl, at least. He loved his job and was very good at it. Leo said he was the best. As for Tony, he and Eden seemed to be getting along as they always had. Still, she dreamed of him; she couldn't help but see his face everywhere.

Even in her glasses she saw him. She blinked, pulled them down from her eyes and stared. It was no phantom, but Tony who stood there on the lanai watching her. Though he looked thinner in the dim golden glow of the lanai lights, hc seemed even more handsome than before, she thought tenderly. She thought she could detect a smile on his lips. Her heart jumped — it was the first time he had smiled at her since the day they had made love.

She waved to him, but quickly reminded herself, We must be civilized about this meeting. We are only friends, like Eden and Leo.

It was harder when they met. He went down several steps, and, meeting her, gently took her two hands in his. All the while she was deeply conscious of his eyes looking into hers.

"How have you been?"

She said brightly. "Very well, as always. And you?"

"Okay."

"Your troubles with the gentlemen of the Congress, they are settled now?"

He laughed. "Oh, sure. Those things come and

go. I've got my cousin investigating it now. We think it was a deliberate plot to set me up." He caught himself, making Jany tense. Was he going to name his enemy? she wondered. It would be someone she knew, obviously.

Who had a better motive than Leo? She was ashamed that her own conduct might have contributed to this. At the same time she felt strong indignation against Leo for seeking such underhanded revenge. Surely this explained why Leo decided to take her on the cruise. It was a second blow to Tony. She could never forgive that.

"Come inside. I will show you Leo's house."

"Leo's? Not yours?"

She shook her head. "Everything is his property, including Jany Friedrich. But he is a kind property owner."

Tony chose not to argue with that.

They walked into the big living room that opened out on the lanai. It was empty, but they could hear voices in another room, behind closed doors.

"Eden and Leo fighting again," Tony guessed.

Jany was startled. "How does she dare? After all, he's her employer."

"Why should Eden worry? This is her fourth nomination for an Academy Award. And all her recent films have made money, which is more than I can say for the two I directed. One was sneaked out and ended up on the bottom half of a Loew's double bill. The other one hasn't even been released. Leo's holding it up."

"It was cruel of him, what they call underhanded. Carl and I always despised people in Paris

566

who behaved like that. With the Boches, you know."

He repeated slowly, "So Carl hates people who are underhanded."

"Very much so."

He breathed deeply, then turned to her impulsively. "Let them see us. I'm going to kiss you."

"*Nom de Dieu!* We do not dare."

"A very little kiss, then."

"I do not think we —"

His mouth touched hers, a mere brushing of lips before they pressed against hers eagerly. In his arms she held tight to his body, excited by it, hungry for him, remembering how she had adored his flesh, his nakedness, how she longed for him so.

# Chapter Thirty-Eight

Eden was shocked when she first saw Leo Prysing. He looked bloated, red-faced, none too steady on his feet, and he had gained considerable weight. She jumped to the conclusion that his appearance had something to do with her own problems.

"My God, Leo. Am I the only one in this love quadrangle who conceals the wear and tear? You look ghastly. So does Tony, and Chiye tells me your little bride isn't looking so hot either."

He waved his double-Manhattan glass. "Are you suggesting that you yourself look ravishing? You don't kid — don't kid yourself."

"Thanks, darling. You've always been a charmer."

"Well, my wife gives me no trouble whatever. She's one hundred percent in my corner. Your husband is another matter. He was annoying her a lot back in L.A."

"So that's why you walked out at the worst possible time for Tony? To make him look guiltier than ever? Why don't you offer me a drink?"

He reached for the ice tongs, automatically poured from the pitcher of martinis and handed her a glass. His big hand trembled.

She took a sip, studying him over the rim of the glass.

"It's more than Jany and my husband, isn't it? Are you sick?"

"Never felt better," he boasted. "But time gets

important when a man reaches my age." He leaned against the edge of the portable bar, felt for a little glass bonbon dish and chewed up a couple of what appeared to be antacid wafers.

So he still had "heartburn." She suspected it was considerably more than it. Probably his heart, period, and he knew it. No wonder he talked about not having time.

"Look, Leo, you want to take things easier. Why don't you stop hounding my husband? Get it off your conscience. Go back to L.A. and talk to the congressmen and the lawyers. Tell them — you know Tony never put any Communist messages in his films."

Leo took a good long swig and wiped his mouth. "Tony always had funny ideas. Spouting off about the unions and the guilds and the right to free speech and the rest." He straightened up. Despite his failing health, he was still an impressive figure, solid and powerful. "But that's not what I've got against him. I may as well tell you. You'll find out sooner or later anyway. He's been sleeping with my wife."

She laughed at that. "How? By long distance?"

"*Nein.*" The word surprised her. He must be very agitated. "While you and I were sealed up in the studio last December, they were together. That strike turned out pretty handy for that slick bastard you married."

"Did your drinking friend McDevlin tell you this?"

"One of the maids snooping around heard them talking in our bedroom. She told Mac."

She felt a sharp pinch of certainty about the story, but made an effort to ignore it.

"You'd accuse your wife of adultery on the word of a self-seeking bum like McDevlin?"

"My wife! Are you crazy? It was that husband of yours with his sly little tricks that seduced her. My Jany wouldn't do anything to hurt me like that. And she's been good as gold since we got out of his reach."

She was beginning to feel frantic, and raised her voice, pleading with him, "All right, all right. Think what you want but just help Tony answer that congressional committee. Your word would mean so much. They know your importance in the industry, and the reputation of your films. Please, Leo."

While Leo was snorting over the idea, Eden examined her colorless drink in every light, telling herself repeatedly how little the evidence of a McDevlin mattered. Maybe they did make love once — weren't those urges natural? But it couldn't have been an ongoing thing. They saw the Prysings many times after the strike, and nothing seemed unusual. All these months later Tony still hadn't wanted to come to the islands. He preferred to stick it out at home.

As arguments to the contrary raced through Eden's mind, the sickening truth kept hitting home — Tony loved Leo's wife.

If her own instincts hadn't told her, she would have guessed the truth when she opened the door into the big living room only a second or two after the two guilty lovers moved apart. She felt queasy, but there was also a surprising relief that numbed her sense of loss.

At this precise moment, standing in the living

room of Leo's rented house, she knew her marriage was over. There would be no patching it up, no pity in Tony's eyes any more when he looked at her. She had dreaded and denied that pity for too long. It was time to be released from it.

Behind her she felt a hand on her shoulder, and devoutly hoped that Leo did not sense what had just happened between his wife and her husband. Though her shoulder still ached from his tight clasp, Leo behaved very well, making Tony's drink with consummate hypocrisy, asking how Tony was handling the Un-American Activities Committee.

By this time several other guests had arrived, most of them anxious to meet the daughter of Oahu's hero, Dr. Nigel Ware.

Because of her love for her father, Eden enjoyed this different kind of fame she received as his daughter. Also, it took her mind off the deep chasm she felt developing at the thought of Tony's drifting away.

There were moments that evening when she wondered what she would say to Tony as they walked home along the beach — if they would. But when the time came, Eden said good night to her slightly weaving host and pale, quiet hostess, and Tony was at her side, as always.

Maybe we'll have a reprieve, Eden told herself, borrowing hope . . . maybe I imagined their feelings. Me and my movie mind . . .

While she helped the servants clear away the party debris, Jany got up enough nerve to ask Leo about his condition. She started to remove the ice

571

bucket but he pulled it out of her hands.

"Leave it."

"But *mon chèr*, it is not good for you."

"How would you know, Frenchie? You Frogs are half-drunk all the time on wine anyway. You know what that makes you? Winos. My wife is a god-damned wino."

She knew he was suffering from chest pains, or he wouldn't speak to her this way. Her guilt made her accept his sharp, ugly tone as a penance, but she wished he wouldn't speak so loudly. Some of the departing guests, especially the Lombards, might hear him. He would be angry in the morning if he found out that they knew about his drinking. And Jany dreaded the possibility of Tony knowing.

She tried to get around him to rescue the glasses that had made rings on the glossy surface of the grand piano. Again, he caught her wrist. Jany was surprised, looking into his bloodshot eyes — usually he kept much better control of himself.

"So the great lover is back in town."

"You're hurting me, Leo."

"I saw the fadeout of that tender embrace scene between you and Eden's pretty gigolo. So did Eden, or I miss my guess."

To hear him insulting Tony was too much for her. She tried to wrench her arm away. All the fire she had conscientiously stifled now blazed out.

"How can you insult him, call him a gigolo? He saved my life in Paris. He was a hero, fighting right alongside Carl in all the street fights. He is as noble and fine a man as my brother."

He held her there for a minute, shaking her hand

and arm. "A perfect comparision. I've suspected all along that your beloved Carl was in back of that Commie tart from Paris. He probably brought her to Hollywood just to stage that little scene."

He could not have said anything more vile. It was a degrading, disgusting lie that reflected only on the man who said it. She freed herself with a hard, painful twist of her wrist and backed away from him.

"You are disgusting! You attack the two people in the world who are my life."

That hurt. She knew it instantly and was sorry, but he had provoked the truth out of her. He reached for her, but she eluded him. She knew he was too drunk to be aware of what he said. She tried again. "Leo, can't we forget tonight? You'll feel better tomorrow."

His voice slurred a little. "Sure. Forget my own wife is carrying on under my nose. I should have known better than to trust Kurt Friedrich's kid. Like father, like daughter. Lice, all of you."

She stared at him, open-mouthed, wondering if he had always felt this way about her and Carl. If that was so, then her marriage had been nothing more than the satisfaction of the old man's lust. It had nothing to do with love and devotion to each other.

She had to get away from him, to think. She had never really made any decisions on her own. Always there was Carl, and sometimes Maman, and always the Church. Now, there was this man who seemed to hate her father and to despise her. She took a few steps backward, away from him. While he fumbled for ice in the bucket, she turned and walked out to the lanai.

He heard her high heels clicking on the steps as she hurried down to the beach. He stirred himself to action. It wasn't easy; he found furniture unexpectedly in the way, and he bumped hard into the door frame before he made it to the lanai railing.

Out in the dark was the enormity of the Pacific. The lanai lights cast a dim golden halo over the water. The rising tide brought the water so close he shook off his alcoholic haze to look more carefully into the creeping white foam. He made out her slender form in its white, ankle-length evening dress with a poufed skirt, like a ballerina's. She seemed to be floating along the water's edge, following the uneven path of sea foam.

She stopped at a distance from the house. The foam seeped around her, washing over her shoes. Leo shook his head, trying to get the fuzziness out. He had said a lot of dumb things that he didn't mean. Or only half-meant. But it hurt like hell to be told that he wasn't one of the two men who mattered most to her.

He had been jealous of Lombard, and with cause, just as he had once been jealous of Tony's father, who seemed to have the same hold over Randi. Well, that one-sided infatuation died from lack of encouragement. But this was a marriage, and it was different. Jany had been as perfect a mate for him as he could find. He was molding her into the perfect wife for a man of his position. He could easily overlook Jany's unfaithfulness during the strike — he knew it was Tony Lombard who must have made all the moves.

Leo raised his head enough to watch the

graceful butterfly-figure of his wife on the water's edge. Then, suddenly, she was gone.

He squinted and stared along the beach that lined the cove. In the distance he made out Tony and Eden just rounding the Crouching Tiger headland. In another minute or two they would be out of sight. He leaned over the railing toward the north. There was nothing but the moonlit waters and the long, desolate beach.

He called out Jany's name, yelling frantically, but the breaking surf blurred the sound of his voice. In a panic he started down the steps, waving both arms and yelling for Eden and Tony.

Tony looked back at the Prysing house as they started around the headland. He thought he saw a figure moving, as though something were wrong. They turned around quickly and retraced their footprints across the damp sand.

By the time Leo got to the bottom of the steps he was panting breathlessly. The pain across his breastbone was like a lashing whip. He kept flailing his arms around frantically. The motion seemed to increase his pain, but he couldn't stop.

"Gone — wife's gone —" Tony and Eden glanced at each other. He was too breathless to make himself coherent. "No! Was here. Just — vanished."

It slowly dawned on Tony what he was trying to say.

"My God, she went out there?"

He tore off his dinner jacket as he ran down the beach, passing Leo, plunging into the first big wave that engulfed him. Leo tried to follow but could only sway, trying to keep his balance.

Eden, who had been weaned on these beaches, reached for him. Holding fast to his body with her left hand and his arm with her right, she dragged him away from the waterline. He fell through her arms, collapsing on the sand. Kneeling over him, she could see that he was in excruciating pain.

"D-damned — heartburn."

"Not heartburn. *Heart,* Leo. Be still, now."

"He find her?" he muttered.

Eden looked up. She made out two figures walking in the waters along the cove where it was shallow. They appeared to be struggling. There was no mistaking Jany's sodden, white evening dress. Eden suspected the two men's panic was wasted. When Tony suddenly stooped over to lift Jany and carried her ashore, Eden was not surprised to hear the girl's angry protest.

"I am not a suicide and I wasn't drowning. I was very angry and I wished to cool down, so I walked into the water. It was a wave that surprised me."

Soaking wet, with his hair plastered to his head, Tony set her down on her feet.

"How was I to know? We came back here and Leo was in a panic. Sweetheart, if anything had happened to you —"

"No, no, *mon coeur.* You were wonderful."

At least poor old Leo couldn't hear all this obvious affection, Eden thought. He was groaning. Her body had partially concealed him from his wife's sight. She moved and Jany discovered Leo. She sank to her knees beside him, calling his name anxiously. Then she looked across his body at Eden.

"What is it? Did he fall? Leo! I'm so sorry. Forgive me . . . *mon pauvre petit.*"

It was ironic, hearing her call this big man, her "little one." The sight of him lying on the beach in the dark terrified her. She remained kneeling next to him, stroking his forehead and crying softly.

Eden attempted to calm her, but it was of little use. Eden looked up anxiously when Leo stopped groaning. "Tony, I think he's having a full-fledged heart attack."

"My God!" Tony started for the house on the run.

While he called the doctor at Kaneohe Plantation, Eden and the guilt-stricken Jany tried to make Leo comfortable.

Eden tried to cut off the tirade of self-accusations the girl sobbed out.

"He's been headed for this for years. And on top of it, all that booze tonight."

Jany put her cheek close to Leo's.

"Forgive me, *mon chèr.* I did not mean to quarrel with you."

Strange girl, Eden thought, fighting off her own jealous prejudices. Jany loved another man — Eden no longer had any doubt of that. But her feeling for this brilliant yet crude man was also sincere. Tears streamed down her face as she raised her head to call after Tony.

"Hurry, please! Tony . . ."

Leo's face contorted. His heavy lips were loose, uncontrolled, but he managed to mouth, "Hi, little one."

Eden touched his chest gingerly, feeling the awful helplessness of not knowing what to do. Why hadn't she watched her father in emergencies?

Jany kept caressing his hands and forehead, hopefully repeating his name.

It was several minutes before Eden knew for certain that his heart had stopped, the pulse gone.

# Chapter Thirty-Nine

Leo Prysing's death rocked Hollywood. It was reported everywhere, from San Francisco, Paris and even Moscow that the screen's most celebrated independent producer, responsible for some of the greatest films of all time, had died suddenly in Hawaii.

*The Hollywood Reporter* and *Variety* hurriedly pulled their morgue files on him and brought them up to date with the full details of his marriage to "a lovely French freedom-fighter." So far, nothing had been mentioned of Mrs. Prysing's brother and the affidavits he quietly submitted to the legal counsel of the House Un-American Activities Committee.

All the same, Tony Lombard discovered a subtle change in the attitudes of his studio friends. He heard that even casual acquaintances referred to him as a "victim" set up by someone outside the industry. Cousin Alec's investigation was the beginning of what proved to be his vindication as a "Communist sympathizer." His only real regret was Carl's part in it. He wanted it kept secret, for Jany's sake, but the idea of Carl's treachery still rankled. To Tony it was incredible that Carl would feel compelled to carry out to this extent vengeance for a man as despicable as Kurt Friedrich.

At Leo's elaborate burial service near other film notables in the Hollywood cemetery, several prominent movie figures stopped before the

Lombard family to wish Tony well.

"Ironic, isn't it?" Tony remarked to his mother and father. "Just as all my friends are in hot water over their politics, I'm suddenly whitewashed. I still don't get it."

"They know you are innocent," Randi said quietly. "There's nothing else to 'get.'"

"Just accept it," Steve advised him, "it's been a long time coming."

Randi and Steve went over to offer Jany their sympathy. She looked small and thin in her black widow's weeds. When she raised her veil she looked worn, much older than her twenty years. Listening to her gentle voice the way he had, in his mind, for three years, Tony heard her complain to Randi for what must have been the hundredth time.

"Carl should have been here. It's not like him to return to Paris so suddenly. And Leo was his friend."

It was an awkward situation, and Tony longed to comfort her, but he owed Eden an enormous debt of gratitude for her conduct and understanding since their return from the Islands. She had even permitted Andrea to visit Jany Prysing once in the grim old house up in the Hollywood Hills.

On the night of the Academy Awards it seemed only natural that Andrea should stay with Jany during the hours that the Lombard family was expected for the presentation. Jany looked forward to that night, too, since she was expecting an overseas telephone call from her brother in Paris. For those who knew, there was a certain sad irony in the fact that Jany might never understand why Carl

Friedrich had given up his Hollywood job and returned to Paris. She continued to talk of "when Carl comes back," and there was nothing anyone could say to stop her.

In spite of Leo Prysing's death, his company figured prominently in the Academy Award nominations. One of the founders of the Academy of Motion Picture Arts and Sciences, he was already being discussed as the model for a new award to be dedicated to foreign-born filmmakers in America. This included so many of the film geniuses during the industry's first forty years that in a way it seemed a redundancy. There was already the Academy's highest honor, the Thalberg Award, which was given for general production excellence. The Academy was still debating the matter on the night the awards were to be presented at Grauman's Chinese Theater.

Riding along Hollywood Boulevard in a rented limousine, Eden and Tony found themselves uncomfortably silent with each other.

Eden slumped down in her seat, giving in to a sudden depression. She knew that Tony's kindness to her was only a coverup for his guilt. He would much rather be with Jany Prysing at this very moment . . .

In spite of herself, Eden sympathized with the French girl. Alone except for servants and a five-year-old child who was not hers, wondering about her beloved brother's absence, uncertain that she would ever be happy again, Jany deserved a little more out of life.

Tony had been tense the entire afternoon, so much so that it rubbed off on Eden. She decided this was the cause of her depression.

"Always a bridesmaid," she murmured, thinking of the Oscar, but also of her husband's love which she knew was clearly lost.

Tony sighed heavily. "Eden. Darling." He reached for her hand. His own was cold.

It's come, she told herself numbly. She was almost relieved. It was that kind of a night. She laughed.

"Okay, honey, but make it short. I don't want to miss any of Bob Hope's quips tonight. I'm going to need all the cheering up I can get."

"I won't be going to the winners' parties with you afterward. Mother and dad will take you."

"I figured that. Going up to see Jany?"

"She needs me. And Eden — ?" His fingers closed on hers. "I need her. I always have. You, on the other hand — darling, you never needed anyone."

"True enough," she said flippantly. "And you want a divorce." She was commendably calm, probably because she had been rehearsing it so often since Leo's death. "I just may leave the theater empty-handed tonight. In more ways than one," she said almost lightheartedly. But deep down, Eden knew she could bounce back from almost anything.

"It isn't possible. Not with your track record. Besides, if Prysing wins for Best Production, you'll be picking up that Oscar for the company."

"True. Leo the winner."

He started to say something, then looked out. They had arrived.

The noise of the fans and the traffic around

them was deafening. The shiny limousine was cheered even before its occupants were visible. The studio chauffeur opened the door. Tony got out, then held out his hand to Eden.

The sounds of a cheering crowd were familiar to her, but the furor that greeted the first sight of her tonight was a real ego boost. Tony smiled at her dazzled look.

"Hear that? They know you're going to win."

She scarcely heard him. She was thinking that he had never looked more dear to her, and after to-night he would be gone from her bed and her life forever. Now, when it was too late, Eden Ware Lombard knew that there would never be anyone who meant quite what Tony had meant in her life.

Surely theirs had been a perfect marriage in many ways.

But people change, she thought wistfully, or they meet someone else. He had met Jany Friedrich. Nothing lasts forever, *especially* perfection.

She smiled and waved to her happy fans in the bleachers, and couldn't remember a single detail about it afterward.

As one of the major nominees, Eden was seated between Tony on the aisle, and Steve and Randi on her other side.

I've got to make a decision, Eden told herself . . . he wants a divorce . . . I've got to give him one. There *is* such a thing as pride. Never in my life have I held onto a man who didn't want me . . .

She settled into her seat, resigning herself to accept what would be her fourth Oscar loss. *Night of the Hero* would go the way of her work in *Journey* and the other two roles she's been nominated for in the past. Only this time she would be losing the big prize: Tony as well as the Oscar for Best Actress. They were inextricably tied up together in her mind.

Steve and Randi had their heads together, whispering to each other. Steve leaned closer to Eden.

"Everything all right?" She nodded. "You're a cinch," he promised her.

She managed a smile. "Not tonight. I've got a feeling it's just not my night."

Randi leaned across Steve to wish her luck. Then the musical director of one of the major studios came into the pit, received his applause and struck up "Hooray for Hollywood." The tense, nerve-wracked audience settled back to pretend this was just another premiere or gala night out.

Eden was a proud woman. She had married Tony only after he had endlessly pressured her to do so. She had warned him she wasn't the marrying type, and reminded him that she was eight years old when he was born. Now, after seven years together they had come full circle and he was discovering that she had been right all those years ago.

She felt desolate, which was absurd. She had always known it wouldn't last, in fact, couldn't last, given the strong independent streak Eden found herself unable to control.

Bob Hope opened the ceremony with a monologue, helping to lift Eden's spirits. She'd laughed at everything he'd said, including "thank you." She was beginning to think she was delirious.

The awards for supporting roles came early. Eden remembered all the former Oscar ceremonies during the war when the evenings had been interminable after her own defeat. She ran her forefinger around her mouth, remembering the fake smile pasted on her lips when such luminaries as Mary Astor and Hattie McDaniel and Anne Revere took the Supporting Oscar against her in previous years.

She nudged Tony. As the orchestra played the year's Best Score, she whispered, "Reno?"

In spite of her effort to show how easily she gave him up, she read the pain in his eyes and knew he was remembering their good times.

Best Direction. Leo's postwar film, *Night of the Hero*, lost.

It had won for Best Supporting Actor, for Editing and for the Best Original Screenplay. But the award for Best Director was the tipoff. Prysing Films would not carry off the majors tonight.

Joan Crawford was introduced, a dazzling example of everything that was Hollywood. She presented the Best Actor Award. This was a shoo-in for one of the screen's greatest actors, equally at home on the New York stage . . . *I'm certainly not in his league,* Eden told herself miserably. She had sunk low enough in her seat so that her knees were locked against the seat in front of her, until one of the earlier losers turned around and gave her a dirty look.

The Best Actor from the year before read off the names of the five Best Actress nominees. Eden lost her hands to Tony and Steve, each of whom grabbed one and squeezed hard. She was astonished by the rolling wave of applause when her name was read, strange and flat, at the end of the list.

The suave, good-looking male star asked for "the envelope, please."

Tony had tightened his grip on her left hand. She thought suddenly of all the nights she would spend without him in all the years to come.

"And the winner is . . . Edith — er — Eden Ware. For *Night of the Hero*."

Eden sank lower, the plastic smile fixed on her frozen mouth. One more defeat. Once more those hideous company parties, to make it all look like Prysing Films had won.

Tugged from both sides, she was pushed to her feet. Tony pulled his legs back but she fell over him anyway. He caught her in the aisle. Confused and unbelieving, she swung around.

"Go to it, honey!" Tony said, grinning broadly. "This is it."

Slowly, she came to her senses. Her stumbling progress down the aisle changed. Unbelievably, she had won. She began to run toward the stage, aware of sympathetic titters from the audience. Somebody got her up to the stage. She hadn't fallen into the orchestra pit, after all. Here were people she had played opposite for years, and there was the microphone.

Long ago she had rehearsed her winning speech. It was witty and short. She couldn't remember anything now. The handsome star who put the tall, surprisingly heavy statue into her hands was an actor who had been light-years her superior back in 1939 when she won her first nomination.

Clutching the lean figure to her breast, wondering if her year-old, slinky, white crepe evening gown was sticking to her body, she began her speech, stammering.

"I — I forgot what I — Anyway, thank you all. And a special thanks to my family, to Andrea and Tony and Chiye, and all I love who gave me what everybody needs in this life. And thank you, daddy and Tamiko, and André." She started away from the microphone, remembered and raised her voice. "And Leo Prysing, of course."

The applause poured over the footlights, engulfing her.

She started toward the steps and her family in the audience, but was caught and roughly piloted backstage. Here in the Tower of Babel, with all the winners being interviewed at the same time, Eden reviewed what she thought she had said in her acceptance speech.

It astonished her to find she had mentioned André de Grasse. André had died long ago, blown up while getting his men off the coast at LaPanne, near Dunkirk. He was her first love. She hadn't thought of him since Tony disappeared over France in '44. Every other man in her life and memory had vanished during the awful possibility of Tony's loss.

She heard her name called out. Like a chain message it reached her. Unable to enjoy this moment of supreme artistic triumph because of the confusion in her personal life, she let herself be shoved out to the wings.

The Best Picture Award had already been announced; Leo's film didn't win. What was this all about? Why did they want her standing in the wings?

The president of the Academy was making a short speech.

"The Irving C. Thalberg Memorial Award is not given every year. It is voted by the Academy Board of Governors to creative producers whose body of work reflects a consistently high quality of motion picture production. During the past eighteen years it has been bestowed only seven times. Tonight will be the eighth."

He sounded solemn. Obviously, he was paving the way for a special tribute.

"The Academy Board of Governors has voted the Irving G. Thalberg Memorial Award this year to Leo Prysing, whose films of consistently high quality have been an inspiration to the entire industry for twenty-four years. He will be sadly missed."

After a breathless hush the applause started. It swelled to a roar. He waited until it gradually died down, then held his hand out to Eden in the wings.

"It is appropriate that this award should be accepted for Mrs. Prysing by her close friend, a bright star in the Prysing firmament and winner of her own award tonight. Miss Eden Ware."

More applause. Still clutching her own Oscar to her bosom, Eden rushed across the stage, wishing to God she had worn a skirt with a wider hem.

She made a little speech without knowing what she would say or what she had said after she finished. The *Hollywood Citizen-News* reported it the next day:

Prysing Films' delightful star, Eden Ware, swept aside all the funereal atmosphere of last night's awards with her brief mention of Prysing's admiration for Thalberg himself.

This award was the finale of the evening. Afterward she searched the crowded room for her soon-to-be ex-husband and in-laws. In the shifting, chattering crowd, Eden made out the tall, slim figure of Tony Lombard, just ahead of Randi and Steve. Steve waved to her. Apologizing profusely, Eden pushed her way through well-wishers toward them. She held the heavy Thalberg trophy over her head with one hand, but the trim Oscar was still locked to her chest.

While Steve and Randi admired the two statues, Tony and Eden said good night.

"You see? I was right," Tony reminded her.

She nodded. Her face ached from her plastered-on smile. "Somehow it hasn't soaked in yet. Maybe tomorrow."

"Tomorrow," he echoed. "Eden — ?"

"I know. Look, Tony. The Thalberg Award. You'd better take it to her. Go along and be happy. And one more thing. Bring back Andrea. Then you are free. Reno calls me."

"Thank you, darling. It was great, while it —"

"— lasted. Amen to that."

He kissed her on the cheek, and winced as he felt her body press against him. "Ouch. That damned statue."

She laughed. "I'm going to sleep with him. Now, run along."

After the broadcast the new maid automatically closed the drapes in Leo Prysing's study. Jany went across the room and opened them again, so she could stare at the great arc lights still illuminating the Academy Award festivities at Grauman's Chinese Theater far below.

Tony was down there on Hollywood Boulevard, in one of those halos of light, with his wife. To Jany as a girl, the devastating, beautiful femmes fatales were women like Garbo and Dietrich and Joan Crawford. It had been much more frightening to realize that women as freespirited as the glamorous Eden Ware were also irresistible to some men. Jany felt guiltily that heaven was on the side of supremely independent women like Eden Ware.

Jany needed Tony so desperately she felt that her present fate was a punishment for Leo's death. She certainly couldn't ask his wife to give him up.

As she stood immersed in her own thoughts, Andrea clip-clopped into the study, absurdly but charmingly swathed in whatever she chose from Jany's wardrobe. Her high heels gave her a tip-tilted look, but she was already beginning to grow accustomed to the evening gowns and fur coats on her own short, childish figure.

Jany held out an arm to her.

"Would you like to see where your mama and papa are?"

"Where? Oh, thank you, Aunt Jany. I see the big lights."

Jany pulled her close. She was so warm and dear that it was easy for Jany to pretend that the child was her own.

Andrea flattened her nose against the windowpane. After a few minutes she asked hopefully, "Could I sleep in the castle tonight, maybe?"

"I don't know, sweetheart. I think your mama

would want you near so you can see her lovely prize."

The ringing of the telephone always unnerved her. She had grown up in a city where private phones were rare, and any time she heard the loud jangle of an American telephone she assumed the worst had happened. She started out of the room at a dead run but Andrea stopped her, puzzled by her behavior.

"Aunt Jany, here's a telephone."

Jany looked around and saw her husband's entire bank of telephones on the big desk that hadn't been touched in days. She picked up the only phone that seemed to have incoming calls for her.

She recognized the younger maid's voice. "For you, Mrs. Prysing. From Paris."

Jany's voice rose a few notes in her excitement. "Carl? *Chèri,* is it you?"

There were intercontinental squawks and hisses before she heard Carl's voice. Then he sounded very real, as though he were in the next room.

"Jany, *ma petite.* Are you bearing up? I worried about you after we talked last week."

"I am perfectly well. It was terrible, how Leo died. I felt that I had killed him. But they say he was sick for many months. Perhaps years. Carl, when will you return?"

"I have a job here. I wrote yesterday to the Board of Directors at Prysing Productions. I explained that it is better for a Frenchman to live in his own milieu."

"Oh, no, *chèri!* You went back to the Ministry of Education? But you were not happy there."

He hesitated. "My post there is filled. In the autumn there will be a retirement and they may take me back. Meanwhile, I am working in Pierre's café."

"Not as a waiter!"

"Why not?" He seemed amused by her shock. "I may tell you I am a very good waiter. We have many customers. The tourists are coming back again. Pierre asks me to embrace you most affectionately for him."

"And return it. But Carl, when will I see you?"

There was a short pause. The international whistling and buzzing noises became more pronounced on the line again.

"Are you going to remain in Hollywood?" Carl asked finally. "I thought it might be that you would be returning home."

She looked at Andrea, who sat playing with Leo's unused phones. Andrea flashed her one of her winning smiles so like her father's that it made Jany's heart beat faster just to look at her. Although Jany and Carl spoke in French, she knew Andrea was a sharp little girl and might repeat what she heard.

"No. I think — it is possible — one day I will marry again. I do not know."

"Tony Lombard."

"There was never anyone else."

"God knows I've always been aware of that. I have much to say to Tony. Explanations for old matters. He is secure now?"

"It is very strange. Nothing is in the press now, and he has friends again. All because of two people."

Carl caught his breath. "Who are they?"

"Louella Parsons, a columnist of great importance. She wrote that there had been stories about the director husband of a famous star but that they were all lies. She said this again on the radio. And there is also a man in New York. A friend of Tony's cousin Alec, a newspaperman named Walter Winchell. He spoke of Tony, too. He said that enemies from without had planted the stories and that none of them were true."

"Good. Tell Tony I am happy for him. I must go now," Carl said.

"You will call again very soon?" she begged.

"Very soon, *ma petite*. Be happy."

The line went dead.

She felt Andrea's hand sneaking around her neck, the child's cheek against her own.

"Don't be sad, Aunt Jany."

"I am not. I am very happy. I talked with my dear Carl."

With surprising insight, Andrea asked, "Do you like Carl better than daddy?"

Jany considered this matter gravely. Her fingers outlined Andrea's face, her round cheek and chin.

"It is very different. I love them both."

"Like I love you and I love mama?"

Jany tried not to look as pleased as she felt.

"Perhaps. But you must never say that to your mama. And now, shall we go and explore this horrid old castle again?"

Andrea was delighted, but they had barely started when they heard the heavy brass knocker sounding on the front door. Andrea squealed, both glad and sorry.

"Oh, it's daddy and mama. That means I have to go home now."

"But you heard your mama win the big statue. You must tell her how happy you are for her. Run, run!"

Andrea ran down the steps, along the tiled lower floor to the door. She beat the maid, who had been hired to replace the discharged McDevlin, but it was Jany who pulled open the door.

Tony stood there alone in his evening clothes and topcoat. He had never looked more handsome. Jany peered over his shoulder.

"Where is Eden? We heard the wonderful news."

He looked strangely pale in the moonlight but his eyes glowed.

"She gave me Leo's award for you. It's in the car. But there is something else she gave me."

Andrea flung herself into his arms and cut off whatever he was about to say. He lifted her high, complaining, "You're getting to be a heavyweight. And what the devil are you doing in Aunt Jany's best clothes?"

Andrea drummed her feet against his legs, giggling hysterically. "I'm playing castle. Daddy, we heard mama on the radio. I'm going to be like mama someday and win things. Can I stay tonight with Aunt Jany?"

Tony kissed her. "I promised to bring you back to mama tonight, but maybe tomorrow, if your mama agrees." Over her head he asked Jany, "Will you be waiting?"

Jany wasn't sure she understood him. "You mean tomorrow?"

Andrea had crawled out of his arms and ran to

the car, shedding Jany's shoes as she went.

"I mean tonight," Tony said, "and forever, sweetheart. Eden is going to Reno."

Jany gasped, unable to believe what was happening.

Returning with the Thalberg Award, Jany took Andrea's hand and walked into the house with Tony on the child's other side, but Andrea's eyes sparkled as she looked longingly behind her at the Hollywood lights far below. She freed her fingers from Jany, who was too hypnotized by her companion to notice. In the foyer Tony held out his arms, enfolding Jany.

The years seemed to fall away from them. They were back in Paris during the hot summer of '44, in their first embrace. He stroked her hair lovingly, his lips lingering against her tender mouth.

Andrea wriggled out through the doorway just before the heavy door closed. Remembering her mother's magical moment earlier that evening, the little girl presented the chunky statue to herself, then held it tightly against her chest, as she'd seen her mother do. All the twinkling lights of Hollywood were spread out before her, reminding her of the lucky stars she was sure she would always carry with her.

The employees of G.K. Hall hope you have enjoyed this Large Print book. All our Large Print titles are designed for easy reading, and all our books are made to last. Other G.K. Hall books are available at your library, through selected bookstores, or directly from us.

For information about titles, please call:

(800) 223-1244
(800) 223-6121

To share your comments, please write:

Publisher
G.K. Hall & Co.
P.O. Box 159
Thorndike, ME  04986